Availabl
from M

S...
by Jessica A...
&
Criminally Handsome
by Cassie Miles

Secret Agent, Secret Father
by Donna Young
&
The Cavanaugh Code
by Marie Ferrarella

The High Country Rancher
by Jan Hambright
&
A Soldier's Homecoming
by Rachel Lee

Hunting Down the Horseman
by BJ Daniels

SECRET AGENT, SECRET FATHER

"There had to be a hell of a reason for me to walk away from you."

Then his mouth was on her. But not with the fierceness she had expected. Still, caution tugged at her, urging her to step back. But it was impossible. And with a groan he deepened the kiss.

A yearning broke free, snapping through her. To be held, comforted. Cherished. Until finally, with a cry, she pushed away. Tears burned her eyes but she blinked them back. She put out a hand, stopping him from grabbing her again. "Please, don't."

His arms dropped to his sides. "Tell me, damn it."

She understood what he was asking. First with his kiss, now with the words. Stricken with embarrassment, she clung to the one thing that straightened her spine, hitched her chin and locked her eyes on his. It was time to lie. Self-preservation dictated it.

"This baby is not yours."

THE CAVANAUGH CODE

"Can I kiss you?"

OK, *not* what she expected to hear. It took all she had not to let her jaw drop. Finding her voice took another good half a minute. She did her best to sound blasé.

"Why are you asking? You didn't the other two times."

"Because we're on your home ground now. And because there are other factors that'll come into play this time around," he told her meaningfully. "Now, can I kiss you?" he repeated, his voice low, soft. Caressing her. Creating incredible havoc throughout her soul.

"Go ahead," she whispered, her breath catching in her throat even before he raised her to her feet and brought her close to him.

All the characters in this book have no existence outside the imagination of
the author, and have no relation whatsoever to anyone bearing the same name
or names. They are not even distantly inspired by any individual known or
unknown to the author, and all the incidents are pure invention.

First published in Great Britain 2010
Harlequin Mills & Boon Limited,
Eton House, 18-24 Paradise Road, Richmond, Surrey TW9 1SR

Secret Agent, Secret Father © Donna Young 2008
The Cavanaugh Code © Marie Rydzynski-Ferrarella 2009

ISBN: 978 0 263 88255 1

46-0910

Harlequin Mills & Boon policy is to use papers that are natural, renewable
and recyclable products and made from wood grown in sustainable forests.
The logging and manufacturing processes conform to the legal environmental
regulations of the country of origin.

Printed and bound in Spain
by Litografia Rosés S.A., Barcelona

SECRET AGENT, SECRET FATHER

BY
DONNA YOUNG

THE CAVANAUGH CODE

BY
MARIE FERRARELLA

MILLS & BOON

SECRET AGENT, SECRET FATHER

BY
DONNA YOUNG

Donna Young, an incurable romantic, lives in beautiful Northern California with her husband and two children.

To Wendy and Jimmy,
I love you, Mom and Dad.

Chapter One

With the pain came consciousness.

It pierced the cataleptic depths with jagged teeth that gnawed through skull and skin.

The man lifted his head, testing. Blood coated his tongue, coppery and thick. He groaned as the nausea tightened his gut, pressed into his chest.

They're coming! The words screamed at him through the blanket of fog, adding a bite to the pain. His eyes fluttered open. Blurred lines altered, then cleared into comprehensible patterns.

Rain trickled in through the half-shattered windshield. The splatter of water mixed with his blood turning the air bag pink in the semidarkness. A light pole lay bent across the top of the sports coupé, its base uprooted from the cement.

How long had he been unconscious? He shifted, trying to relieve the pressing weight on his lungs, focusing on the half-deflated air bag wedged between the steering wheel and his chest.

A shaft of white heat impaled his right shoulder. He let out a slow hiss.

After a moment, he pulled his other arm in from the driver's side window, noting for the first time he held a pistol tight in his grip. The silver flashed in the night. The cold steel felt good in the palm of his hand. No, more than good, he thought. Familiar.

He fumbled with the safety belt, released the lock. Tightening his jaw, he shoved his good shoulder against the car door, stiffened at the new surge of pain, the wave of dizziness. Metal scraped, glass crackled. Another push and the door gave way. Slowly he slid through the opening and then stood, using the mangled roof for support.

Sirens wailed in the distance. Instinctively he turned. Bile rose, burned his throat. The ground tilted beneath him. Swearing, he fell to his knees and vomited.

They were coming for him. Cops. Rescue workers. It didn't matter which. Both filed reports.

Reports left paper trails.

With gun in hand, he waited a moment for his stomach to settle, using the time to get his bearings.

Rows of houses, dull with age and earth-toned brick, flanked the street. Each with covered porches that lay behind picket fences or scattered hedges. Each containing onlookers, mostly white-haired couples, their arms tightly wrapped over their chests, holding closed a variety of plaid and terry cloth robes.

Those who didn't brave the elements took protection from the rain behind the narrow bay windows of their homes. Their fingers held the curtains slightly apart, while eyes squinted with curiosity and fear, deepened the grooves of their features.

Enough fear to keep them away from the armed stranger who had invaded their quiet suburban neighborhood.

Carefully, he turned his head, his eyes searching the shadows of the road. How far was he from her?

A bent street post lay no more than five feet from the wrecked light pole. Proctor Avenue?

Too far, his mind whispered. Too far to help.

The sirens grew louder placing his rescuers no more than a few minutes out.

Hot needles pricked his eye sockets and images began to swim. A black fog seeped in, setting off another wave of dizziness. Struggling against the void, he rammed his injured shoulder into the car. Pain exploded through his arm, jarring his spine, driving consciousness forward, forcing the obscurity back.

Sheer willpower put him on his feet. He swayed, then stumbled. *Warn her,* his mind screamed. Before he passed out. Before his enemies found him.

Or worse, the whisper came. *Before they found her.*

Chapter Two

A storm swept over the outskirts of Annapolis. The air crackled and snapped, alive with the hum of lightning, the boom of thunder. Below, stinging sheets of rain pounded water and land with heavy fists, spurred by the fierce Chesapeake winds.

Grace Renne stood by her bay window holding one billowing curtain in her grip. When the bark of the storm reached her, a twinge of sadness worked up the back of her throat.

For the last several years she'd lived on the bay, admiring the city's fortitude, appreciating its history. It was a city born amidst the turmoil of the American Revolution. Time-honored traditions cemented every cobblestone, forged every piece of iron, framed every structure for more than three hundred years.

Grace caught a whiff of burning wood—fireplaces combating the early autumn chill. Underneath the smoke lingered the richer scent of the sea and sand. Slowly, she drew in a deeper breath, enjoyed the bite of salt on the back of her tongue.

She loosened her grip until the curtain fluttered against

her fingertips. Scents, textures…intuition were her tools to live by. Characteristics, her father insisted with irritation, she'd gotten from her mother.

She'd gotten her mother's looks, too. The pale, blond hair that hung in a long, straight curtain. The light brown eyes that softened with humor, narrowed in temper. Delicate features—until one looked close enough and saw the purpose, the character that shaped the high cheekbones and the feminine jaw.

She shut the window, smiling as Mother Nature beat at the framed glass. Any other time, any other mood, she would have let the storm have its way. Her eyes swept over the oak trim of her cottage, the barreled ceiling, the endless stacks of half-packed boxes. But the cottage was no longer hers, sold only days before to her friend and bar manager, Lawrence "Pusher" Davis. The reformed ex-con had bought her home as his first step to becoming a real-estate mogul. And she was sure he wouldn't appreciate water damage on his new hardwood floors.

"We won't have nor'easters in Arizona, baby," she murmured and patted her stomach, a habit begun to soothe the first trimester bouts of nausea.

And now? Grace stopped midmotion. What did her father say? A subconscious attempt to soothe a restless spirit?

Better than no spirit, she'd countered and brushed off the ache just beneath her heart.

With the window shut, the air grew thick with the sweet scent of baking cookies. A grin tugged at the corners of her mouth. "I'd say, handsome, that patting you is a self-defense mechanism to divert your constant cravings for warm milk and chocolate chip cookies."

Her oversized, navy sweatshirt fell to midthigh—its Annapolis insignia covered her midriff like a big yellow target. The shirt, combined with the thick cotton of her dark leggings, provided more than enough warmth to allow her to go barefooted.

Still, she threw another log onto the fireplace's burning embers. Its muted glow matched her melancholy mood.

Overstuffed furniture of glossy, dark oak and warm tweeds filled the room. She hadn't packed up the rich, brown chenille throws that draped the back of the couch. Putting it off had been a silly defiance, she thought. But even as she did, her hand ran over the nearest throw, her fingers curled reflexively into its thickness. After five years, she wasn't quite ready to give up the first true home she'd ever known.

The buzz of the oven timer broke through her thoughts, but the growl of her stomach prodded her into the kitchen. Tiles of white and cornflower-blue checked the six-foot counter—effectively separating the kitchen from the main room without diminishing the cottage's warmth.

For once, Charles Renne had agreed with her decision to move. In fact, her father encouraged her. Surprising, since he hadn't agreed with any of her choices in years. She'd been fourteen when her mother had died. But the war of wills had started long before.

She snapped off the oven and opened the door. The heat blasted her in the face. She hesitated over a long, drawn-out and downright decadent sniff.

The small flutter in her belly told her she'd gotten the baby's attention. She laughed, low and easy. "Okay, sport, one plate of cookies and glass of milk coming up." With an expertise born from cravings, she took the cookies from the oven and slid them onto a nearby cooling rack.

Lately, her battles with her father had flared to a whole new level. One that heightened after her refusal to reveal the baby's father.

The baby was hers. Only hers, she thought stubbornly.

That characteristic she inherited from her father. But it hadn't made the past pleasant for either father or daughter.

Four years ago, she'd stopped by a cigar bar called The Tens to meet a group of college friends.

The pungent smell of whiskey and the more earthy scent of imported cigars drew her in, but it was the low murmur of conversations and clink of glasses—a backbeat to the smoky jazz—that seduced her.

Two weeks later, she dropped out of premed and bought the bar with the rest of her trust fund. An emancipation of sorts, she thought in hindsight.

For the past several years, she'd indulged her passion for fast cars and jazz clubs and leaned ever more closely toward liberal ideas. And the more she indulged, the more distant her father grew. The more distant he grew, the more she hurt.

But over time, the freedom she'd gained became precious and the pain bearable.

The doorbell rang, startling her. She glanced at the mantel clock.

Almost midnight.

Unease caught at the base of her spine. She pushed it away, annoyed. "Who is it?" she asked, but heard no response. Only the wind whistling through the crack beneath, tickling her toes. She curled them against the floor. A look through the peephole proved useless.

"Hide." The command came low, splintered. Still, she recognized the underlining timbre, the slightly offbeat drawl that turned one syllable into two.

"Jacob?" She yanked open the door. He sat next to the door pane, his back propped against the side of the cottage. Blood coated him from top to chin, dripping off the slant of his jaw onto his torn shirt and his black dress slacks. "Oh my God. Jacob!" She fell to her knees beside him.

His eyes fluttered open, focused for a brief moment, one black pupil dilated to more than twice the size of its partner. Blood rimmed the iris until no white could be seen. "Hide, Grace." He rasped the order. "Before they kill you."

His head lolled back. Fear gripped her. Quickly, she placed her hand under his shirt. *Please, God.* The rhythmic beat of his heart remained steady beneath her palm. She closed her eyes briefly against the sting of tears.

The rain and wind spit at them. She raised his hand to her cheek, felt the ice-cold fingers against her skin. She glanced around and saw no car. How had he gotten here? Walked?

Her nearest neighbor was down the beach, too far to call for help. If she left him outside, he'd be worse off by the time the ambulance got there.

A few weeks ago, the doctor had said no heavy lifting. What would he say if he knew the father of the baby lay half-dead on her porch?

"Jacob!" She screamed his name, but he didn't stir.

She scrambled inside and grabbed her purse from the counter. She'd call the ambulance from the front porch—

Then she heard it, the familiar ring tone of her cell phone.

She dumped the contents of her handbag onto the counter, ignoring the lipstick and keys that fell to the floor. She snagged her phone, saw the displayed name and punched the button.

"Pusher?" She flipped the overhead switches on. Lights flooded the room, making her blink. A glance to the doorway told her Jacob hadn't moved. She ran back to his side, checked the pulse at his neck.

"Grace? Thank God." Pusher Davis paused on a shaky breath. "Are you okay?"

"I'm fine but I need you to—"

"Then you haven't talked to anyone?"

"Talked…" she said, momentarily off balance. Using the cuff of her sweatshirt she wiped the blood from Jacob's forehead, trying to get a good look at the injury beneath. "Pusher, I don't have time for this." His skin grayed in the porch light. She had enough experience to know he'd lost too much blood. "I need you to—"

"Helene's dead."

"Helene?" Tension fisted in her chest. "Dead?"

"Grace, I found her body outside The Tens. In the back alley."

Helene, dead? The fist tightened, catching her breath on a short choke of surprise. It couldn't be true. She'd just seen Helene earlier that day. They'd met at their favorite sidewalk bistro for a farewell lunch.

"It's Monday night. The bar should've been closed. She shouldn't have even been there this late. What happened?" The question slipped from her lips, but a prick at the nape of her neck told her the answer.

"She'd been shot," Pusher answered, then paused. "Grace, last time I saw her she was with Jacob Lomax."

She studied the wound in Jacob's shoulder, forced herself to inhale. *Hide, Grace, before they kill you.*

"Did you hear me?"

"Yes," she answered, then took another breath to steady herself. "Are the police there?"

"Not yet. But I've called them."

"Pusher, listen to me." She nearly screamed the words. "I need you to stall them when they get there. They're going to want to talk to me, but I can't right now."

"I don't think you understand, Grace. Helene has been murdered—"

"I understand." She cut him off, not trying to stop the urgency of her words. "Jacob Lomax collapsed on my porch a few minutes ago. He's been shot, too," she added, deciding to put her trust in Pusher. "And until I find out why, the police will only complicate things."

"But if Lomax is there—"

"I told you, he is."

"Then why the cloak-and-dagger, Grace? If Jacob has been shot, this could have been a robbery. A simple case of wrong place, wrong time. I've seen it before."

"I don't think it is and I need some time to make sure."

"Why? Do you think he shot Helene?" He said the words almost jokingly. But when she didn't respond, he swore. "You do, don't you?"

"No," she snapped. "I think his life is in danger."

When the manager didn't say anything, she added. "I can't explain right now. And I can't do this without your help, Pusher. Please," she whispered.

"Okay, okay. Lord knows, I owe you," he answered, the uncertainty thickening his Texas drawl. "I can probably stall them until morning. A little longer if they get ahold of my rap sheet. Will that work?"

She could trust Pusher to take care of the police. The ex-con had certainly sold her on hiring him a few years back, against Helene and her father's wishes.

"Yes, that will work," she said. "Thanks, Pusher."

"It's been a while since I've been in an interrogation room. Was feeling a little homesick, anyway," he mused before his tone turned serious. "Grace, watch your back. The cops aren't your only worry. I won't ask again why you think Jacob's in danger. But if you're right and he is a target, you could become collateral damage."

"I'll be careful."

She hung up the phone. Calling an ambulance was out of the question now. Not until she found out what was going on. She glanced at Jacob before hitting the speed dial.

The phone clicked on the fourth ring. "Hello."

"Dad, it's Grace."

"Grace. Do you realize what time—"

"Dad, I need your help." Jacob's wound couldn't wait for her father's lecture. "Your medical help."

Suddenly, his tone turned sharp. "Is something the matter? Is it the baby?"

"The baby?" She gripped the phone tighter. Deceit warred with desperation inside of her. "Yes, it's the baby."

"Are you spotting again?"

"No," she answered, not wanting to add that possibility to her father's worry. "But I can't explain over the phone. I need you to come over here now. And don't tell anyone where you are going. I want to keep this private."

"Don't tell… Grace Ann, maybe you had better explain—"

"Not now, Dad. Please," she added to soften her order. She moved her hand over Jacob's heart, took reassurance in its steady beat against her palm. "And bring your medical bag."

"I will, but I want to know what's going on when I get there."

"I promise full disclosure," she agreed. "And Dad, do one more thing for me?"

"What?"

"Hurry," she whispered.

Charles Renne hesitated for only a split second. They might not understand each other's views, but he was a father. One that understood fear. "I will."

Grace snapped the phone shut and shoved it into her sweatshirt pocket. Her father would take a good hour to reach her from Washington, D.C. Jacob couldn't wait that long.

"I can do this but you need to be easy with our baby, okay big guy?" It took some shifting, but she managed to maneuver herself behind him. Rain soaked her sweatshirt, plastered her hair to her forehead. Impatiently, she brushed the blond strands away, then slid her hands under his arms and around his chest.

Jacob was a good six inches over her own five-eight frame, and had well over fifty pounds on her. He was built lean, with the firm muscles and long limbs of a distance runner. Grateful her taste didn't run toward male bulk, she settled him back until he rested against her chest and shoulder.

The clatter of metal ricocheted in the night air. She glanced down. A pistol lay on the cement, its barrel inches from her feet.

His? Once again, her mind rejected the idea that Jacob had shot Helene. No matter what secrets he carried, he wasn't capable of murder. From the moment Helene had introduced Jacob to Grace, there was no doubt about the close friendship between the two.

Ignoring the weapon, she gripped him between her thighs. Slowly, she scooted him back through the doorway. Using the strength of her legs and arms, she tugged and pulled in short bursts of energy. The struggle took more than twenty minutes. Twenty minutes in which she pleaded, prayed, begged and swore. But she managed it.

Once inside, she scooted back toward the fireplace and lowered his shoulders gently to the floor. Quickly, she closed the door, grabbed a pillow and placed it under his head.

For months, she'd worried about him, raged at him—yearned, grieved, loved him—silently through the long, dark nights.

But not once had she been terrified for him.

Until now.

His face was pale, stark against his deep brown hair, now darker with rain, sticky with blood. His features cut in razor-thin angles. Sharper, leaner since the last time she'd seen him. A four-inch gash split the hairline above the middle of his forehead. Blood and bruises covered most of his features.

She knelt beside him, saw him shiver. Cursing herself, she threw a few more logs on the fire.

But it was his shoulder that worried her the most. Blood was everywhere. His face, neck and arm were coated with it. From his head, or shoulder, or both. She couldn't be sure which.

Her pulse thickened with fear, making her hands heavy, her fingers tremble. She shook them, trying to settle them and her nerves, then removed his suit jacket. A shoulder holster crowded under his arm. Something she hadn't noticed when dragging him in. Quickly, she unbelted the holster and tossed it aside. Within minutes, she had him stripped to his underwear and covered him to the waist with her comforter.

The bullet had torn a hole through his right shoulder, leaving an exit wound on the back side.

Fear and confusion warred within, but right now she had time for neither. Instead, she crossed to the linen cupboard and pulled out a clean, white hand towel.

After running the cloth under warm water, she returned to his side with it and her biggest pan filled with hotter water. She tucked the blanket around him, knowing she couldn't do anything other than clean the wound until her father got there.

With gentle fingers, she brushed a lock of hair from his forehead, then systematically dabbed the blood away from the gash.

"I'll give you one thing, Lomax," she whispered. She rinsed the towel out in the water, watched it turn pink, before she switched her attention to his shoulder. "You sure as hell know how to make an entrance."

Chapter Three

"He's coming, Mr. Kragen."

Oliver Kragen sat on a park bench as dawn broke over the Chesapeake Bay. His enforcer, Frank Sweeney, stood no more then ten feet away, his bulky frame eclipsing the sun behind him. Dressed in an Armani suit, the man appeared more like a pro football player ready to renegotiate his contract than the mercenary he was.

And that's exactly why Oliver had hired him.

"I'll give you odds the bastard screwed up."

Oliver didn't acknowledge Sweeney's comment. Instead, he waited until the click of shoe soles sounded behind him. Rather than turn in greeting, Oliver tossed the remainder of his Danish to a nearby pigeon. After all, Boyd Webber wasn't a peer, he was an employee.

"She's dead."

Oliver glanced at Sweeney, a silent order to leave. Once the big man stepped away, Kragen spoke up, but his focus remained on the pigeons at their feet. "How?" The question was low, pleasant.

Boyd wasn't fooled. But he didn't care, either. The ex-marine had more than two dozen kills under his belt and had survived more horrors than the bloodiest special effects ever created. Nothing on this earth made him afraid of dying. Least of all a weasel like Kragen. "The Garrett woman had a gun. They both did. It forced my hand."

"They forced your hand because they were armed? They're government operatives. What did you expect, Webber?" Kragen's voice hardened. "If I remember right, I told you it was imperative that the Garrett woman was to be brought to me. Alive."

"It was a mistake. They killed one of my men, wounded another. The third man targeted Lomax, but somehow the woman took a stray bullet in the chest."

"And this third man?"

"I killed him."

"To save me the trouble? Or him the pain?"

"I was…angry." More than angry. Infuriated. Enough to lose his cool and shoot until the woman was dead. Enough to murder another man—one of his own—who had witnessed his transgression. "My man should have been more careful," he lied.

In Webber's opinion, Helene Garrett deserved no better than to die in a gutter. She had betrayed Senator D'Agostini. Slept with him, used him, stolen from him. End of her, end of story. Or it should have been. But the files were still missing.

"Did you clean up your mess?" Kragen's eyes shifted to his coffee cup. He took a sip, burned his tongue and swore.

"I thought it better to leave things." Resentment slithered down Webber's back, coiled deep within his belly. He studied Kragen's profile with derision. Kragen was the poster-boy politician. The meticulous, trimmed blond hair that enhanced the high slant of the cheekbones, the aristocratic forehead. A nose so straight that Webber would bet his last dime that Kragen had it cosmetically carved. All packaged in a five-figure topcoat and custom suit. All done to hide the trailer-park genes that ran through Poster Boy's veins.

"You killed your man without consulting me first." Oliver glanced up then. Twin metallic-gray eyes pinned, then dismissed the mercenary in one flicker.

"I consulted with the senator beforehand," Webber responded.

Oliver noted the verbal jab, but chose to ignore it for the moment. "Did you search the bar? Her apartment?"

"She'd moved out of her apartment days ago and left nothing behind. And we had no time to search the bar. Lomax was the priority."

"The woman had the files and the code," Oliver insisted. "I want the bar searched. And I want Lomax found."

"Shouldn't take long. We winged Lomax before he slipped away. We found his car wrapped around a light pole."

"Did you follow the blood?"

"Witnesses told the police he took off down the street but the rain washed away any bloody trail."

"And the police? What do they say?" Oliver prompted, his annoyance buried under a tone of civility. More than the Neanderthal deserved, in Oliver's opinion.

To say that Webber was ugly would have been polite. He had the face of a boxer, flat and scarred from too many alley fights, and a bulbous nose from too much booze. Like Sweeney, he wore a tailored suit, had no neck and too much muscle. Unlike Sweeney, he sported a butch cut so close it left the color of his hair in question.

"The police are questioning the bar manager. An ex-con by the name of Pusher Davis."

"If the man is an ex-con, they'll suspect him first," Oliver observed. "Tail him, just to be sure. I don't want any loose ends."

"There won't be. The police won't get anywhere. Helene Garrett will become just another statistic in a long line of unsolved homicides," Boyd explained.

For the moment, Oliver ignored the arrogance underlying Webber's words. "They have Lomax's blood on the scene."

Webber snorted. "Won't do them any good if they have no records to match it with. Right now, the cops don't have any information on either of them. Or the senator's connection to her."

Webber was right. Oliver had gone to great lengths to keep the senator's relationship with Helene Garrett private. A precaution he practiced with all the senator's mistresses. "That won't get us the Primoris files or the code. We need to find Lomax."

"My men are checking nearby hospitals and clinics."

"You actually expect him to show up on some grid? He's injured, not stupid, Webber," he snapped, annoyed over the fact that this wouldn't have happened if Helene hadn't slipped under their radar.

Oliver had investigated Helene months before the senator had started the affair. With his contacts, it took Oliver no more than a few calls to get everything from her finances to her elementary school records. False records, as it turned out.

"From the look of his car seat, he's lost a lot of blood. If he passed out, he'd have no choice. Someone might have taken him to the hospital."

"Find him."

"It would help if you could give me more than just his name."

"I gave you his name *and* the time and place of the meeting." Oliver paused, his eyes critical. "It should have been enough."

"I told you, they forced my hand. It couldn't be helped."

"Just find Lomax and keep him alive. I don't care what it takes," Oliver ordered, already making plans to advise the senator to call an emergency meeting. The others would have to be informed. "That bitch stole the Primoris file. I want it back. Do you understand?"

"I'll take care of it," Boyd responded automatically. "And the police?"

"I'll make a few calls. Jacob Lomax won't be on their data banks unless I arrange to put him there."

"Are you thinking of making the murder public?" Webber questioned.

"No." Any unwanted attention at this stage could sabotage their plans. "At least not for now." Not until the others met and reevaluated the situation. They were too close to their goal.

"How about her partner?" Webber asked. "Grace Renne?"

Oliver considered the possibility. "She might know something. Or at the very least, have seen something." Oliver remembered faces, names. It was vital in his world. He'd met Miss Renne once at some sort of political function—one of many. At the time, the association between Helene and Doctor Charles Renne's daughter seemed coincidental—and, in his mind, added to Helene's credibility. But now...

"They had lunch yesterday afternoon," Webber prompted.

"Then you should have already had someone talking to her this morning." Oliver stood, his gaze back on the horizon. He didn't like disloyalty within his ranks. And those who were foolish enough to betray him suffered. "I'm here in Washington, D.C., with the senator until after the fund-raising ball tomorrow night. You know how to get hold of me. And I mean me, Webber. The senator is too busy with the upcoming election to be bothered with this. Do you understand?"

Not waiting for an answer, Oliver turned to Sweeney. "Frank." He waited the moment it took for the enforcer to join them. "You're with Webber. Make sure he does his job this time."

"Now wait a minute—"

"Yes, sir." Sweeney stepped behind the mercenary, boxing the man in between Kragen and himself.

"One more thing." Oliver grabbed Webber's wrist. When Webber automatically jerked back, Sweeney clamped down on his shoulder, holding him in place with a viselike grip.

"I want to make sure they don't force your hand this time." Slowly, Oliver poured the cup of coffee into Webber's palm. Within moments, the hot liquid raised blisters. "Be diplomatic, Webber," he cautioned with noncommittal coolness.

Webber nodded, his jaw tightened against the pain until the skin turned white under his ruddy complexion. "And if the Renne woman doesn't want to cooperate?"

Oliver dropped the mercenary's wrist and tossed the cup to the ground. "Then be discreet."

Chapter Four

He wasn't dead. It took a moment for the thought to seep through. Another for the layers of fog to dissipate.

He surfaced gradually, registering the extent of his injuries. The throbbing at his temple, the ache over his brow. When his right arm refused to move when commanded, he shifted his shoulders no more than an inch. Pain rifled through him, setting off waves of nausea that rocked his belly, slapped at the back of his throat.

But his heart beat.

For a full minute, he concentrated on the rhythmic thumping, worked on breathing oxygen in and out of his lungs.

A keen sense of danger vibrated through him. But when his mind searched for details, he found nothing but the urge for caution. And an underlying edge of danger.

Slowly, he opened his eyes. The ceiling beams doubled, then danced before finally coming into focus. His gaze slid from the white ceiling to the white bandage on his shoulder.

With his good hand, he carefully searched the bed around him but found nothing. He let his arm fall back to his side. Molten heat blasted through his upper body, setting his shoulder and ribs on fire and telling him he'd been carelessly quick with the motion.

Cloth brushed leather, drawing his attention. Slowly, he turned his head. No more than four feet away, a woman straightened in the leather wingback chair. She uncurled her long legs in one slow, fluid movement. The morning light washed over her in soft pink rays, coating both her skin and pale blond hair in a hazy blush.

"You're awake." Her sleep-soaked voice reminded him of crushed velvet, rich and warm. But it was caramel-brown eyes that caught his attention. Carmel dusted with gold, he realized as she drew closer.

And edged with concern. Enough to tell him she'd spent the night in the chair.

"Is the pain bearable?" Her face was scrubbed clean, revealing a few freckles dotting her nose. With long, blond hair tied back into a ponytail and clad in jeans and a black, zipped hoodie two sizes too big, she looked no older than a first-year college student.

The back of her hand drifted over his cheek. Her cool, soft touch soothing. So much so that he felt a curious ache in his chest when it dropped away.

"No fever, thank goodness. How are you feeling?"

He caught her wrist with his good hand and jerked her closer. It was a mistake.

Skin pulled against stitching, bones ground against cartilage. A curse burst from his lips in a long, angry hiss.

"Where is it?" His question was barely a whisper. Dried bile coated his tongue in a thick paste, leaving his throat sandpaper-dry.

"Where is what?" she demanded. But a quick glance at

his shoulder kept her from tugging back. He didn't have to look because he felt it. Blood—thick and warm—seeped from his wound into the bandage, dampening the gauze against his skin.

"The 9 mm. Where is it?" he repeated, pushing his advantage. Whoever she was, she wasn't smart to let him see her concern.

"In the nightstand drawer. Both the gun and the two clips." Her temper surfaced, sharpening her tone.

He didn't take her word for it. Instead, he reached down with his bad arm—grunting at the shock of pain—then opened the drawer with his fingers.

But his actions took effort. Sweat beaded his forehead, his arm shook against her when he grabbed the pistol.

"Let go of my wrist." The fact she kept her words soft didn't diminish the anger behind them.

Or the concern.

Immediately, his hand dropped to the bed. More from weakness than her demand, he knew.

"Trust me, if I wanted you dead, I wouldn't have saved your butt last night." She rubbed her wrist.

Jacob resisted nodding, not wanting to set off another wave of dizziness. But he tightened his grip on his pistol. "What am I doing here?" His voice was no more than a croak.

She poured him a glass of water from a pitcher on the bedside stand and offered it to him. "Recovering."

When he didn't sit up, she lifted the glass to his lips. The cool water hit the back of his throat, immediately soothing the raw, burning heat. After he finished, she placed it back on the nightstand.

"What happened?" he murmured, resting his head back

against the pillow. The room tilted a little. That and the water made him queasy.

"You have a gunshot wound in your right shoulder, a forehead laceration and a concussion. You were lucky the bullet only caused minimal damage. We've stitched your wounds, but only rest will help the concussion," she explained, her voice softening once again with concern on the last few words.

First he digested her reaction, then her explanation. A bullet hole meant he'd lost a lot of blood. A hindrance, but not debilitating. "Who is we?"

"My father." She hesitated over the words, enough to obstruct any natural warmth in them. "He'll be back in a moment."

"How did I get shot?"

"I was hoping you could tell me."

The sunlight grew brighter, casting beams across the bed. When he grimaced, she crossed the room and pulled the curtains shut.

"And you are?"

She stopped midmotion, her eyes narrowing as they pinned him to the bed. "If you're trying to be funny, I suggest you work on your timing. Because whatever sense of humor I might have had, you destroyed it about five months ago."

What the hell was that supposed to mean? "Trust me, the only joke here is on me." His laugh was no more than a savage burst of air. "So why don't you tell me who you are and we'll go from there."

"Grace. Grace Renne."

Grace. He took in the serene features, the refined curves of her face that sloped into a slightly upturned nose, a dimpled chin and a mouth too wide to be considered movie-star perfect. But full enough to tempt a man, even a half-dead one like himself, to taste.

"You don't recognize me?" she asked. Disbelief—no, he corrected, distrust—lay under her question.

So she didn't trust him? Seemed fair enough, since he didn't trust her.

"Should I?" Vague images flickered, their edges too slippery to grasp. He focused beyond the disorientation, the fear that slithered from the dark void.

Again, he found nothing.

"Yes." She turned back to the curtain, took a moment to tuck the edges together until the sun disappeared. "We were friends. Once."

Her voice trailed in a husky murmur. A familiar bite caught him at the back of the spine. He swore under his breath.

"Once. We're not friends now?" He wasn't in the mood for cryptic answers or a prod from his libido. Obviously, his body needed no memories to react to its baser needs.

Sledgehammers beat at his temples, splitting his skull from ear to ear. He used the pain to block out her appeal.

"I'd like to think so," she responded. "What do you remember?"

"Not sure." Admitting he remembered nothing was out of the question. Clumsily, he shoved the thick, plaid comforter off him. Immediately the cool air took the heat and itch from his skin. She'd stripped him to his boxer briefs, he realized. Bruises tattooed most of his chest and stomach in dark hues of purple and brown.

He tried again, searching his mind until the headache

drove him back to the woman for answers. "A bullet didn't do all this damage," he remarked even as the void bore down on him with a suffocating darkness. He took a deep breath to clear his head, paid for it with a sharp slice of pain through his ribs.

"Feels like I've been hit by a train." Anger antagonized the helplessness, but something deeper, more innate, forced a whisper of caution through his mind.

"Someone tried to kill you last night." She spoke the words quickly, as if simple speed would blur the ugliness of them. "They almost succeeded."

Frustrated, he swung his legs over to the side of the bed before she could stop him. He fought through the vertigo and nausea. But the effort left him shaking.

"Where are my pants?" If he needed to move quickly, he didn't want to be naked doing it.

"You don't need them right now. You have a concussion." She glanced toward the door. "You need bed rest."

"What I need is my pants." He glanced up at her, saw the anxiety that tightened her lips, knit her brow. But once again, it was the fear dimming the light brown of her eyes that bothered him. He hardened himself against it.

The woman was definitely on edge. He tried a different tack. "Now," he ordered. For a moment, he was tempted to raise the gun, point it at her, but something inside stopped him.

As if she read his mind, she glanced from the weapon to his face, then surprised him by shaking her head. "You won't shoot me over a pair of pants."

"Don't bet on it," he growled. Right now, for two cents, he'd put a bullet through his own forehead just to relieve the pounding behind it.

"Then go ahead," she said before she swung around, leaving her back exposed. The movement cost her, he could see it in the rigid spine, the set of her shoulders. He'd scared the hell out of her but she didn't give an inch.

"Damn it." She had guts for calling his bluff, he gave her that. "All right, it seems I'm more civilized than I thought."

When she faced him, she didn't gloat.

She had smarts, too, he thought sarcastically.

He placed the gun on the nightstand beside him and ran his free hand over his face, ignoring the whiskers that scraped at his palm. "Look, for the time being, I'll accept the fact that you and I are...friends. But whoever did do this to me is still out there somewhere. And I assume they'll try again. Agreed?"

"Yes," she replied, if somewhat reluctantly.

"If I have to face them with no memory and very little strength, I'd at least like to have my pants on when I do it."

"Your pants and shirt were covered in blood. I burned them in the fireplace."

When he raised an eyebrow, she let out an exasperated breath. "Fine. There is a change of clothes for you in my closet."

She waved a hand toward the double doors beside a connecting bathroom. Another good idea, considering the state of his bladder.

But he'd be damned if he'd ask for help. He'd wait a moment for his legs to stop shaking. "Do I usually keep clothes in your closet?" he asked, knowing the answer would explain the pinch of desire he felt moments ago.

"You forgot them here," Grace explained and glanced toward the open bedroom door.

"And here is?"

"Annapolis." She paused for a moment, the small knit on her brow deepened. But when she brushed a stray hair from her cheek, the slight tremble of her fingers gave away her nervousness. She tucked her hands in her pockets. "You really don't remember, do you?"

"Right now, I don't even know what the hell my name is."

"Jacob Lomax."

He searched his mind for recognition. Found nothing that was familiar. His headache worsened, making it difficult to think. "How long have I been unconscious?"

"Since midnight last night." She glanced at the alarm clock on the nightstand. "Ten hours."

"Which makes today, what?"

"Tuesday. The twenty-third of September."

Slowly, he scanned the room, searching. The curtains and comforter, while a yellow plaid, were both trimmed with white lace. The latter was draped over a pine-slotted sleigh bed that sat more than three feet off the floor. Positioned across the room were its matching dresser and mirror.

Jacob studied his image. The blade-sharp cheekbones, the strong, not-quite-square jaw, covered with no more than a day's worth of whiskers. He rubbed his knuckles against the stubble on one cheek, hollowed more from fatigue he imagined than from pain. A bruise dominated the high forehead, spilled over in a tinge of purple by the deep set eyes of vivid blue.

No flashes of recognition. No threads of familiarity. Nothing more than the image of a stranger staring back.

His focus shifted down. Assorted lotions and powders cluttered the top of the dresser, along with a few scattered papers and a stack of books.

Packing boxes sat opened on the floor. Some were full, others half-empty, but most lay flat, their sides collapsed.

"You're moving?"

"Yes—"

"You're awake." A man entered the room, the black bag in his hand and the stethoscope around his neck identifying him as a doctor.

Grace met the older man halfway across the room. Jacob deliberately said nothing and waited. But his hand shifted closer to the gun beside him.

Her father was on the smaller side of sixty, with a leanness that came with time on a tennis court, not a golf course. His hair was white and well groomed, combed back from a furrowed brow.

After a few murmured words, he patted her shoulder, then approached the bed. "Jacob, my name is Doctor Renne. Grace tells me you don't remember what happened."

"That's right." Since the older man didn't ask Jacob if he remembered him, Jacob assumed they'd never met.

"How's the headache?" Doctor Renne pulled a penlight from his pocket and clicked it on. He shined the light in Jacob's eyes. First one, then the other. The bright flash set off another series of sledgehammers. He winced. "Bearable."

"Look up...now down." Another flash, another jolt of pain.

"How did I get here?"

"Since there was no car, we assumed you walked. Grace discovered you on her porch last night." The doctor clicked the light off and tucked it back into his inside pocket. "Stay focused on my finger without turning your head."

Jacob followed the doctor's finger, this time ignoring the pull of discomfort behind his eyes.

"There's definite improvement." The doctor waved his daughter over to the bed. "Grace, I'll need your help. I want to check his shoulder."

They eased Jacob back against the headboard. The doctor examined the bandage. "There's blood. You're moving around too much. I didn't spend hours stitching you up for you to take it apart in five minutes."

"Thanks, Doc. I'll remember that," Jacob commented wryly. "I'd tell you where to send the bill if I knew where I lived."

"Your driver's license says Los Angeles, California," Charles answered. "Seems you're a long way from home."

Home? Why did the address, even the word, sound so foreign?

Grace leaned over to adjust his pillow. A light floral scent drifted toward him. For a moment he tried to identify the flower, but came up with nothing. Still the fragrance was distinctive. Feminine. Clean.

"Do you remember a woman named Helene Garrett?" Grace asked without looking up.

Frames of shadow and light passed through Jacob's mind, but nothing he could zero in on, nothing to bring into focus. "No, but…" Suddenly, a snapshot—vivid but brief—flashed across his mind. A woman laughing. Her cheeks and nose pink from the falling snow. Her smile wide, her eyes brimming with…happiness?

No, he realized suddenly. Not happiness.

Love.

Chapter Five

"You." Jacob nodded slightly toward Grace, then frowned. "I see you."

"From last night or this morning?" The doctor asked, then took Jacob's wrist and checked the younger man's pulse against his watch.

"From a ski trip." Jacob closed his eyes, for a moment, trying to bring the image back. "I remember her hovering over me." When he opened them again, he caught the surprise in the doctor's features.

The doctor didn't know about me. Jacob decided not to mention how the scent of her shampoo triggered the memory. Not until he understood more.

"You were skiing? Where?"

Grace nearly groaned aloud at her father's questions. When she'd found out she was pregnant, she'd told him the father of the baby was no one he knew. Just someone she'd met skiing.

Lifting her chin, she met her father's glare head-on. "In Aspen. A few times."

When her father said nothing, her gaze shifted from him to Jacob. But her smile was forced, her teeth on edge. "You fell the first time we were there." What she didn't add is that he had faked the fall, pulled her into the snow and spent the next twenty minutes kissing her breathless.

She hugged her arms to her chest and walked over to the window.

She didn't want to see the anger—the disappointment—emanating from her father.

"Who's Helene Garrett?" Jacob's question snapped the thread of tension between father and daughter.

"A business associate of yours. And my partner. Ex-partner. She introduced us," Grace admitted reluctantly, but she continued to stare out the window. The bay's waves crashed against the sand and dock, not quite over its temper from the night before. She'd stayed awake all night helping her dad, jumping at every sound the wind and rain made. But no one came after her. No one pounded on the door or jumped from the shadows.

Hide, Grace. Before they kill you. The words floated through her mind for the thousandth time. But was the threat real or a side effect to his amnesia?

"Someone shot and killed Helene last night outside our bar." Grace could feel Jacob's eyes on her, studying her like some specimen in a jar. Something he'd done while they dated. Before his habit unnerved her, now it just annoyed her.

Amnesia. Her nerves endings snapped and crackled. She didn't believe him at first, but that lasted only a few moments. Admittedly, she had expected Jacob to clear up the confusion—the fear—that plagued her all night. How can you fight your enemies when you have no idea who they are? Or hadn't known they even existed until only hours before?

"And you assume because I took a bullet, I was there, too," Jacob said coolly.

He wasn't asking a question, but her father answered anyway. "It's a logical assumption."

"Did Helene have a gun on her?" Jacob asked, his tone flat.

"Yes, but you didn't shoot her. And she didn't put that bullet in your shoulder, either. The two of you were very close," Grace insisted, but she didn't face him. Not yet. Not when her emotions could be seen in her expression. The doubt, the fear. Everything in her being told her he wouldn't harm Helene. She had to believe that, for now. "You might not remember who you are, but I know what kind of man you are. And you aren't a murderer."

"Well, for all our sakes, I hope you're right," Jacob replied grimly.

"I am." Her chin lifted, defiant; she was under control again. She was betting her life on it. More importantly, their child's life. "How long do you think his memory loss will last, Dad?"

The doctor had remained quiet. She swung around, challenging. "Dad?"

"I can't give you a definitive answer, Grace. We're dealing with the brain. Anything can happen. The concussion, while it's nothing to dismiss, doesn't appear serious enough to have caused permanent damage. Of course, I would prefer to order him to undergo some tests and a day or more of observation to be sure." The words came out rigid, censured. "Without them, I believe we're dealing with more of a dissociative amnesia. A loss of memory due to a shock rather than an injury to the brain."

"Traumatic as in Helene's murder," Jacob replied. "So this is mental rather than physical."

"In my opinion, yes," Charles answered, but he prodded

Jacob's head wound, checking it. "If that's the case, my guess is that your memory will return in bits and pieces over the course of time." Her father took off his stethoscope and placed it in his bag.

"What span of time?"

"There is no telling how much will come back or how long it will take."

"He remembered his gun," Grace commented. "First thing when he woke up."

Dr. Renne glanced at Jacob, surprised. "You did?"

"Yes." He flexed his right hand, spreading his fingers. "I know I've been trained to use it. Even if I don't remember the when and the why." The confidence reverberated deep within him, hollow echoes from an empty void.

"That explains the other marks you're sporting. Two bullet scars on your back and a six-inch knife scar on your hip."

Charles Renne moved from the bed, his bag in hand. "Some traits—like combat training or studied languages— will surface instinctively. But most memories are triggered by emotions, reactions, physical evidence. A scent. A song. Any number of things. Experiencing them might eventually help your recollection, but there are no guarantees."

"He also remembered my name. Last night, before he passed out, he called me by my name," Grace inserted.

"If that's true, why don't I remember you now?" Jacob asked.

"Something must have happened while you were unconscious. Your brain could've just shut down from the emotional shock," Charles said. "If that's the case, your mind will decide if and when it's ready to remember."

"If?"

"There's always the chance you might not regain any of your memories," Charles indicated. "Especially those from last night."

Jacob considered the doctor's words. The sense of danger intensified after the mention of Helene Garrett. Could he have killed a woman he considered a friend? There was no doubt he had killed before. The certainty of it resonated through him.

Obviously, some things amnesia couldn't erase.

"I can make arrangements—"

"No, Dad. No arrangements. If he isn't wanted for murder, he soon will be."

"He carries a gun, Grace. One that might be a murder weapon. Do realize the implications of that?"

"Do you mean to your reputation or to my safety?"

"For once in your life, don't be irresponsible," Charles retorted impatiently. "So far this morning, we've been fortunate. It won't take long for the police to show up on your doorstep. Then what will you do?" Charles's gaze dropped to her stomach. "It's not just you I'm concerned for. You're not thinking about—"

"We agreed last night that it's not your decision."

"I'm required by law to report a gunshot wound," Charles snapped. "If I don't, I could lose my practice."

"Do what you have to do, Dad," she answered, the truth lying bitter against her tongue. It wasn't the first time she'd defied him. But a few moments earlier, when his eyes moved from her stomach back to her face, it was the first time she'd ever seen fear etched in his features.

"Damn it, Grace. I don't want to turn this into the same old argument. The man was shot. Your friend was killed.

This is not about the fact that once again I'm choosing my practice over—"

"Over what? Me?" Grace rubbed the back of her neck, trying to loosen the tension. Even she couldn't ask him to go against his oath. "You're right, Dad." She sighed. "I put you in this position with my phone call and I'm sorry." The words were sad, made so by their unending conflict. "But I'm not going to budge on my decision, either. He stays with me until we figure this out."

Jacob had been about to agree with the doctor. No matter who he was, hiding behind a woman wasn't acceptable. But the undercurrent of emotion in the room changed his mind. Something wasn't being said and Jacob wanted to know what it was. Better to wait and get the information from the daughter.

"I'm safer with Jacob. Trust me, Dad." When he said nothing, she added, "Please."

Finally, it was Charles who turned away. "The pain is going to get worse. You're going to need morphine in a short while, Jacob. Enough to take the edge off. I can give you some but I have to go get the prescription filled." He closed his bag and turned to his daughter. "I'll be back in an hour."

The threat was there, Jacob knew. He had less than an hour to find out what the hell was going on.

Chapter Six

"Why didn't you tell him?"

"Tell him what?" Jacob asked.

"That you won't take the morphine he's bringing back."

She was right, of course. He couldn't risk being doped up if trouble started. "For a person who doesn't know me, you understand me pretty well," he commented dryly.

"One doesn't discount the other," she countered. Her gazed drifted over his face. "You've lost weight."

"Really?" Jacob's mouth twisted derisively. "I wouldn't know."

"Yes, well—"

"I didn't tell him I didn't want the morphine because I thought you needed some breathing room," he lied. "But I agree with your father, Grace."

"A man you just met."

"Technically, I've just met you, too."

Her body grew rigid. "You remembered Aspen."

He'd hurt her with his comment. A vulnerability he could take advantage of, if needed. "I stand corrected."

"For the record, I agree with my father, too." At Jacob's raised eyebrow, she added, "To a certain point. But that doesn't mean I can do what he wants. We need to get you out of here before he gets back."

"We?"

"I have to find out what happened last night and you're my only lead to the answers."

"I thought I was to have bed rest."

"I couldn't risk his overhearing anything else," she said impatiently. "He would've stopped us. You're not safe here."

"What if I don't ever remember, Grace?" When she didn't answer, he continued, "Why not let the police handle it?"

"They can't be trusted. Not yet. Not until we find out who killed Helene. Don't you see?"

"If I remember right, the police are the ones who find murderers."

Her head snapped up, and what he saw was genuine fear. "Not if they've already decided on a suspect."

"Me." When he tried to maneuver his feet to the floor, she placed a hand against his good shoulder.

"Please, let me help you. If you move too fast, you could break open the stitching." Before he could stop them, her fingers drifted across his skin.

He caught her wrist, but this time with gentle fingers. His intent was to stop her, but the action brought her closer.

He caught her scent, breathed it in. Without thought, his thumb skimmed her pulse. When it jumped, his did, too. Slowly, he pulled her toward him until her hand rested against his chest. Her eyes met his and what he saw made him stop. The desire was there, but more than that, he saw panic.

He let her go. "I'm not so weak I can't put a pair of pants on."

Pink flushed her cheeks, but from embarrassment or temper, he wasn't sure.

She stepped back, letting her hands drop to her sides, but not before she made them into fists.

Temper, then.

When she walked to the closet, her actions were fluid, almost regal. And when she yanked open the door, he almost smiled.

She skimmed the hangers with her hand, pulled out a pair of slacks and a sweater. Judging from the high-end material of the charcoal V-neck sweater and the black chino slacks, he wasn't hurting for money.

"These should do."

"I guess they will." When he reached to take the hangers from her, pain exploded in his shoulder. He swore and grabbed at his arm, locking it to his side. "I'm going to need your car."

She tossed the clothes onto the corner of the bed. "Don't be stupid. You're not in any condition to drive."

He had to give the woman credit; she did snooty with a certain sex appeal.

"You're going to need someone to get you around."

Pointedly, he glanced at his gun. "I have a feeling I'm pretty self-sufficient."

But what he wasn't was flush. He needed cash.

Money, he knew, would open many more doors. "Did I have a wallet?"

She picked a slim, brown wallet from the dresser and handed it to him. "There's almost a thousand dollars, a few credit cards and your driver's license in there."

Instead of opening the billfold, Jacob laid it on the bed beside him. He'd search through it after she left the room.

"Now, do you want my help dressing?"

"No, I can handle it myself." He was in no mood to deal with the fluttery touch of her hands against him again.

"There's a brand-new toothbrush in the bathroom's medicine cabinet and fresh towels on the rack," she noted, then walked over and turned on the bathroom light for him. "You're not strong enough yet to take a shower. And even if you think you are, you can't risk getting your bandages wet."

"I'll manage." He leaned back against the headboard and studied her through half-closed eyes.

"You didn't take me to the hospital because I'd be vulnerable." The fear was back with his statement, tightening her features, only for a heartbeat but long enough for him to see. And understand.

"Running will only protect me for so long. And like your father said, puts you at risk whether you're with me or not."

"I told you I want answers. And once your memory returns I'll get them," she replied. "And I'm hoping neither of us will need protection."

"About my other scars." When her eyebrow lifted in question, he clarified. "You wouldn't know how I acquired them, would you?"

"No. We were never that close," she replied evenly. But at what cost, he thought.

"Then why is it that little bits I am remembering seem to revolve around you?" Even without her reaction to him a few minutes prior, his instincts were telling him they'd been intimate. The tightening of his groin, the itch at the base of his spine, told him that if he didn't watch himself, they just might be again.

"Maybe because I knew Helene."

"Maybe," he replied, but he didn't believe it. "Do you have a picture of her?"

"Yes." She went to her dresser and slid open the top drawer. After a moment of digging, she pulled out a newspaper photo. She crossed the room and gave it to Jacob. "This was taken the day we opened The Tens. Our bar. Her bar," she corrected, then sighed. "Actually, I have no idea whose bar it is now."

"We need to find out," he decided. "Could be the new owner wanted a premature switching of titles and I got in the way." He studied the picture. It was a waist-to-head shot. Even with that, Jacob could tell the woman was tall and on the athletic side but not enough to detract from her overall femininity. He glanced at the deep cut of the buttoned jacket with no blouse to ruin the sleek, cool effect of the navy business suit.

One of Helene's arms was casually looped around Grace's shoulders. Her hair was a deep red, spiked softly around the sharp angles of her cheeks, emphasizing a long nose, its feminine point.

"Do you recognize her?"

"No," he said, taking one last look before glancing up. "Can I keep this?"

When she nodded, he placed it by his wallet.

"Do you need help to the bathroom?"

He contemplated the wide span of hardwood floor between him and the bathroom door. "I can manage," he said and hoped he was right.

"Then I'll make you some toast. And some coffee." She turned to leave.

He waited until she reached the door. "Grace. Were you telling the truth earlier? Are you absolutely sure I didn't kill Helene?"

She hesitated for a moment, her hand clenched on the doorknob. "I'm not absolutely sure of anything. Least of all, you."

JACOB COULDN'T SAY he felt better, but he felt more human after cleaning up and putting on clean clothes. The itch was off his skin and his stomach had settled. His shoulder and head still throbbed, but he managed to find some aspirin in her cabinet. He'd found a razor and new blades also, but decided against a shave. No use causing more damage with a shaky hand.

Like the bedroom, the bath had a decidedly feminine appeal. The combination hardwood floor and bead-board paneling presented a casual coziness that was only emphasized by a pedestal sink, distressed vanity and an eclectic collection of candles.

Curious, Jacob grabbed the shampoo from the corner of the bathtub. He took a whiff, then read the bottle. Honeysuckle.

A small mystery solved.

For the first time, he simply focused on the facts of his situation and systematically sorted through what he'd learned over the last half hour.

In his mind, he saw flashes of pictures. From parks to fields to coliseums. He couldn't bring names to mind, or locations. He couldn't say if he'd been to these locations or merely seen them in photos or on television. They held no connection to him on any level.

The only thing, only person who seemed familiar to him was Grace.

A lead—his only instinctive lead. One he planned on pursuing.

The coffee aroma hit him as he stepped out of the bedroom. "Smells good."

The neutral colors, the rustic pine floors triggered no memories, but this time he hadn't expected them to. "How often have I been here?"

"Many times. Too many to count."

The walk to the kitchen caused his legs to shake. Enough that he was grateful for the stool when he slid onto it.

"Go ahead and have some while I get things together." She placed a travel mug in front of him, along with a plate with toast. "You liked your coffee black."

He lifted the mug. "Let's see if I still do." When he took a swig, the heat of it punched him in the belly. Enough to make him grunt and draw a slanted look from Grace. "It's good. Thanks."

"You're welcome." She grabbed two chocolate chip cookies from a nearby plate.

"So, do you and your father disagree often?"

"No more often than most fathers and daughters." She came around the counter and leaned a hip against the side. "I turned on the news while you were getting dressed and checked my computer. The shooting wasn't mentioned on either."

"You just changed the subject."

"You noticed." She took a bite of her cookie, chewed, then waved the remaining piece like a pointer. "Helene's death should have made the morning news."

"A murder would be hard to keep out of the press," he reasoned, even as a cookie crumb settled on her cheek, distracting him. "But the police have done it before."

Giving in to the urge, he leaned in and brushed the crumb away with the pad of his thumb. But instead of keeping the touch light, the gesture simple, he found himself cupping her face in his palm—told himself that he was only searching for memories. Answers.

"Jacob—"

"Shh." His thumb stopped her mouth, midmotion, leaving her lips slightly parted. He slipped between to the warm smooth touch of her teeth, felt her intake of breath rush over his skin—

The doorbell sounded, jolting them both apart.

Jacob swore, low and mean. His body went rigid, his hand already reaching for the gun in his back waistband. "Your father?"

"He wouldn't ring the bell," she answered, trying to get her heart back down from her throat. Not from the interruption but from the realization that in another minute, probably less if she were honest, she'd have been in Jacob's arms.

"Is your car out front?"

"Yes. It's parked under my carport."

"Then you'd better answer." Jacob's face turned cold, almost savage. The fact he reached for his gun only fed her trepidation.

"Leave my plate. It will look like you're eating breakfast alone. I'll wait in the bedroom," he whispered while he checked his clip. "But I'll be watching, so no worries." This time when he cupped her cheek, it was for reassurance. "You'll be okay. Just stay calm."

After Jacob disappeared into the bedroom, she walked slowly to the front door.

A second chime rang out just as she peered through the peephole. Two men stood on her front porch, both dressed in navy-blue suits, both holding badges in their hand. The law enforcement insignias glared in the sunlight.

"Who is it?"

"Annapolis Police, Miss Renne. We need to speak with you."

Her hand tightened reflexively on the knob. She glanced at the closed bedroom, unlocked the dead bolt and opened the front door. "Can I help you?"

"Miss Renne?" At her nod, the thinner of the two, a nearly bald man with a flat face and heavy eyelids, stepped forward.

"I'm Detective Webber." He pointed to his partner, a man with steroid-typical muscles packed into a tailored suit and crisp, white shirt. "This is Detective Sweeney. We're both with the Annapolis Police. Homicide Division."

"How are you, Miss Renne?" Sweeney's smile was a grim line but it was his gaze that drew her attention. Gray eyes studied her from under two rather thick eyebrows, before shifting past her shoulder to sweep the room behind her.

Grace resisted the urge to shut the door. "Fine, but uncertain how I can help you, Detective."

First one, then the other flipped his badge closed and pocketed it. "Can we talk to you about Helene Garrett?" Sweeney asked, his gaze back on hers.

"My bar manager called me earlier about her death and I'm really not up to answering any questions just now."

"You mean your ex-manager, don't you?" Sweeney placed his foot in the doorway. "It's either here or downtown, Miss Renne. Your choice," he advised. His tone, while professional, left her with no alternative but to believe him. "We have a murderer on the loose. What happened to your friend wasn't a robbery or an accident. And I'm sure you would want her killer caught as soon as possible."

"Of course, I do."

"The longer we wait, the less chance we have of catching him." Sweeney pushed against the door with his knee with just enough pressure to emphasize his point—if she wanted them to get physical, they would.

"All right, gentlemen." Grace released the door, allowing the two men to enter. She led them to the middle of the room, but didn't offer them a seat. "How can I help you?"

"You can start by telling us where you were last night at approximately eleven o'clock." Webber fished under his suit and pulled out a notebook and pen.

"I was here baking cookies." She gestured to the plate on the counter.

Neither man glanced over. "Was anyone here with you?" Webber continued.

"I'm afraid not."

"Did Helene Garrett have any enemies? Anyone who might have wanted her dead?" Sweeney asked. Once again those gray eyes skimmed the room, touching on the closed bedroom door before moving over to the window and back to Grace.

Grace shifted until she blocked his line of sight. "No one that I know of."

"How about her friends?" Webber remarked, his frustration breaking through. "Do you know anyone who was close enough to Miss Garrett to give some insight into the last few days of her life?"

"Helene didn't have friends, she had business acquaintances. Too many for me to know."

"You mean to tell us that after three years of being partners, you have no idea how Helene Garrett conducted her life? Who she associated with? Can't make a guess at who could have killed her?"

Grace hesitated.

Are you absolutely sure I didn't kill Helene?

No.

She put her hands in her sweatshirt pouch and pressed her palms against her stomach. She felt the weight of her baby against the burden of her decision.

The police would do their best to keep her safe. But she understood deep down that their best would not be good enough.

"I'm telling you exactly that, Detective Webber," she said. "Helene was a private person. She didn't share much about herself with anyone. And I wasn't her only partner. Her capital was tied into many business ventures."

"We're finding that out," Sweeney admitted wryly. "You recently sold your half of the club to her, right?"

"That's right."

"Did you know the new owner is Jacob Lomax? He was one of those business acquaintances you mentioned earlier." The shock of Sweeney's statement nearly shattered her rigid hold. But then Webber smiled with venom and Grace's nervousness gave way to anger.

"No, I didn't know Mr. Lomax was the new owner, but I'm not surprised."

"How well did you know him?"

"Not very well at all. In fact, I didn't remember him until you just mentioned his name. I met him briefly, about eight months ago, but shared no more than a handshake." Grace and Jacob had kept their affair private. But if the police dug deep enough, they would discover the truth.

"Even if I had known, it wouldn't have mattered." She nodded at the boxes in the living room. "As you can see, I'm moving. Out of state, actually. And I didn't want to manage a business long-distance. Helene understood that."

"Can I ask why you are moving?" Sweeney walked over to the nearest box and lifted the flap.

Grace swallowed a nasty comment about minding his own business. "A change of climate."

"When was last time you saw her?" Sweeney asked, before returning. He glanced over to the counter, took in the breakfast dishes.

Another lie was there on the tip of her tongue. But too many people could have known about their meeting the day before. "Yesterday at the bistro down on Main. We had lunch together. A farewell of sorts."

"Do you mind?" He nodded toward the cookies.

"Not at all."

"Thanks." Sweeney helped himself to a cookie, took a bite and nodded his approval. "You and Miss Garrett parted on good terms?"

"Yes, we did." The hair prickled at her nape. There was no doubt in her mind that Jacob was observing her conversation with the detectives. "Is that all, gentlemen?"

"For now." Sweeney finished his cookie in one more bite, then reached into his suit pocket and pulled out a business card. "If you think of anything else that might help us, please contact me."

Grace didn't take the card from him fast enough and it dropped between them. Sweeney bent down to retrieve it and paused, his eyes on the hardwood floor. "Miss Renne, did I mention that Helene Garrett managed to shoot her killer just before she died?"

"No, Detective. You didn't. But I don't see how that—"

"There are bloodstains on your floor."

Grace followed his line of vision. More than a few red streaks smeared the varnished cherrywood. Marks she'd missed in her hasty cleanup the night before. "Those are mine. I cut my foot yesterday on some broken glass. I must have missed a few spots when I cleaned up."

Sweeney automatically looked at her bare feet. "There's no bandage."

"It was a small cut." Her chin lifted. "I'm not going to show you the bottom of my feet, Detective."

"She's lying," Webber inserted, obviously pleased by the prospect. He shoved his notebook back into his pocket.

Indignation worked its way into her words. "You honestly cannot think that I'm somehow involved in Helene's death—"

"You're right, I don't." Sweeney stood, scuffed the stains with his foot. "Where is he?"

Webber took a threatening step toward Grace. Out of sheer willpower, she stood her ground.

"Where is who?"

The blow came from out of nowhere. Pain ripped through her cheek, burst behind her eyes. She staggered back, just managing to keep herself from hitting the floor.

"My partner is much more polite than I am," Webber warned. "Where is Jacob Lomax?"

Grace straightened, her legs shaking. She could taste blood on her lip, but her hand automatically went to her belly. "I told you I haven't seen the man in months."

When Webber raised his fist again, a gun exploded from behind Grace. Screaming, the big man doubled over, one meaty hand wrapped around the other. Blood oozed through his fingers and dripped to the floor.

"Move, Grace." The words came low and mean. Grace automatically stepped out of reach, giving Jacob an unobstructed view of the two men.

"Looking for me?" With one shoulder against the doorsill, Jacob shifted his 9 mm slightly until it pointed at Sweeney. Jacob's face hardened into savage lines.

Slowly, Sweeney raised his arms away from his sides, but shock flickered across his face before he masked it. "I am if you're Lomax."

"That's what I hear."

"You son of a bitch," Webber wheezed. He slumped to his knees and cradled his injured hand to his chest. "You just shot a police officer."

Jacob let out a derisive snort, ignoring Webber's gasps of pain. "Most cops don't hit potential female witnesses. Or wear suits that cost more than a year's salary."

Sweat broke out on Jacob's forehead. Grace could see the tremors in his left hand and understood he wouldn't stay standing very long.

He tilted his gun, just a bit to put Sweeney's chest in his crosshairs. "Want to try telling me who you both really are?"

"We work for a private investor that is extremely interested in your relationship with Helene Garrett," Sweeney answered, cautious.

"And this is how you get your information?" Jacob mocked. Out of his peripheral vision, he caught Grace wiping the blood from her lip. Rage strained against reason, pushing the limit of his control. "I think you boys need to work on your approach."

With a growl, Webber grabbed for his gun. Jacob fired and Webber stumbled back. Blood flooded from the man's neck.

He struggled, groping the wound with his hands even as he crumpled choking on his own blood.

Sweeney charged Grace. Reacting swiftly, she slid on her hip, taking out his legs and toppled Sweeney like a bowling pin.

Jacob slammed his pistol into Sweeney's head, knocking him out cold. "Let's see how you like headaches," he murmured, then dropped to his knees, shaking.

"Jacob!" Grace sat beside him. Immediately, she found herself drawn tight against his side. "I thought—"

"Are you all right?"

"Yes." Grace leaned into him, grasped his sweater in one hand to make sure he didn't pull away. Finding reassurance. Just for a moment, she buried her face against his chest. He smelled of soap. Basic. Clean. Reassuring against the heavy metallic scent of blood that already thickened the air.

"Do you need help?" she asked.

"Not yet." He blew air out through his mouth, trying to get a grip on his rolling stomach, his shaking limbs. "Who in the hell taught you how to take someone down like that?"

"You did." She tried to smile, but her lips wobbled. "That day in the snow."

Chapter Seven

"Looks like you were right." Jacob found handcuffs on Webber's belt and snapped them on Sweeney's wrists. "Do you have any cash?"

"About a hundred dollars."

"Make sure you grab it," he ordered. "And your keys."

The scent of blood grew to a sickening stench. Grace glanced down at Webber, his face now a contorted death mask of crimson. His expensive suit was no more than a soggy towel saturated with his blood.

With effort, she took a few deep breaths through her mouth to avoid the scent, drive away the nausea.

"Are you going to faint on me?"

"No." She dug her nails into her palm to prove it.

Swearing, he grabbed a throw from the couch and covered Webber's body. "That's the best I can do for you, Grace."

"Thank you." Her voice quivered, but with Webber covered, the queasiness started to fade. "Aren't we going to question Sweeney?"

"Questioning a prisoner takes stamina. I don't have any right now." He checked the two men's pockets, pulled out their wallets. "Let's see if they are who they said they were." He took out the badges. "Fake. Crafted well, though."

"How do you know?" Her panic faded under curiosity.

"Just do." Jacob shrugged, storing the information away for later. He was working on instinct and right now it was telling him to move. "But like my weapons training, I couldn't tell you how long I've had the knowledge or where I picked it up from."

He took the money from each of the wallets. "Whoever pays them pays them well. They're carrying over three thousand between the two of them." He handed her the cash. "We're going to need this. Credit cards put us out on the information grid."

"You were carrying almost as much in your wallet."

"Maybe we have the same boss," he answered derisively.

"Sweeney was in charge. If that's his real name. Anyone with this caliber of forgeries, probably works under a dozen different aliases." He patted a few more pockets until he found their keys and cell phones. He glanced at the phones. "All the numbers are deleted. These boys knew what they were doing. Still, if his boss decides to call, I want to be available." He pocketed Sweeney's cell phone, then handed Webber's phone to her.

"Crush it." Jacob's face paled to a sickly gray; his lips were bloodless. A sheen of perspiration covered his skin, dampened his hair. "I'd like to know what the hell they want from me."

Grace stomped on the phone, shattering it. If he was placing his life on the line, the least he deserved was the truth. "It's not you they want, Jacob."

"Say that again."

"It's not you," she repeated, grinding the last of the phone under her heel. "It's me."

He sat back. "Go on. I'm listening."

"Last night, you were still conscious when I found you. In fact, you knocked on the door, then collapsed on the porch."

She rubbed the back of her neck, suddenly feeling the weight of the world there. "You told me to hide. That someone wanted to kill me."

"I didn't say who."

"No. You didn't."

"Grace, Sweeney came looking for me. Not you."

Startled, she could only look at him. "You're right. He wasn't concerned with me at all. But that doesn't make sense."

"It does if we're dealing with two separate problems," he reasoned.

"You mean we're being chased by two different people?" She dropped to her knees, her hands braced on her legs. Her gaze was fixed on his. "But it still doesn't answer why whoever wants me came after you and Helene first. I can be found by anyone who has a phone book."

"Maybe someone chased me to your house and I was afraid you would get in the way," he reasoned. "Or maybe I was just delirious from my head injury."

"No, the threat was real," Grace argued. "I'm sure of it."

"And since I brought the message, you think you can trust me to help you?"

She looked pointedly at his shoulder. "That's what friends do," she whispered. "Besides, who else can I trust if it isn't the guy who warned me?"

After a moment, he nodded. "Okay, pal, grab whatever you can hold in your pockets. We don't have time for anything else." Jacob tossed Sweeney's keys under her couch. He was standing by the time she returned from the bedroom. "What kind of car do you drive?"

"A Jag," she shouted from the bedroom. "I filled the tank yesterday."

"Good. We might need something with some power."

She pushed her wallet into her sweatshirt pocket and phone into the back of her jeans. She grabbed her keys off the counter.

Before she could react, he opened the front door and fired a few bullets into Sweeney's tires. "How well can you drive?"

She glanced at the deflated tires and thought of Webber. "Better than you can shoot."

THE JAG WAS THE COLOR of hot salsa, with saber-chromed wheels and butter-cream leather seats. If a car could preen, this one would have a reason.

"Nice ride." Drained, Jacob shifted back into the passenger seat. The throb in his shoulder took on an edge of heat. He shifted using the armrest to brace his bad shoulder. What he needed was some time to regain strength and to sort through their situation.

"Thanks. That's what you said when you helped me pick it out."

"I did?"

"I wasn't lying to you," she replied. "We were friends." But like *father,* he noted, she infused no warmth into the word *friend.*

"Were we more than friends?" It seemed natural to cock his head, lift one eyebrow.

"No," she said, but with enough hesitation to feed his doubt.

"Am I gay?"

Her lips curled into a tolerant smile. "No."

"Are you?"

She laughed then. "No."

He decided he liked her laugh. It rolled through her, erupting in a slightly breathless chuckle. He realized he wanted to hear it again.

Her gaze turned to the road and he used the opportunity to take a long look. He took in the slope of her neck, the pulse at the base of her throat. A flush crept up over her cheeks, telling him she was aware of his scrutiny, but Jacob continued to study her nonetheless.

He'd distanced himself from his emotions, accepting the situation. Though, even at its best, it was nothing more than a maze of smoke and mirrors.

But something inside—an echo of what was, or what could've been—kept him from gaining that same emotional distance from her.

"You're sure we weren't more to each other?"

"Yes," she said, exasperated. The pulse quickened, the flush darkened. Her response was more than a little breathless, but this time there was no chuckle.

Did her reaction mean they had been involved and she was lying, or she'd thought about it and was embarrassed? Self-preservation either way, Jacob decided. And that he could understand.

"What happened?" This time the push wasn't for the truth, but for the reaction. Damn, he found her blush charming.

"Nothing really. You left."

He rested his head against the window, enjoyed the cool

glass against the pounding in his temple. "What do you mean? Did I leave the state? Or leave the country?"

"Both." *You left me,* Grace thought, keeping her pride intact but at the cost of another crack in her heart.

"So why did I leave?"

"I don't know." At least in that Grace could be truthful. She downshifted, taking a hairpin turn with the ease of a race car driver. She heard his reluctant grunt of approval. "You never explained. One day you were here, the next you weren't."

"Can't say I was a very good friend, then."

"You had no reason to be, really." She stopped the ache that threatened to harden the edges of her response. Just.

"How long had we known each other?"

"Not long," Grace hesitated, pretending to do the calculations. "Two months. Almost three." Eighty-one days.

Jacob realized she was choosing her words very carefully. A person only did that when they didn't want to offend or, more importantly, wanted to defend. From the white-knuckled grip she had on the steering wheel, he tended to believe her choice was the latter.

"I had accidentally interrupted a business meeting between you and Helene. I didn't know you were in our office and I burst through the door all excited about a jazz band I had just booked. One we'd been trying to get for months. She introduced us."

Helene again. Shooting Sweeney's partner had showed Jacob he was capable of killing. He'd felt no remorse, not even a twinge of regret. Webber needed killing. Period. But somehow Helene's murder didn't sit right. Almost as if murdering her didn't fit his sense of self.

"What you told Sweeney about Helene, was it true?"

"More or less," she acknowledged. "We had lunch together and she gave me the final copies of our sales contract. We ate. We laughed. We hugged. We cried a little, then said goodbye."

"What did you talk about?"

"Business details. Plans to meet again," Grace said, then glanced in his direction. "You."

"What about me?"

"She told me she was meeting you later that night and wanted to know if I had a message to pass on." Actually, Helene had threatened to tell Jacob about the baby. "I said no."

"I see." Grace's fingers flexed against the steering wheel. "Did anyone stop by your table?"

"Only the waiter," she said. "But he's been there forever."

"How about her demeanor? Did she seem angry? Afraid?"

"No—" She stopped. "Wait. When I came back from the bathroom after we ate, she seemed…" Grace thought for a moment. "Impatient."

"She could've been spooked."

"Or she could've had a hard time saying goodbye."

"Maybe. But if she kept herself distant, why would she be upset?"

"At least she said goodbye." The retort was out of her mouth before she could stop it. "I'm sorry, that was unfair."

"Why? Because I don't remember?"

Her lips smoothed out into a grin. "Well, it does put you at a disadvantage, doesn't it?"

"I suppose it does." Then seriously, he added, "I'd like to think I had a good reason, Grace. Maybe it even has something to do with what we're in now. But either way, if and when I do remember, I'll tell you everything."

Grace shook her head. "I don't expect you to—"

"I know," he said quietly. "Why would Helene leave me the bar?"

"She trusted you."

"But why didn't she leave it to you?"

"I told her I wasn't coming back to Maryland."

"Did Helene give you anything? Warn you about anything?"

"Nothing," she answered. "I told you, it was like every other lunch we've had together. Other than saying goodbye, of course."

"Did Helene ever talk about me? I mean, before the lunch?"

"No. Never. Her business was her business."

"Yet you trusted her."

"Implicitly," Grace said without hesitation.

"Why?"

"I don't know. Instinct, I guess."

"Is that why we became friends? Because you instinctively like me?"

"You could be charming when you wanted to be." Again there was no hesitation.

He watched the roadside for a moment. A few mailboxes, some scattered buildings. Remote, but not so remote a person had to travel far for food or fuel. "It's frustrating. I know this road, yet I'd swear to you that I've never seen it before."

Grace laid her hand on his thigh and squeezed. "It will come. We need to give it time."

"That's the problem, if Sweeney is any indication. We don't have time."

"So I'll tell you what I can and hope it prods your memories."

"That bothers me, too," he acknowledged. "After three months of being together, the only information I shared with you was my name? And that I'm a business associate of your ex-partner?"

"Yes." Sadness underlined her words, not resentment. "That's why I left, isn't it?" His eyes flitted over her, the blue in them flat and unreadable. "Because you pushed me to open up?"

"I told you I don't know why you left." More buildings loomed as they passed a sign welcoming them to Eastport. She glanced at the side mirror and changed lanes. "You didn't share that with me, either."

"Talk about irony." His laugh was harsh, tinged with self-deprecation. "If I had told you about myself, we both might have a better idea about the mess we're in. Even my driver's license is from out of state."

"Jacob, Helene had moved out of her place and into yours a few months ago. She told me she'd rather rent from a friend than a stranger. But she didn't advertise it. She told me she needed some peace and quiet away from work."

"Where?"

"You have a renovated boathouse. Down south off of the bay."

"And you were going to tell me this when?"

"Excuse me for being distracted," she muttered.

"Point taken." His sigh was long, ragged. "I guess that's where we're headed, then. If Helene left any clues behind, it would be either there or at the club."

"Shouldn't we go by the club first?

Jacob shook his head. "The police will be watching it. I'm not up for another confrontation."

"You might have spoken too soon." Grace glanced at her rearview mirror. "I think we're being followed."

Jacob studied the side mirror. "The black sedan?"

"Yes."

"Turn your blinker on like you're going to turn right. Then take the next left."

Grace gripped the steering wheel, taking the turn on a squeal of tires.

A few moments later, the black sedan skidded around the corner. The driver gunned its engine, picking up pursuit.

"Looks like I didn't smack our friend hard enough," Jacob commented dryly. He pulled out his gun and checked the clip.

Grace punched the gas.

"How did he get a car so fast?" Grace demanded.

"Why don't you ask the guy in the passenger seat with the machine gun?"

Grace didn't take her eyes off the street. Instead, she swung the Jag into a sharp right. The back end fishtailed, but a second later Grace regained control.

The traffic light flashed red at the end of the block. "Run it," Jacob ordered.

"Hold on." Grace dodged a delivery truck with another twist of the wheel but didn't ease up on the accelerator. Pedestrians scattered, screaming as they dove for the curb.

Rubber squealed against cement. Bullets pinged off her side panel. "Are they crazy?"

"You don't have to be crazy to kill." His fist hit the window button before he released the safety belt and swung around in his seat. He thrust the gun out the window and fired at Sweeney.

"There's too many people, Jacob." Real fear caught hold of her. One slip, one bad reaction, and she could kill an innocent person.

A taxi cab skidded across the intersection. Grace slammed the brakes and wrenched the wheel, spinning the car into a one-eighty. People screamed and scattered, diving and ducking behind parked cars.

Jacob's shoulder slammed against the passenger door. Pain ripped through him from his elbow to his skull.

Swearing, Jacob righted himself and fired a few more shots. "Keep the car straight, damn it."

"You're kidding, right?" She shoved the stick into Reverse and hit the accelerator. Jacob's back crashed into the dash. Metal crunched metal as she hit the car behind her. She threw the Jag into gear, heard the whine of steel breaking loose from the back end.

"Was that straight enough for you? I just lost my bumper." Not waiting for a reply, Grace charged through the pattern of cars clogging the city streets, weaving when she could, cutting others off when she had to.

Grace hit her brakes, barely missing the back end of a bus.

Suddenly, their friends in the sedan skidded past them. Sweeney slammed the brakes, fishtailing against a corner mailbox.

Jacob's bullets pelted the sedan, doing very little damage to their windows. "The glass is bulletproof."

Sweeney reversed on a squeal of tires. Wide black stripes burned the pavement, smoked the air.

Grace floored the accelerator and shot forward, once again putting them into a two-vehicle race.

"Construction?" She nearly screamed the word. Orange barrels spotted the street in uneven lines, narrowing into a blockade across the highway on-ramp.

"We need that ramp, Grace. We can lose them on the stretch without traffic lights."

"You're out of your mind, Lomax." The back window exploded, shooting shards of glass into the air.

"Scoot down, damn it."

Grace couldn't get down far, not if she wanted to keep control of the car.

Jacob dropped his empty clip and shoved the second into his pistol. "They're using the machine guns. I can't hold them off very much longer."

"Damn!" She hit the steering wheel with one fist.

"Take the ramp." Jacob punctuated the statement with two shots from his gun through the back opening.

The sedan sped up, closing the distance between him and Grace's car. Close enough that Grace could see Sweeney in the driver's seat.

Grace waited a long few seconds, swerved toward the blockade of wood and barrels, her foot heavy against the accelerator.

The Jag hit the barrier, jolting them both. She gritted her teeth. "This car isn't even a year old."

"At the rate we're going, we'll probably be dead before the day's over. So I'm not too worried about it."

She pushed away thoughts of her baby. "Not if I can help it."

In the distance, she heard sirens. Felt the prickle at her

back. "Hold on." Grace took the car flying over the dirt and broken cement.

Police cars raced toward them, their red and blue lights flashing, their sirens screeching.

"We need to lose your car. It's too conspicuous."

"You think?" Grace commented as two more police cars joined the chase.

"You've got five cop cars on your ass."

"I saw. Now all we need is a chopper and we can have a party." Grace swerved, just missing a parked construction backhoe. One of the police cars wasn't so lucky. It bounced off the digger, spun and hit another cop car head-on. Air bags exploded. Grace said a small prayer hoping the bags did their job.

"Two down," Jacob said, his voice grim.

Wheels hit flat cement and Grace shoved the car into high gear. The Jag raced onto the expressway.

"Let's see what we can do with some elbow room." When she floored the accelerator this time, Jacob saw the needle shoot past one hundred.

Grace jerked the wheel sending the car onto the shoulder, creating her own lane as she passed cars one by one.

"Don't tell me. I taught you this on the mountain, too."

"No, we only had time for some light hand-to-hand combat," she said, and swerved two lanes to the right without touching the brake. "I learned this on my own."

The sirens behind them lessened, telling Grace the police cars were losing ground.

"Where are our friends?"

Jacob dropped his clip, checked the number of rounds left, shoved it back in. "Lost them when the police joined the party."

He glanced up and caught the sign for Chesapeake Bay. "Take this street."

"It leads to the harbor. Limits our options."

"Take it."

She saw the blood-soaked shirt, the gray-tinged skin. He'd ripped open his stitches and was losing blood. "Are you okay?"

"I'll manage."

The pier loomed ahead. Monday midmorning traffic had already congested the main path with tourists.

A barrage of bullets hit the car from the side. Suddenly, Sweeney was there again. This time close enough for Grace to see the grim slant of his features. "Where did he come from?"

"Look out!"

Grace swerved, barely missing a biker and his dog. But it cost them. The car slammed through the metal guard gate blocking the pedestrian's crossing and shot down the main pier. People screamed and scattered in mass panic. Grace slammed on the brakes, but there wasn't enough time.

The car skidded, the tires screeched. A heartbeat later, the car splintered the side railing and plunged into the water.

More screams shattered the air.

But this time, Grace realized, they were hers.

Chapter Eight

When the car hit the water, both air bags exploded, driving Grace back into her seat. Instinctively she struggled against the bags' suffocating weight. Water rushed in from the floor, a gush of icy liquid that sucked the oxygen out of the car, smothering what little gasps of air she managed.

Without warning, the car shifted nose up. Water gushed through the blown-out back window. Tossed backward, Grace stifled a scream. She clawed at the bag, trying to get leverage.

"Stop struggling, Grace." The order came in a short burst of air by her ear. Suddenly her safety belt broke free. "Hold your breath!"

The car submerged. Her breath backed up into her lungs. Out of nowhere, Jacob grabbed her hand and tugged her toward him. Blindly, she shoved the deflating air bag away.

Jacob pulled her through the back window behind him. The ragged steel scraped at her sweatshirt, snagging her like a fish on a line. Panic pressed in on her chest. She yanked on the material but it held tight. Quickly, she unzipped it and pulled free, leaving the jacket behind.

Her head broke the surface a few seconds before his. She

dragged oxygen into her lungs in huge swallowing gulps. The gritty water and air burned her throat and lungs.

The black sedan skidded to a stop by a small diving equipment rental shack. Both men jumped from the car, but Sweeney's passenger was faster. A machine gun appeared in his hands a split second later.

"Dive!" Jacob ordered. Gunshots peppered the water in front of them.

She gasped for breath and plunged below again. This time swimming deep as bullets whizzed past her.

Only when the blood pounded at her ears and the air slipped from her lungs did she kick to the surface.

Jacob reached for the semiautomatic in his waistband just as Sweeney grabbed the machine gun and smashed it into the other man's face.

Jacob heard Grace surface, coughing. "Stay behind me." With his feet he tread water, ignoring the pain that seared his back and shoulders. Instead, he scanned the rental shack. Racks of oxygen tanks lined one side of the front door. Pedestrians scattered, running away from the gunmen.

Jacob didn't hesitate. He fired into the rack of divers' oxygen tanks. An explosion ripped through the air. The gunmen hit the deck, but Sweeney's partner was too close. A fire stream shot from the ground behind him, the flames engulfed the man.

Jacob looked at Grace. "Are you okay?"

When she nodded, he said, "Follow me."

Jacob swam under the nearby fishing piers, looped out and followed an invisible line of water down south. Several minutes later, both he and Grace rode the waves onto the beach well away from the crowd of onlookers at the pier fire.

"This isn't good, Jacob." Grace stood and let the water lap

against her calves. Sand sucked at her feet. Her legs trembled, but with the effort from wading ashore or from sheer shock, she couldn't be sure.

"It's not done, either." He came abreast of her and stopped.

He was right, of course. She tried not to think about it. Instead, she pressed her hand to her belly, took comfort in the round swell of it, and then said a silent prayer that at least for now, they were all safe. "What's our next step?"

When Jacob didn't answer, Grace turned fully toward him. But his eyes weren't on her face.

Panic tripped down her spine as she followed his gaze to her stomach.

A thin cotton tank top stuck to her body, a second skin that outlined the fullness of her breasts, the more than slight roundness of her stomach. Her hand plucked at the material, pulling it away from the damp skin beneath.

But he barely noticed. His mind flashed back to Grace's house and her confrontation with Sweeney. He saw her hand dip to her belly when Webber hit her, saw her father's eyes drop to Grace's stomach during their argument.

"You're pregnant?" Suddenly, Jacob exploded with a string of curses.

"It seems you remembered some of your favorite words."

"You think this is a joke?" Pain ripped through his shoulder, down his arm. Bits of sand caught under his bandage, burned like acid in his wound. Sheer willpower kept him on his feet, fighting the waves that slammed against the back of his legs. "Since this morning, you've been shot at, punched and nearly drowned." He jabbed at the sky with his finger. "And the day isn't even half over yet." It wasn't a question, so he didn't expect an answer. But what he didn't expect was her chin to hitch, her eyes to narrow.

Her temper enraged his own. He grasped on to the anger with both hands, knowing if he didn't the thought of what could've happened—what might still happen—would make him shudder with fear. "How far along are you?"

"Almost five months."

He stood there for a moment, where the bay hugged the sandy shore, knowing that with her statement she'd just upped the risk. "Of all the idiotic—" He glanced at her, then stopped. Not because he'd gone too far. He was justified, damn it. But for the first time, he looked beyond her temper, beyond the stubbornness that kept her back rigid, her features tight. And he saw the hunted glaze of her eyes, the paleness of her skin.

The need to protect her rolled through him, knocking the breath from his chest. "Let's go." Annoyed, he shoved the pistol into his back waistband with his good hand and yanked his sweater over the handle. "Act normal."

Pregnant.

With a quick glance, he scanned their surroundings. The beach was fairly large with a parking lot that ran for more than a block. Just beyond lay a playground spotted with children and their parents.

"Stay down. Use the cars for cover."

Grace couldn't stop shivering. The brisk wind beat against her damp skin and jeans. "We're wet and you're bleeding." She nodded toward his shoulder. The sweater was more crimson than not across the shoulder and chest. "How normal do you think we can act?"

They walked briskly, cutting through several rows of cars, avoiding mingling families and other groups of people.

"Over here."

Farther down toward the back of the parking lot sat a truck with a camper shell attached to the bed. A classic, if you counted the early seventies, with more rust than paint across its hood and tailgate.

The driver's window stood half-open. Far enough for Jacob to reach in and unlock the door.

"Watch for trouble." Jacob opened the door, shoved over a baseball cap that lay on the seat. Shifting, he managed to squirm under the dashboard. He grabbed the wires from under the steering column and pulled them free.

"You're hot-wiring a car?" Grace scanned the surrounding area. She strained her ears for any signs of sirens but heard nothing but the wind whip through the cabin.

"It's better than walking." The engine revved, punctuating his remark. "Get in. You're driving."

Jacob maneuvered out from under the dash and let out a long hiss when his shoulder bumped the steering wheel.

She needed no other prodding and slid into the driver's seat. "Let's go," Jacob ordered. Then he grabbed the baseball cap and shoved it onto her head. "Can you drive?"

"It's an automatic," she said, throwing the car into gear. "If I run into trouble, I'll make sure you're the first to know."

"You do that." Gas fumes and stale vinyl filled the air. Her stomach rolled in protest but Grace resisted the urge to hold her breath.

Within seconds, she backed them out of the parking spot and drove away. "Are we safe?"

"For the time being." He noticed her shivering. He reached over and switched on the heat. "Where's my house?"

"If we go there, they might be there waiting."

"Doesn't matter. It's a chance we're going to have to take. Right now, that house might be the key to getting my memory back."

Grace tensed. Her home. Her father. "Jacob, I forgot about my dad." She groped at her pocket. "I need to warn him."

"Do you think you'll be doing him a favor?"

"What if he'd walked in on Sweeney?" She took her phone out of her pocket, biting back a curse when she flipped open the lid. The LED screen was cracked.

"Sweeney followed us too quickly." His eyes studied her for a moment. "Chances are that your father discovered Webber's body after Sweeney left. Which means he called the police. Which means he'll be questioned by the authorities—if he isn't being questioned already. He has no idea what happened. He can be honest with the police and tell them about me. Your father has no reason to trust me now. If you contact him, they'll know and realize you're not being kidnapped but a willing accomplice. We don't know who we're dealing and until we do, I'm not going to take a chance; it might be the police themselves."

"An informant?" She shook the water from the phone. When that didn't work, she used her teeth and popped open the back cover. Maybe if she dried off the battery and placed the phone to the heater vent…

"Let me do that."

"Not a chance. You'll throw it out the window." She glanced over at him. "My dad's better scared than dead? Is that what you're saying?" She balanced the phone across the steering wheel and used her finger nails to pry out the battery. "You think that my dad is involved with this?"

"Someone is holding Sweeney's leash. And until I discover who it is, the only person I'm sure didn't kill Helene is you."

"The only thing my father knows is that you are a friend of mine in trouble—"

The battery popped out and fell into her lap. Grace froze. "Jacob, there's a note."

"What?"

"A small note folded in half." She took out the thin strip of wet paper that clung to the underside of the battery and handed it to him.

Carefully he separated the back from the front. "It's a series of letters and numbers." Quickly, he counted them.

Grace shot him a side glance. "It's Helene's handwriting," she said. "Are they readable?"

"Yes. Only the edges are smeared a little," Jacob replied. "Did Helene have access to your phone yesterday?"

Did she? Grace went over the lunch yesterday in her mind. "I turned my phone off because I didn't want to be interrupted during lunch. We were sitting in a booth, so I set my keys and phone on the window ledge."

"Why not in your purse?"

She studied the road ahead, thinking. "It's a habit. Not one of my better ones. I'm constantly misplacing things."

"You said Helene became impatient at the end of lunch. Was it after you came back from the bathroom?"

"Yes," she replied, then remembered. "Actually, she had already paid for lunch and stood when I came to the table.

She handed me my keys and phone. Then jokingly she told me not to lose them." She jerked her gaze to his. "You don't think—"

"The hell I don't," he answered. "Where are your keys?"

"In the ignition of my car. At the bottom of the bay."

and the co...

Chapter Nine

The Victorian mansion stood five levels high. Anything less would seem impoverished to a United States senator, Frank Sweeney thought derisively. And D'Agostini was anything but impoverished. A sophisticated blend of old and new, the mansion boasted an embassy-sized ballroom, an art gallery, a wine bistro and a media room with an adjoining twenty-seat cinema.

All with coffered ceilings and herringbone floors. All tastefully gilded, draped and cosseted by one man's wealth and affluence.

But Frank wasn't here to see D'Agostini. He ignored the bodyguards flanking the entryway and the nearby elevator. Instead, temper had him climbing the grand staircase. Each jarring step increased the tempo of the hammers that beat the inside of his skull and added to his sense of self-punishment.

He'd screwed up. He hadn't anticipated the kick from the girl. Whether he wanted to admit it or not, the sight of Lomax standing in the doorway caught him off guard.

The third floor opened into a wide lobby. With quick strides, Frank walked to the far end where two oversized mahogany doors stood. Not bothering to knock, he opened the doors quietly, already hearing the battle that went on from the other side and not wanting to disturb it.

At one time, the gymnasium stood as a ballroom, now renovated into a modern miniature health club. While the vaulted ceiling remained, the walls were covered with mirrors, the hardwood floor with mats. Weights and machines flanked one side, while a bar, sauna and hot tub stood opposite.

In the middle, he saw Kragen take a short jab to his mouth. His sweat-darkened hair plastered to his head. His teeth gleamed white as he wiped blood from his lip with the back of his knuckle.

"All right, Tomas." He taunted his opponent and waved the other man forward with his fingers. "Come on."

Frank knew the instructor—a wiry martial arts expert—was left no other choice. And he had to give the man credit for taking that step forward. Mistake or not, Tomas drew blood, setting the tone for the workout. No apologies would be accepted.

Both fighters were of equal height, and equal in build. A good match for workouts. Tomas attacked with a right round-house kick to Kragen's face. At the last moment, Kragen sidestepped, grabbed the man's ankle and slammed his elbow into his opponent's face. Frank heard the bone crunch against cartilage, saw the blood gush.

But Frank knew Kragen wasn't finished. A second later, Kragen twisted the leg. This time, the bone snapped and Tomas screamed. Kragen followed his opponent's momentum and slammed Tomas's head into the floor. "I think we're done for the day, don't you?"

When Tomas nodded, Kragen left the man rolling in agony on the mat.

Frank opened the door, waved the guards in and watched them carry Tomas out. A dislocated knee is a small price to pay for keeping one's life.

"You keep going through instructors like that, you won't have anyone to tear apart when you really get angry," Frank commented.

"I told him I had a meeting later with the senator. He failed to pull his punch." Oliver wiped his lip again, then grabbed a towel from the edge of the mat and patted his face.

After a moment, he studied Frank's bruised features. "It appears that I fared better than you, Frank." He threw the towel back onto the mat and walked over to the bar. "I see you found Lomax," he commented, smiling. "Or did Webber do that to you?"

Frank snorted, but took the insult. He deserved it after all. "Webber's dead."

"Really?" Oliver's smile thinned. He reached under the bar and pulled a bottle of juice from the refrigerator. "Did you finally get a stomachful or did Lomax kill him?"

"Lomax," Frank admitted. "But he only beat me by a few seconds."

"What happened?"

"I found blood on the woman's floor, suspected it was Lomax's. Before I could question the woman, Webber hit her. Pissed me off. Took my focus off of her and the situation just long enough for Lomax to catch me unaware. He burst into the room like some damn hero."

"It's not like you to blame others for your mistakes, Frank."

Frank's gaze drifted pointedly over the bar, searching.

"What are you looking for?" Kragen asked.

"Hot coffee," Frank answered, referring to Kragen's earlier meeting with Webber.

Oliver laughed and chugged some of his juice. "With your tough hide, I'd use acid," he said, but the underlying tone of truth raised the hair on the back of Frank's neck.

"The only mistake I made was not killing Webber before we even got to Grace Renne's place," Frank admitted, but the muscles in his back stayed tight. "The screwup at The Tens should have never happened."

"I agree. But then again, the senator handpicked Webber to take care of it, didn't he?" Oliver commented dryly. "Did you take care not to leave any evidence at the Renne woman's house?"

"I did, but it wouldn't hurt to make another phone call."

"It wouldn't hurt you," Oliver said noncommittally. "But the more I cover up, the more chance of exposure." He grabbed a nearby towel and hooked it around his neck. "What about Miss Renne? Is she involved?"

"Now? Definitely," Frank added, thinking of the small plastic case in his pocket.

"What about the father?"

"We're still uncertain. Webber said he'd shot Lomax. The blood I found was obviously from his wound," Sweeney said carefully. "But it couldn't have been serious. The Lomax I saw looked healthy enough. Although, his face is banged up a bit. If I had to guess, I'd say the father wasn't a problem. But he might be part of our solution."

"Webber is dead and Lomax is gone. Neither will please the senator," Kragen advised. "If we decide to pressure a prominent Washington physician, it had better be for a good reason."

"Show the senator this," Frank reached into his pocket, pulled out the miniature DVD case and handed it to Kragen. "I think you'll have your reason."

Chapter Ten

The sun had faded into the ember-orange blur of a cloudy
Chesapeake dusk. In the distance, herons swooped and fed
from the bay waters, their long, white bodies graceful, their
eerie calls mournful.

The evening breeze picked up enough that the ends of her
hair tickled her shoulders, touching off a chill that skittered
down her spine. Grace stepped from the truck and hugged
her arms to her chest to fight another bout of shivers.

The air was thick with the smell of pine and earth—and
heavy enough with moisture that she could taste a hint of rain
at the back of her throat.

Her jeans, damp and stiff, chafed against her skin with
each step forward, but she ignored the discomfort.

"Not what I expected." Jacob observed from behind her,
startling her.

"I think that's why you liked it," Grace admitted slowly,
her heart still up in her throat.

Positioned out over the water, the four-story home stood
on stilts of steel and cement. The design shouldn't have
worked amongst four acres of wood, beach and bay. But
it did.

The sleek, straight-lined style defined contemporary architecture with its square yet modern windows and a lone tower resting comfortably on the flat roof. Only the occasional right angle kept the design from being too boxy and gave the home enough class to be unique, not boring.

"Most homes around here are more traditional," she said, breaking through the silence that had settled between them. At one time, she'd foolishly dreamed of living here with Jacob. "Tell me again why we are here and not chasing down my keys?"

"We're going to wait until the city fishes the car out of the water. Let them do the hard work."

"How long do you think that will be?"

"Considering that we parked the car in the middle of a boat channel, I would say relatively soon," Jacob commented, slanting her a sardonic look. "And if we're lucky, they'll take the car to city impound."

"So we start making calls to find out where we go looking. Then we break in later tonight?" The shivers rippled through her. She hugged her arms to her chest to keep them contained.

"There's no we," Jacob acknowledged. "You're not going, Grace."

"Why?"

"You're pregnant," he snapped.

"And you've got a bum shoulder and no memory. That's more of a disadvantage than being pregnant if we run into a bad guy or two."

"If I don't think, my reflexes take over. Like they did at your house with Sweeney."

"That doesn't mean—"

"What happened with Sweeney and the car chase should tell you they're not going to stop. Hell, you're lucky that baby didn't get harmed when we took our dip in the bay."

"He's tougher than he looks. And so am I," she said, but she had thought the same thing and shivered once more. But this time it wasn't from the cold.

"Well, you scared the hell out of me," he replied, his voice tight. "Once we get to my place, you're going to stay put until I figure out what is going on."

"Jacob, I'd go insane waiting for some faceless predator to hunt me down in a dark corner."

"It wouldn't be a dark corner. It will be a whole different country if I have anything to say about it."

"You don't think they'd find me?"

"Not before I'd find them," he growled. "And that's a promise."

"No."

"You have no choice." His eyes snapped to hers.

"There's always a choice." Stubbornness set her jaw, but fury had her grinding her teeth.

"Why didn't you tell me you were pregnant?"

More than anything she had wanted to tell him. Had come here to his house looking to do just that and found it deserted. Her heart bled just enough to remind her she wasn't immune to the hurt yet. Better a baby without a father than a baby with a father who remained distant.

A lesson Grace learned from her own childhood.

"Because I was trying to avoid this argument," she snapped. "We have no idea who is behind this. At least with you, there's a chance you might remember."

"And the baby?" When she didn't answer, he continued, "Are you willing to put your baby at risk?"

"My baby is already at risk," she answered, pushing back the fear and doubts that threatened to suffocate her. She swiped at an annoying strand of hair that clung damply to her cheek. "Whoever gunned down Helene is still out there. I wouldn't be here right now if you had left me at my house. I'd be lying on the floor beaten and bloody from Webber's fists," she insisted, touching the sore spot on her lip with her tongue. "Even if I thought to hide at that point, he changed my mind. Nowhere is safe for me or my baby until we get to the bottom of this."

He was angry. She saw it in his features. But rather than scare her, it surprised her. The Jacob she knew never lost control, never gave anything away. This man wasn't covering up any of his emotions.

"Damn it." He pinched his nose between his thumb and forefinger. "Tell me, did I ever get the last word with you?"

"Yes. One time," she murmured. But he had to walk out on her to do it, she thought grimly. She turned her head away from him, stared out over the water until the tears stopped pricking her eyes.

"Well, the argument must have been pretty insignificant, then."

"You thought so."

"What the hell is that supposed to mean?"

"Nothing." Her tone was clipped, more out of annoyance with herself than him. "Look, I'm sorry. You don't deserve me taking shots at you."

"Just because I don't remember it doesn't mean I didn't

deserve it. Either tell me what I did or wait until I gain a point of reference for the hostility. All right?"

"Yes." She watched him for a moment, saw the set of his jaw hadn't relaxed. "But I want your word, Jacob, that you won't leave me behind."

He gave her a long, considering look. "You have it."

Until the old Jacob returned, she thought. "Fine," she said, but with much less conviction.

"How are we going to get in?" She followed him over the graveled driveway to the front porch.

"Don't suppose I keep a spare set of keys under a nearby flower pot?"

"You're not the type," she mused. His sense of humor hit her with a rush of pleasure. Enough that she almost forgot their reason for being there.

Almost.

"Can you pick the lock or something?"

"Actually, I'm doing the 'or something' part." He ran his hand down around the reinforced steel door until his fingers located the security trigger. "The mechanism is too sophisticated. I don't have the right tools. A problem I'm going to have to correct soon enough." He pulled out his gun, checked the clip before placing it back in his waistband. "We seem pretty isolated. How close is my nearest neighbor?"

"My best guess would be a mile in either direction. Why?"

"Because I have a pretty damn good security system, but not a linked one."

"You mean, no police are going to show up on your door step if you trigger the alarm."

"Exactly. And if I trigger it, you might have to cover your

ears. I don't expect an alarm to activate, but it's only a guess. Either way, you're not to move from the front door. No matter what. I don't want to shoot you by mistake. Got it?"

"Yes."

Without thinking, he leaned down and kissed her on the lips. A quick butterfly brush of the lips. "For luck."

Grace went still, paralyzed. Not from the touch of his mouth against hers, but from the longing the simple gesture invoked.

"I've done that before, haven't I?"

A simple gesture that gutted her from rib to belly. Grace tried to answer, tried to nod but managed neither.

He grabbed her arm, just above the elbow, shook it. "Tell me."

She managed a short nod then, but the words took another second to push past the tightening in her throat. "It was somewhat of a ritual you did when you left on one of your business trips."

She saw the shift, the laser sharpness that entered his gaze. Knew the rejection, the long-ago hurt showed in hers.

"Hell." He muttered the curse even as he dropped his hand. "Stay here. Don't move."

For a moment, she watched him melt into the semidarkness and almost laughed. Would have if she could have been sure hysteria didn't spur the urge.

Leave, he said? She took a deep, shuddering breath, realizing hysterics weren't so far-fetched.

Just where in the hell was she supposed to go?

FATIGUE RODE HIM HARD, making his movements slower, more sluggish than he would've liked. But it was the rage, the frustration over Grace's pain that drove him deeper into the shadows. That and the sweet taste of her still lingering on his lips.

Jacob worked his way around the perimeter of the house, stopping every few steps to listen, to wait. The wind rustled the trees, making the leaves dance and the branches whistle. In the background, the water rushed the beach, slapping foam and grit against the rocks in its path.

She'd stood her ground against Webber, he'd give her that. Held her own in a car chase, too. With five cops on her tail. Hell, she even managed to take down Sweeney without Jacob's help.

He played the last through his mind in slow motion. Damn, he thought he'd lost her that time. All it would've taken is one of Sweeney's meaty hands squeezing her neck.

His scowl brought a sharp tug of pain from the stitches in his forehead. He'd get her into the house, then he'd get some answers.

As darkness settled in, his eyes adjusted. He quickly discovered his night vision worked well enough for him to place most shadows into decipherable patterns.

From what he could see, there were no thermal or motion detectors. Considering the house sat on the edge of the woods, he wasn't surprised. Too many deer to hinder that kind of security.

Soundlessly, he worked his way to the back, noting the freestanding generator, two satellite dishes and a series of solar panels.

It seemed the house was set up to be independent of outside sources. The simplest way to maintain anonymity, if that was one's goal.

Considering they were two miles off the nearest main road, intentional isolation had been a distinct possibility.

Toward the back, he discovered the attached garage housing an SUV and a black Mercedes. Both locked up tight.

It wasn't until he investigated the boat dock, that he felt a deep pull of satisfaction in his belly. Wide enough to house two boats, the dock sat snuggly underneath the stilts of the house.

He sure as hell hit the jackpot.

The prize? A midnight-black Malibu speedboat moored to the steel posts—its keys still in the ignition.

ONE MINUTE STRETCHED to five, then ten. Agitation worked Grace's nerves until she was forced to pace back and forth to ease her anxiety. In the dark, the shadows seemed to grow and stretch. But it wasn't the shadows that left her on edge.

"Grace."

She screamed, swung around and realized too late that it was Jacob who stood in the doorway behind her.

He caught her fist with a smack against his palm.

"Damn it," she swore, more at herself for being jumpy. "Make some noise when you walk up behind me."

Inside the door, a security box buzzed. He dropped her hand, then reached over and broke open the box with the gun. He ripped out the inner wires.

The buzzing stopped.

"How did you get in?"

"Through a back window," he answered, tossing the lid onto the floor. "I broke the pane with the butt of my gun."

"It was that easy?"

"Not quite."

"But what if they come here?"

"There are other ways to protect us." He shot her a sardonic look. "Besides, if everything else fails—" the cold-blue of his eyes flickered to his weapon "—this seems to work well enough."

"Until it runs out of bullets," she retorted before following him through the doorway.

He shut the door behind them and turned the dead bolt. But made no other move. Instead, he leaned back against the door and folded his arms.

He glanced at the ceiling. "Lights on."

Track lights flipped on, hurting his eyes.

"Lights eighty percent capacity."

The relief was minimal, but acceptable. "How did you know to say that particular phrase?"

"I didn't think about it." The harshness of the light emphasized the unyielding lines of his features. "I think it's time you and I had a discussion."

"Jacob, I'm tired—"

"It's called, 'she said, he believed.' And it won't take long," he continued, ignoring her gasp of protest. "She said they were friends. He believed they were lovers."

"This is ridiculous," she replied, striving for nonchalance, but the small quiver in her voice and his raised eyebrow told her she'd failed.

"She said the baby she carried was another man's. He believed it was his."

Suddenly in two quick strides, he was in front of her. His hands gripped her shoulders, preventing her retreat. "She said he left with no goodbye. And for no reason."

Her head tilted back. "And?" she whispered, torn. "What did he believe?"

"There was no goodbye. But no reason?" he murmured as one hand slid up the back of her neck, cupping her head with enough pressure to bring her up against him. Her fingers curled into his sweater, holding her there suspended. "There had to be one hell of a reason for me to walk away from you."

His free arm slid around her, curving her body into his. Giving her only a second to adjust to the heat, to accept the primal intent that set his features into hard lines.

Then his mouth was on hers. But not with the fierceness she had expected. Certainly not with the same fierceness that her heart beat in her chest or the blood pounded through her veins.

His lips settled into a persuasive tempo that swept her up, rolled her under, left her trying to find her feet under their tender assault.

Caution tugged at her, urging her to step back. But the warmth of his body, the stroke of his hand up her spine blurred her thoughts, spiked her emotions until her arms slid up and around his neck.

With a groan, he deepened the kiss. He used his tongue to coax her mouth open. Then used it again to reward her, when her lips parted. Stroking, tasting.

A yearning broke free, snapping through her, catching her in a backlash of need. To be held, comforted. Cherished.

With a cry, she pushed away. Humiliation coursed through her, its ugly head rearing up, sniping at her soul, making her nauseous.

"Grace?"

Tears burned her eyes, but she blinked them back. She put out a hand, stopping him from grabbing her again.

"Please don't."

His arms dropped to his sides, but his hands became fists. The shadows cut edges into his already sharp features, turned his eyes into hard blue stones. "Tell me, damn it."

She understood what he was asking. First with his kiss, now with the words. Stricken with embarrassment, she clung to the one thing that straightened her spine, hitched her chin and locked her eyes on his. Self-preservation.

"This baby is not yours."

Chapter Eleven

"If I'm not the father, who is, Grace?"

"My baby doesn't have a father. Not in the sense you mean, anyway." Her eyes burned—from fatigue or the tears, she couldn't be sure. She rubbed them gently with her fingertips. "Besides, I met him after you left, so you never knew him."

"Did you tell him?"

"No," she said, using that part of the truth as her defense. "He isn't father material."

"Compared to whom?"

"I guess to my own." She sighed, suddenly so weary her bones ached with it. Lord, why couldn't he have forgotten his stubbornness along with his memory? "Look, Jacob. I don't want to be analyzed. Not tonight. Okay?"

"Fair enough," he bit out, exasperated.

She glanced around, striving for a lightness she didn't feel. "The house hasn't changed since I've been here."

"How long ago was that?"

"Four months," she answered, but didn't explain the reason. Jacob didn't push her. Instead, he studied his home. If you could call it that, he noted dryly.

Exceptionally renovated, the main floor was laid out in a

wide, airy space. The entranceway opened into a two-story living room with a loft and a black mahogany circular stairway that led from the boat dock beneath and to the third level above.

"Looks like I kept a pretty simple existence." Jacob looked around, trying to find something familiar.

Paintings covered the walls—expensive, judging from the vivid colors and the broad strokes. His tastes obviously ran toward abstract and modern, he thought, eyeing a particular flamboyant red and blue bust of a naked woman over the inset fireplace.

"The word is *impersonal*," Grace commented quietly.

Quiet, he noted with growing admiration, not cowed.

"Do you realize that while you don't necessarily know my history, you really do seem to know me?"

"That's not true—"

"You know I like my coffee black," he pointed out. "What else do you know?"

"Nothing, really." She paused. "Maybe little things."

"So if you had to guess, what would be my favorite color?"

"Black," she answered, using her hand to sweep over the room. "Most things you own are black. Your cars. Your clothes. Your boat. Even your furniture."

"That's gloomy, isn't it?"

"You told me once it kept you from having to worry about coordinating problems."

"Seriously?"

"No, you winked at the time. But now that I think back on it, there might be some truth there."

"And my favorite music?"

For the first time she realized she did know many things about the man. Maybe not what he did for a living or about his background and family. But the man himself. Why hadn't she realized that before?

"Jazz. Blues. Rock—most of the vintage, less of the contemporary. And wine. You built a wine cellar to hold a pretty extensive and quite expensive collection."

"I'll have to try a little later," he mused. "Go on."

Grace shifted until she could see his profile, giving in to the sudden urge to study his expression while she gave him details. "You have a small addiction for a good cigar. One that you rarely indulge. A bigger addiction to fast cars— which you indulge frequently. You like five-star hotels, secluded tables in restaurants and are always willing to pay the money for good service."

"So I'm a big tipper."

"One of the biggest I've ever met," she teased. "*Huge* tips."

He gave her an exaggerated frown. "That's hard to believe."

"You don't play into the metrosexual trend and wouldn't be caught dead getting a manicure. But a good, deep massage by an attractive woman's another story. You'd keep it professional, but why turn down good eye candy while you're relaxing?"

Jacob got the distinct impression she was teasing him, but instinctively he knew better than to pursue it. For the first time, he'd gotten her to open up and he didn't want to spoil the mood. "Anything else?"

"You've told me details about countries that only someone well traveled would know. And as you said, you speak several different languages. I've heard French, Spanish and Mandarin."

"Sounds like I'm well rounded if you add in the weapons training." He stopped just short of sarcasm.

Her features softened into uncertain lines. "One time, you mentioned your mother."

"What was she like?"

"You didn't say," she replied, shrugging her shoulders. "You just told me that she would've liked me. But I don't think you meant to."

A pang of regret shot through Jacob, catching him off guard. He searched for an image or memory of his mom. A whispered word that would remind him of her voice, but it was a futile effort. "The one aspect of amnesia I never expected to deal with were the echoes of emotion."

"I don't understand."

"I had figured from the beginning that bits of my past would come back to me a little at a time or in one sweeping rush," he acknowledged. "But it's the emotions that are taking the jabs at me."

When Grace didn't say anything, Jacob glanced her way. But her face was turned from him. "What is it?"

When her eyes found his again, there was a sadness there. "It's just you've never said anything like that to me before. You never shared your thoughts."

"Maybe that will change," he said quietly before shifting his attention back to their surroundings. "I took a quick look around on my way to the front door. One bedroom. No office. If I'm a businessman, why wouldn't I have an office here? Or somewhere?"

"You told me once you never felt the need to have an office."

"No office. Sterile living quarters. Weapons and language expert. Doesn't seem I'm adding up to be an everyday Joe, does it?" Jacob glanced at the sleek black cabinets and hi-tech appliances. "Do I like to cook?"

"Not really. So I guess we can rule out chef," she answered and ran her hand over the granite top. "But you once told me you had an associate who loved to cook, so you kept your kitchen stocked for him."

"No name?"

"None."

Grace slid onto the bar stool next to the counter.

"Are you okay?"

Grace nodded. "Just tired." Exhausted really, but she didn't want to give him another reason to hold her. Comfort her. Not while her nerves were still snapping from their last encounter.

He studied her for a moment. "My fault," he murmured, the words more of a caress than an apology. The pleasure from them shot through her, an arrow to the belly. One that left her insides more than a little quivery.

"Why don't you get out of those clothes and take a shower. I want to check around the house some more, anyway. See if I can find anything that might prod my memory."

A shower sounded wonderful. Just what she needed to shake the chill from her bones, wash the feel of him from her skin. But she could wait. "Actually, I think we should change your bandage. See how much damage you've done."

"All right. But let's at least change our clothes. I'm sure we can find something warm to wear in the bedroom. Then you can change my bandage." He grabbed her hand and tugged her up the stairs behind him. When they reached the master bedroom, Jacob walked to the closet.

"Helene's?" He nodded to a row of dresses hanging on the rod.

"Yes." Startled, her eyes skimmed the pile of chiffon and sequins. "She moved in a few months back. About a month after you left."

Slowly, she picked out a black sarong evening gown. "I've seen her wear most of these dresses."

"Were she and I lovers?"

"Maybe at one time, but it would've been long before I met her or you." Grace frowned, trying to remember Helene over the last few weeks. "Actually, she was never involved with anyone seriously."

"Even lately?"

"I don't know. If there was, I never met him," she said. "Helene went through men pretty quickly." Grace studied Jacob. "She might have told you."

"Which doesn't help at all," he commented, then sorted through some of his clothes on the opposite side.

Moments later, Jacob scanned the bedroom. He took in the crisp, clean lines of the platform bed. With drapes and linens of tan and the sleeker base of black wood—nothing else was needed to highlight the masculine edge.

"Do you recognize anything?"

"No." His eyes followed the curved stairway in the corner. Of the whole house, this was his favorite feature. An exclusive access to the tower room on the roof.

"If I was hiding papers, I'd want them close and protected. I'd want to be able to grab and go." His eyes worked their way around the walls. "Something hidden in plain sight."

"Would it be small or big?"

"Small. Travel light." The disconnection gnawed at him. "But it wouldn't be in here. Too obvious."

Grace laid her hand on his forearm and squeezed. "Give it time."

"We don't have time." He tugged his hand free, not liking the empathy behind the words, not when somewhere deep inside he wanted more than that from her.

Fatigue paled her porcelain skin, left dark smudges beneath her eyes. "Look, why don't you get dressed first? I'm sure you can find something here. Meanwhile, I want to take another look at my boat."

A smile tugged at the corners of her mouth. "That boat was your baby."

"Might still be," he responded, a small grin of his own tugged at his mouth. "After, I'll take another turn around the perimeter before it gets dark."

"Perimeter?" Grace asked. "That's military, isn't it?"

"Goes with the weapons training, I imagine," he answered. "Go change. I'll be back before you know it."

Without thought, he went to gather her close. An automatic instinct to comfort. But just as quickly, she sidestepped him, placing more than a few feet of distance between them.

"Don't." The word wasn't a plea or an order. A hint of desperation underlined it. Enough that he couldn't even be sure she directed the statement solely at him. "All right?"

Jacob stiffened, finally understanding. The fear had never been of him or that he might harm her again. Although, in his mind, he must have certainly warranted it.

No, she feared herself—or her reaction, he corrected. She didn't trust herself.

He watched her leave the room, not waiting for his reply. A good thing, since he had no intention of answering her.

Not yet, anyway.

GRACE STEPPED OUT of the bathroom a half hour later feeling refreshed and in control once again. She'd found Helene's emerald-green velour jogging suit and decided it would be perfect for pajamas. Helene was one size larger than Grace, but that worked in Grace's favor. She rolled down the waist until it hung low on her hips and gave some relief on her stomach.

"You look comfortable."

Grace stopped midstride and glanced up. Jacob stood across the room wearing nothing more than a worn pair of jeans.

"So do you." He was barefooted and bare-chested. The dim glow of the bedroom light surrounded him, softening the harsh bruises and the white gauze of his bandage, shadowing the lean, hard form of his chest and the sleek, tight muscles of his arms.

Her gaze traveled down the masculine contours of his ribs, drawn like a moth to the flickering light that danced over the taut skin of his belly. Her mouth went dry as she followed the line of sable hair that started slightly below his navel and disappeared into the open vee of his unsnapped waistband.

"Are you ready?"

"I'm sorry?" Grace forced her eyes upward and caught the slight flexing of his jaw muscles, telling her he hadn't missed her perusal.

"I asked if you were ready to change my bandage," he

repeated, but each word was low, raspy. Each syllable ground against the next, sandpaper on sandpaper.

"Yes." She forced herself to take a long, steady breath.

"I found this in the boat." He grabbed a first aid kit from the bed and held it up. "Are you sure you're up for this? The wound isn't going to be pretty."

"It's nothing I haven't seen before," she managed, forcing her legs to walk toward him. "Who do you think took care of you before my father got to my house?" When Jacob raised his eyebrow, she added, "I was premed when I dropped out of college."

"Okay, Doc." Jacob nodded toward the bathroom. "I'm all yours."

She waited a moment to get her heartbeat under control, then followed him in.

Jacob sat on the bathroom counter, putting his shoulder eye level for Grace.

Grace murmured her apologies, concentrated on cutting away the bandage. Soon she was finished, and she took a deep breath.

"How does it look?"

"The wound is crusted with dried blood, but otherwise the sutures are still intact."

She dipped a clean washcloth into some water from the sink and started to wash away the blood.

"Tell me about your mom," Jacob said softly.

Because it kept her mind off their proximity, she obliged him. "Her name was Claire. She met my father during the Vietnam War. She worked for Senator Langdon, although he was a colonel then."

"And your father?"

"He was an army surgeon. The way my father tells the story, my mom came in to deliver some papers and it was love at first sight." She laid the wet towel down and used another to pat his wound dry. "They were married a little over twelve years when she died."

"How?"

"She was in a plane crash with Senator Langdon. He was seeking reelection."

Ignoring the slight trembling in her fingers, she applied some antibiotic cream.

"You must look like her."

She opened the package of square bandages, pulled one out and placed it against his wound. "Yes. Very much so." Carefully, she taped the bandage down.

Jacob's fingers played with a thick lock of her hair, testing its weight, the texture. The scent so familiar, something inside him strained to break free. "Honeysuckle," he murmured, reining the emotion back as her fingers fluttered and stroked him. Not with the heat of passion, but with the softness of concern.

"I'm sorry?" She shifted closer in order to start wrapping the gauze over his bicep first.

"Your shampoo is called Honeysuckle Sweet. When I remembered the trip to Aspen, it was because I recognized the scent of your hair. I looked in your bathroom when I couldn't remember the name of the flower."

"The fact that you noticed surprises me." Her gaze snapped to his. A moment later, she noticed how the dampness of the bay and wind clung to him. How the scent enticed her to lean in closer. "I didn't mean that in a rude way."

"I understand," he said, the truth of it saddening his words. "Maybe I didn't then. Who knows? But I'm noticing a lot of things now, Grace." He rubbed the strands of her hair between his thumb and forefinger. "Why is it I can remember the texture and scent of your hair, but nothing else?"

"Maybe because I was the last person you saw before you passed out." She saw the flash in his eyes, the desire that took the blue to slate. Her hand went to his chest to hold him off, but she ended up curling her fingers in the soft hair.

"My memories revolve around scents. Textures." His finger slid down her cheek, settled at the corner of her mouth. "Tastes."

Her body shuddered at the images his words invoked. "Stop, Jacob."

"I've tasted you before." His lips replaced his finger trailing down her cheek to the hollow beneath her ear. He nibbled, groaning softly when her body jerked in reaction. "Sweet." His mouth followed the line of her throat. Her head tilted back giving him more access. "Help me remember, Grace."

The heat of his mouth licked over her skin, seeped into her pores. Help him remember? She couldn't even think. Couldn't breathe.

The heat became dizzying. She reached out, tried to hold on. Suddenly, Jacob broke off the kiss. He swore. It wasn't until then she noticed her hand gripping his shoulder.

Fear made her drop her hand, but it was embarrassment that made her take a step back.

"Well, nothing like a little pain to kill the mood." Jacob strained for light humor, but couldn't get it past the rasp in his throat.

"No more," she whispered on a shaky breath. Her eyes darted to his. "I won't be seduced—"

"Again?" He shrugged and moved off the counter. "All right. We won't go there. For now."

When he stepped out of the bathroom, she found herself following him. "I mean it," she insisted, even if the words sounded lame to her own ears.

"All right." He tugged on a dress shirt, buttoned it half way up. "I could use something to eat. How about you?" When she didn't answer, he continued, "We only have a few hours before we go after your keys. I suggest you eat something, then take a nap." When he walked past her, he kissed her gently on the forehead. "You look like hell, Grace."

"I what?" But her words fell on an empty room. Annoyed, she followed him into the kitchen.

"There's milk, eggs, an assortment of take-out leftovers." Jacob straightened from inside the refrigerator.

"The house looks hardly lived in."

"You've always had a cleaning service—" Grace froze.

"What is it?"

"I've figured out a way to call my father."

"No," he declared. "The authorities will be watching your father."

"He has a housekeeper. Her name is Carol Reed. The police wouldn't have tapped into her cell phone, right?"

"Probably not, but that doesn't mean—"

"I can call her—"

"I said *probably,* Grace," he emphasized. "Even if the police overlooked her phone, would you trust her not to report back to them?"

"Yes. She's been with my father for years."

"It's too much of a risk," he said after a moment.

"If he's talked to the police, he might be able to help us," she pressed.

"It's still too risky. There's equipment out there. Laser microphones, for instance. A good one will pick up conversations from a hundred yards away."

"A what?"

"A microphone that…" He shoved his fingers through his hair. "Never mind."

"If I promise to not give out any information, we should be safe. Right?"

"What if Helene's murderers have a tap on your dad? What makes you think they won't use him to get to you? If you're not worried about your safety, worry about his."

"I am. That's why I want to warn him, Jacob." Her statement drifted between them. A hushed whisper filled with fear.

Jacob swore. "All right. Is his house fairly large? Bigger than this one?"

"Yes."

"Then have him walk into the closet or another room without windows."

"Why?"

"If they haven't bugged the house or the phones, they would have to use a laser microphone, which needs a window to record voice vibrations."

"These are big 'ifs.'"

Jacob handed her a disposable phone. "Make it short, simple. And no information. You can tell him you're safe. Even tell him not to worry. But don't tell him anything else. Then hang up."

"He might have information." She punched Carol's number into the phone.

"Then he better give it to you quickly. No more than a minute, Grace."

The phone picked up after the first ring.

"Hello?"

"Carol, it's Grace." She heard the housekeeper gasp, pictured her small, round face going slack with shock. "Please don't say my name out loud. And listen for a moment. I need you to go to the nearest room without window. A bathroom or a closet, okay?"

"Okay. One moment."

"Thank you, Carol." She waited until she heard a door shut. "Where are you?"

"In the pantry." Carol paused, seemingly shaking off her upset. "Grace. My god, where are you? Your father is sick with worry."

"I know," she replied, grateful the housekeeper had followed her instructions. "Tell me. Have the police been there?"

"Not the police. But someone from the government. FBI maybe," Carol answered, her voice lowered to a whisper. "They did not talk to me, so I can't be sure. But they spent over an hour in the library with your father."

"Is he there?"

"Yes. He hasn't left since he discovered you missing at your home."

"I'm going to hang up, Carol. I want you to get my dad and make sure he stays in the pantry with your phone. Tell him I'll ring him in five minutes. Okay?"

"Okay, Grace," the older woman acknowledged. "I don't know what you're involved in, but please take care of yourself."

"I will. Thank you." Grace hung up the phone before the housekeeper responded.

For the next five minutes, Grace paced the floor. Neither she nor Jacob spoke but the hard set of his features told her he wasn't happy.

Finally, Grace hit the phone's redial.

Her father answered on the first ring.

"Grace?"

"Hi, Dad." She paced back and forth, ignoring Jacob's frown.

"Thank God. Are you okay. Are you safe?"

"I'm safe," she answered. "Are you in the pantry, Dad?"

"Yes, yes," he said impatiently. "Where are you? When I got back to your house I found—"

"I know what you found. Look, I don't have much time," she said. "Have you been questioned by the police?"

"Of course. I walked right into their crime scene," he answered. "Why did you run away?"

"Dad, those two men tried to kill us. They broke into the house—"

"There were two?"

"Yes, Jacob knocked the second unconscious."

"Grace," Jacob warned, his hand reaching for the phone. She jerked away.

"Grace, where are you?"

"I told you, somewhere safe." She glanced at Jacob.

"Come home. The police can protect you."

"No. These men are dangerous, Dad. I think they have connections. Until I'm sure, I need you to be careful."

"The police think you're dead. Murdered by the same person who killed Helene," her father said, his tone low, suspicious. "They suspect it's Jacob."

"Did you tell them he was there?"

"No. But if they search hard enough, they'll probably turn up his DNA." Her father paused. "Is Jacob Lomax the baby's father?"

"Yes."

Her father swore. Something he never did. "Dad—"

"Never mind that, Grace. They questioned me about Helene's computer. Do you have it? They said it wasn't in the office or her home. They seem to think it holds the key to her murder."

"I don't have it. I thought it was at the bar."

"Grace," Jacob prompted.

"I've got to go, Dad. Please be careful. These men are dangerous," she whispered, blinking back tears. Words caught like shards of glass, shredding her throat until it burned like hellfire. She hung up the phone.

"I couldn't say it." Tears formed, then spilled. "I couldn't tell my own father that I love him."

Suddenly, Jacob's arms were around her. He led her to the couch and cradled her in his lap.

And she cried. Long, gut-wrenching sobs that set her body quaking. The problem was, she didn't know what she was crying over. Helene. The baby. Her father.

She cried because, at that moment, she had no more left in her. No more courage. No more strength.

Nothing left but the need to release.

For what seemed like hours, Jacob held her. Rocking her close to his chest. And when that didn't work, he whispered soothing words against her temple.

When the tears stopped and she settled, he kissed the wetness off her cheeks, rubbed her back until the shaking stopped.

"Feel better?"

She nodded into the hollow of his neck. "I don't suppose we can blame my hormones for that?"

His laugh rumbled deep within his chest. She tucked her hands between their chests, used his heartbeat to soothe.

"I'd probably blame exhaustion myself."

"I can see your point. A good cry is always draining." Her lips curved into a smile against his throat. "I'll tell you what. When it's your turn for a bout of hysteria, I'll hold you. Then after, we'll blame yours on the hormones."

"Deal." He shifted, reclining back on the couch. He pulled her down to him, tucking her head beneath his chin, her legs caught between his. "I think we both could use a nap."

She snuggled her cheek against the open vee of his shirt, enjoying the clean, masculine scent, the comforting rhythm of his heart beneath her cheek.

She'd missed this. The closeness with another human being. The simple act of holding someone, touching him, comforting him.

Loving him.

The crying, she understood now, had been the catalyst she needed to clear her head, help her mind catch up to what her heart already understood.

She'd never fallen out of love with Jacob.

Chapter Twelve

"We should have made the eleven o'clock news," Jacob commented while Grace cleared away their dinner dishes.

She'd woken up earlier to the sizzle of bacon and eggs frying.

"Guess the murder wasn't as big a deal as we thought," she said wryly.

"Or instead of the police covering up," Jacob answered, his brows lowered into a frown, "someone in the media is stopping it. Or both."

"You're saying that whoever is involved in Helene's murder owns the media in this area?"

"It's a definite possibility."

A chill went down Grace's spine.

"Tell me about Helene."

Grace wiped her hands on a nearby dish towel and leaned against the counter. "No-nonsense. Sexy in a cool, untouchable way. You were very much alike. You could have been formed from the same mold. A his and hers. I think I envied that about both of you."

"How did you meet?"

"At a political event. I was dating an up-and-coming lobbyist at the time."

"Was she political then?"

"Yes. Extremely so. Very much like my father. She enjoyed living amongst the Capitol Hill elite. Especially lately."

"Why do you say that?"

"The presidential election is only a few months away and she had been following the coverage very closely. She always seemed connected to everything. Politics, business, the world economy. She attended the right dinner parties, always escorted by the right people."

"You sound like you envied her."

"Only her decisiveness. She had the courage to back up her choices."

"From where I'm sitting, she has nothing on you."

"You wouldn't say that if you remembered her," she prodded mildly.

"Maybe she considered you her friend."

"She did. I think you and I were her closest, and still I didn't know much about her," Grace replied. "And now she's dead and I don't even know who to notify."

"Did she have a safe? Anything that she kept her personal papers in?"

"None that I knew." Grace stopped, slapped her hands on the counter in quick succession. "That's wrong. She kept most of her business records on her computer. One of those new, sleek laptops."

Grace swung to him. "Dad said the police were interested in finding her computer. At the time, it didn't register because I was overwhelmed emotionally. But he said the police couldn't find the laptop at the bar or her apartment."

"If she had always had it with her, it would have been at the bar, right?" Jacob glanced around. "Or here."

"Pusher." A slow smile slid across her face. "With everything going on, I forgot about Pusher."

"Who's Pusher?"

"Pusher Davis. My bar manager. Ex–bar manager." She straightened from the counter. "If I'm right, Helene had her computer with her. She never went anywhere without it."

"So it's at the bar."

"No, Pusher has Helene's computer."

"How can you be sure?"

"Because Pusher is an ex-con." She paced the floor, trying to sort through the steps the bar manager would have taken after discovering Helene's body.

"I'm not following."

"He's an ex-con who did time for cybercrimes. With a specialty or passion, I guess, for hacking into corporate and federal accounts. And my understanding is that he was the best."

"So, the first thing he would've noticed was—"

"Helene's computer." She sat on the couch, drew up her knees. "He would've taken it. Out of loyalty, if nothing else. Pusher hates cops. The only thing he hates more, he says, is dirty cops."

"First, we find Pusher," Jacob reasoned. "Then we get your keys from the impound."

LAWRENCE "PUSHER" DAVIS stepped off the apartment's elevator. The red carpet, well-lit hallway and pristine chandeliers spoke high-class in volumes.

Pusher lived on the trendy side of Washington, D.C.

Overblown, expensive but in the game he played, it was all about image.

The paper bag rattled a bit in his hand when he dug for his key. Because it played well to anyone happening by, he shifted the bag up into the crook of his arm like a sack of groceries.

For a moment, the irony struck him as funny. Pusher Davis carrying pretend groceries. It wasn't too long back that he'd been forced to go for days without food.

Pusher had grown up with a Baptist mother in South Texas. His father was nothing more than a temporary lover with enough cash to keep his mother in bourbon. Not that Pusher cared. His mom wasn't a mean drunk. On the contrary: the deeper into her stupors, the more genteel she became— spouting one slurred Bible verse after another until she passed out.

Until one day, she passed out and choked to death on her own vomit.

Barely ten years of age and homeless, Pusher took to the streets with only one valuable lesson—the need to survive superseded any laws of man and God.

At the age of twelve, he learned that cops held the same attitude.

And at the age of thirteen, he learned that information, of any kind, was power.

That's when he stole his first computer.

Now he was a grown man, one whom the ladies recognized as a charmer and a rogue. He kept trim, because it was expected, and his muscles were defined, not bulky, because that's what filled a tailored suit well.

He'd been born poor, but knew from the Bible that people

better than him had risen from dirt. A kid on the street, he watched people. He educated himself, studying only the people others stepped out of the way for. How they walked, how they styled themselves. Some he followed for days, studying their lives from the shadows of his own. Eventually, he'd embraced the best of their qualities and shed their worst like a snake's skin.

And when he dug deep and still couldn't find what he needed, he stole it—by mimicking those he'd watched or taking advantage of the poor souls he hadn't.

He had no doubts about who and what he was, but, more importantly, about what he'd done and had become.

The rest was God given. Six feet in height, ice-blue eyes and a boy-next-door grin. Add to the package sun-kissed blond hair—groomed on the short side, styled in the trend of messy chic—and a keen mind.

He held no ill will toward his mother. In fact, he'd always thank her and the sweet Lord for giving him a Texas accent and knowledge of the Bible. Both proved irreplaceable as tools for a hi-tech con man.

Now reformed.

He smiled at the word. As much as a con man could ever reform. His talent ran toward conversation and computers. To him, that made him just an everyday businessman. After all, in his opinion, some of the best cons were pulled by businessmen.

He set Helene's computer on his desk and started it up. The fact he was breaking his parole by just carrying the laptop didn't phase him a bit. The point was just not to get caught.

As predicted, the police had run his rap sheet. He'd been

dragged down to the station and questioned to all hours of the morning. Accusations were thrown back and forth between him and the cops.

He enjoyed the hell out of it. It was an enlightening meeting. Getting grilled gave Pusher a good opportunity to find out more about what was going on. Not by what was said, but more by what wasn't.

Pusher flipped on the lights and went directly to the kitchen. He grabbed a dark ale—his favorite import—from the refrigerator.

A few hours into the interrogation, it all suddenly stopped. They released him with no explanation. In fact, if he had to guess, the investigation was no longer a priority. If it made the local news, he'd be surprised.

The computer flashed on, its screen asking for the password. It would take time, but he would break it. And then he'd find what he was looking for.

Opportunity.

Chapter Thirteen

The meeting hadn't gone well. Richard D'Agostini hadn't expected it to. These men and women were the elite one percent of the world. Bankers, politicians, media moguls, royalty. They were not accustomed to failing, and now they were vulnerable. They had agreed, albeit reluctantly, to a small window of time to let him deal with the situation.

And deal with it he would.

Tall, stoic and somewhat bald, he had the older, notable features of a Harvard scholar. And he played the distinguished, upper-class role of Senate Majority Leader like one who'd risen to royalty. He wore his pedigree like a tailored suit—custom-made and fitted, with a well-honed charm and a sense of diplomacy.

A quick knock on his suite door drew his attention. "Come in."

Oliver Kragen loosened his tie as he shut the door behind him.

"Oliver. Have a seat." Richard indicated one of the high-back leather chairs. "Do you have a situation report?"

"Lomax killed Webber," Oliver said without preamble. "Not that it was a loss."

"You mean because Webber was my man." It was a statement, not a question, but one Richard wanted answered nonetheless.

Oliver had been working for Richard for too many years not to understand his answer had better be an acceptable one.

"No, because Webber was an encumbrance. Lomax escaped from us twice because of him." Oliver sat in the chair and rested his ankle across one knee.

"He didn't allow Helene Garrett past his guard. You did." Richard paused, sensing rather than seeing Oliver's annoyance. Oliver was too good at what he did to show any reaction to Richard's baiting, but the senator couldn't help twisting the knife just a little bit more. Sometimes Oliver needed reminding of who pulled his strings. "And it seems the score now is three for Lomax, one for you." He walked over to his minibar and picked up the decanter of Scotch. "It appears Mr. Lomax is getting the better of you, Oliver."

He poured two glasses and brought one over to the younger man.

"Lomax is containable, Senator," Oliver commented, then took the glass and finished it in one swallow.

Something Richard would never consider doing. "Suppose you tell me how you plan on containing him." Richard took a drink from his glass.

"Once we have the Primoris files and the code back, he becomes less of a threat," Oliver reasoned.

"First we have to get them back."

Oliver pulled a disk from his pocket and walked over to the television. "Helene and Grace Renne had lunch together yesterday at a local bistro. Sweeney got his hands on the restaurant's security tapes. Seems the owner is somewhat of a techno nut and has a pretty decent security setup." He placed the DVD into the driver and hit the button. "Here's something you might want to see."

"You took a video from someone," the senator stated.

"Not me. Sweeney."

"At gunpoint?" Richard understood Oliver certainly wouldn't have hesitated to do the job himself. Something Richard never approved of really. As his top aide, Oliver needed to curb his tendencies toward violence.

Oliver shrugged. "Does it matter? I'm sure he was discreet."

A picture flashed across the television screen of Helene Garrett at a table, alone.

Oliver froze her image. "Take a look."

"What is she grabbing?" the senator asked as he watched, his drink held midair.

"Grace Renne's phone and keys."

"So what?" He took another swallow, then set the glass down.

"Watch." Oliver hit the slow motion button. Both men watched as Helene brought the phone and keys under the table into her lap. Two minutes later, she got up to leave.

"She kept her hands under the table," Oliver observed. "I think Helene made the drop to Grace Renne before she even met with Lomax last night."

"Looks like someone is keeping secrets from us," Richard mused. "So are we assuming Grace Renne now knows?"

"I think we must assume that, sir,"

"Then take care of her. I want to see this over, Oliver," Richard ordered. "Now."

"It will be," Oliver agreed. "By the way, I had Lomax's DNA run through the government databases."

"And?"

"If he's an operative, the government buried him deep. One of my associates is working on it."

"It doesn't matter. Whoever he is, we'll find him," he murmured, and gazed out over the city. "And with him, we'll have the Renne woman and the Primoris file."

THE WIND PICKED UP pieces of garbage, whipped them around like confetti in front of the strip club. Its only neon light flashed its name, Chancellor's, in a hot-pink flare that drew more than the casual crowd off the street.

"Are you sure this is safe?" Grace asked.

"It's packed in here. Pusher made a good choice. Would be hard to find us in here."

"Good evening, sir." The dark eyes of the doorman—a guy on the younger side of thirty with more tattoos than hair—were curious but steady as they swept over Grace. "Club rules require that I search our guests. Do you mind?"

Grace tensed next to Jacob. He slid his arm around her and drew her close. "Not at all." Jacob smiled easily.

With a quiet efficiency, the bouncer patted Jacob down and checked Grace's purse.

"Thank you." The bouncer handed Grace back her purse and stepped to the side. "Enjoy your visit."

After walking through the door, Grace slipped the gun from under Helene's navy peacoat and gave it to Jacob. "How did you know he wouldn't search me?"

"Educated guess."

The music was loud, the air thick with cigars and perfumed oils.

A woman appeared, her black jacket and matching mini-skirt identifying her as one of the bartenders. "Mr. Lomax?"

"Yes," Jacob answered, his hand cupping Grace's elbow.

"Mr. Davis asked me to escort you to his table. This way, please."

They followed the woman to a semihidden booth in one of the far corners of the club.

"Pusher." Grace sighed in relief. She stepped away from Jacob to give her bar manager a hug. "I'm so glad to see you're okay."

Pusher pulled Grace into the curved booth beside him and kissed her cheek. "How are you doing?" His eyes darted down, just enough for her to get his meaning. She gave him another quick hug. "Fine. We're both fine."

"Lomax." Pusher rose slightly, reached across the table for a handshake. "Sure am glad to see you again."

"Glad to be seen," Jacob said noncommittally.

When Jacob didn't reach to shake, Pusher's hand dropped to his tie, smoothing it down. "Act like your having a good time. Otherwise, we're all in trouble." He waved a few fingers, signaling the waitress.

Within moments, a waitress dressed in a French maid's outfit appeared at their table. The woman was slight in build, teetering on the unhealthy side of one hundred pounds. A short cap of blond curls framed thin, delicate features, adding almost a comical edge to the slashes of red blush across each cheekbone and the matching crimson lipstick that slicked puffy lips. But it was her eyes that drew Grace's attention, caused her to settle uncomfortably in her seat. The big, sky-blue irises glittered with an unnatural intensity, rapidly shifting back and forth beneath long, mascara-laden lashes. "Hello. What can I get you all?"

Pusher smiled, revealing a perfect set of straight, white teeth. "A vodka martini for the gentleman, Maggie my darlin'. And another highball for me." Pusher glanced at Grace. "A glass of tonic water for the little lady."

"Sure thing, Mr. Davis." Maggie picked up Pusher's glass and set it on her tray. "The bar is really crowded tonight so I might be a few extra minutes."

"No problem, honey," Pusher responded with a slow wink. "We're in no hurry."

When Maggie left the table, Grace let impatience get the better of her.

"Since when do you hang out in strip bars?" She glanced pointedly beyond their table to the row of steel poles set on a long narrow stage. Half a dozen woman clad in a rainbow selection of G-strings worked their way around the poles in slow, seductive twirls and slides.

"I don't usually, but under the circumstances…" Pusher shrugged. "A few years back, I did the owner a few favors. That's why I asked you to meet me here. We're practically among friends. Besides, it's easier to keep my ear to the streets here. Fish out information on what happened to Helene."

"Did you find out anything?" Jacob asked.

"Word has it that Helene had hooked up with a major player in the city. Someone who foots big parties for even bigger clients."

"Who?" Jacob snapped out the question before Grace could.

"At this point, it can be anyone. But whoever it is has their fingers in every underground business in this district. Drugs, prostitutes, gambling. You name a sin, they've got the market cornered."

"Do you have Helene's computer?"

"Yes," he said. "I grabbed it before the police arrived. Trouble is, I've accessed most of the files and come up with nothing that might give us a clue why she was murdered."

"Did you bring it?"

"Under the table." Pusher took the stirrer from his glass and tossed it onto a nearby napkin.

"We need that computer, Pusher," Jacob said. "Whoever killed Helene might be after what's in her files."

"You can take it with you. I made a copy of the files to play with them a little more, just in case there is something encoded."

"What did you find on the computer?" Grace asked.

"That's the interesting part. Other than regular business files for the bar, like accounts and supplies, I discovered a couple of dozen dossiers on some pretty important people."

"Such as?" Jacob leaned forward.

"Articles and notes on the upcoming presidential election. The candidates, the voting, their supporters. A complete workup on Richard D'Agostini. From his college days."

"The Maryland senator?" Grace asked, puzzled.

"The one and the same." Pusher paused. "But he's much more than that. He's the Senate Majority Leader and a pretty powerful force on Capitol Hill."

"Here ya go folks," Maggie stepped up to the table and placed their drinks in front of them. "If you need anything else, just wave me down. Otherwise I'll check back with you in a little while."

"Thanks darlin'," Pusher said, then waited until Maggie left once again.

"If you were looking for Helene's major player, D'Agostini would be the one at the top of the list," Jacob commented.

"Sure would be." Pusher studied Grace for a second.

"What is it?"

"There was also a file on Alfred Langdon."

"Who is Langdon?" Jacob asked.

"He's the man my mother worked for." Grace frowned. "She was his top aide. He was running for reelection to the Senate. They died together in a plane crash right before the election that year. D'Agostini ran in Langdon's place and won the Senate seat."

"There's a coincidence."

"If you believe in them," Pusher acknowledged. "I don't."

"But why would Helene have that information?"

"She had more than that. She had a complete file on you, Grace."

"Me? Why?"

"Maybe she investigated you before she decided to become partners with you," Pusher commented. "She also had an extensive file on both your parents."

"Did she have anything on me?" Jacob asked.

"Some contact information. Phone numbers. Addresses," Pusher observed. "Didn't realize you were worth so much in worldwide real estate, Lomax. Otherwise I might have been nicer to you."

Jacob raised an eyebrow at that.

Pusher drained his drink. "It's all here." He reached under the table, pulled out the small laptop bag.

"All of it?" Jacob repeated, his tone sharp.

"I don't double-cross friends, Lomax," Pusher said, his own tone showing the same edge. "Not that you're my friend, but Grace is. I owe her my life. I don't pay my debts with betrayal."

Jacob studied him for a moment, then gave a quick nod. "The file you want is listed under Primoris."

"Primoris?" Jacob frowned. "That's Latin for first or foremost. So the only good lead we have may be in one of those files."

"How did you figure out the password, Pusher?" Grace asked.

The bar manager shrugged. "I didn't. I bypassed the security and deciphered it afterward."

"You think one of those files will tell us who is behind this?" Grace asked.

"It didn't help me get any closer," Pusher responded. "But it's all we have at the moment. How are you two set for money and transportation?"

"We're fine for now. We're staying—"

"Out of sight," Jacob finished for Grace.

Pusher nodded, understanding.

"One other thing, Pusher. I need to go shopping for some equipment. Hi-tech stuff. Know anyone who doesn't ask questions?"

"Sure." Pusher pulled out a pen from his pocket and wrote an address on the napkin. "The dude who runs this place can hook you up. His name is on the napkin. Just tell him I sent you."

He handed Jacob the information. "If I get more information, where do you want me to contact you?"

"We'll contact you," Jacob said easily enough, then pocketed the napkin. "Soon."

Grace leaned down and kissed the bar manager's cheek. "Thanks, Pusher."

He caught her arm when she was about to turn away. "Be careful, darlin'."

"She will." Jacob cupped her elbow as they made their way through the tables. Suddenly Jacob stopped and swore. "We've got company.

A head above the crowd, it was easy to spot Frank Sweeney. Just then, the enforcer turned. His eyes caught Grace's and she gasped.

"Let's go!" Jacob yelled.

He snagged her hand and pulled. They shoved their way through the crowd, making little headway.

"They're coming." A quick glance told her Sweeney would catch them if she didn't think of something. She reached into her purse, grabbed a handful of cash and threw it up in the air behind them. A wall of people screamed. Strippers, bartenders, customers rushed the floor, diving for the money.

"Of all the—" Jacob swore. "I didn't give you half of our cash, so you could toss it away."

Quickly, they burst through the front doors, then ducked down the side street where they'd left the truck.

"It worked, didn't it?" Grace demanded, when they reached the truck. She automatically stepped to the driver's side. They were broke but safe. That's all Grace cared about.

"I'll drive." Jacob said, his voice barely containing the anger.

"What's the matter?"

"I'd like to know how Sweeney knew we'd be at Chancellor's."

"You don't think Pusher—"

"I won't if you can give me a better explanation."

Grace didn't say anything, simply because she couldn't.

Chapter Fourteen

Pusher threw money on the table and headed out the back. Since he didn't see Jacob and Grace in the throng of people, he'd just have to trust the man could take care of Grace.

He opened the door to the women's dressing room. A few of the girls screamed—mostly the half-naked ones—while others threw clothes and shoes.

"Sorry, ladies," Pusher said with a smile, dodging them and their sailing shoes. Quickly, he made his way to the back exit and stepped out into the alley behind the club.

He took a deep breath, clearing his head of the smoke and stale air. A slight shift in the shadows had him taking a step back and reaching for the pistol in his suit pocket.

"You look like a man with a problem, Pusher." Maggie, cigarette in her hand, stepped into the rim of light.

"Maggie, darlin'." Pusher let his hand fall back to his side. "You scared the hell out of me." He nodded toward the cigarette. "I thought you told me you'd quit those a few weeks ago."

She dropped the butt and smashed it under her heel. "I did, but today…" Maggie stopped. "Never mind."

Pusher liked Maggie. She'd pulled herself up from the gutter. Word had it that she had battled a drug problem for over a year and won. "Look, Magpie, I wish I could hang tonight. But I have important business to take care of. I'll catch you later, okay?"

"Sure, Pusher. I'll see you later."

He straightened his tie and stepped past her. Suddenly a hand gripped his shoulder from behind. Pain shot from his neck to his head. His knees buckled.

"Going somewhere, Pusher?"

The hand turned Pusher just far enough so he could see a man's face.

"Do I know you?"

"The name is Sweeney." The big man looked at his associate. "Pay the lady, Miller."

The second guy took a couple of hundred-dollar bills from his wallet. A big, bullish man with droopy lips and heavy eyelids, Miller wouldn't win any beauty contests, Pusher thought wryly.

"Sorry, Pusher." Maggie stuck the bills into her bra, her eyes meeting his with a quiet defiance even as they filled with tears. "I needed the money." With a sad smile, she turned back down the alley.

"I don't suppose we can talk about this, gents," he said, trying to ignore the death grip on his shoulder.

"Oh, you'll be talking. But to a man named Kragen," Sweeney commented. "He wants discuss a few things with you regarding Grace Renne and her new friend. I suggest you give the right answers, because your life will—" the smaller man grunted in pain as Sweeney squeezed his collarbone to emphasize his point "—depend on it."

"I guess I can spare a few minutes of my time." Pusher's struggle for nonchalance was lost in a painful rasp.

"Glad to hear it. Now I'd rather you walk to our car on your own two feet, but if you, say, get the urge to run, I have no problem throwing you in the car in a few broken pieces. Your choice."

Pusher didn't fight his way from the streets without learning a thing or two about survival.

"If I say okay, can I have my shoulder back?"

Sweeney let go and Pusher hit the ground. Pain exploded through his kneecaps, but he didn't cry out. He rolled his shoulder, helping the blood flow back into his muscles. "I'll have a chat with Kragen. But I'm not quite sure how I can help him."

"By having answers, Pusher. Because if you don't, I can guarantee you won't be able to help yourself."

"Lead the way, gentlemen," Pusher joked before he stood and dusted off his suit.

Sweeney shoved him forward. "You first."

Chapter Fifteen

The impound lot was located on the outskirts of town and hard to miss. As far as Grace knew, it was the only ten-foot-high chain-link fence topped with spirals of barbed wire in a fifty-mile radius of Annapolis.

"There's a good chance the perimeter is wired," Jacob muttered. He glanced down at his arm. "I'm going to cut through the fence. Which means I'm going to need your help."

Grace raised an eyebrow, wondering how much it cost him to make that confession. "Shouldn't we wait until midnight? Ten o'clock seems a little early."

"They shut down at six. The security guard is the only one we have to worry about." He handed her his Glock. "Ever shot a gun?"

"No." The steel was warm and smooth against her palm, surprising her. She expected the steel to be cold, the grip rough.

"Keep an eye out for the security guards. And for God's sake, don't shoot them."

"Then why give me a gun?"

"Because our friends might be out there, too. If you see one of them, aim for their chest and empty the clip."

He grabbed a small laser cutter from the backpack at his feet. "I'm going to keep the cuts low, so both my hands are going to be busy."

"I'll keep watch." Grace scanned the yard. More than a hundred parked cars lined the lot under the yellow glow of flood lights. It was like looking for the proverbial needle in a haystack.

As if he knew what she was thinking, Jacob said, "You're wasting your time. We don't need the car, we need the keys."

He nodded toward the trailer office to the left of their position. "I'm betting the keys are hanging in there."

The chain-link fencing broke free. Just as he lifted the bottom edge to slide under, dogs barked in the distance. "Figures. Cops' budget. Cheaper security and no pension plans."

Jacob cursed, then glanced at the gun.

Understanding, Grace whispered. "I'm not shooting the guard dogs."

He shrugged, letting the fence fall back into place. "Just a thought."

"Find another."

Suddenly, two German shepherds hit the fence at a dead run, their barks shattering the night air.

"How fast can you run?"

Grace watched the animals growl, their teeth bared back to their molars. "Not funny."

Jacob sat back on his heels. "Okay, let's go with plan B."

"What's plan B?"

"Back to the car."

Grace followed him to the truck and slid into the passenger seat. "We're just going to leave?"

He glanced at her. "Buckle up." Then he twisted wires together, starting the ignition. With suppressed annoyance, he shoved the truck into Reverse. "Hold on to something," he ordered, then punched the gas.

Too late, Grace realized his intention. The truck plowed through the locked gate of the lot.

"Are you crazy?" She screamed and grabbed for the dashboard.

He whipped the truck around and aimed for the wooden porch in front of the portable office trailer.

Within seconds, they plowed through, smashing the wood and scraping the side panel with a loud screech.

"Roll down your window and get ready to get us the hell out of here."

Within seconds, he crawled over her and climbed out the window and up on the roof of the truck's cab.

The dogs hit the truck, their teeth bared, their bodies trembling with anger as they jumped up against the driver's window.

Jacob kicked the trailer door in on the second try and slid from the roof in through the office doorway.

Immediately, Grace slid over to the driver's seat. "Come on," she murmured and gripped the wheel. In the distance, she could hear a set of sirens, certain they were heading in their direction.

A few minutes later, Jacob tossed a garbage bag full of keys in through the passenger window before climbing through himself.

"Go!"

Grace hit the gas and sped out of the parking lot, relieved when both dogs stopped their chase a block away from the impound.

She glanced over at Jacob. "Your shoulder is bleeding."

"I probably ripped open the stitches." He leaned his head against the back of the seat and closed his eyes. The wind washed over him, cooling the damp sweat on his skin. "But no dogs were hurt."

She nodded toward the bag. "You didn't know which keys were mine."

"Nope. So I grabbed them all."

"They'll know now that I helped you. There were cameras."

"Grace, there are always cameras."

In his mind's eye, he saw the flash. Helene was laughing at him—her face masked, her body sheethed in black spandex climbing gear. They were suspended from the side of building, hanging on ropes with pulleys.

Be careful, we've got cameras at two o'clock.

Darling, Helene laughed softly, there are always cameras.

The image faded into a frustrating void. He waited for more of the memory to break free. But no more came.

Earlier, when they left the house, Grace followed the truck with the SUV. "Time to ditch the truck. The front headlight is out, so be careful. We can't risk getting pulled over before we get it out of the way."

They left the truck parked on a deserted street and walked to Jacob's SUV two blocks away. "Do you have a key chain for your keys so I can find them easier?"

"It's a USB thumb drive in a black leather key chain." Grace stopped. "Do you think it would be that simple? She could've switched my USB with one of hers at the restaurant yesterday. I wouldn't have noticed."

"If she did, it won't be simple. Those keys sat at the bottom of the bay for a good three hours or more."

Once in the SUV, Grace drove while Jacob searched for her keys. It took a good fifteen minutes before he finally located them. "The leather case protected it to some extent but it's still wet."

"Does that mean it's ruined?"

"Possibly." He examined the small thumb drive. "But a USB memory stick has no moving parts and we're at the north end of the bay. With all the rains, that part of the bay is likely more fresh water than salt water right now. We could get lucky."

"We need a blow-dryer," Grace suggested.

"Blow-dryer might damage it. Our best bet is to let it dry naturally," Jacob reasoned. "But we might not have the time."

"Could the password code from my phone be for the files?"

"Hell, we don't even know if this holds the missing files. For all we know, it could be Helene's grocery list."

"I CAN APPRECIATE a man who wants to deal, Pusher." Oliver Kragen leaned against the bar in the gymnasium. "But some things I just don't haggle over."

Earlier, he ordered Sweeney to handcuff the bar manager to a chair. Not because he expected the younger man to escape but simply to keep him in the chair once the interrogation started taking its toll.

Which, in all honesty, the bar manager passed a good hour before the toll showed.

Pusher's head dropped forward against his chest. Blood dripped from the broken nose and split lips, soaking the shirt beneath.

Kragen nodded to Sweeney, who placed a bottle of ammonia under Pusher's nose to bring him around.

"Pusher, we need to establish some kind of rapport here."

He grabbed the younger man's hair and forced his head back until he was looking straight up into Oliver's eyes.

Pusher's face was no more than blood and ripped skin. Not surprising to Oliver, considering skin never held up well against leather-covered fists.

"Now, I'm going to ask you again where Helene Garrett's computer is."

"I told you Lomax has it," Pusher answered, his words slurred by his swollen lips.

"But you failed to tell me where Lomax is."

"I don't know. They were to get in touch with me."

"About what?"

"Updates on Helene's murder."

"And this disk I found in your pocket?" When Pusher's head lolled forward, Oliver slapped it back. "The disk!"

"I don't know. Haven't had a chance to look at it yet."

That earned Pusher another backhand across the face. Oliver nodded to Sweeney, who walked over to a nearby desk. He slid the disk into the laptop computer.

"We need a password," said Sweeney after looking at the screen. "I could probably find someone to break it."

"That would take too much time. Besides," Oliver reflected, as he glanced down at Pusher, "I have the feeling the answer is right here on the tip of Pusher's tongue. We just need to convince Mr. Davis that giving us the password might just save that same tongue."

"Take a look at this, Jacob."

It was after two in the morning, but Grace wasn't willing to go to bed until they read Helene's computer files.

"Oliver Kragen. Top aide to Senator D'Agostini." She

rubbed the gritty fatigue from her eyes. Then looked again. "I've seen this guy before."

"With Helene?"

"I don't remember. Maybe at a political event."

"Pusher said she had detailed files on a lot of people."

"Including me, my father and mother. From the time my parents met in the military to my mother's death. And my father after."

"According to this," Jacob said, scrolling down, "your dad had top security clearance."

"What do you mean? He was a spy?"

"Not necessarily. He could have been in charge of a specific project, or even a specific part of the government or war department." Jacob pinched his nose between his forefinger and thumb. Without thinking, he walked to the kitchen cabinet, found the aspirin and took a few.

It wasn't until he finished swallowing the tablets dry that he realized what he'd done. Obviously, on some level he remembered where the pills were located.

"She's got complete files on several of her business acquaintances. And on Pusher and myself, too."

"But?" Jacob glanced at Grace, impatient.

"Pusher was right, she has nothing on you, Jacob." She paused, considering. "Other than a few addresses. Why?"

JACOB HEARD BRANCHES banging against the house. He tensed, and then relaxed. He blinked away the grit in his eyes and slowly flexed the stiffness from his bad shoulder.

He glanced over at Grace, gave in to the urge to smooth away the stray strand of hair on her cheek. Why had he walked away from her? She shifted closer, partially lying on him.

It took him a while to convince her to share the bed with him. But he did so on the pretense he didn't want to mistake her for an intruder.

She accepted his suggestion only after he agreed to sleep on top of the blankets. But in the end, it didn't matter. She moved restlessly in her sleep and kicked off her covers.

His hand automatically came up, drifted over her spine. She'd changed her clothes, finding a pair of black jogging pants to use for pajamas and a thin cotton T-shirt as her top.

The hem had worked its way up past her waist. Unable to stop himself, he placed his hand over her belly, just above her panty line. The pregnancy had hardened her stomach. Something in him shifted. Something he didn't look at too closely. Not yet.

He noticed a tattoo just inside the curve of her hip. His fingers slid over the delicate tracings of the butterfly wings.

Why a butterfly?

She smiled, running a hand up over his hip. Why the scar?

The memory stopped him. It wasn't the first. He'd been having bits and pieces all night since the one of Helene.

But the few he had after were all of Grace.

Her on a lounger beside a pool. Both of them sailing the bay. Romantic dinners. Evenings at the theater. Even more evenings at her home in front of the fire.

Each memory connected. Each ending with them kissing or making love.

But when? Five months ago? A year? He didn't know. Winter. Aspen. Long enough to have fathered the baby? He'd suspected all along, but suspecting and having proof were two different things.

Restless, he snagged a pair of jeans by the bed, slipped them up over his hips, only to pause before zipping.

It was there, just at the top point of his right hip. A jagged, raised mark six inches in length.

Why the scar? she'd asked.

Frustrated that he had no answer, he grabbed the phone off of the nightstand, then slowly climbed the stairs to the tower.

Once up at the top, he tried Pusher's number. But after letting it ring several times, he hung up.

Where in the hell was he?

He heard it then, the soft pad of her feet against the wood steps. "I didn't mean to wake you."

She sighed. "The baby decided to sleep on my bladder. But since you'd been gone so long, I wanted to make sure you were okay. What time is it?"

"After five in the morning," he said and sat on one of the window seats. He forced himself to look at her, study the delicate lines of her face, the soft waves of blond hair that settled on her shoulders. Beautiful, rumpled and decidedly feminine. Something moved inside him. The queer mixture of fear and vulnerability that came with the sense of inevitability. "You should go to bed, Grace. You need rest. If not for you, for the baby."

"The baby is fine," she murmured and stepped closer. He caught a new scent, the spicy scent of his soap she'd used earlier. A fist of desire tightened his gut, caused him to shift away.

Annoyed at his retreat, Jacob pushed the phone into his front pocket, drawing her attention.

"No answer still?"

"None. I think something happened to him."

"Something bad?"

"Something. I don't know what. He could have skipped town. Got thrown in jail again. Defected to the other side."

"I won't believe that. Not Pusher."

"Well, we aren't doing anything about it until tomorrow." Jacob looked out the window at predawn sky. "We'll start with the strip club and work our way from there," he said, then rubbed the back of his neck. "Look, Grace, I don't want you hurt—"

"Then I guess we better figure this all out soon," she responded softly. "Okay?"

The set of his jaw told her it wasn't okay. "Since we're both up anyway, let's see if we can prod your memory," she suggested, trying to distract him with a change of subject. Giving in to impulse, she brushed a stray lock of hair from his forehead.

"Tell me something I didn't know before when we were together," he insisted. He caught her hand, tugged on it until she sat in his lap.

"I was named after a prayer."

"Which one?"

"The Serenity Prayer," she said, her words lost against his neck as she rested her head against his good shoulder. She missed this, the closeness.

As if sensing her thoughts, his arms tightened around her, keeping her safe if only for that moment. "What were the words?" He whispered the question against her hair, making her smile.

"'God, give me grace to accept with serenity the things that cannot be changed, courage to change the things which should be changed, and the wisdom to understand the difference.'"

"Who wrote it?"

"No one knows for sure." After a moment, she added, "It was my mother's favorite, though."

"God, give me Grace," he repeated. She could feel his smile against her ear. "Honey, it's probably a good thing you're mother didn't name you Serenity."

Grace pulled back until her eyes met his. "That's exactly what she used to say." She winked, slow and deliberate. The surge of pleasure rolled through Jacob, catching him off guard. How could he forget a look like that?

"In fact, she swears that when they decided on my name, the earth trembled, just enough for her to know she was in trouble."

"You miss her, don't you?"

"Very much."

Jacob watched the moonlight halo her head, setting the golden highlights on fire. He gave in to the impulse and captured a few strands in his hand. Just then a second flash of memory hit him. "I kissed you here, before."

"Yes."

"It wasn't a friendly kiss, Grace."

"No, it wasn't."

He leaned in until his mouth hovered just above hers. "Anything you need to tell me?"

"Not if I can help it—"

He covered her mouth with his and breathed in her sigh, keeping the kiss light until a sexy purr rounded off the edge of her breath. It took him from comfort to desire in a millisecond.

What man wouldn't take the kiss deeper to hear that sound again, feel the roll from her throat to his gut?

His hand twisted in her hair, keeping her head still in case she wanted to pull away. He dove this time, swallowing her in one, long erotic gulp of sin and sex.

But Grace couldn't pull away. She couldn't think. She couldn't breathe. All she could do was leave herself open under the onslaught. Matching him stroke for stroke, taste for taste, texture upon delicious texture.

When that wasn't enough, when it didn't come close to enough, he brought her up against him, his body hard as much as hers was pliant. When her knees threatened to knock, she thought for a moment of sliding off his lap, giving herself some space, regaining some sanity.

But then he dove again and she managed not to think at all.

Jacob's hand cupped her thigh, keeping her in place. But she had no thought of moving. He squeezed gently, kneading the flesh beneath his fingers, letting his thumb stray in long lazy circles, tempting her to shift and then, moments later, to move against him when he upped the tempo.

When she trembled, Jacob slipped his hand over her belly, groaning when it quivered beneath his fingers.

He nuzzled her neck, followed the cord of it to her collarbone, suckled her nipple through the cotton of her tee. The tremors ripped through her as his fingers slid between her thighs, stroking her until her hips writhed, her muscles quivered.

"Let it go, let me see."

The warm, moist demand against her ear sent her over the edge. Grace erupted, clenching herself around his hand, riding the release, melting into him as it played out.

"I can't believe I've forgotten that," he whispered the

words against her neck. Visibly affected, he kissed her, soothed her trembling body with long, draining kisses until she quieted beneath his touch.

"You're shaking," Grace whispered against his chest. "You're whole body…you've never—"

He raised her chin with his hand, ignoring the slight tremor in his fingers. "Maybe you are finally seeing the real me. Maybe we both are. With no memories, I have nothing to guard against."

The truth of his statement hit her square in the chest. "A relationship with you is impossible, Jacob. You're still the same man. When all is said and done, those guards will go back up once the amnesia is gone." She softened the harsh words by kissing his neck. "You didn't want me then. What good would it do to become lovers again, after all this time?"

"Damn it, we never stopped being lovers, Grace."

"Yes, we did. The minute you walked away from us."

He stilled. "Us?"

"You and me," she snapped, using her finger to point back and forth between them.

For a moment, he'd thought she meant her and the baby. That he'd left her and the baby. "I really did a number on you, didn't I?"

Her silence gave him her answer.

"I'm sorry, honey. I think if I could take it back—" he murmured, then stiffened.

"What?"

"Shh." He instinctively placed his hand over her mouth. Then he heard it again. A car door shutting.

"We've got company." He looked out the tower window and saw two sedans parked outside. "Sweeney."

Grace tensed. "But how?"

"Ask Pusher," Jacob said grimly. "In fact, I'll ask him the next time I see him."

A trunk slammed shut. "They're not worried about surprising us."

"Why?"

"Probably because of all the guns their carrying."

Chapter Sixteen

Hugh Miller was the first to speak up. "Are they there?"

"Don't see them, but Lomax would be smarter than that," Sweeney answered, looking through infrared binoculars. "If I were a betting man, I'd say the odds are in our favor. This was the closest address of Lomax's on the list."

Sweeney took his pistol from his side holster. "If they are there, I want them taken alive. Got that?" Sweeney waved the other three men over. Miller checked his clip. "We need them breathing. Anyone who kills them by accident will be dead before Lomax or Renne hits the ground. Understand me?"

The other men nodded.

"Then let's go."

"GRAB YOUR JACKET and shoes! Now!"

They raced down the tower's stairs to the bedroom beneath. "The car?"

"No. It's too late for that. We're going to have to go across the bay."

Grace followed him down to the lowest level, her own sneakers in hand.

"Get down in the boat."

Within moments, she lay flat on her belly, curled at the bottom.

"No matter what, I don't want you sitting up." Jacob grabbed a nearby gas container and started pouring it over the dock.

The fumes caught in her throat, making her gag. "What are you doing?"

"Making sure they can't follow us."

He jumped into the boat and untied the rope from the post. It wasn't until then he noticed the anchor had been set overboard.

Quickly, he pulled it to the surface.

He swore. Grace glanced over and in the darkness she could see a large bag tied to the anchor weight.

Jacob tossed it into the boat. "What do you want to bet I've found my stash."

He left it and grabbed a life jacket. "Put this on." He took a lighter from his pocket, hit the switch and tossed it onto the dock. Flames immediately spread. "Hold your shirt over your nose."

"Your house, Jacob. You're burning—"

"If I'm as rich as you say, I'll have it rebuilt later."

He slammed the accelerator forward. Gunfire peppered their boat as Sweeney's men shot out from the dock, but none of the bullets hit close.

Grace peered over the side, saw headlights turned on in the distance. "They're following us," Grace yelled the words across the din of the motor.

"It will be hard to follow us without a boat." Jacob studied a bank of trees crowding the beach in the distance. He brought the boat around until it pointed directly toward woods rising over the crest of land.

"Hold on." He jerked the steering wheel until the boat headed straight for the beach. "This is going to get rough."

Chapter Seventeen

In the daylight the Chancellor's was nothing more than drab. Drab brown paint, drab gray cement. Even the neon light, blinking in the afternoon sun, lost the power to catch and hold the gaze of the few pedestrians who strolled past.

Jacob and Grace arrived at the strip club before its doors opened for the nooners escaping their jobs for a lunch hour of distraction and drinks.

"There she is," Jacob murmured, his gaze settling on the street about half a block down from their rented silver sedan.

It took over two hours to find a stretch of beach to ditch the boat, steal another car and head back into the city. And then another hour or so to secure the rented car and check Pusher's apartment.

"Let's go." They had been leaning against the car, waiting. Jacob cupped her elbow and guided her across the street until they intersected with Maggie at the alleyway entrance beside the club.

The blonde tossed her cigarette into the gutter just as they approached. Half expecting her to bolt, Grace braced herself, blocking the waitress's path.

"Hi, Maggie, do you remember us?" Jacob asked.

"Sure, you're Pusher's friends."

She folded her arms across her stomach. But it was her bloodshot eyes that drew Grace's attention.

"Actually, we're looking for Pusher and wondered if you'd seen him."

The waitress looked at Jacob. "You a cop?"

"No."

"You've got the smell of a cop."

"Pusher's my friend, Maggie," Grace said quietly.

"Well, hoorah for you."

"Last night, I got the impression Pusher was your friend, too," Grace added mildly.

"Then you got the wrong impression." Maggie tried to step past but Jacob grabbed her arm and held her in place.

"Let me go." She jerked her arm away, but Jacob gripped tighter. "I'll call a cop."

"You do that, Maggie, and you'll lose out. I'm willing to pay for information."

"How much?"

"Two hundred."

"Make it five and you have a deal."

"Okay, five."

Her eyes narrowed with suspicion. "Show me."

Jacob pulled out his wallet and took out five one-hundred-dollar bills. "They're yours if I get the answers I want."

Maggie stared at the money for a moment. "Okay. That guy who chased you last night? His name is Sweeney."

"We already know that."

"Well, what you don't know is that Sweeney and his goons went after Pusher a few minutes after you left," she said. "Yesterday, one of Sweeney's guys put the word on the street that he wanted to talk to Pusher. He left his card at all of Pusher's haunts. Rumor was that Sweeney was looking for something Pusher had. Said he'd pay good money to just talk to Pusher."

"So when Pusher showed up here yesterday—"

"I called Sweeney. I told him you two were with Pusher and Sweeney went ballistic on the phone, ya know? He started cussing a blue streak. I thought he was going to hang up but then he told me if I saw you start to leave before he arrived, I was to stall you if I could."

"Why didn't you?"

"Before I could think of something," she said, then nodded at Grace, "your girlfriend threw all the money on the floor." She shrugged. "I stopped and grabbed a few twenties myself since I couldn't reach you anyway."

"You still haven't told me what Sweeney did with Pusher."

"Give me half first."

"Two hundred," Jacob said and handed over two of the bills. She stuck them in her bra.

"Sweeney cornered Pusher in the alley last night. He forced Pusher to go with him. Sweeney said some guy named Kragen wanted to have a talk with Pusher." She glanced up the street. "I don't know what about. I'd already gotten my money so I left."

"Did you say Kragen? As in Oliver Kragen?"

"I don't know. I just heard the last name."

Jacob took the last three bills and stuffed them into her bra himself. "Thanks. I'll make sure I pass along your story to Pusher when I see him."

"You do that." Maggie tossed over her shoulder as she walked toward the club. "If you need anything else, sugar," she added, deliberately adopting Pusher's accent, "you all don't forget to look me up."

For the first time, Grace noted Jacob's hands fisted in anger. "We need to find Pusher," he said. "I'm pretty sure I'm the type that would rather give an apology in person."

"Where do you think Sweeney took him?"

"I don't know, but I do know who does."

"Kragen," Grace stated.

"How would you like to attend a presidential election ball tonight?"

"I think I'd love to."

Chapter Eighteen

The Lakelear Grand Hotel stood on posh Connecticut Avenue. Labeled as more of a resort than hotel, Grace had to admit she'd never had the budget for a suite.

She glanced over at Jacob as he pulled up to the front entrance. "How much money was in that bag?" They had already used a good chunk, she thought, to shop for clothes, suitcases and other necessities.

"Enough not to worry about staying here for a while."

The valet opened the door. They had traded the sedan in earlier for a black Porsche. Grace swung her legs out, deliberately waiting to catch the valet's eye before stepping out of the rented Porsche.

"Welcome to the Lakelear."

"Thank you," she said, smoothing her carmel suede mid-thigh skirt back into place.

His smile slowly disappeared as Jacob rounded the hood of the Porsche. "Welcome to Lakelear Grand, sir."

Jacob just nodded, having already given his key to another valet. He cupped Grace's elbow. "Ready, darling?"

"Yes."

The hotel lobby lived up to the glamour and wealth of the D.C. elite, with its marble inlay floor and gold-trimmed reception desk.

"Welcome, sir. May I help you?" A man stood behind the cherrywood counter. His small mustache twitched only slightly.

"My name is John Eckert. My secretary made arrangements for a suite earlier today."

"Yes, Mr. Eckert we've been waiting for you. My name is William Fremont and I'm the assistant manager here at the Lakelear. All your arrangements have been taken care of." He nodded to include Grace, hesitating a long second.

Jacob pointedly ignored the silent request for an introduction. He didn't want to take any chances that her voice would be recognized as his secretary's.

The assistant manager shifted his gaze just over Grace's shoulder. "George will be happy to escort you to your suite." He handed the card to a young man in a bellboy uniform. "The Mayflower Suite, George."

"Follow me, sir."

"One moment." Jacob turned back to the assistant manager.

"Yes, sir."

"It seems one of our pieces of luggage has been forgotten and we'll need replacement clothes for our evening plans. I'll need to be measured for a tuxedo and have several gowns delivered to our room from your clothing boutiques. Have them call our room for the details."

"My pleasure, Mr. Eckert."

Jacob placed his hand at the small of Grace's back as they followed the bellboy.

"ROOM SERVICE work for you?"

It had already been a long afternoon. The boutique had sent up a selection of gowns and the men's shop had sent up their tailor. Both Jacob and Grace were ready for their appearance later that night.

"Maybe a vanilla shake, if you don't mind. My stomach is a little queasy," Grace added, thinking about Pusher. "The shake will help settle it."

As if reading her thoughts, Jacob walked over to her and pulled her to him, wrapping his arms around her. "No, I don't mind but I'm going to order some fruit and a sandwich with it. Try to eat what you can. Pusher will be fine. They won't do anything to him, for a while at least. They want what's on the USB thumb drive. Until they get it, they can't be sure what part he plays in this."

Grace knew Jacob was exaggerating, but there was an underlying truth to his words.

"I'm also worried that someone might recognize you," Grace reasoned. "Unlike me, you wouldn't have any idea who your friends or your enemies are at the ball."

"From what you've said, I don't have too many friends to worry about. That should narrow the playing field."

"That's not funny."

He sighed and placed his forehead against hers. "No, its not. And neither is this situation," he said apologetically. "Look, I've had time to think about the amnesia, Grace. There's nothing I can do about getting my memories back, so I'll just have to learn to punt. Seems that's second nature to me anyway."

"I can't disagree with that."

His hand cupped her jaw, then lifted her face up until she met his gaze. "But I don't think it's second nature to you. That's why I don't want you with me. It's too dangerous. For you and the baby."

"We're going to a swank ball at the Senate Majority Leader's mansion, not a drug dealer's lair."

"Bad guys don't have a dress code."

"I'll be fine," she said. "If there's trouble, I'll lose myself in the crowd like we agreed. Then leave after you've caused a diversion."

"I'll have to accept that, for now," Jacob said. "Why don't you go have a shower? The food will be here by the time you get out. Then after you eat, you can try and get some rest. It's going to be a long night."

"A shower sounds good." But they both noted she didn't comment on the rest of Jacob's statement.

"Most of this kind of work is a waiting game, Grace. We've got hours before the ball."

"What kind of work?"

"Government work," Jacob said automatically, then froze. He tried to follow that same train of thought, only to draw another blank. "Damn it."

"It's a start, Jacob," she said softly and kissed his cheek. "If you worked as an agent, you'd have to keep that from me, wouldn't you?"

"More than likely," he admitted. "But I wouldn't let me off the hook that easily, Grace. For all we know, I could be one of the bad guys."

"No way," she quipped, walking toward the bath. "You dress too nice."

His laughter followed her into the bathroom, making her smile. The old Jacob rarely laughed. So whenever she managed to get him chuckling, she counted it as a victory.

She stripped out of her clothes. On impulse, she studied her image in the mirror. Her breasts had gotten larger, the nipples much darker. A small hard bulge in her tummy told her the baby was growing. The small flutters she'd been feeling on and off told her he was getting more active. For precautionary reasons, she checked for spotting before folding her clothes and placing them on the vanity nearby.

It was hard for her to believe that less than forty hours earlier, she'd been in her house, taking it easy and baking cookies.

Alone.

Chapter Nineteen

On the Hill, there was a saying: Good politics require great staging.

Which made Senator D'Agostini's presidential campaign ball a full-blown Hollywood extravaganza.

Palladian windows were draped in patriotic blue, while diamond-infused chandeliers glittered and sparkled from twenty-foot coffered ceilings.

A sea of satin, silk and tailored tuxedos crowded thirty square yards of glossy herringbone wood, while a fifty-piece orchestra stood in the corner delivering a jaunty but sophisticated big-band sound.

"Dance with me."

Before Grace could react, Jacob's fingers skimmed over the small of her back, urging her forward into the crush of waltzing couples.

They made a striking pair. Jacob had opted for a basic black tuxedo. Severe in cut, the sleek but simple material complemented his broad shoulders, his lean hips. The arrogance of the cut went well with his predatory gaze, the dangerous slant of his chiseled features. A panther, she thought, stalking his prey.

He pulled her to him, holding her in the close intimate

circle of his arms. Making it apparent to anyone watching that they didn't want to be disturbed.

He bent his head close to hers. "Relax," he murmured.

"I am," she whispered back, hoping that saying the words out loud would make them true. Gaining access had been relatively simple. All one needed was to mingle, to laugh and part with a compliment or two about one's golf game or latest insider news on Wall Street. "My role is easy. I'm just the arm candy."

And for that purpose, she'd chosen a strapless gown of ivory silk chiffon. Feminine and alluring, the overlay material flowed from a bodice that hugged her breasts before falling gracefully into a cascaded drape of shirred layers.

She pinned her hair up high on her head, drawing more than one male gaze to the slope of her neck. And more than one female's glance to the diamond solitaires that winked at her earlobes.

"God, you're beautiful." His fingers drifted carelessly over the delicate point of her shoulder, sending ripples of pleasure down her spine.

His arm pressed her closer, until the heat of him seeped through the thin layers of her gown. Grace got lost in the sway of their bodies. She breathed in his warm, masculine scent. Caught the underlying hint of aftershave. She rested her head on his shoulder, promising herself only one song.

Suddenly, he went rigid against her. Her gaze snapped to his. The blue of his irises glittered with a fierceness, a cold savage fury that she'd never seen before. An air of violence suddenly surrounded them both like a tight leash.

A small flutter of panic worked its way up at the back of her throat. "Jacob?"

JACOB HEARD HIS NAME, the plea in Grace's voice through the static of sounds, the rush of images.

Suddenly, he was in an alley. It was dark. Pitch-black, he remembered. Glass crackled beneath his feet—the remnants of the alley's light, shattered by a bullet.

Gunfire spattered the Dumpster above Helene's head. *Get behind me.* But the warning came too late.

Pain exploded in his shoulder, but it was Helene who'd screamed, Helene who'd fallen. Frantic, Jacob reached for her, firing his pistol as he pulled her into his lap.

Blood covered her chest, rattled her lungs. *"Jacob...find Grace."*

The grief welled up inside, then seeped through his pores.

He grabbed her tight, willing her to live.

"Jacob. You're hurting me."

Relief poured through him. He blinked, refocusing.

"Jacob," Grace whispered, her voice harsh with worry or fear, he couldn't be sure.

"Grace." He glanced around the dance floor, satisfied no one really cared that they'd stopped dancing.

He automatically took up the rhythm of music.

"Are you okay?"

"Yes. Just had a flashback, but I'm fine now." He shifted, forcing the muscles in his back to relax.

"Kragen's here."

"Where?" The muscles snapped into tight rubber bands.

"Over your left shoulder."

He maneuvered her around in a slow, lazy circle. Oliver stopped across the room in front of an older gentleman. Jacob recognized the tall, thin, almost frail build. The gray ring of hair that circled a nearly bald head. "D'Agostini," Jacob commented.

Oliver leaned in to the senator, whispered something by the older man's ear, then stepped back again. The senator nodded. Within moments, the senator excused himself from the ball.

"Where are they going?"

"I don't know but we need to find out," Jacob said, realizing the need for revenge had been forgotten—until now. "He's our only lead to Pusher."

Jacob cupped Grace's elbow and led her off the floor.

OLIVER KRAGEN wasn't happy. There was nothing left to get out of Pusher Davis. The man had taken a beating without uttering one word of information. But for some reason, the senator wanted him kept alive.

"Going somewhere, Kragen?" Before Oliver could react, his arm was shoved up and behind his shoulder. Pain rushed up his back and exploded into his rotator cuff.

It would take very little pressure for Lomax to separate his shoulder. He felt a gun jab in his side. "How the hell did you get in here?"

"Doesn't seem your security is worth the money you pay," Jacob answered. He did a quick search of Kragen's pockets. "Although I have to say that you dress them well.

"Now unless you want to get intimately acquainted with a dialysis machine for the rest of your life, I suggest you do as I ask."

"And that is?" Oliver asked.

"Pusher Davis."

"Who?"

Kragen hissed with pain as Jacob applied pressure to his arm, moving it farther up his back. "I don't think you want me to snap your shoulder out of joint, do you?"

"Okay, say he is here. He's…incapacitated at the moment. You would never be able to get him out without notice."

"You let me worry about that, Oliver. All you need to do is take me to him," Jacob replied, his tone mild. "Agreeably. Pretend we're long lost friends." He punctuated his order with another jab of his pistol.

"And if we're seen?"

"You better hope we're not. Because you'll be the first person I'll want out of the way."

Kragen led them to a room on the third floor. In front stood a man, one of the personal bodyguards Jacob assumed. He jabbed at Oliver's side.

"It's okay, Miller. These people are associates." The tone of Kragen's voice was smooth but firm.

"Grace."

Grace pulled out a small revolver, aimed it at Miller and fired. A dart imbedded itself in Miller's chest. No more than three seconds later, the giant crumpled to the floor.

Jacob shoved Oliver into the door. The senator's aide punched in the key code with his free hand.

Jacob opened the door. "Go, Grace."

Grace stepped through the door and stopped. Pusher lay unconscious on the bed, his wrists in handcuffs, his face nothing more than raw meat and blood.

Jacob stiffened at Grace's cry of alarm, turned slightly to make sure she was safe.

Without warning, Kragen rammed his elbow into Jacob's gut and twisted away. He grabbed for the gun, but Jacob let go of the grip, catching Oliver off guard. Instead, Jacob nailed the aide in the throat, then slammed his elbow into the man's face. He grunted in satisfaction when he felt the bone give beneath the impact.

Jacob snagged the pistol as Oliver went to his knees. He forced the man's head back by his hair and shoved the barrel under his chin.

Kragen gasped, trying to find his breath through the bruised larynx.

"Jacob. Don't."

Something in Jacob went cold. Grace's plea saved Kragen's life. He slammed the pistol against Oliver's temple and watched him crumple to the floor.

He turned to Grace, took in the fear on her ashen face.

"I didn't kill him."

The savagery of his features told her he could've killed him, would have, if she hadn't been there.

Quickly, Jacob went back to the doorway and dragged Miller into the room. "There's a chance he hadn't been spotted yet by the security cameras."

Grace barely heard. She was already at Pusher's side. "How are we going to get him out of here?" she asked.

Jacob didn't answer. Instead, he handed her the gun and lifted Pusher up and over his good shoulder. His features tightened with the effort, but he didn't waver.

"Let's go. I noticed a service elevator farther down," Jacob said, shifting Pusher slightly. "The only way to do this is make a dash for it."

They headed down the hallway, the thick carpet masking their footsteps. Grace's hand trembled against the gun. Nausea reared up in her stomach, swiped at the back of her throat. But she refused to give in to the queasiness. If they ran into one of D'Agostini's men, she wouldn't hesitate to shoot.

When they reached the elevator, Grace hit the button. Neither of them spoke. With the hall empty, their voices would carry. In the distance they heard a door slam, then muffled footsteps.

Suddenly, the chime sounded and the door slid open. The voices morphed into screams of rage.

"Go!" Jacob ordered, but Grace was already through the door. Panicked, Grace hit the basement floor first. Then punched the Close button with her fist.

"That won't make it shut any faster."

"I know, but it sure makes me feel better."

"We'll be fine, if we don't have to stop," Jacob said and took the gun from Grace. It wasn't until she looked down, she saw how badly her hands were shaking.

"It's all right, baby. You did good." He raised the gun, barrel up, ready to shoot when the doors slid open once again.

No one was waiting. Relief threatened to buckle her knees.

As if reading her mind, Jacob said, "We're not out of the woods, yet."

Suddenly, gunshots punctuated his statement.

"Move, Grace." They burst through the kitchen doors. Kragen followed less than a minute later. One of the cooks, a small man brandishing a knife, tried to stop them. Jacob laid him out cold with one punch.

"They'll have guards coming at us from both directions," Jacob said as they strode through the maze of ovens and counters. The kitchen staff yelled and cursed until they saw Jacob's gun. Then they screamed.

Suddenly, fire alarms exploded around them. The lights went out. The screams hit a higher pitch as people scrambled for exits.

"Jacob, here," Grace shouted. She stood in front of large garbage chute, holding its steel door open. "It should be big enough."

Quickly, he shoved Pusher down the garbage slide. He picked up Grace and tossed her in, ignoring her scream as she flew down the steel ramp.

Swearing, he dived in after her, a flurry of bullets exploding around him.

"Go!"

Grace jumped out of the Dumpster. Jacob grabbed Pusher and literally threw him into Grace's arms before jumping out himself. Once again, he slung Pusher over his shoulder. With gun in hand, Jacob joined Grace and they headed for the valet parking lot.

People poured from the mansion in a surge of chaos and indignation.

"What's going on?" A young kid, no more than twenty years of age, pulled up in a four-door sedan. His valet badge identified him as Peter. "Is it a fire or something?"

"Why don't you go check it out?" Jacob walked right up to the car and placed the gun in the young man's face. "Now."

"Yes, sir." The guy stumbled out of the car. "I don't want any trouble."

"Then go."

When the kid took off over the lawn, Jacob handed Grace his gun. "You're going to have to drive." He brought Pusher around to the back of the car. With difficulty, he laid the unconscious man in the backseat and then climbed into the passenger seat.

As soon as he was in the car, Grace hit the accelerator and took off through the gate and down the street.

"How are we doing so far?" She blew a stray lock of hair off her forehead.

Jacob checked the side mirror. "We're safe enough for now, but I think it's time to regroup back at the hotel."

"In a stolen car?"

"We'll ditch the car."

She glanced at Pusher through the rearview mirror. "We're going to look petty conspicuous walking into to a hotel like this."

"Who says we need to walk in?"

OLIVER SLAMMED OPEN his office door, nearly taking it off its hinges.

The bruise across his nose had turned purple, but the swelling was down. Oliver held a white kerchief up to the side of his head, stemming the stream of blood still oozing from the cut.

"Who set off the fire alarm?"

Unflustered, Frank Sweeney followed his boss into the office. "Still working on it. But Lomax and the woman got away."

"Of course they did." Kragen slammed his free hand against the desktop. "I want it on the news. Now! If we can't locate them, we'll market them as criminals and hang them out to dry. By tomorrow, I want their faces splashed across every channel in this country. Fugitives wanted for murders."

"I don't think that's the answer—"

"Did I ask your opinion?" Oliver sneered.

"You should. Your man is right, Oliver." D'Agostini walked into the office, his voice grim but the steel of his eyes unbendable. "I'm surprised at you. I don't think you've ever let your emotions rule your decisions. Can't say I like this side of you, Oliver, but I guess it's understandable. Lomax has certainly gotten the best of you over the last few days, hasn't he?" His eyes took in the bloody features. "In more ways than one, it seems."

Oliver forced himself to sit back in his chair.

"I'm going to tell you what we're going to do," Richard said. "Instead of flushing them out and bringing more unnecessary attention to this problem, we're going to do what we should have done in the first place. We're going to bring them to us."

"And how do you propose to do that?" Kragen said with sarcasm. "Call them up for tea?"

Richard D'Agostini's features subtly took on a hard edge. "Oliver, I'll excuse the impertinent behavior, simply because I know you're not at your best. But make no mistake. While I've found your services and devotion exceptional in the past, I will not tolerate insubordination among my people. Do you understand me?"

"Yes," the aide agreed, but inside he seethed.

"I have arranged a meeting tonight. A very important meeting." Richard said. "One that will take care of Jacob Lomax. You just make sure you're here to greet the couple when they show. Understand me?"

"Yes."

"Now, I think you've had a long day, Oliver," Richard observed. "I want you to get a good night's sleep. I'll take

Mr. Sweeney here for my meeting. He will inform you of what happens later."

Kragen fisted his hands. The senator was giving him a disciplinary slap by making him go through his own subordinate for information. Kragen looked at Frank, but the enforcer was smart enough to show no reaction over the change of plans.

"Of course," Oliver responded, his lips tight. "I'll be here, waiting."

Chapter Twenty

Pusher had made himself comfortable with a sandwich from room service. Although the man moved slowly and chewed even more slowly, Jacob was relieved he would suffer no permanent damage from his injuries.

Jacob showed the ex-con the paper from Grace's phone. "Try this."

Pusher took a look at the series of numbers. "It's not the right type of code for the USB. I don't know what this is for, but it's not the one I need."

"Is the thumb drive working?"

"So far so good. But I won't be really able to tell until I can access the information," Pusher explained. "How much time do I have to decrypt this?"

"Less than ten hours."

"I'll do my best."

Jacob arched an eyebrow.

"Ten it is."

Jacob placed a hand on the younger man's shoulder. "Thanks, Pusher."

"No problem." The younger man's smile went lopsided

under the swelling. He winced and touched his lips. "Besides, I owe them a little back."

Grace walked up to the men. "Will we be safe here?"

"Yes," Jacob lied, knowing they wouldn't be safe until he finished this. "At least until tomorrow. The senator is going to be dealing with the aftermath of the commotion tonight."

"Why don't you two get some rest," Pusher suggested. "If you want me to crack this, I'm going to need some quality time alone."

Grace smiled. "Okay, Pusher. I need to talk to Jacob, anyway."

Jacob followed Grace into the bedroom. During the ride home, emotions and memories stampeded through him, leaving his inside battered, his mind overloaded.

"Do you think the fire alarm was a coincidence?"

"Maybe." But neither of them truly believed it.

Suddenly, he heard the click of the lock before she crossed the floor to him. "All I could think when we were running over the lawn was what would have happened if we'd been caught."

With a gentle hand, she pushed him until he sat on the bed. "And I knew what they had done to Pusher wouldn't have even been close to what Kragen would've done to you."

"Grace—"

"I saw Kragen's eyes, Jacob. That man wanted to tear you apart."

Jacob felt the flutter of her fingers across his forehead as she brushed his hair back, then kissed his wound. "Grace."

"I decided then, at that moment, what I wanted."

"And what's that?"

"You," she said softly. "For tonight, tomorrow. For as long as we can have."

"You mean, for as long as my amnesia lasts," Jacob corrected. "And when my memory returns?"

"We'll have a decision to make."

When she stepped closer, he cupped the small of her back with his palms, brought her body in tight to his. "The baby is mine, isn't it?"

"Yes."

He had anticipated her answer. Still, his hands flexed against her in reaction.

"Jacob, I couldn't tell you before—"

Tears swelled in her caramel eyes, then spilled. He wiped the dampness with his thumb, tracing the bones of her cheek, the soft line of her jaw. "Shh. Tomorrow. We'll deal with it all tomorrow."

He studied her mouth, loving the soft curves, the slight tremble of anticipation.

"I've missed you," he murmured, then covered her lips with his own, catching the next quiver, soothing it with his tongue until she whimpered with pleasure.

His fingers moved to the back of her hair, releasing the pins, letting them drop—forgotten before they hit the floor.

The silky ends of her hair fell, then flowed over his hands.

One of them shuddered. He didn't know which one. He only knew he didn't care.

Her lips softened under his. She sighed, then shifted, trying to fit her body to his. He tasted the sweet curve of her shoulder while his fingers traced the bare skin of her back.

He caught her dress zipper between his thumb and forefinger and tugged, letting the side of his hand ride the bumps of her spine down to the small hollow above her hips.

"Wait," she murmured.

Slowly, he pulled back, but no more than a breath away. She reached up, took one end of his tie and slid it free. The silk whispered against his shirt in a long, seductive hiss. She dropped it to the ground.

Her fingers found the buttons of his shirt and slipped them free one by one. His heart picked up speed and he moved her hand to his bare chest. "See what you do to me, Grace?"

"What if I want to do more?" Loose, her dress slipped to the floor in a long, sexy sigh, leaving a puddle of chiffon at her feet.

She wore nothing now, except a wisp of white lace just under the round swell of her belly, a small scrap of material that provided no protection from his gaze. "How much more?" he rasped, as his eyes followed the long lean lines of her legs up to the gentle flare of her hips and back again to her belly.

A stab of possessiveness shot through him, on its heels a jolt of the need to protect her and his baby inside her.

"So much more," she murmured. She started to slip out of her heels, but a hand on her thigh, stopped her.

"Not yet."

Grace smiled, a wicked curve of the lips that thickened the blood in his veins.

Slowly, she stepped out of her dress, slid into his lap and straddled his waist. She guided his hand from the curve of her hip, down the length of her leg, stopping only when his palm flexed against the curve of her ankle and his fingers slipped under the strap of her sandal. "I never knew high heels turned you on."

Jacob shuddered, absorbing another punch of desire, before his hand gave in to the need to feel the silk of skin again. "I didn't, either," he admitted, while his fingers traveled back to her hip. "Let's find out what else I like."

His hand cupped the roundness of her belly—soft in tenderness, lingering with possessiveness.

Then he jerked back, his eyes wide.

The baby bumped his hand again.

Grace would've paid good money to be able to laugh. But the emotion caught at the back of her throat. She didn't think it was often that Jacob got caught off guard.

But he recovered quickly, she thought with delicious pleasure. His lips skimmed her shoulder, followed the delicate curve of her neck, tasted the hollow of her collarbone.

With a sigh, she leaned back. Just for a moment. Just for support. His mouth settled over one sensitive nipple, tugging, tasting. Little electric shocks exploded under his lips, setting her nerves humming.

He moved slowly, maddeningly so. Nibbling here, stroking there. She tugged off his shirt to show her impatience. When that didn't change his tempo, she fisted his hair, holding him still until her mouth found his. Hard, hot, impatient.

Suddenly, Grace was beneath him, the final barriers gone. The wisp of lace, torn and thrown. His pants peeled away and left beside her gown.

Jacob used his elbows for support, not wanting to crush the baby, but wanting—needing—it between them.

A double-edged sword of pain and pleasure sliced through skin, gut and bone. How could he have turned away from this, turned away from her?

He shifted back, bringing her hips to the edge of the bed. Her calves slid up over his shoulders. He absorbed the pleasure with the pain when one balanced over his wound.

His hands found the soft cheeks of her derriere. Because he could, he squeezed each, heard her gasp before he hitched her hips higher.

She felt open, exposed, balanced on the edge. Her heart beat, fluttering with fear. Of what, she didn't know. She gripped the covers in tight fists, trying to keep from falling.

At that moment, he slid into her.

They both groaned. "I'm a selfish bastard, honey, but I need to hear you say it."

Grace understood. His face was savage despite the endearment. The pain became unbearable, the words burned the back of her throat. Too much pain already, she thought. She looked into his eyes and stepped off the edge. "I love you, Jacob Lomax. I always have and I always will."

His muscles bunched reflexively against her, telling her what she needed to know.

The only way she needed to know.

He took her then, on a long, shuddered sigh—sweeping her into a rhythm that had her rising, cresting, tumbling into a free fall.

And for the first time in a long time, she wasn't afraid.

Chapter Twenty-One

I love you, Jacob Lomax.

Jacob watched Grace fall asleep in the crook of his arm. Lord, he hoped so. But even as she spoke the words, he understood they wouldn't get her through the next twenty-four hours.

The flashes of memories were coming at breakneck speed, tumbling over each other, battering the wall that had held them back for so long.

Jacob had parents, still living. Still together after almost forty years. Grace had been wrong. He had family, he had friends. No more than a handful, but friends he trusted.

He also had a past.

The memories of Helene remained just out of reach. But they were right there, lingering on the edge of the others. They would come soon, he knew. And then he'd be prepared.

Determined, he gathered Grace closer, closed his eyes and planned.

A SLIGHT TAP ON THE DOOR had Jacob up and out of bed. He reached for his gun on the nearby nightstand.

"Lomax." The bar manager let out a long, low whistle through the door. "We just opened Pandora's box."

Jacob opened the door, stepped through, then shut it quietly behind him. "Show me."

For the next hour, Jacob scanned the Primoris files. "Can this be copied?"

"With a little time," Pusher replied, concern deepening his accent. "I have to bypass more security codes."

"How long?"

"At least a few more hours," Pusher answered.

"We don't have a few hours." Jacob grabbed the USB from the side of the computer. Their escape from the party tonight had terrified him. Now that he understood what he was dealing with, he wasn't going to let her near the situation.

"I need you to watch over Grace." He handed Pusher his pistol. "See that door? No one gets through that door alive."

"Hey, man, my specialty is computers—" Pusher stopped. "Hell. All right. Why not."

"Thanks. I'll be back as soon as I can."

"She's going to want to know what happened to you."

"Tell her I'm taking care of some business," answered Jacob as he picked up the phone and punched in the number. When the other side clicked, he said. "It's me. I've got the files."

CHARLES RENNE PARKED his car in the parking garage on the west end of the city and waited.

When headlights flared in his back window, he opened the door and stepped out.

Sweeney approached him and quickly patted Charles down. "The senator would like to have a word with you, Doctor Renne."

Charles said nothing. Instead, he waited until Sweeney opened the limousine door.

When Charles slid onto the seat beside him, D'Agostini didn't bother with the usual pleasantries. "They showed up at the fund-raiser last night. They could have done serious damage to our plans."

"Who? Lomax?"

"With your daughter. They managed to escape with Pusher Davis. I need to know where they took him."

"And I told you, I need time."

"You've had time, Charles. More than I've allowed anyone else. Now I am out of patience. The election machines are waiting to be shipped from the warehouse. I need that source code."

Anger rose in Charles, burning hot until it threatened to spew from every pore in his body. "If Sweeney hadn't showed up at Grace's house, I would've contacted you and taken care of everything myself. But your man Kragen had to send in his enforcer. He put everything at risk. Not me."

"That was unfortunate," the senator said. "But you had assured me from the beginning that your daughter would not be a complication when you told me about Helene's deception. And here she is right in the middle of the problem."

From the first time Charles had met Helene, there had been something vaguely familiar about her. But it was only a few days ago that he placed her as Langdon's daughter. She was the identical image of her mother.

"I need you to contact Grace."

"I told you, I can't find her."

"I have a hard time believing that, Charles. What I need you to do is persuade her to meet with you. And have her bring the Primoris files and the code."

"And how am I supposed to do that?"

"Tell her you're in danger," D'Agostini suggested.

"You really think she'll believe me?"

"Yes, because if she doesn't, your being in danger will be the truth."

Fear, dark and ugly, slithered beneath Charles's skin. "I will do whatever is necessary. After all these years, there should be no question of my loyalty. Didn't I warn you that Helene was an imposter? Didn't I tell you about her meeting with Lomax? Once Grace mentioned she'd be at the club that night—"

"Your loyalty was bought and paid for, so it's always in question. What I'm concerned about is your devotion to your daughter. Will it become an obstacle?"

"None whatsoever," Charles argued. "You forget, she's never been my daughter."

Chapter Twenty-Two

I've missed you.

The memory nudged Grace from hazy edges of sleep. But it was the actual words that had her sitting straight up in Jacob's bed.

A glance around the bedroom told her he'd left. He wouldn't desert her. She knew him too well now. But he'd certainly protect her.

Even if it meant breaking his promise.

She drew her knees up under the sheet, then rested her forehead against them. He was putting his life at risk to save her and their baby.

Grace got up and slipped on Jacob's robe, hugging it close.

The scent of coffee drifted through the open door.

Her heart jumped. She smiled, chiding herself.

She rushed down the stairs, not caring if she wore her heart on her sleeve. "I thought you'd left."

Pusher stepped out from the kitchen. "He did."

He handed her some tea. "He gave me his gun and told me to protect you."

"Protect me." She nodded. So she had been right.

The phone rang, startling her. She automatically reached for it. Only Jacob knew where they were.

Carol's number. Her father.

"Dad."

"No, Miss Renne. This is Oliver Kragen. We met last night."

"How did you get this number? What have you done to Carol?"

"We have not harmed your housekeeper. In fact, she probably hasn't even realized her phone is gone."

"Then how—"

"Your father. Of course, he gave it to us somewhat reluctantly. Which is one of the reasons I'm calling."

"You better not have harmed him—"

"Or what?" Kragen laughed, a savage sound that chilled Grace to the bone. "You're going to send Jacob Lomax after me? Why don't you put him on the phone. I'd rather cut out the middle man anyway."

"He's in the shower."

"Please, Miss Renne, don't play—" Kragan stopped. "He's not there, is he?"

She could hear him smiling over the phone. "Well, well. Is he out hunting up the bad men for you?" Kragen asked. "Seems the father of your baby is an undercover government operative. Independent contractor, actually, which is why it made it difficult for us to find out information on him."

"He's not the father—"

"Please. I told you, I have been talking to your father." Kragen chided. "Not that it's important. What's important is that I have someone here who needs to speak to you."

"Grace, it's me."

His voice was harsh, ragged. As if he had run a marathon or was in pain. "Dad."

"They want the input code and the Primoris files, Grace. Helene stole both from them. Don't give—"

Kragen came back on the line. "In fact, Miss Renne, we want it back so much, that we're willing to kill for it. Starting with your father here. Now I know you're alone, so this should be relatively easy. I'm going to give you very specific directions on where to meet my car in fifteen minutes. I'll be waiting. If you're a second late, you'll be an orphan."

"I won't be. Just tell me where to meet you."

"In front of the Library of Congress."

"How do I know to trust you?"

"You don't."

The phone went dead.

"No, Grace. Don't do this. Let Jacob handle this one. He'll save your father."

"Pusher, I need you to stay here in case Jacob comes back."

"The hell with that. If he comes back and finds you gone and me still here, I'm worse than dead. No thanks, I'll take my chances with that psycho Kragen again."

"No."

"Yes," Pusher insisted. "They think you're going in alone. I'll just tag along at a distance. Watch your back until Jacob saves the day." He winked. "What do you think?"

KRAGEN PUSHED OPEN the double steel doors and motioned Grace in with his pistol. "The senator's waiting."

The warehouse smelled of cardboard and antiseptic. But, for a warehouse, it seemed unnaturally quiet. Only the squeak of her sneakers against cement echoed through the half-acre-large building.

Senator D'Agostini stepped out from behind a shelf filled with crates. "Were you followed, Oliver?"

"No. But we did pick up a hitchhiker." Miller stepped forward and shoved Pusher to the ground. "He tried to tail my car."

"Mr. Davis. This is a pleasant surprise," Richard said with a smile that didn't quite touch the cold, gray eyes.

"The pleasure's all mine."

"Really?" He nodded to Miller. The big man swung his foot, connecting hard with Pusher's ribs. The bar manager grunted, and rolled into a tight ball from the pain.

"Don't," Grace screamed and stepped forward.

"Shut up." Kragen jerked her back, his fingers digging hard into her skin.

"And Lomax?" Richard asked, his gaze on Grace. "Has he disappeared?"

"For now. But he'll show up soon enough once he realizes we have her." Kragen pulled Grace's phone from his pocket. "He'll call to check in and I'll make sure he knows where to find her."

"And Sweeney? Where is he?"

"Checking the perimeter with his men. I want to be ready when Lomax puts in an appearance."

"Well, let's get to it, then," Richard replied. "Do you have the code, Grace?"

"No. But I know where it is." She glanced at Pusher, caught the defiant anger in his eyes. "I can take you there, but first I want to see my father."

D'Agostini laughed. "You've watched too many movies,

Grace." He walked over to Oliver and nodded toward his pistol. "May I?"

Before Grace could react, the gun exploded next to her ear. Pusher cried out, grabbing his shoulder. Blood seeped through his fingers.

"Pusher." Grace would've run forward, but Kragen grabbed her arm and jerked, sending her to her knees.

"Now, I will start putting a bullet in your friend each minute you wait. And trust me, it will take several before he dies from loss of blood."

"Don't, Gracie," Pusher ordered. "Trust me. You tell them, you're dead. I'm dead, anyway."

Miller reached down and squeezed Pusher's shoulder until the younger man cried out again from the pain.

"Do you think you can stand here and watch us take your friend apart, Grace?" Richard's lips thinned over his teeth in a feral smile. "You would be amazed at how much pain the human body can take when the bullets are well placed."

D'Agostini took aim at one of Pusher's knees.

"I don't have it, damn you!" Fear cramped her belly, bile rose to the back of her throat. "I was bluffing. I don't have the code or the key."

"Then you'd better hope, Miss Renne, that your lover does," D'Agostini said. "Miller. Find out where Sweeney is. Inform him to watch for Jacob Lomax. If Miss Renne doesn't have what we are looking for, Lomax does. If he has the code and key on his person, you may kill him. If he doesn't, I want him brought to me."

Chapter Twenty-Three

A platform of crates stood in front of the machine, still hooked to the chains that lifted it from a nearby storage pit in the floor.

For a moment, Frank Sweeney toyed with the idea of climbing the stack to get a good look from overhead, but quickly discarded the idea. If he got spotted, he'd put himself in a bad position.

Lomax was one canny son of a bitch. There was no doubt in the enforcer's mind that Lomax would show up sooner rather than later.

But that was fine with Frank. He was more than ready to get the show on the road.

A series of low grunts drifted from across the warehouse. On its heels came the echo of scuffling feet, the thud of a body slammed against a nearby wall.

Frank grabbed the gun from his shoulder holster and circled toward the sounds.

Suddenly, Miller stepped from behind some crates and grinned at Frank. He waved his gun toward Lomax, who knelt on the floor in front of the big man's feet. "Look what I found, boss."

"Good work." His eyes swept over Lomax, taking in the

blood at his mouth, the look of disgust that hardened his features.

Frank raised his gun and fired. Miller grunted and fell to the floor dead, the back of his skull splattered the crates behind him.

"I've had it with you, Lomax. First you call me out of the blue and tell me you're on your way here," Frank snapped. "Then you let that idiot catch you by surprise. How in the hell did that happen?"

"He just caught me and we'll leave it at that," Jacob snarled out and wiped his mouth with the back of his hand.

"So you decided to trust me and not run away this time?" Frank snagged Jacob's gun from Miller's hand and gave it back to his partner.

"I wouldn't have run away from you the last time except I didn't know who the hell you were." Jacob dropped the clip, checked it and shoved it back into the pistol.

"What the hell does that mean? If you're trying to pull some crap because I owe you a crack on your skull—"

"It's the truth. I had amnesia. I'll fill you in later." Quickly, Jacob scanned the warehouse. "I have the files and the code. And I've already called in the cavalry. They should be here anytime now."

Frank swore. "Jacob, they've got Grace. The moment this place fills up with agents, she's dead."

"I left Grace at the hotel—"

"She came here to save her father."

"What? Her father?" Jacob scowled. "Did she find him with D'Agostini?"

"No. And she's not going to handle finding out he's a traitor."

"I'll deal with that."

"Pusher Davis is with her. The man needs to stick to bartending. D'Agostini's using him for bullet practice to make Grace give up the Primoris files. I had to choose you or him. I'm hoping Grace keeps him alive. Hate to see him die, especially after I helped save his butt the other night. He took a hell of a beating before you showed your ass up to save the day."

"You set off the fire alarms."

"You're damn right I did." Frank grinned. "Felt good, too. Didn't like watching that Pusher kid take a beating." Frank cocked his gun. "Let's go save your lady friend before the troops get here."

"No. You go stop the troops and anyone else who gets in the way. I'll get to her and keep her safe until everything's clear."

"Okay, man. But watch your back. Kragen's with D'Agostini and that man is no pushover." Frank turned to leave, then stopped. He placed a hand on Jacob's good shoulder. Gave it a gentle squeeze. "About Helene. I didn't know they made her, Jacob. I would've gotten a warning to you somehow. Webber handled the hit—"

"It's okay, Frank. We all know the score. Helene more than anyone. Just bring our friends in quietly until I give you the all clear. It's time D'Agostini got his payback."

"You got it. And when we're done, I'm taking a vacation."

"Me, too," Jacob murmured as he watched Frank slip back into the shadows. "But mine's going to be a honeymoon."

"I wouldn't count on it, Lomax." Kragen stepped from behind a nearby crate, his pistol pointed at Jacob's chest.

"WHERE'S Sweeney?" Kragen took Jacob's gun and tossed it across the floor.

Jacob shrugged, using the movement to loosen the tight muscles between his shoulders. "Around."

"How long has he been working for you?"

"He works with me," Jacob mused. "And we work for the good guys."

"Was Helene Garrett just one of the *guys,* then?" Kragen snorted. "It doesn't matter. Within a month, we'll be the good guys as far as the nation is concerned."

When Jacob didn't respond, Kragen said, "They won't believe him, you know. Too many people involved with too many connections. Frank doesn't stand a chance of convincing anyone without the disk."

"What makes you think he doesn't have it?"

"The fact that your girlfriend is just past those doors with the senator. You need the disk to save her. Not that it will help. She's probably dead already."

Fear slithered up Jacob's spine, coiled in his chest.

"I don't want the disk as much as the senator. You see, my name isn't on it. I made sure of that."

"And Frank Sweeney?"

"Once I kill you, there will be no one to protect him."

When Jacob didn't respond, Kragen waved his gun. "We could use these and have our own version of the shootout at the O.K. Corral. Or we can have our own little Tuesday night takedown. What do you say?"

Keeping his gun drawn, Kragen slipped out of his suit jacket, folded it in half and laid it over the nearest crate.

"I'm willing, considering my disadvantage right now."

Kragen laughed and tossed his own gun by Jacob's. "Now we're on equal ground."

Lomax waved his fingers, crooking them at Kragen. "Let's get it done then, Oliver. Why waste time?"

"That's right, you have the girl to save."

Kragen rushed Jacob, backing him up with a flurry of kicks and punches. Jacob blocked most with his forearms and absorbed others with his upper body before he dove underneath and rolled. He came up into a roundhouse kick that connected with Kragen's jaw.

Kragen stumbled back two steps. He rubbed his jaw. "Not bad."

"Want more?"

Kragen charged Jacob again. At the last minute he pivoted, catching Jacob off guard. His heel slammed into Jacob's forehead. Razor sharp stars burst behind Jacob's eyes.

He caught Kragen's leg, came up to jam a knee in his groin. Kragen immediately collapsed his other leg, sending both men to the floor.

Both men rolled, grappling for a death hold. Jacob grabbed Kragen from behind, his forearm wedged under Kragen's neck, squeezing.

Choking, Kragen reached behind, grabbed Jacob's shoulder and gouged. White-hot pain shot through Jacob's arm and up his back, forcing him to let go of Kragen.

Kragen flipped away, but remained on the floor. Both men blew the oxygen in and out of their lungs.

Blood trickled into Jacob's eye. He wiped it away with the back of his hand. "Come on," he growled, scrambling to his feet.

Kragen kicked, aiming for Jacob's wound again. Pain exploded, knocking the breath from him. But this time, Jacob was ready for the jolt. He staggered but stayed upright.

He heard it then, the sound of shots. Grace's scream.

With a savage cry, he fought past the pain, focusing his mind on the one obstacle between him and his family.

His family.

Jacob rammed Kragen in a football tackle, smashing them both into the crates on the nearby pallet. Oliver grunted, his hands grappling for a hold on Jacob's neck. "She's dead, Lomax. Can you feel it?"

Kragen forgot the neck and aimed a fist into Jacob's ribs, knocking himself free. "You think you can stop this? This is bigger than you or me. Bigger than the United States. We're talking world domination, Lomax. The most powerful men in the world have come together. World bankers, world leaders. Industrial giants. Do you really think you can stop that?"

"Maybe not, but I will stop you." Jacob got his feet under him. "Let's finish it."

Kragen moved, knocking Jacob back into the chains. Jacob grabbed hold of one chain for balance, kneed Kragen in the groin. Kragen fell backward onto the controls. Suddenly, the floor shifted beneath them.

Kragen tackled Jacob, rolling to the edge of the platform as they rose toward the warehouse rafters. His hands were around Jacob's neck squeezing the oxygen from his throat, forcing Jacob's head back. "Tell Helene hello from me when you see her."

Jacob's neck muscles corded, straining against Kragen's strength. At the last moment, he pivoted, bringing his good arm down on Kragen's hands, breaking the contact.

Jacob went to his knees. He wrapped his bad arm around a chain for balance as he heaved in bursts of oxygen.

Kragen charged, intending to knock Jacob off the platform.

Jacob grabbed Kragen's shirt and yanked, using the other man's momentum against his attack. The weight of both men flipped them off the platform. Jacob grunted in pain as the chain caught his bad arm, keeping him suspended midair.

"Go to hell," he rasped as he let go of Kragen's shirt.

Kragen screamed, his hands flying, grabbing at air as he fell. His body dropped into the pit. Jacob heard it bounce, once…twice with sickening thumps before hitting the floor. Jacob dangled for a moment, while his eyes searched the floor beneath. Kragen's head lay at an unnatural angle, his sightless eyes open and gazing up.

With his good arm, he maneuvered himself back up on the platform and hit the button. As soon as he could, he jumped to the floor, snagged his gun and ran. His mind was repeating the only word he could think of. *Please. Please. Please.*

D'AGOSTINI PLACED HIS GUN at Grace's belly. "Just think if I fire now, I will be killing two birds with one bullet, don't you think?" A thin line of madness underlay the senator's laugh.

"Why don't you join us, Mr. Lomax? I'm sure you'll want to hear what I have to say to the mother of your child."

Jacob approached, relief making his muscles shake. Grace was okay. Her cheek was bruised, her mouth was bleeding, but she was alive.

Pusher was another matter. The bar manager lay on the floor, bullet wounds in his shoulder and thigh.

"He's not dead yet. Only unconscious," Richard stated. "Like you, who should've died many times over. Maybe I should have hired you instead of trying to kill you."

"I'm particular about who I work for, Senator. Garbage, even the human kind, tends to come with a stench. One that I don't abide well."

Richard shrugged. "Charles Renne didn't seem to mind. Your father was easy to recruit, Grace."

"My father has nothing to do with this," she bit back.

"You are naive, aren't you? First your father, now your lover?"

"I have no idea what you're talking about."

"Betrayal. I'm talking about betrayal and how it does strange things to people.

"You see, once upon a time, your father suspected your mother was having an affair with Senator Langdon. So one night he drugged her. When he questioned her, she confessed everything.

"At the time, we suspected that Senator Langdon was gathering information on us. We had already decided he was a complication we needed to get rid of.

"What we didn't know was that your mother was privy to her lover's plans. She divulged many names, including mine. So when your father approached us, we took care of things for him."

"You caused the plane to crash?"

"I have to admit, he didn't expect us to kill your mother. But after, we convinced him that extreme actions are sometimes necessary. In this case, we saw his potential and needed something to guarantee his...loyalty.

"After her death it was easy enough to get him to drug

others, gather intelligence. He was already involved. Neck deep, so to speak. When his reputation grew here in Washington, D.C., so did his role in our organization. He became our truth serum expert. Allows us to keep others loyal or destroy them. Whatever we deem fit."

"I don't believe you. My father couldn't hate my mother that much. Not to stand by and let her—"

"Die with her lover?" D'Agostini laughed. "How about once he found out that you weren't really his daughter? That the affair had been going on for quite a long time. How old were you when she died? Ten?"

When Grace didn't answer, he shrugged. "I guess once you were conceived, your biological parents parted ways. Seems when Senator Langdon failed to divorce his wife, your mom slept with Charles on the rebound. Up to your birth, she didn't know who the father was. But as the years passed, and she hadn't conceived any more children, it became apparent that Charles wasn't your father."

"And you're telling me that Langdon and my mother reconnected and that was the ultimate betrayal."

"Washington, D.C., is no more than a small town that loves to gossip. Whether they did or not, your father was being laughed at behind his back."

"I don't believe you."

"But you see, Grace, that isn't even the best part of this story," D'Agostini taunted. "Senator Langdon had a family, too.

"A wife, who later committed suicide after falling into a depression." He paused. "And a daughter."

Grace froze, knowing what was coming. "Helene."

"And here I thought you weren't clever. Much quicker

than I was, actually," he added ruefully. "Helene was a few years older than you at the time. Old enough to suspect the plane crash had been deliberate. You see, her father was an excellent pilot. She knew it because she spent many hours up there with him. Bonding time, I guess."

Was it true? She glanced at Jacob, saw the answer in his eyes. Grace locked her knees to keep her legs under her.

"She must have panicked when her sister fell in love with her partner and got pregnant."

Grace jerked with surprise.

"Oh yes, don't you think your dad would've told me? He told me so much more," D'Agostini mocked. He reached into his pocket and pulled out a recorder.

Grace heard her father's—no she corrected, Charles Renne's—voice. *"You forget. She was never my daughter in the first place."*

Everything inside her turned cold.

"Grace Ann." The whisper was harsh from behind her. She turned to see Charles step forward with a gun in his hand.

Jacob recognized it as Kragen's pistol.

"I said what I needed to keep D'Agostini from suspecting." Charles tilted the pistol up, pointing it at the senator. "It's over Richard," he added.

"It's a little late to play the hero now, isn't it, Charles?" Richard responded derisively. But Jacob noticed the senator kept his gun pointed at Grace's belly.

Jacob could feel the cold steel of his own 9 mm dig into the small of his back, but he couldn't take the risk.

"Let go of my daughter or I will shoot you."

"Shoot and I will kill your daughter. Oh wait, she's not

your daughter," Richard said, snapping his fingers. "I keep forgetting."

"It's over, Senator. I have the code to the voting machines. I also have the files on your operation," Jacob said, his gaze flicking to Grace.

"And you think I won't get it from you?" The senator shook his head. "This is no mere operation, Lomax. An operation is run by two-bit criminals. Your small-mindedness is the reason you will fail."

"I haven't failed."

"You think what you have will bring Primoris to its knees?" His laugh was savage, the lines of his face distorted in his insanity. "All it will do is set back our timetable for a decade, maybe two at the most. There will be others. Primoris is a global power. It goes far beyond the banks and governments. We control the militaries, the sciences, technologies, economies and the law, whether it's martial or otherwise. Do not kid yourself. We control the very air you breathe, the food you eat, the ground you walk on. And like sheep, you exist because of our benevolence," D'Agostini spouted, his voice raging at Jacob. "We are the elite, the one percent. We have no sympathy for the weak." Suddenly, the senator swung his gun toward Charles and fired.

Startled, Charles fired a split second later. His bullet hit D'Agostini directly in the heart. The senator looked down at the blood as it gathered on his chest and slowly sank to his knees. Looking at Charles with astonishment, he fell forward, dead.

Grace turned to her father just as he crumpled to the ground. Hurrying to him, she turned him over onto his back and saw that the bullet had entered his chest. Charles looked up at Grace and tried to speak, only to cough up blood.

"Dad." Tears flooded her eyes. She gathered him close into her lap. "Hold on, please!" she whispered urgently. "Call an ambulance!" She screamed the words at Jacob, but when he didn't move, she whispered, "Please."

"It's too late, Grace," her father rasped, while a deep, moist rattle shook his lungs.

"I love you." Tears formed in her eyes, causing his face to blur. Angrily, she wiped them away with the back of her hand. "You have to hold on. Everything will be fine but you have to hold on!"

Charles reached up and cupped Grace's cheek in his hand, using his thumb to rub away a tear.

"Don't cry, honey. Not for me," he whispered. His hand dropped back to his chest. "It had to be this way, don't you see?" Blood bubbled at the corners of his mouth. "You're safe. That's all that matters."

"No, Daddy." Grace started crying in earnest now, her tears dripping unheeded onto her father's shirt. "Please, don't give up," she begged him. "Don't you dare die on me!"

Charles wrestled back another cough, but it cost him. "What I did to your mother, it was a mistake. I didn't…" He tried to inhale. "I love you…"

Grace shook her head, gripped him closer. "Don't. Don't, Dad. Stay with me."

But she knew Charles didn't hear her, didn't see her.

"Grace, I'm sor—" Jacob began.

"Don't say it. You remember, don't you?" she said dully, her eyes still on her father. Gently, she closed his eyes.

"Yes," Jacob answered, his tone flat with remorse.

"When?" She choked back the sob, the excruciating pain that sliced through her. Gently, she laid her father on the floor, then stood.

"Last night."

Her hands fisted before she could stop them. It took effort, but she forced them to relax. Anger wouldn't help, wouldn't make the facts any less harsh. "Before we—"

"Yes."

The word was a knife that severed an already damaged heart.

"Grace, its not—"

"Get away from me." She could've contained the rage, the slap of betrayal if he hadn't reached for her. Blindly, she struck at him when he tried to hold her. The second sob caught her off guard, then a sweep of them couldn't be stopped.

She cursed him, each word punctuated with the pounding of her fists against his chest. She didn't want to be touched, consoled. She wanted to grieve, to rage. She wanted to inflict the same pain that ripped her from chest to stomach.

Jacob took the hits, blocking them only when he thought she'd hurt herself. Eventually the screaming turned to guttural sobs, then desperate whimpers. Only then did he gather her close.

Drained, Grace couldn't, didn't resist. Minutes blurred together until Grace lost all sense of time.

Finally, when she gained some control, she moved away. "I'm okay now."

When he stepped to her again, she raised her hand. "Don't."

"Grace, we need to talk."

"You left me. You gave me your word. And at the first

moment you had to make a decision on whether to be truthful, you left. I thought I understood why, that you wanted to protect me and the baby. But this—" She waved her hand toward her father. "You had no right to protect me from this." Her stomach hurt, the insides twisting painfully with the betrayal. "Leave me alone, Jacob."

"I wasn't about to let you get killed, damn it."

"And as you can see, your plan worked out well." With gentle fingers, she reached down and brushed the hair away from her father's forehead. "I'm safe."

His sharp intake of breath told her she'd hit home. But she was already beyond caring. What he'd done, no matter the reason, wasn't forgivable.

"Grace, let me explain."

"No." She placed a hand to her stomach, willing the pain to stop. "You could've explained everything last night before you left me, damn you. We were in this together."

"I work for the government. Helene was an operative. One of my contacts."

"I don't care—"

"Listen!" He talked over her, almost believing that if he got the words out, she would understand. Maybe forgive. "She and I were meeting the other night because of the code. The one in your phone. It's the code that accesses the voting machines. Officials click on certain numbers and letters hidden on the touch screen and they can flip the vote to whatever party they want to win."

"I told you I don't care now," she said dully. "Last night, I might have cared. It might have made a difference. But you're too late."

Emotion, hurt, love, longing shot through him, catching

in his chest, catching him off guard. He stepped back, reeling as memories flooded. Pain-filled memories of the first time he'd left her.

"Grace. The senator was right. Primoris is worldwide. Helene managed to gather intelligence on over a hundred men and women working toward global domination. Prime ministers. Generals. Presidents."

"I told you, I don't—" A harder pain hit her this time, deep within her belly. She bent over, fighting against the next spasm.

"Grace!"

She realized the cramping hadn't been from fear or the pain of losing her father. She looked down, saw the blood spotting her pants.

"Jacob, the baby," she whispered, terrified. But the next spasm hit on another wave of gut-wrenching pain. "No, please—"

Jacob caught her before she hit the floor in a dead faint.

Chapter Twenty-Four

Two weeks later.

Mount Hope Cemetery was no more than a spot of grass and a grove of trees meshed between high-rises and skyscrapers on the streets of Washington, D.C.

But its history had long been established before the first historical monument had been erected. Long before the first war, even the first church. And Jacob had no doubt the cemetery would stand long after the last structure crumbled with age.

Gravestones dotted the small, rolling knoll. The cemetery was certainly more eclectic than the famed Arlington, but no less loved, if the flowers adorning most graves were any indication.

The newest of the gravestones was small, but so pristinely white it almost hurt the eyes. It lay by two others, no bigger, no more worn, but matching in a sallow-gray marble.

With a sigh, Jacob laid the pink roses against the white marble.

"Helene loved roses. She would buy them from the street vendor for our office."

He'd heard her, of course. Long before she spoke. The

scent of the honeysuckle hung in the air, had mingled with the roses.

"I remember," he said. "She preferred red, but for some reason…it didn't feel right."

His eyes swept over Grace from behind mirrored sunglasses. He hadn't seen her since the hospital. The day her father died.

"Isn't it too soon to be up on your feet?"

The concern in his voice warmed her heart.

"No." She shook her head when what she really wanted to do was take his hand, touch his face. Reassure him. "The doctor gave me her approval.

"She said I was to avoid stress, among other things." Her hand slid over her stomach, more pronounced than ever under the V-neck sweater, the loose cotton pants. But she wasn't surprised after a week of rest and spoiling from Carol.

"What other things?"

"Sex. Mainly," she teased and almost smiled at the growl that rumbled deep in his chest.

"I'm joking, Jacob.

When he didn't answer, her tone grew serious. "The pain had been from the stress, not the baby. And the blood—" even now, she had a hard time saying the words "—had been my father's."

She stepped closer to Helene's grave. Saw her parents' nearby. It had been her decision to bury them together. One she didn't regret. "A whole family destroyed because of power."

"I wish I could say it will never happen again," Jacob answered. "But corruption goes hand in hand with money and power."

She turned to him then, curious. "You know, you never explained why Helene went into business with me."

"I haven't seen you."

"Yes, you haven't explained that, either."

"I wanted to give you time. To heal. To adjust." He glanced at her, his gaze sharp and watchful. "To work through the anger so when I did see you, I wouldn't have to worry about injuries."

"And Helene?"

"Helene had government access to your whole life profile. It didn't take her long to discover you were her half sister. I think she just couldn't walk away from an opportunity to get to know you better. That outweighed any risk she might have been taking. But when you got pregnant, it changed everything."

"Why?"

"She wanted your baby to have a father. A good father, like she never had."

"And I never had," she added solemnly. "That's ironic if you think about it. I didn't want you to know because I didn't want the baby to have a father like I had. Emotionally removed. And Helene was going to tell you because she wanted the baby to have a real father. One who could love the baby. Helene had more faith in you than I did."

"Helene had an advantage. She knew my family background. Something I couldn't share with you. Not at the time. Not without risking your life."

Even now, it could hurt. The fact that he'd shared his life, his past with another woman so easily—trusted her so completely as a friend. "And now?"

"Now," he said, drawing out the word until it became two syllables, "I'd like to know what you're doing here."

"Pusher said you had left the bar with a bouquet of flowers. This was a logical conclusion. He says you've bought a bouquet every day."

"Not every day, but most days. I miss her, Grace."

"Me, too." Tears pricked the back of her eyes. She wasn't ready to talk about them yet. "How's the bar going?"

"I didn't realize when Helene left me the bar, she left me Pusher, too." He sent her a sexy, sidelong glance. "I don't suppose you'd come back as my partner?"

"I'm going to be really busy soon." She patted the flutter in her stomach, took a deep breath to settle the flutter in her heart. "Don't have any plans other than to get plenty of rest at my father's house."

"You're staying, then?"

"For a while. My father's being hailed a hero. His reputation is still intact. The only ones who know the truth now are you, me, Frank and Pusher," she said. "So I know his secret is safe."

"It is."

"What about you? I figured you'd leave Pusher in charge and head off on another mission."

"I'm retiring, actually. And thanks to Helene, I have a legitimate business to manage."

"What about your properties?"

"I can still manage them, too," Jacob said. "I'm staying at a hotel for right now, but I'm thinking about having the boathouse rebuilt. Make some improvements. Make it a real home."

"You mean, you're staying here for good?"

"I left that first time to complete some unfinished business. I had every intention of getting back with you after

I helped Helene bring down Primoris. Long before I found out you were pregnant."

She looked at him, startled.

"Helene told me the night she died. About you. About the baby. About the fact that she had to pass the information off to you. It frightened her, putting you in jeopardy like that, but she had no choice at the time. She had moved into the boathouse as an added precaution, but still suspected her cover had been blown. She thought someone had followed her to your lunch date. That's why she made the switch. When we were ambushed, I was on my way to you. The bullet that hit my shoulder went through me and caught Helene in the chest. She used her last breath to tell me she loved you."

Tears backed up in her throat. "I loved her, too. She was a sister to me in so many ways. I just never realized it until she was gone but she was my family."

"And Charles?"

"I still love him," Grace admitted. "He will always be my father. I haven't sorted it all out in my mind yet—or my heart—but I'm sure I will eventually."

"I guess that's it, then," Jacob said, his eyes resting for a last time on Helene's grave. "So you've told me how you found me, but you never told me why you came out here."

"We're having a baby girl. I found out this morning."

"We are?" The muscle in his jaw clenched and unclenched. "Grace, I don't have a right to ask your forgiveness—"

"Neither do I. But I'm going to ask you anyway. Will you forgive me, Jacob?"

"Forgive you?"

"What I said to you when my father died—"

"Was deserved." Jacob gathered her into his arms and kissed her softly. "I love you, Grace."

"I love you, too."

He hugged her to him for a moment, then pulled back. "I thought you wanted to be surprised with the baby's sex?"

She laughed. "I've had enough surprises for a while."

"Do you think you can handle one more?"

Her eyebrow rose, suspicious. "Depends on the kind of surprise."

"My dad is retired military. He and my mother own a bed-and-breakfast in Maine. I want you to meet my parents, Grace. I want you to look at my baby albums, see my old tree fort." Jacob buried his face in her neck, inhaled the sweet scent of honeysuckle. "While my parents are out playing bridge, I want to make love to you in my old bed, like a horny teenager. Then later whisper all my hopes and plans for our baby girl against your belly."

Love tightened her chest, squeezed a shimmer of tears from her eyes. Jacob was giving her more than his love, more than his trust. He was showing her his vulnerability. A precious gift from a man with so much control.

"I like Maine." Her arms circled his neck and for a minute she leaned into him, letting their hearts beat against each other. "But I don't go anywhere with strange men."

"Strange?"

Stiffening, he tried to pull away, only to relax when she chuckled, tickling the base of his throat.

"Frank told me Lomax wasn't your real name."

"He did? When did he tell you that?"

"When he called for my chocolate chip cookie recipe,"

she replied. "He's the friend you have that likes to cook, huh?"

"Yes, he is," Jacob admitted. "He's also my partner. And my uncle."

"Your what?"

"My uncle. He's the one that got me into government work, much to my mother's dismay. He's her younger brother."

"And you hit him on the head?" She gasped. "No wonder he looked so shocked when you walked through my bedroom door."

"Shocked is putting it mildly. I guess for a moment he was relieved, until I didn't lower the gun. That's why he grabbed for you. He knew he could buy some time using you as a bargaining chip until he could figure out what the hell was going on. I think at one point, he assumed your dad had used some kind of brainwashing drugs on me."

"You hit him really hard, Jacob." Her brow lifted. "He's not going to forgive you anytime soon, is he?"

"I'm already forgiven."

"That easily?"

"Hell, no. I didn't say it was easy," Jacob growled. "I had to give him my boat."

Grace laughed. She had a feeling Frank was going to be one of her favorite people. "So, Lomax, what is your real last name? Frank wouldn't tell me."

"Alexander."

"Jacob Alexander," she murmured, nodding. "I like it."

"Me, too," he joked. Then picked her up and twirled her in a circle. "But I like Grace Alexander more."

Epilogue

Four months later

Grace watched Jacob hold his daughter. The two-day-old lay comfortably in the cradle of her daddy's arm, her belly full, her eyes half-closed with sleep.

Jacob sat next to her on the bed, near enough for Grace to rest her head on his shoulder.

"You're asking for trouble if you go ahead with this," Grace insisted. But Jacob wasn't listening. He was too pre-occupied with the baby.

"I can't get over how thick her hair is," he whispered, running light fingers over the honey-brown locks, then tickled a tiny ear before brushing across the delicate cheek. "And how small she was. Remember?"

"Yes, she still is." And Grace was remembering other things. The slight shake of his hand when he held his daughter for the first time. The way his jaw clenched and unclenched to fight the emotion that overwhelmed him. The first time he kissed her small forehead, and held them both in his arms together.

Tears pricked at the back of her eyes, shuddered deep in her chest.

"Now, what were you saying about trouble?"

"You know exactly what I am saying. What you're planning on doing is worse than tempting fate, Jacob," Grace admonished, but the temper was no longer there. If anyone could take on fate and win, it was Jacob Alexander.

"I don't have the faintest idea what you're talking about, do you, honey?" he stage-whispered to their daughter, who was busy staring into the identical blue eyes of her father.

She bit her lip to keep the smile from getting the best of her. "You're spitting right in its face, and don't think I won't say 'I told you so'—"

"It's perfect. And you know that as well as I do." He held out his finger, smiling with pride when the baby grabbed it with her hand. "She's perfect."

How could you argue with a man who was driven by love?

A nurse walked in the door. The woman was young, with a short, bouncy bob of red hair and bottle-green eyes that took in Jacob in one long, feminine sweep.

"Are you ready for me to take her, Mr. Alexander?"

Grace glanced from father to daughter and felt her own heart quickening. "Not just yet," she answered for Jacob.

"All right. Call me if you need anything."

"I will. Thank you." The nurse started to leave, only to stop by the door. "By the way, the doctor wanted to know if you've decided on a name for your baby girl?"

Jacob glanced at his wife.

Grace didn't bother sighing. Instead, she took a deep breath, thought of her mother and waited for the ground to tremble. "All right," she agreed, resignedly. "But don't say I didn't warn you."

Jacob laughed and turned to the nurse. "Serenity. We're naming her Serenity."

* * * * *

THE CAVANAUGH CODE

BY
MARIE FERRARELLA

Marie Ferrarella has written almost two hundred books, some under the name Marie Nicole. Her romances are beloved by fans worldwide. Visit her website at www.marieferrarella.com.

To Charlie,
who I love more today
than yesterday,
but not half as much as tomorrow.

Chapter 1

The way Detective Taylor McIntyre liked to work a homicide was to put herself in the victim's place. Not just into his or her place, but into their actual lives.

To get a full sense of the person, she needed to walk through their homes, touch their things and imagine what it felt like to be this person who had fallen victim to a homicide.

In essence, Taylor, a third-generation law enforcement agent, wanted to walk in their shoes and examine what they normally had to deal with on a daily basis. She couldn't accomplish that from a distance. And she had come to learn that sometimes the smallest of details was what eventually allowed her and her partner to find the killer and solve the crime.

Just because her partner, Detective Aaron Briscoe,

was on a temporary leave of absence, immersing himself in the head-spinning roller-coaster ride of first-time fatherhood, and the precinct was shorthanded, didn't mean that she had to change her approach. She just had to go through the paces alone rather than have Aaron stare at her as she wandered around, patiently waiting until she needed to use him as her sounding board.

Taylor had no doubt that her partner of almost three years considered her approach unusual, but he'd made his peace with it and generally went along with her method. That was what had made them such a good team and she missed him now, missed the sound of Aaron's grunting as he squatted down to examine something close-up.

She even missed the way Aaron sometimes unconsciously whistled through his teeth, even though it had driven her crazy periodically.

Taylor half smiled to herself as she pulled up in front of an impressive, sprawling four-story apartment complex where the cheapest lease went for the paltry sum of $4,000 a month.

You just never know, do you? she mused. Right now, she'd welcome that awful sound Aaron made. It meant that he was thinking. And two heads were always better than one.

Entering the parking structure, she drove underground and parked in one of the spots designated for guests. Taylor got out and walked toward the elevator located against the back wall.

The late Eileen Stevens's apartment was on the fourth floor. That made it The Villas—as this particular complex was whimsically named—penthouse. And, given the fact that the building was situated at the crest of a hill, anything above the second floor actually had a decent view of the ocean in the distance.

The Villas, a nine-month-old complex with rounded corners and panoramic windows, was situated directly across the street from a newly constructed, exceedingly popular outdoor mall. The mall boasted pricey stores of all sizes, exotic restaurants, a twenty-one-screen movie-theater complex and even had a merry-go-round located smack in the middle. It also promised a skating rink for the winter months. With Christmas less than a month away, there was one now. Hordes of humanity seeking entertainment and diversion swarmed there every Friday and Saturday night. The rest of the week saw a healthy dose of foot traffic, but it was the weekends that put the mall on the map.

Eileen Stevens would no longer be among the people frequenting that mall, Taylor thought, getting out on the fourth floor. Because Eileen Stevens, thirty-eight-year-old dynamo and newly made partner at her prestigious law firm, was found dead in her opulent, cathedral-ceilinged bedroom this morning. With a key to the apartment for emergencies, her personal assistant had come by to see why Eileen hadn't shown up at the firm this morning and wasn't answering her pager or her cell phone.

Upon seeing her dead boss, the young woman, Denise Atwater, had become so hysterical she'd had to be sedated by one of the paramedics summoned to the scene.

Death could be ugly, Taylor thought.

Marble met her heels. The resulting contact created a soft, staccato sound as she made her way from the elevator to Eileen's apartment. In direct contrast to the holly decorating the walls, yellow tape was stretched out across the extra wide door, warning everyone that a crime had been committed here and that they were not allowed to cross the line.

With a sigh, Taylor lifted the tape, slipped beneath it and began to unlock the door. As she turned the key, she realized that there was no need. Someone had failed to lock up.

Sloppy.

Probably a patrolman. Good help was hard to find these days, she mused wryly. But then, life moved at such a fast clip, everyone she knew was juggling three things at once. Oversights were no longer as rare as they had once been. Made the job that much harder to do.

According to the thumbnail bio she'd gotten from the woman's law firm, Eileen Stevens was currently juggling twice that. A criminal lawyer intent on leaving her mark on the world—and making a great deal of money while she was at it—Eileen was regarded as being at the top of her game. The list of clients that the law firm's office manager had surrendered earlier indicated that all of Eileen's clients were high-profile people, people who could pay top dollar for top-notch representation.

Someone obviously didn't think that Eileen was so "top-notch."

Closing the door behind her, Taylor stood for a moment just inside the foyer, trying to imagine what it felt like to come here at the end of a long, bone-wearying day. A sense of antiseptic sterility slowly penetrated her consciousness. Even the Christmas tree, silver with ice-blue decorations, felt sterile as it stood aloof in the center of the room.

"Home" to her had always meant a feeling of warmth and security.

Well, not always, Taylor silently amended.

A feeling of warmth and security was the atmosphere her mother strove to create for her and her three siblings when they were growing up. It had actually been achieved only when her father was out on assignment. An undercover cop, his work would take him away for weeks at a time. Her mother, Lila, also on the police force, came home nightly, no matter what. She was there to check their homework, to make sure they behaved. There to give them the love and support they needed so that they could turn out to be decent human beings.

To give him his due, her father had been an okay guy in the beginning. Taylor could remember laughter in the house when she was very young. But the laughter faded in the later years as jealousy started to eat away at her father. He blamed it on her mother's partner, Brian Cavanaugh, a kind, handsome man who came off larger than life. Initially friends, it got to the point that her father loudly complained that he couldn't compete with or compare to Brian. The growing insecurities that haunted her father, giving rise to arguments, made for an atmosphere of almost stifling tension whenever he was home.

And then everything changed.

Her mother was wounded in the line of duty. Lila

McIntyre would have died if Brian hadn't stopped the flow of her blood with his own hands, holding her until the paramedics arrived, refusing to be separated from her even as she was driven to the hospital.

Her father used the incident as an excuse to shame Lila into retiring from the force, saying a mother of small children had no business putting herself in harm's way. Wanting only peace, Lila went along with it for the sake of her marriage—and her children—until Frank, the youngest, was in high school. Against her husband's wishes, she came back to the police department. Trying to compromise, she took a desk job rather than go back on the street.

Life took a few really strange twists and turns after that. Taylor's father, still working undercover, was suddenly executed, a victim of a drug dealer's hostility. Only it eventually turned out that it had been her father who was the hostile one, staging his own death and stealing the enormous amount of money that was to have been used to stage a sting.

In the end, justice was served. Her father was really dead now and Brian Cavanaugh, a man she had tremendous respect and admiration for, was her stepfather. It was only fitting since over the years he had been more of a father to her and her sister and brothers than her actual father had been.

Brian, now chief of detectives, had been the one to send her out on this case. He'd also offered to restructure a few things within the department so that she could have a temporary partner assigned to her until Aaron and his whistling teeth came back.

But she hated disrupting things and said she'd go solo until Aaron's leave of absence was up. Besides, she didn't relish the idea of breaking in someone new, especially if it was just for a finite amount of time. She could muddle through.

Taylor frowned now as she looked around. She had no doubt that what Eileen had probably spent to furnish just the living room could have kept the children of a third-world nation eating oatmeal for breakfast for the next two years. Maybe three. And yet, for all its tasteful, enormously expensive decor, there was absolutely no warmth to be found in the room.

No warmth anywhere, she concluded as she moved about the area with its snowstorm-white furnishing, making her way to a state-of-the-art kitchen that was too immaculate.

All amenities seemed for show, with no soul evident anywhere. Was the late Eileen Stevens an ice princess, or just haughtily devoid of color and shading?

Taylor found herself feeling sorry for the woman.

"What were you trying to prove, Eileen?" she murmured.

Plastic gloves on, Taylor skimmed her fingertips along the pots hanging from the ceiling like so many slavishly dusted, oversize wind chimes. There had to be a reason for all this decadent hemorrhaging of money, she thought.

"What were you trying to make up for? Were you trying to bury your conscience? Or was there an insecure little girl hidden inside those Prada suits, thumbing her nose at anyone and everyone who had ever made fun of her while she was growing up?"

She made a mental note to find out if the woman had any relatives in the area.

Living well was supposedly the best revenge. And although this was not living well—just living expensively—Taylor knew that many felt their success, their actual self-worth, was reflected in the amount of "toys" they managed to amass.

"Didn't do you any good, did it, Eileen, spending money on all this?" she murmured under her breath. "You still turned out to be mortal." She walked back to the living room. "Who got to you, Eileen? Who did this? An ex-lover? A jealous underling you treated like dirt? Or some client who wanted his money back because you couldn't get him off the way you promised?"

She had yet to carefully go through Eileen's caseload. She made a mental note to do that first thing in the morning, review the woman's past clients as well as her current ones. With any luck, by morning the medical examiner would have gotten around to doing the autopsy. He was a prickly man who marched to his own drummer and refused to listen to anyone else's. But he was good.

"She didn't have any lovers."

Her heart instantly jumping up to her throat, Taylor spun around on her heel. She had her weapon out before she completed the turn. Both hands were wrapped around the grip, its muzzle pointed and meaning business, by the time she found herself facing the source of the voice behind her: a tall, good-looking, dark-haired man in his early thirties.

"Hands in the air!" Taylor ordered, aiming her revolver dead center at his head.

Rather than jump to obey, the stranger watched her as if she was the one who was out of place, not him. "Hey, calm down, honey," he cautioned. "I'm one of the good guys."

Honey?

The hell he was. Taylor found the man's deep, steady voice with its hint of a smile irritating, not to mention patronizing.

Honey? Was he for real?

"Hands in the air!" she ordered again. She cocked the trigger, her blue eyes blazing. "I'm not going to tell you a third time!"

"Yes, ma'am." The stranger acquiesced. But when he raised his hands, they went only as high as his shoulders. At what looked like six-three and in excellent physical condition, he all but towered over her.

There was definitely amusement in his eyes.

Was he a psychopath, coming back to review his handiwork? Eileen Stevens had been found bound and gagged. Cause of death looked like strangulation. From the wet marks on the comforter beneath her body, a wet leather strip had been tightly tied around the woman's throat and then apparently allowed to dry. As it did, it slowly shrank, depriving her of air until she finally choked to death.

It had struck Taylor as a particularly cruel way to kill someone.

Was this man capable of that? She tried her best to make a quick assessment.

In the meantime, more immediate questions needed answering. "What are you doing here?" she demanded.

He began to shrug and drop his hands. She quickly motioned for him to raise them again. Her eyes told him she meant business. Or thought she did. For the sake of peace, he raised his hands again.

"Same as you," he answered casually. "Looking around." And then he added with an amused smile, "Except I'm not talking to myself."

She had no doubt that the man was accustomed to getting along on pure charm. She knew any number of women who would probably go weak in the knees just looking at him.

But the circles she moved around in were full of good-looking men. The Cavanaughs had all but cornered the market and her own brothers didn't exactly look as if their secondary careers involved house haunting. All in all, that made her pretty much immune to the ways of silver-tongued charmers.

Her eyes narrowed now. "No, but you'll talk to me. Turn around," she demanded, whipping out a set of handcuffs from the back of her belt.

The stranger obligingly turned around for her. "Now, nothing kinky," he warned. Taylor found herself wanting to hit him upside his head for his mocking tone. "We haven't even been introduced yet."

As she came close enough to the man to slip on the handcuffs, he suddenly swung around to face her and in a heartbeat, Taylor found herself disarmed. He had the gun now.

"Never let your guard down," he counseled.

The next moment, the tables turned again as the stranger received a sudden, very sharp jab from her knee. Pain shot from his groin into the pit of his stomach, radiating out and making him double over.

"Right," Taylor snapped. "Good advice." She wasted no time as she grabbed one of his wrists, snapping a handcuff into place.

"You're making a mistake," he protested as the second handcuff secured his wrists behind his back.

Taylor rolled her eyes, stepping back and training her gun on him. "Oh, please, I expected something more original than that."

For the first time, the intruder seemed put out, but only marginally, as if he still thought of her as a minor annoyance. "Lady, who kicked you out of bed this morning?"

"That," Taylor informed him crisply, "is none of your business."

The fact that there was no one in her bed, no one currently in her life, was not a piece of information she was about to share with a lowlife, no matter how good-looking he was or how well he dressed. Given the charm he radiated, she pegged him as a successful con artist.

The stranger shook his head and a sigh escaped his lips. "Okay, let's back up here—"

"Too late," Taylor countered. She glanced around to see if anything had been moved from this afternoon, when she'd first come on the scene. It didn't appear so, but she couldn't swear to it. "This is a crime scene and nobody's supposed to be here."

"You are," he pointed out glibly, trying to look at her over his shoulder.

Taylor couldn't resist tossing her head and saying, "I'm special."

He eyed her for a long moment. "No argument, but—"

The smile on his lips went down clear to her bones. Taylor shook the effects off, but it wasn't as easy as she would have liked.

"No *but*," she said sharply. "Just move. Now," she underscored.

He took a step toward the door, then glanced at her again. "Okay, but I have a perfectly good reason for being here."

Taylor fought the temptation to jab him in the ribs with the muzzle of her gun. "This is a roped-off crime scene. There *is* no perfectly good reason to be here— unless you're Santa Claus making an early pit-stop or you're a cop." Her eyes swept over him. "You're definitely not Santa Claus. Are you a cop?" she demanded, knowing perfectly well that he wasn't. She knew all the cops on the force, and, due to her mother's marriage, was now related to more than just a few of them. Even if she hadn't known so many, she would have taken notice of this one had he been on the force.

But he wasn't. She'd never laid eyes on him until a couple of minutes ago.

"No," he answered as nonchalantly as if he were taking a telephone survey, the outcome of which had absolutely no consequence in his life.

"Then, *again,* you shouldn't be here. Now *move.*" She brought her face closer to his. "Don't make me tell you again."

The expression in his eyes said that he knew he could take her. Even with his hands secured behind his back.

But then he merely shrugged and grinned affably—as well as irritatingly.

"No, ma'am," he answered in a voice that was far too polite to be believable, "you won't have to tell me again. I'm moving. See?" he pointed out. "Feet going forward and everything."

What kind of a wise guy was he? Taylor wondered. In the next moment, she silently answered her own question. The kind, she realized, stopping dead, who had managed to get her to stop her normal mode of investigation.

For a reason?

Was there something this man didn't want her to see? *Was* he the killer? Or could he be working for the killer? Had he hidden something, or had she come in time to stop him?

"Hold it," she ordered.

The stranger turned around to look at her. "Come to your senses?" he asked mildly.

"Never left them," Taylor informed him tersely.

Moving behind him, she removed one handcuff and then, rather than undo the other the way she knew he expected, she cuffed his hands around the Doric column that rose up from the center of the living room like an ambiguous statement.

"Now you stay here until I'm finished."

To her surprise, he offered no protest, no angry words at being shackled in this manner. Instead, he merely watched her for another long moment, then asked, "And just what is it you're going to be doing?"

Why did that sound so damn sexy? As if he was implying that she was about to have her way with him instead of just surveying the apartment the way she intended?

It occurred to Taylor that she didn't know his name and hadn't even asked. But then, she had no doubt that he would probably just give her an alias. There was no point in asking.

"What I came here to do," was all she said.

"Then I'm guessing it doesn't have anything to do with me."

"First right answer of the evening," Taylor replied curtly. About to walk away, she stopped and tested the integrity of the handcuffs—just in case. To her satisfaction, they didn't budge. "Now stay put. I'll be back when I'm finished."

"I'll be waiting," he called out after her.

"Damn straight you'll be waiting," Taylor muttered under her breath in exasperation as she walked out of the room and headed for Eileen Stevens's bedroom.

The last place the criminal lawyer had gone alive.

Chapter 2

Taylor stood in the walk-in closet that was bigger than her own bedroom. Surveying its contents, she shook her head.

How did one woman manage to accumulate so many clothes? Moreover, nearly half of them still had their tags on. Eileen hadn't even gotten around to wearing them yet.

Was there some inner compulsion that made her just buy things to have them, not necessarily to use them?

"Who's going to wear them now, Eileen?" Taylor asked softly, examining a designer original evening gown that sparkled even in the artificial overhead light. "What drove you, Eileen? What?"

Taylor stopped talking and cocked her head, listening. Was that…?

It was.

The sound of the front door opening and then closing. Instantly alert, her journey in the other woman's shoes immediately suspended, Taylor pulled out her weapon again.

Had someone else come in?

What was going on here, anyway? It felt as if she'd wandered into an open house instead of an official crime scene. Holding her breath, Taylor cautiously made her way to the living room again.

And then stopped dead.

The handcuffs she'd used to secure the intruder were neatly lying on the white rug before the Doric column, nothing but air held within the metal circles.

She rushed over to the cuffs and grabbed them, exasperation bubbling within her veins as she scanned the room. The intruder was nowhere to be seen. He'd pulled a Houdini on her. How? These weren't fake cuffs or a prop. The average person couldn't have gotten out of them.

Hell, *she* couldn't have gotten out of them. But he had. Just who the hell *was* he?

"Damn it!" Taylor exclaimed, scanning the room again as if the second survey would somehow uncover the man for her.

What if the door opening and closing was just to throw her off?

She looked around for a third time, tension weaving in and out of her. Taylor half expected the stranger to come charging at her from one of the corners.

Adrenaline still rushing through her veins, weapon drawn, she swept from one room to another, checking closets, bathrooms, the balcony. Anywhere the man could have folded his lengthy form and attempted to hide. All to no avail.

The man was gone.

Who the hell was he and how did he fit into all this? she silently demanded, her exasperation growing exponentially. This scenario wouldn't have gone this way if Aaron had been with her. Damn him, anyway.

No, Taylor upbraided herself tersely the next moment. This wasn't Aaron's fault, it was hers. She was the one who'd gotten sloppy, unconsciously getting too accustomed to someone having her back at all times.

She knew better.

On this job, no matter what, you had to remain vigilant because there were no guarantees and even the best of partners could be caught napping.

Just like she had this evening, she thought in disgust.

Crossing to the front door, Taylor locked it, then tested the doorknob to make sure it held. It did. Even so, she dragged one of the chairs over and placed it in front of the ornate door. If "Houdini" decided to come back and pick the lock, he'd still wind up hitting the chair. The scraping noise the feet would make against the marble would alert her. She didn't want to be caught off guard a second time.

Most likely, she mused, the intruder wasn't going to come back. He was probably just happy to get away. Not that she planned to let him. She intended to find him, but that was something she'd deal with later. *After* she did what she came here to do.

Glancing toward the door one final time, Taylor went

back to Eileen Stevens's bedroom. Somewhere amid
all the woman's things she hoped to get a handle on the
late lawyer's life.

No doubt about it, Eileen Stevens had led an extremely busy life, Taylor concluded more than ninety
minutes later, finally driving home to her own apartment. A busy life, but, as far as she could ascertain, it
had been far from satisfying. The few photographs that
did grace the walls in the lawyer's study were of Eileen
and the other, older partners from the firm. Eileen
appeared very formal in them.

Didn't the woman have a personal life?

From everything she'd found, it didn't seem so. There
were no love letters stashed in a bottom drawer, held fast
with a faded ribbon, no secret photographs tucked away
in an album of someone who had once made her pulse
race. There was nothing to indicate that Eileen had made
any kind of personal contact with anyone.

The only scrapbook the woman had kept was filled
with newspaper articles about her cases. Cases she had
won. It was all about winning for Eileen.

Can't take a court victory to bed with you at night,
Taylor thought.

"Looks like you lost, big time," Taylor murmured
under her breath to a woman who could no longer
benefit from any insight she might have to give.

Is this any better than your life? an annoying voice
in her head mockingly asked. *Here it is, way past your
shift, and what are you doing? Poking around a dead
woman's apartment.*

Taylor unconsciously stiffened her shoulders. Eileen Stevens's life *wasn't* like her life, she silently insisted. *She* had a life, *she* had a family. A family that meant the world to her and who were always there for her anytime she needed them, or just wanted to kick back. Just because she wasn't spending her nights with a lover didn't make her anything like the dead woman.

She blew out a breath as she pulled into her apartment complex, a modest collection of garden apartments with carport parking and bright white daisies planted all along their borders.

"Great, so now you're arguing with yourself. Maybe you *should* go back to Brian and have him assign that temporary partner to you," she said out loud in disgust.

Taylor pulled into her carport and turned the engine off. For a second she sat there, listening to crickets calling to each other. In the distance was not-so-faint music coming from the pool area. Someone was having another party.

Someone was *always* having another party this time of year. She felt no desire to go.

Maybe you should go, anyway. Might do you good.

She shook her head. Andrew Cavanaugh saw to her social life. The former chief of police and family patriarch held enough gatherings at his place to take care of any spare time she had.

Tonight she was just tired. Tired and disappointed in herself for allowing that cocky intruder to get away. *Tomorrow would be better,* she silently vowed getting out of her vehicle. All she needed was a good night's sleep and then she'd be back on track.

The good night's sleep she'd planned on had eluded her.

Oh, she'd slept all right, but rather than a restful, dreamless event, her night was packed full of dreams. One dream flowering instantly into another, all involving the sexy intruder.

The dreams played out so vividly that she'd had trouble separating reality from fiction. In several versions, the intruder got the drop on her rather than she on him. In the last dream, things inexplicably heated up. Her clothes disappeared just as she realized that he wasn't wearing any either.

That was when she bolted upright, waking up.

It was 7:00 a.m. and her pulse was racing. Her breathing was so shallow she thought for a moment she was going to hyperventilate. The downside was that she felt far more tired than when she'd first fallen asleep.

Exhausted, her breathing finally under control, she dropped, face forward on the comforter for a moment longer.

Who the hell was that man and how did he fit into Eileen's life? Taylor wondered for the hundredth time.

She knew she wasn't going to have any peace until she answered those questions, especially the first one. Sitting up again, Taylor sighed and dragged her hand through her tousled, long blond hair. First thing this morning, she would see about getting together with the sketch artist, before the intruder's features faded from her memory.

She should be so lucky.

Throwing off the covers, Taylor marched into the bathroom. She rushed through her shower and was drying off in less than ten minutes. Dressed, she ran her fingers through her hair as she aimed the hair dryer at several sections, impatient to be on her way. She was determined to find out the man's name and bring him in before the day was out.

Breakfast was a banana she peeled and ate between leaving her front door and reaching her vehicle in the carport.

She was on her way to the precinct less than half an hour after she'd woken up.

Tracking down the mysterious intruder turned out to be a lot easier than she ever imagined.

Arriving at the precinct, Taylor went straight up to her squad room. Her intention was to drop off her purse at her desk and then go in search of the sketch artist.

She stopped dead ten feet short of her goal.

The intruder was there, sitting in the chair beside her desk, looking as if he didn't have a care in the world.

Taylor's first instinct was to draw her weapon, but she banked it down even though training a gun on him would have been immensely satisfying. The man obviously wasn't a criminal. A criminal didn't just waltz into a squad room and make himself at home. Although, approaching the scene from another angle as she played her own devil's advocate, that could actually be the perfect cover.

Either way, the stranger obviously had a hell of a lot of nerve.

Taking a deep breath, Taylor crossed the rest of the way through the room to her desk.

As if sensing her presence, the stranger turned his head and looked right into her eyes a moment before she reached him.

"You," she spat out, making the single word sound like an angry accusation.

An accusation that apparently left him unruffled. The stranger merely smiled that maddening smile she'd previewed last night.

"Me," he affirmed.

Instead of throwing her purse into the bottom drawer, she dropped it in. But she satisfied her need to blow off steam by kicking the drawer shut.

"Who the hell are you?" she demanded, barely keeping her voice down. "And how did you get out of those handcuffs?"

"Handcuffing your dates these days?"

Focused only on the stranger, Taylor almost jumped. The question came from her brother, Frank, another homicide detective. Frank had chosen that moment to come up behind her. Fresh off solving a serial-killer case and riding the crest of triumphant satisfaction, her younger brother grinned at her.

"You know the department frowns on taking their equipment for personal use." He moved so that he stood next to the annoying stranger.

Taylor struggled to keep from telling her brother to butt out. "This isn't a date, this is a suspect," she bit off.

"A suspect?" the intruder echoed, still smiling that annoyingly sexy smile that seemed to undulate right under her skin, shooting straight to her core and warming it. "For what?" he asked innocently.

As if he didn't know. "For the murder of Eileen Stevens," she snapped.

"A suspect?" her brother repeated in disbelief, then looked, stunned, at the seated man. "Laredo?"

Taylor's eyebrows narrowed over eyes the color of the midmorning sky. "Who the hell is Laredo?" she demanded.

"I am," the stranger told her affably. The next moment, he half rose in his seat and extended his hand to her. "J. C. Laredo," he introduced himself. "I came in to see if we might be able to have a successful exchange of information. I would have asked last night," he went on, "but you looked a little too hot and perturbed to listen to reason."

"Taylor hardly ever listens to reason," Frank told the man as if he was sharing some sort of a family confidence.

"Taylor also has excellent hearing and is standing right here," she pointed out angrily to her brother, struggling to hang on to her temper.

She felt Laredo's eyes slide over her torso as they took full measure of her. Slowly they went from her head down to her toes. It took all she had not to shiver.

"You most certainly are," Laredo agreed in a voice that told her he highly approved of the body he'd just inventoried.

Frank leaned his head in toward Laredo and said, "I think you got her angry. I'd be careful if I were you. Taylor bites heads off when she's angry." With that, Frank began to retreat.

"I'll keep that in mind," Laredo promised. His eyes shifted over to Taylor. "Taylor, is it?" he asked, rolling the name over on his tongue as if he were tasting it for sweetness. Satisfied, he smiled. "I think we got off on the wrong foot last night."

Frank was obviously still within hearing range because she heard her brother chuckle to himself and murmur, "Like *that* never happened before."

Taylor took a deep breath, struggling to get her surprisingly frayed temper under control. She was going to kill Frank when she got the chance. Never mind that he was two months shy of his wedding. She'd be doing her almost-sister-in-law a favor. Frank could be god-awful annoying when he wanted to be.

"All right," she said, her voice straining to sound civil as she faced the man sitting at her desk. "This is the season for goodwill toward men. I'm listening, Laredo. What were you doing at Eileen Stevens's apartment last night?"

Since the man had gotten out of the handcuffs, she saw no point in asking how he had managed to elude the security guards in the building's lobby. That had obviously been child's play for him.

Laredo answered without missing a beat. "Probably the same thing as you."

She didn't like playing games unless they involved a board and little colored game pieces. "You said you weren't a cop."

The look on his face was innocence personified. "I'm not."

"Then you weren't doing the same thing that I was,"

Taylor concluded curtly. "And you weren't supposed to be there."

Instead of arguing the point with her, Laredo surprised her by nodding his head. But just as she began to wonder why he was being so agreeable, he admitted, "I bent the rules a little. But I am investigating her death."

She highly doubted that there were two investigations going on at the same time. They hardly had enough people to sufficiently cover all the city's crimes now. If another branch of law enforcement was involved, someone would have told the Chief of D's, who in turn would have warned her.

Handsome or not, this character, she concluded, was full of hot air. "By whose authority?" she asked, thinking that she was just giving him enough rope to hang himself.

She wasn't expecting the answer he gave her.

"Indirectly, her mother, Carole Stevens. I'm actually doing this as a favor to my grandfather. He used to date the dead woman's mother," he confided.

Taylor felt far from enlightened. Was this man just making this up and hoping his charm would fill in the gaps?

"You're contaminating a crime scene as a favor to your grandfather?" she challenged incredulously.

"I know enough not to contaminate the crime scene," Laredo assured her in a voice that she found as irritatingly patronizing now as she had the night before. The next moment, he reached into his pocket. Every nerve ending went on the alert and she started to reach for her sidearm out of habit.

Laredo noted her reaction. "Relax," he told her in a voice that could have easily been used to gentle a wild animal. "I'm just reaching for my wallet, not my Saturday night special."

She deeply resented the smirk she heard in the man's voice.

"Do you own one?" she wanted to know.

The term referred to a weapon that was the common choice of thugs and penny-ante thieves more than two decades ago, before far more colorful, sophisticated and seductively affordable weapons hit the streets.

"I own a lot of guns," he informed her easily, placing his wallet, opened and face up, in the middle of her desk.

Taylor looked down at the private investigator's license he was showing her. The photograph in the corner was a surprisingly good one. But then, the thought whispered along the perimeter of her mind, the photograph was of a surprisingly good-looking man.

"John Chester Laredo, private investigator," she read out loud.

Taylor raised her eyes quizzically to his. Chester? Who named their kid Chester these days, even as a middle name?

"That's me," he responded, taking his wallet back and tucking it into his pocket.

Taylor blew out a breath, trying to put a positive spin on things. At least she didn't have to waste time with the sketch artist. Now, instead of arresting the annoying man, she just had to get rid of him.

"All right," she allowed, "for the time being, let's just say you're on the level."

Was it her imagination, or did his grin just get more annoying? "Let's," he agreed.

She frowned. "That still doesn't give you the right to be there, 'bending rules,'" she said sarcastically, "and poking around."

"I wasn't 'poking,'" he corrected affably, "I was looking. And obviously, if I thought the police would object to what I was doing—" he leaned forward slightly "—I wouldn't have come out and made myself known to you last night, now, would I?"

For a second, he had her. She was willing to admit he had a point.

But then, the next moment she realized that there was no way for him to have known that she was with the police department. She could have been with the housing management—or even a thief, drawn to the apartment by the yellow crime scene tape to see what she could make off with.

"You're a little large to hide, even in a place as big as that," she pointed out. "It seems to me, given a choice, you decided that it was best to take the bull by the horns."

His grin was *really* starting to get to her, which made her increasingly uneasy.

"I wouldn't exactly use the term *bull*," Laredo told her. "I have a lot of friends on the force. I didn't think anyone would mind."

Taylor's eyes narrowed. *Think again, Laredo.* She didn't like anyone even remotely messing with her crime scene. "Well, then you thought wrong," she informed him tersely.

Chapter 3

Laredo had gotten to his position in life by reading people correctly. Innate instincts had trained him to be an excellent judge of character. Consequently, he knew when to push and when to step back.

He also knew when a little extra persuasion might help him wear down barriers. He had a feeling that the sexy-looking blonde with the serious mouth did not respond favorably to being either opposed or coerced.

Moving slightly forward in the chair so that his face was closer to hers, Laredo looked into the woman's eyes. They were a shade lighter than his own. And very compelling. You could tell a lot about a person by the way they looked at you and her eyes never wavered, never looked away.

"C'mon, Taylor," he coaxed, "what's the harm in sharing information?"

She didn't want him getting familiar with her. He wasn't her friend, he was an annoying man and she was still debating having him arrested for tampering with evidence.

"It's Detective McIntyre," she informed him stiffly, and then added, "and I don't talk about ongoing investigations with civilians." And that, she hoped, would bring an end to any further discussion of Eileen Stevens's murder.

The corners of Laredo's mouth curved in what she could only think of as a devilish grin. A wicked expression flared in his eyes as he said, "I'll show you mine if you show me yours."

Taylor would have felt better if she'd thought that the air-conditioning system had broken down that morning. At least then she would have had something to blame for the sudden overwhelming wave of heat surging through her body, leaving no part untouched.

Stalling for time as she tried to get a grip, Taylor blew out a breath. Laredo's eyes, she noted, never left hers.

The way she saw it, she had three ways to go here. She could keep sparring with this annoying private investigator and, most likely, get nowhere while taking precious time away from her investigation. That option held no appeal because she was already behind without a partner's help.

Her second choice was to get someone to eject this overconfident ape from the premises, but she had the uneasy feeling that Laredo wasn't lying about having friends in the department. If he knew her brother, he had to know others as well. Trying to get him thrown out might make her seem like a shrew—and it probably wouldn't work anyway.

Or, door number three, she could toss Laredo a crumb in exchange for finding out exactly what he knew. There was the chance that he had stumbled across something. After all, he had managed to get to Eileen Stevens's penthouse apartment before she had. Who knew how long he'd been there or what he might have seen—and taken?

Door number three it was.

Taylor braced herself. "All right, what do you have?"

She watched as his smile unfurled further. Why did she get the feeling that he was the spider and she was the fly, about to cross the threshold into his open house?

"I believe I said, 'I'll show you mine *if* you show me yours.' That means that you go first, as it should be," he added, "since my mother taught me that it should always be ladies first."

Try as she might, Taylor just couldn't form a mental picture of the woman who'd given birth to this larger-than-life, annoyingly sexy specimen of manhood.

"You have a mother?"

The question had slid from her mind to her tongue before she could stop it. What the hell was he doing to her manners and, more importantly, why was she letting him do it? Once this case was over, she was definitely going on vacation. Her batteries needed recharging.

"Had," Laredo quietly corrected, his seductive grin toning down several wattage levels—and becoming all the more lethal for it.

Taylor did her best to steel herself. For all she knew, Laredo could just be orchestrating this to make her feel guilty. If she felt guilty enough about stumbling onto this sensitive area, he might think she'd fold easily.

It made sense, but even so, she couldn't shake the feeling that she'd just stomped across ground she shouldn't have. She was extremely sensitive when it came to matters that concerned family. Family was, if anything, her Achilles' heel.

Her family was chiefly responsible for who and what she was today. She'd joined the force and become a police detective because her mother had been one before her. And, because of what she'd seen transpiring in her family as a child, she was gun-shy when it came to relationships. The moment one appeared to go beyond being an inch in depth, she bailed, remembering what her mother had gone through with her father. No matter that her mother's second marriage seemed made in heaven; it was the tempestuous first one that had left its indelible mark.

Taylor found it ironic that while she had implicit trust in the men she'd been partnered with when it came to life-and-death situations, she absolutely refused to trust any man with her heart. Taylor staunchly opposed revealing her vulnerability.

Rallying, Taylor squared her shoulders. "Okay, here's what I've got." She deliberately ignored the touch of triumph she saw enter his eyes. "Graduating fifth in her class from Stanford Law School, Eileen Stevens worked her way up extremely fast. She became a much sought-after criminal lawyer who rarely lost a case. None in the last five years. Her list of clients reads like a who's who of the rich and famous—or infamous," she added, thinking of a couple of so-called "wiseguys" who were on the list. "She was made partner at her law firm six months ago. According to the electronic calendar they found by her bed, the woman ate and slept work 24/7. She didn't appear to have a social life that wasn't connected to the firm."

Taylor paused for a moment, wishing she understood how a woman with no social life could end up the victim of a very personal crime. "But someone hated her enough to tie her up and wrap a wet piece of leather tightly around her neck, then wait for the strip to dry and strangle her. My guess is that the process took at least a couple of hours."

"How do you know they waited?"

Laredo didn't look impressed by her conclusion, just mildly curious, like someone asking study questions they already knew the answer to.

She told him anyway. "The carpet is thick and lush— my guess is that it's fairly new. There was a set of shoe prints set in it next to the bed, like someone had stood there for more than just a minute. The killer, watching her die." The comforter beneath the woman's body had been all tangled, as if Eileen had thrashed around while tied to the bedpost, trying to get free, but Taylor didn't add that, waiting to see if Laredo would.

He didn't. Instead, he merely nodded at her narrative. "So far," the private investigator told her, "we're of a like mind."

"And you have nothing to add?" she demanded. He was playing games with her, just trying to find out what she knew. She didn't like being duped.

"I didn't say that," he told her evenly, his gaze locked on hers.

"So?" she asked impatiently.

"I don't have anything from the present—yet," Laredo qualified. "But what I do have is more of a background on Eileen."

Taylor crossed her arms before her, waiting. "Go ahead." It was an order, not a request.

Laredo obliged and recited what he'd learned since his grandfather had come to him with this.

"Eileen Stevens was thirty-eight and the complete epitome of an obsessed career woman. But she wasn't always so goal oriented. When she was a seventeen-year-old high school junior, Eileen got pregnant." He saw the surprise in Taylor's eyes and knew she wouldn't be challenging the worth of the exchange between them. "Her mother wouldn't allow her to have an abortion. The baby, a boy, was turned over to social services the day he was born. From what I gathered, the experience made Eileen do a complete one-eighty. She turned her back on her former wild life and buckled down to become the woman she is today."

"Dead," Taylor couldn't help pointing out.

A hint of a smile touched his lips. "I don't think that was in her plans."

If Laredo was trying to undermine her by laughing at her, he was in for a surprise, Taylor thought. She'd survived growing up with Zach and Frank, expert tormentors both.

"Anything else?"

Laredo spread his hands wide. "That's it so far."

She doubted it, but she had no way of keeping him for interrogation at the moment. "And who did you say you were working for?"

"I'm doing this as a favor," he told her even though he was fairly certain that she hadn't forgotten. She was probably just trying to trip him up, which was all right, he thought, because in her place he probably would have done the same thing. "My grandfather used to date Eileen Stevens's mother. Carole Stevens was a single mother who worked double shifts as a cocktail hostess to make ends meet. That didn't exactly leave her much time to be a parent and from what I gathered, as a kid Eileen needed a firm hand. After she graduated high school, they became estranged for a number of years—"

"Because her mother refused to allow her to have the abortion." Taylor guessed.

Laredo inclined his head. "That was part of it, yes," he acknowledged.

So he did know more than he'd just admitted. "And the rest of it?"

He shrugged. "Just the usual mother-daughter animosity."

She didn't like the way he just tossed that off. Taylor felt her back going up. Something about him made her want to contradict him no matter what he said.

"It's not always 'usual,' Laredo."

Her defensive manner aroused his interest. "You never clashed with your mother for no other reason than just because she was your mother?"

She definitely didn't like his way of stereotyping

people, she thought. "Not that it's any business of yours," she told him coolly, "but no."

He didn't say anything for a moment. It seemed rather obvious to Laredo that Taylor McIntyre was headstrong and stubborn. He couldn't visualize her being easygoing about things and letting them slide unless she wanted to.

"Not once?" he prodded.

"No," she repeated. Less-than-fond memories had her adding, "That was for my father to do." Then, realizing that she had said far more than she'd wanted to, she shot another question at him. "If Eileen and her mother were so estranged, why is her mother asking you to investigate who killed her daughter? Is there a will involved?"

As far as she knew, the police hadn't even found out that the murder victim had a mother in the state. She'd left her next-of-kin information blank on the law firm's employment form.

"I don't know about a will," Laredo admitted. "But as far as Carole and Eileen's estrangement went, my grandfather said they'd reconciled just a few months ago. According to him, the reconciliation was all Carole's doing," he added. "Carole said she felt that life was too short to let hurt feelings keep people apart. Personally, I think my grandfather gave Carole a little push in the right direction."

For a reason? Taylor wondered. "And your grandfather, how does he figure into all this? Beyond the little push, of course."

Sarcasm always rolled off his back. Most likely, the

long-legged detective was trying to get something more
out of him, some "dirt" she probably thought he'd con-
veniently omitted.

Sorry to disappoint, Taylor, Laredo thought, doing
little to hide his amusement.

"He's just a nice guy who's there for his friends,
that's all."

"Or, in this case," she reminded him, "volunteering
you."

He certainly couldn't argue with that, Laredo
thought. But then, in the scheme of things, it was the
least he could do. If he spent the rest of his life as his
grandfather's right-hand man, he wouldn't begin to
repay the man for everything that he had done for
him.

"Something like that," he agreed.

Time to stop dancing, she decided. She'd already
spent too much time getting next to nothing. "What is
your grandfather's name and where can I find him if I
want to talk to him?"

"His name's Chester Laredo," a familiar, deep voice
behind her said.

Taylor didn't need to turn around to know that the
voice belonged to her stepfather. At the same time, she
thought to herself, so much for the mystery of why
Laredo's middle name was Chester.

The next moment, Brian Cavanaugh, Aurora's chief
of detectives, came around her desk, extending his hand
to the man she'd been trying to pump for information.
Brian smiled broadly at Laredo.

"Frank mentioned he saw you here. How are you,

Laredo?" he asked warmly, shaking the younger man's hand. "And what's your grandfather up to these days?"

"I'm fine and he's been running a security firm for the last five years," Laredo told him, sitting down again.

"A security firm?" Brian laughed, shaking his head. "I never thought he'd leave The Company. I thought they'd have to take him out, feet first."

"He thought it was time," Laredo told him. "He didn't think he could move as fast as he used to."

"Chet?" Brian asked incredulously. "That man could pop open any lock and disappear faster than anyone I ever knew."

That would explain the handcuffs, Taylor suddenly thought. And then the initial sentence played itself over in her head.

"The Company?" Taylor echoed, looking from her stepfather to the man at her desk. "Your grandfather was with the—"

"Yes," Laredo said, cutting her off before she could mention the CIA. "He doesn't like it getting around these days. Afraid it might scare off more clients than it attracts," he explained.

Brian looked as if that made perfect sense to him. "Well, tell him I said hello and if he ever feels like catching up, he knows where to find me."

Okay, this was another new turn, Taylor thought. What did Brian have to do with a member of the CIA? "Catching up?" she asked.

Brian left it deliberately vague. "We collaborated a couple of times back in the day."

Taylor blew out a breath. She wasn't going to get any

more than that and she knew it. For all his affability, Brian Cavanaugh was extremely closemouthed when he wanted to be.

She moved on. "So you're vouching for him?" She nodded at Laredo as she asked.

"Absolutely. I've known Laredo for as long as I've known you," he told her. "Bounced you both on my knee—just not at the same time," Brian added with the wink that she knew was her mother's undoing. Brian shifted his eyes toward Laredo. "If I can help you in any way, just let me know."

"I'll do that," Laredo promised. "But right now, I've got no complaints with the way Detective McIntyre is taking care of me."

Brian smiled, affection brimming in his eyes as he looked at his older stepdaughter.

"Never doubted it for a moment. She's one of our finest. Good seeing you again, Laredo," Brian repeated just as his cell phone began to ring. He sighed. "No rest for the weary," were his parting words as he walked away quickly, taking out his phone. "Cavanaugh here."

"He's a great guy," Laredo said to her. There was genuine admiration in his voice. There, at least, Taylor thought, they were in agreement.

"Yes, I know." She turned her attention back to the man at her desk. "I guess if he vouches for you, I can trust you." She couldn't help the grudging note that came into her voice.

"With your life." Laredo sounded completely serious as he said it.

But she still couldn't help wondering if he meant it, or was trying to throw her off. Ordinarily, if Brian vouched for someone, that was enough for her. But something about the way Laredo looked at her had her struggling to keep her guard up.

For the second time, she told herself to wrap it up. She had witnesses she needed to question and an investigation to kick off. Damn, but she missed Aaron. The man wasn't due back for another six weeks. They stretched out before her like a long, lonely desert.

"All right," she announced to Laredo, "if you have nothing else to tell me—"

The same sexy, lazy smile traveled along his lips, straight into her nervous system.

"I have lots of things to tell you," he assured her, his voice deliberately lower than it had been, carrying only the length of her desk. "Preferably over a lobster dinner with soft music in the background and some champagne chilling beside the table."

Nine times out of ten, that line probably worked, she thought. But not on her. "You're a player."

He smiled. If it bothered him to be caught, he didn't show it. "When the occasion arises. The rest of the time, I'm pragmatic."

You had to admire a guy who didn't give up, she thought despite herself. "And plying me with liquor would be which?"

He looked at her for a long moment before saying, "A little bit of both, most likely."

If she hung around him any longer, she was in danger of getting lost in those blue eyes, Taylor warned herself.

"Well, I have a job to do, so if you'll excuse me." With that, she rose to her feet.

Laredo did the same. And as she went out of the squad room, he was right there, his steps shadowing hers until they both reached the elevator.

She had no recollection of issuing an invitation, Taylor thought.

Pressing the down button, she turned to face him. "Look, if you think you're coming with me just because my stepfather bounced you on his knee—"

A touch of surprise entered his eyes. "Brian Cavanaugh's your stepfather?"

It was something she assumed everyone knew because, in the world she inhabited, for the most part they did. "Yes."

He nodded, as if approving. "Your mother's got a good man."

She was *not* going to get sidetracked. "Be that as it may, you're not coming with me."

"I didn't think I was."

She pressed the down button again. "Then why are you following me?"

"I'm not," he told her innocently.

Where was the damn elevator? There weren't that many floors. "Right."

"In case it might have slipped your notice, 'Detective,' cars are supposed to be parked outside the building and I haven't trained mine to come when I call so, consequently, if I want to use it, I have to go to the car." He gave her an amused look. "Same as you, I suspect."

She was about to press for the elevator a third time

when it arrived. She saw that the car was almost filled to capacity. Ordinarily, she would have waited for the next car, but she wanted to get away from this man as quickly as possible. So she slipped into the car, trying to make the most of the space that was available.

As did he.

Taylor discovered that ignoring a man she found herself pressed up against was next to impossible no matter how hard she tried.

Chapter 4

Hours later, out in the field, Taylor could swear she could still feel the blush from that morning creeping up her neck. It lingered, breathing color along her cheeks as they traveled down in the elevator to the first floor.

To his credit, Laredo had made no reference to being packed against her like an amorous sardine, but it was obvious that he was thinking about it. One look at the smile in his eyes told her that.

Damn annoying man, Taylor thought now, not for the first time. If her stepfather and Frank hadn't indirectly vouched for Laredo by the way they'd both greeted and interacted with the man, J. C. Laredo would have definitely been at the top of her list of suspects to investigate. She wasn't sure if she would have bought into his story about investigating Eileen's murder as a favor to his grandfather if it hadn't been for them.

Even so, she still might look into his background once she finished interviewing the people on the victim's list of clients. She'd been doing that for a good part of the day, as well as talking to the other tenants in Eileen's building. So far, she felt as if she was just spinning her wheels. Slowly.

After getting back into her car, Taylor closed the door and then just sat there for a moment, looking over the remaining names on the list of clients. Because they were all celebrities of varying degrees, getting past their bodyguards and arranging for a few minutes of conversation was turning out to be almost a Herculean effort. She wouldn't mind if she felt that this helped the investigation, but it didn't.

A gut feeling told her that she was probably just wasting her time. Maybe she needed to talk to Eileen's mother.

That was when it occurred to Taylor that she'd been so eager to get away from Laredo, she had completely forgotten to ask for Carole Stevens's address.

With a sigh, she dug out the card the private investigator had pressed into her hand just before they parted company.

"In case you change your mind and decide you want to collaborate," he'd said, punctuating his statement with a rather unsettling wink just before he'd sauntered off to his car.

She recalled thinking, almost against her will, that Laredo had the tightest butt she'd ever seen on a man. That was when she'd almost thrown his card away. But there weren't any trash containers in the immediate vicinity, so she'd temporarily stuffed it into her jacket pocket.

Looking now at the plain white card with its bold, raised black lettering, Taylor read the cell number twice, repeating it under her breath before putting it into her own phone.

The phone on the other end rang four times. She was fairly certain it would go to voice mail, but then she heard a noise. The next moment, a deep male voice rumbled against her ear and she was certain she had the real deal, not a recording.

"Laredo."

Something suddenly and unexpectedly tightened in her gut. Annoyed with herself—and him—Taylor almost flipped the phone closed. Damn it, she was acting like some indecisive schoolgirl, she upbraided herself. This just had to stop. *Now.*

"That you, Detective McIntyre?" she heard the deep voice ask when the silence stretched out. She could *swear* she heard a smile in his voice.

"Yes," she bit off grudgingly. "It's me." How had he known? It wasn't as if she'd indicated that she was *ever* going to call him, at least, not until such time as the Winter Olympics took place on the frozen terrains of hell.

As if reading her mind, he said, "Didn't expect to hear from you so soon. Miss me?"

"Like a toothache." Taylor could almost see the smirk on his lips. "I need Carole Stevens's phone number and address."

He was the soul of cooperation. "Sure thing. Got a pencil and paper?"

"Of course I do," she answered, quickly opening her glove compartment and tossing things onto the passenger seat in a frenzied attempt to locate the items.

"I can wait," he offered, as if he could see her rummaging.

The man made her exceedingly uneasy. "The address," she repeated, issuing the words like a direct order.

"Yes, ma'am."

Carole Stevens lived in the older part of town, Taylor thought as she wrote down the street address. Had those been Eileen's roots as well? she wondered, quickly writing down the phone number Laredo recited.

"Thanks."

"Anytime, Detective McIntyre," he replied cheerfully.

Last time, Taylor countered mentally. She quickly terminated the connection before he could say anything else.

Why the hell was her heart racing? Taylor silently demanded as she turned the key in the ignition. There was absolutely no reason for it to be beating as if she'd just completed a hundred-meter dash.

She really needed to go on that vacation. The minute that Aaron came back, she would take off for a couple of weeks. Let *him* go solo for a while. It would serve him right, leaving her in a lurch like this.

What *was* the matter with her? Taylor thought the next moment, guiding the car to the main thoroughfare. She was happy for Aaron. She knew how much he and his wife, Rachel, had wanted this baby, how long they had tried to get pregnant. They *deserved* to enjoy their little girl.

Taylor sighed, her hands tightening on the steering wheel. Just when had she turned into the Wicked Witch of the West?

Since her path had crossed Laredo's. There was no point in denying it. She didn't know what it was about the tall, muscular private investigator with the intrusive manner, but he made her feel as if she was walking on a foundation made of gelatin.

What she needed, until she could go off on that mythical vacation, was to hang out a few mornings at Andrew's house. The former chief of police threw his doors open every morning, making gastronomically thrilling breakfasts for whichever member of his family happened to wander into his house. The man loved to cook and he loved his family. And everybody knew that. The atmosphere within Andrew Cavanaugh's house was energizingly positive and right now, she could use a little positive reinforcement.

Since her mother was married to Brian, Andrew's younger brother, that connected her to the family patriarch. Not that she actually needed an excuse to show up. Andrew considered most of the people on the police force his extended family.

How the hell did that man manage to keep enough food around to feed everyone? she couldn't help wondering. It was like one of Aesop's fables come to life, the one about the bottomless pitcher of milk. No matter how many glasses were poured, the pitcher always remained full. In this case, it wasn't a pitcher, it was a bottomless refrigerator.

Someday she would have to ask Andrew about that.

* * *

There were two cars in Carole Stevens's driveway when Taylor pulled up twenty minutes later. Did the woman have company? she wondered as she parked her car at the curb.

Maybe it was a friend, offering condolences to the poor woman. Taylor was grateful that she wouldn't have to break the news to Eileen Stevens's mother about her daughter's murder. There was nothing worse than having to tell a parent that their child wasn't coming home again.

There should be a chaplain on the force who took care of that sort of thing. It was hard enough getting through each day alive, always running the risk of being shot—or worse.

Making her way up the front walk, Taylor took out her detective shield and ID. She held it up so that it would be the first thing that the woman would see.

There was a Christmas wreath on the door, in direct contrast to the sorrow that now resided within. Taylor rang the bell. It opened almost immediately.

"Mrs. Stevens?"

The question was merely for form's sake. The tall, thin woman who opened the front door was an older version of Eileen Stevens. And, eerily like Eileen, the light had been drained out of her eyes.

"Yes."

Taylor raised her shield slightly, calling attention to it. "I'm Detective McIntyre—"

"Yes, I know." It was then that the woman opened the door further, allowing Taylor to see that Carole Stevens wasn't alone. She had a six-foot-three guardian angel next to her. "Laredo told me you'd be coming."

Taylor's eyes shifted to Laredo, who smiled at her. She allowed her mouth to curve, but there was no humor in the expression.

"How thoughtful of him."

Laredo acted as if they'd just exchanged a hearty greeting. "Nice to see you again, Detective."

"I can't say the feeling is mutual," Taylor murmured under her breath. Eileen's mother didn't seem to hear her, but she was certain that Laredo did. His smile widened.

"Laredo is just here to support me," the woman told her, her voice echoing the hollowness that she obviously was feeling inside. Carole glanced at the man beside her and did her best to smile her gratitude. "Chet thought it might be a good idea."

Taylor looked from Laredo to the woman. Where'd she heard that name before? "Chet?"

"My grandfather," Laredo reminded her.

The man had a gift, she thought. Without uttering a single, derogatory word, he made her feel as if she were the intruder.

Taylor got down to business. "This isn't going to take long, Mrs. Stevens," she promised the woman, doing her best to cut Laredo out of the mix by turning her back toward him.

"I've got nothing but time," Carole told her sadly just before she turned on her heel to lead the way into the living room.

Mrs. Stevens sat down on the sofa, clasping her hands before her as if doing so would give her strength to get through this horrible ordeal. Laredo sat down beside her. Leaving Taylor to take a seat on the chair opposite the sofa. Again she felt isolated, like an outsider.

"I really don't know how I can help you," Carole confessed. "I don't know much about her life." It was obvious that the admission was painful for the woman. "Eileen and I just recently got back together again. She'd been angry at me for years, holding me responsible for nearly ruining her life." The sigh that escaped her lips was ragged. "Those were her words, not mine." Carole raised eyes that were bright with tears. "Do you have any children, Detective?"

The fact that Laredo eyed her with interest, waiting for her answer, didn't escape Taylor. "I'm not married."

A sad smile curved the thin lips as a faraway look came into Carole's eyes. "Neither was I."

Taylor caught the woman's point. She shook her head. "No, no children."

Carole nodded, as if she hadn't expected any other answer. "Then you have no idea how that can hurt, having your child hate you."

"Eileen didn't hate you, Carole," Laredo interrupted, his voice soft, kind, as he took the woman's hand and squeezed it, as if to give her support. "You made her take responsibility for her actions. You actually caused her to turn her life around and make something of herself. If anything, she should have been grateful to you."

Gratitude filled Carole's eyes. "I wish I could believe that, Laredo"

"Believe it," Laredo urged as if this was the one truth she could hang on to.

Rallying, Eileen's mother straightened, squaring her shoulders. She looked at Taylor as if she'd suddenly become aware of her presence. "I'm sorry. This is all still very new to me."

"I understand and I am sorry for your loss," Taylor told her with genuine feeling. No mother should have to outlive her child. She knew how devastated her own mother would have been if anything were to happen to any one of them.

Carole nodded. "Thank you." She took another bracing breath, then asked, "So, how can I help you?"

Taylor took a small, worn notebook out of her pocket. She'd thought to take it with her after writing down the woman's address.

"You can tell me about Eileen," she urged, watching the woman's face. Sometimes an expression said more than actual words did. "When the two of you got back together, did she say anything about being afraid of someone? About somebody bothering her or maybe sending her threatening letters?"

She had already asked the same questions of the victim's coworkers yesterday and gotten no feedback, but maybe Eileen had felt more at ease around her mother.

Carole shook her head. "Nothing. She never mentioned anything like that. All she talked about was her work. She was very excited about being made a partner."

"But?" Taylor let the word hang between them, picking it up from the tone of Carole's voice even though it hadn't been spoken out loud.

"But she didn't seem happy," Carole conceded. "Driven, but not happy. It was as if something was missing out of her life." At an apparent loss for words, Carole helplessly added, "Like everything she had just wasn't enough."

Funny that the woman had mentioned that. It was the exact same impression she'd come away with, walking around the victim's apartment last night.

Working with what Laredo had told her this morning, she tried to piece things together. "Your daughter got pregnant when she was seventeen and gave the baby up for adoption, didn't she?" Taylor asked Carole, approaching the sensitive subject slowly.

"Yes." Caution entered the woman's features. "What about it?"

Taylor knew she was grasping at straws, but sometimes that paid off. "Could Eileen possibly have been experiencing some remorse over that? Maybe feeling that she shouldn't have given the baby up?" As she spoke, ideas popped into her head. "Could your daughter perhaps have been considering trying to find her son after all these years?"

Carole almost laughed out loud. "Oh, God, no. When he was born, Eileen didn't even want to look at that poor child. I had second thoughts about giving him up, but she pitched a fit, insisting that if I kept him, she'd run away." Carole shrugged helplessly. "My first duty was to my daughter, so I let him go. Once she went off to college, I didn't see her anyway. I should have kept him," she whispered almost to herself, then roused herself and said with conviction, "No, Detective, I don't think she tried to get in contact with her son. Eileen never talked about him or the pregnancy. The second she left the hospital, it was behind her.

"My daughter didn't like children," Carole confided. "She never did. Thought that they were nothing but trouble." The woman's voice was sad as she continued. "I can show you her old room and pictures of Eileen when she was a little girl, but I really don't think any of that will help you."

Taylor never liked leaving any stone unturned. "You never know, Mrs. Stevens," she said encouragingly. "Sometimes it's the smallest thing that winds up solving a case."

A glimmer of hope passed over the woman's lined, concerned face. "I really hope so," she murmured, more to herself than to either one of the people in the room with her. Slightly unsteady, still dealing with the shock of the last twenty-four hours, Carole rose to her feet. Laredo was quick to take her arm and give her support. She smiled her gratitude. "You're a lot like your grandfather," she told him.

"I take that as the highest compliment, Mrs. Stevens," he replied.

Carole's eyes shifted toward Taylor. "This way," she urged, pointing down the hall to the back of the house before she walked in that direction.

Well, that was an hour of her life that she would never get back, Taylor thought after thanking Carole Stevens for her time and saying goodbye. There was no enlightenment to be garnered from her daughter's old room, other than the fact that in appearance, it was light-years away from the penthouse apartment that had seen the end of her life.

It was as if the two bedrooms had belonged to two very different people. The bedroom she'd just been in had, for all its disorganization, a kind of warmth to it that was glaringly missing from the one in the trendy, expensive penthouse. In the bedroom she'd just left there had been photographs pinned onto a bulletin board in a haphazard, overlapping fashion. The younger Eileen had had people in her life, friends she shared her time and her feelings with, not to mention the boyfriend who'd gotten her pregnant in the first place.

From all appearances, the successful Eileen slash murder victim had had only clients and acquaintances in her life. There was no evidence that she even *had* a personal life.

Did that mean something more than she was seeing? Was she missing something right there in front of her? In plain sight?

Taylor heard Carole saying goodbye again. Thinking the woman was calling out to her, she turned around only to realize that Carole wasn't talking to her, she was saying goodbye to Laredo. He was leaving, too.

Did he intend to follow her?

Instantly alert, Taylor waited until Carole closed the door, then went back up the walk to confront the not-so-private investigator.

"Just what exactly were you doing here?" she asked.

"Offering Mrs. Stevens some support," he answered amiably. "I thought we already cleared that up." And then he flashed that annoying smile of his, the one that seemed to wind itself like a corkscrew right into the center of her being. "You might not know this, but you do have a tendency to come on a little strong. I thought that I could act as a buffer for Carole if you got too carried away. After all, I was the one who told you where you could find her. If you rattled her, it would be my fault."

Taylor's eyes narrowed. "I don't appreciate being second-guessed."

"No guessing was involved," he countered. "I figured you'd come on like gangbusters. With me around, you didn't. Simple," he concluded.

"This might offend your ego, Laredo, but I don't temper the way I do things because you're around. And, now that I'm on the subject, I would really appreciate *not* having you around from now on." She pinned him with her eyes. "Agreed?"

The expression on his face told her that the answer to that was a resounding "No."

"Look, Detective McIntyre, it's a known fact that two heads are usually better than one. Why don't we just, off the record, join forces until we find out who killed Eileen Stevens? Think of the perks."

She refused to ask him what perks, fairly certain that he was going to say something about having him around for extracurricular activity should the desire hit.

"That way," he continued as if she'd asked him to elaborate, "you won't look so strange, talking to yourself. People'll think you're talking to me."

The man was a walking ego. "You think you're pretty clever, don't you?"

He lifted his shoulders in a casual shrug. "I have my

moments, but I'd rather think that I'm more intelligent than clever. How about it? Temporary partners? Off the record?" he pressed, extending his hand.

She looked down at his hand for a moment, then turned her back on it and him and returned to her car.

"I'll get back to you on that," was the last thing Taylor said before she got into the vehicle and pulled away.

"Yes, you will, Detective McIntyre," Laredo said to himself, watching her car make its way out of the development.

Chapter 5

Several hours later, after questioning more of Eileen Stevens's former clients and the people on the lower rung of her law firm, people who were more likely to pass on gossip, Taylor was no closer to solving the woman's murder than she had been before. Nobody loved the woman, but everyone respected her and felt she was an excellent lawyer. As far as she could determine there were no grudges, outstanding or otherwise.

Desperate for any kind of a decent lead, Taylor decided to return to the late lawyer's building. But this time, she wasn't going to wander around the tomblike apartment or talk to any of the woman's overly busy neighbors. Taylor wanted to question the security guard who had been on duty the evening Eileen had been murdered.

The young man, Nathan Miller, seemed surprised

to see her again. She'd already questioned the guard once and he had sworn that Eileen Stevens hadn't had any visitors. Anyone who didn't live in The Villas had to sign in and indicate who he or she was there to see. There'd been no name next to the dead lawyer's name.

"I'd really like to help you, Detective," Nathan told her with feeling. "But nobody went up to see her—unless they scaled the outside of the building," he added with an odd little smile, enjoying his own joke.

"What about the other residents?"

His forehead furrowed as if he was trying to make sense of her question. "You mean, did any of them go to see Ms. Stevens? I'd really have no way of knowing that. The residents get together all the time. That's why this place is so popular. We've got the fully stocked gym, the Olympic-sized pool, the—"

She held her hand up before Nathan could go, verbatim, through the features listed in the slick sales brochure. She'd already taken a copy with her and perused it. The Villas came across more like a spa slash mini-mall than a residence. From what she'd gathered from the neighbors, no one ever saw Eileen Stevens make use of any of the facilities she was paying so dearly for.

"No, what I want to know is did anyone come in to see any of the other residents that evening?" When the guard looked at her blankly, she elaborated. "A pizza delivery boy, a visitor you might not have recognized, a—"

Taylor knew that she was probably shadowboxing in the dark, but there had to be something. Someone had to have gotten to her. No way could Eileen Stevens have tied herself up like that.

Nathan shook his head to her suggestions and then abruptly stopped. "No, no—wait." His brown eyes widened as he looked at her.

She tried not to sound eager. "You remember something?"

"Yeah. There was somebody who came in, but he wasn't here for Ms. Stevens." Taking out the logbook housed on a shelf, he flipped back two pages. "Here it is," he read, then looked up, his hand spread out across the entry and holding down the page. "Mrs. Wallace had flowers delivered to her a little after seven."

Yes! "Did you see the delivery boy come back down?" Taylor pressed.

"No. But I was on my break," he explained quickly. Nathan looked crestfallen. "He could have left without me seeing him."

"You don't have security cameras?" Even as she asked, she looked toward the front doors.

"No. The residents consider it an invasion of privacy. I'm supposed to be enough," he added in a chagrined voice. "It's my fault, all my fault."

She felt sorry for him. He looked so young and inexperienced. Reality was taking a hard bite out of him. "Sometimes things happen that you just can't anticipate, Nathan," she told him. "Nothing's going to change if you beat yourself up over it. Do you know if Mrs. Wallace is in?"

He nodded his head. "She hasn't gone out on my shift," he told her.

He was qualifying his statements like a man who'd had his faith in himself shaken. "What floor is Mrs. Wallace on?"

"Second," he said with no hesitation. "But she's all the way over on the other end."

Taylor merely nodded. That didn't mean that the killer hadn't walked up one flight and then gone over to the dead lawyer's side. It *did* mean that a lot of planning had gone into Eileen Stevens's murder.

And she was still no closer to finding out why. Taylor banked down a wave of frustration as she went up to the other woman's apartment.

Dorothy Wallace was a widow in her late sixties who had a young woman's sparkle in her eyes. Dressed to show off all her best features—a body that was a combined product of religiously faithful workouts and the clever scalpel of a top plastic surgeon—Dorothy was just on her way out to meet "this young stud" for an early dinner "and 'whatever,'" she added with a broad smile.

Apologizing, Dorothy explained that she could only give her ten minutes because the "stud" apparently grew impatient when he was kept waiting.

"Flowers?" Dorothy repeated when the question of the delivery was put to her. Appearing perplexed, she slowly moved her head from side to side. "No, I didn't receive any flowers." A grin nothing short of wicked curved her carefully made up lips. "Not that night at any rate. I do get my share, though," she confided. "Don't you just love the old-fashioned type? The ones who know how to properly woo a woman?"

Now there was a word she hadn't heard lately, Taylor thought. Did anyone actually "woo" these days? She sincerely doubted it. Then she thought of Brian and her mother and decided to revise her conclusion, at least just a little. But outside of them, she was certain that men and women no longer had time for things like slow, languid courtships. Everything, including relationships—and breakups—seemed to occur in a hurry. Sometimes she had the feeling that life was almost over before it could even begin.

Philosophy aside, she had the answer she came for. Eileen Stevens's killer had gotten access to the building by posing as a delivery man for someone else.

After thanking the woman for her time, Taylor went back down to the ground floor. The security guard seemed impatient for her return.

"Well?" Nathan asked the moment the elevator doors opened.

Taylor shook her head. "Mrs. Wallace didn't receive any flowers."

"Oh, damn." He groaned as if he'd been physically punched in the stomach. "You mean that I let in the killer?"

"Maybe." She tempered her response only because he looked so terribly distraught. Taylor focused on the positive side. They finally had a lead. "Do you think that you could describe this guy to a sketch artist?"

"Maybe." Nathan thought a moment, then his head bobbed up and down. "Yeah, yeah I could," he decided. "Let me just call my boss and get someone to take my place. I can't just walk off my post."

"Except for breaks," she reminded him.

He slanted her a look she couldn't quite fathom. "Except for breaks," Nathan mumbled, sounding deeply ashamed.

Armed with the sketch of the so-called flower delivery man, Taylor returned to Eileen's firm.

The senior partner commented that he might have to put her on the payroll if she kept turning up. His one attempt at humor faded as he looked at the sketch and shook his head. He appeared genuinely disappointed when he told her that he'd never seen the man before. Neither had any of the other people at the law firm. No one she questioned even remotely recognized the man.

Five days into the murder and she felt as if she was banging her head against a wall. Still, for now this was her only lead and she wasn't about to give up on it.

She couldn't get over the feeling that she was missing a piece. Something that was out in plain sight and she just didn't see it.

It drove her crazy when, after several more days, her thoughts didn't gel. But neither did the feeling disappear.

"Try backing away from it," her older brother counseled. Zach had swung by her desk to ask if she wanted to grab some lunch. She'd been so preoccupied that she hadn't even heard him come up. He'd said her name twice before she even looked up. "Maybe it'll make more sense to you if you take a break."

Taylor laughed shortly. "The security guard at Stevens's building took a break and Eileen Stevens wound up dead."

Zach shook his head as he lowered himself into the

chair beside her desk. "Now you're just babbling. As your older brother, I'm telling you to come to lunch with me."

But she shook her head. "Sorry, I can't." She gestured at the empty desk that was butted up against hers in the cubicle. "Aaron's still away and I'm doing double duty."

Zach looked unimpressed. He knew the kind of workaholic his sister could be.

"So both of you need to eat. To keep your strength up and all that good stuff." As Taylor began to shake her head to turn him down again, he added, "Okay, as senior detective, I order you to come with me."

"Pulling rank?" she laughed.

He could remember when doing something like that would set her off. But they'd been kids at the time and squabbling had been a way of life. "If that's what it takes, you better believe it."

Taylor began to waver. Now that she thought of it, she could feel her stomach pinching. Had she had breakfast? She couldn't remember. She supposed nothing earthshaking would happen if she did stop to get something to eat.

And then it did.

"McIntyre," Lieutenant Harrigan called out, walking out of his glass-enclosed office. When both Zach and Taylor looked his way, he amended, "The pretty one."

"That would be me," Zach told her, rising. "Sorry, kid."

"Yeah, right." *Now what?* Taylor wondered, rising to her feet. "Yes, Lieutenant?"

The expression on the older man's face was stern. "You caught another one."

Confused, she looked at him blankly. "Another one what, sir?"

"Homicide." The single word hung in the air, lethal and treacherous.

She felt a little frayed around the edges. The last thing she needed was a new murder to pile onto the one she hadn't solved yet.

"No disrespect, Lieutenant, but aren't one of the other teams up?" She gestured vaguely around the room. Most of the desks were unoccupied, but that was only because the teams were out to lunch or in the field. "I'm still—"

Harrigan cut her short. "Same M.O. as your dead lawyer," he told her. "Hands and feet tied up and a leather strip around the neck, choking off the air supply."

Once was bizarre. Twice was eerily unbelievable. "You're kidding."

The lieutenant gave her a look that said she should know better. "When have you known me to kid?"

The flicker of hope died ignobly. "Right. Where's her body?" Taylor asked as she took her oversize, carry-everything purse out of the bottom drawer and slung it over her shoulder.

"His," Harrigan corrected. Both Zach and Taylor looked at him, obviously taken aback. "His body."

"His body?" Taylor repeated incredulously.

The barest hint of a smile came to the older man's lips. "Aced your hearing test, did you?"

Taylor blew out a frustrated breath. "So this wasn't personal, this is just some homicidal wacko getting his jollies."

"Draw no conclusion before its time," Harrigan advised. He handed her the slip of paper with the dead man's name and address on it. "Here you go. Dispatch just called."

"Terrance Crawford," she read out loud then saw the address. "Lakeview Middle School." She raised her eyes to the lieutenant's. "He's a teacher?"

"Not anymore," Harrigan contradicted with a heavy sigh.

"Okay, guess you're off the hook," Zach said to her as the lieutenant retreated to his office. "I'll take a rain check. But you get yourself something to eat, hear me?" She nodded dismissively, her mind already working on this newest twist. Was there a connection between the homicides, or was this killer just an opportunist? "If you're going to be the godmother of my kid," Zach told her as he began to walk away from her desk, "I want you healthy."

Taylor's thoughts vanished as her mind came to a skidding halt. She grabbed her brother's arm and turned him around to face her.

"Hold it!" she ordered. "What godmother? What kid?"

"You," he said in a mild tone, struggling to keep a straight face. "Mine."

"You don't have a kid." And then she backtracked. "Do you?"

Zach grinned. "According to Kasey, who's much more of an expert on these things than I am, considering she's a doctor, it's the size of a peanut. But it is mine. Ours," he amended with all the pride that flowed through a newly minted father's veins.

"Oh, God, Zach! A baby!" Excited, thrilled, Taylor threw her arms around her brother. There were a lot of babies of varying ages and sizes in the Cavanaugh family, but this was the first one for the McIntyre contingent. "Does Mom know?"

"Officially?" he asked, then shook his head as Taylor released her hold on him. "No. But she probably just heard you scream it out. Kasey and I thought we'd tell her and Brian over dinner tonight. Want to be there?" he offered.

Taylor knew her location tonight was still up in the air, depending on what she was going to learn at this new crime scene, but she said what was in her heart. "I'd love to."

Like the rest of them, including their mother, Zach had no illusions about the demands of the job. He read between the lines.

"I'll understand if you're not." He took his leave, saying, "Now go solve this damn thing before we have to set up another task force."

Taylor paused only long enough to kiss her brother, give him another warm, fierce hug, and then she rushed off. She had a body waiting for her.

It almost didn't seem right to feel this happy while going to investigate yet another murder but this ultimately kept them all going. The small, deep, unexpected pockets of happiness that they dipped into to sustain them.

Otherwise, it was all sorrow, all darkness in the worlds they occupied. She knew without exploring it that she wouldn't have been able to cope with that. Most likely, none of them could.

Thank God for her family. How would she have ever maintained her sanity without them? It was a rhetorical question.

Pulling up to Lakeview Middle School, Taylor parked her car right beside the patrol car and got out. It appeared to be the last parking space. The lot was completely filled with cars that undoubtedly belonged to the teachers who worked here.

Out of the corner of her eye she noticed one car parked off to the side that looked vaguely familiar, but then she shrugged it off. Lots of cars looked familiar at this point.

She wondered how the students were coping with this turn of events, or if somehow the teachers had managed to shelter them from the traumatic truth. The irony of the situation wasn't lost on her. This made twice. Two murders in two neighborhoods deemed exceedingly safe. Patrolmen were more likely to hand out tickets for failing to wear a bicycle helmet or not coming to a full stop at a stop sign than deal with the grisly details of a murder.

Walking up to the wood-framed double glass doors, Taylor took a breath and braced herself. She pulled open the right door with one hand, holding her badge in the other.

As she crossed the threshold, she found she didn't have to say anything. The principal, a Mrs. Hammond, was waiting for her and she pointed out the way as she fell into step beside her.

"I don't know what to say to the parents," Mrs. Hammond confessed, tension radiating from every pore as she obviously struggled to hang on to her composure. "Nothing like this has ever happened here before. Nothing," she repeated, her voice cracking.

"You need grief counselors," Taylor advised kindly. She paused for a moment, looking through her wallet. Finding the card she wanted, she handed it to the woman. "Call this number," she told her. "You'll get the help you need. Meanwhile, what can you tell me about the teacher who was killed?"

Mrs. Hammond swallowed before answering. "He didn't call in today."

Taylor looked at the stately woman, confused. "Excuse me?"

The principal ran her tongue quickly across her dry lips. "He wasn't here this morning and he didn't call in. I thought it was rather strange. He's one of our most dedicated teachers," she explained, her voice speeding up nervously with each word she uttered, her distress very evident. "He was always volunteering for after-school programs. The kids all love him. Loved him," she corrected. "And then, Jack opened up the closet where the equipment's stored—"

"Jack?" Taylor interrupted before the woman could continue.

But it wasn't the principal who answered her.

"The maintenance man," Taylor heard an all-too-familiar voice say.

No, it couldn't be.

But it was.

She didn't know which she was more, angry or stunned. "What the hell are you doing here, Laredo?" she demanded, swinging around to face him.

He appeared nothing if not easygoing as he answered, "Just lending a hand." Then, to placate her, he added, "I own a police scanner and heard the call being made to dispatch."

Trying to maintain her temper, Taylor turned to the principal.

"I'd like to talk to you later, Mrs. Hammond. Will you be in your office?"

"Yes." There was almost an echo in the woman's voice.

Taylor nodded. "Good. And please, make that call," Taylor pressed, indicating the card that she had just given her.

The principal glanced down at the card numbly, nodded and then retreated. She looked like someone on automatic pilot.

The moment the woman was out of earshot, Taylor whirled around to face the private investigator who was turning up more often than the proverbial bad penny.

"This is getting more than a little suspicious, Laredo."

He nodded, gazing down at the body that had fallen out of the closet at the frightened maintenance man's feet. "That's what I think, too."

She wasn't about to get sidetracked. Taylor pulled on his arm to get him to look at her. "I'm talking about you, turning up here and at the other crime scene—"

In a patient voice that instantly got under her skin, he reminded her, "I already told you what I was doing at the first scene. As for this one—" he looked back at the body again "—it's just too much of a coincidence not to be our boy."

He was really starting to tick her off. "*We* don't have a *boy*. *I* have a suspect."

He raised his eyes to hers, interested. "You do?"

He was making her trip over her own tongue. "I mean I would if I could find the guy who supposedly delivered flowers at the building the night Eileen Stevens was killed." To cover all bases, she'd spent the better part of one afternoon calling every florist within a twenty-mile radius. No one had a delivery scheduled to anyone at The Villas. She really hadn't expected them to.

"There was a delivery guy?" Laredo asked. "Who told you that?"

"The security guard. Nathan Miller," she added in case he'd talked to another one.

The information surprised him. "Funny, he never mentioned that to me when I talked to him."

"Maybe you're not as persuasive as you think," she couldn't resist saying.

"Maybe," he allowed. And then he smiled at her. "Maybe we could go out to dinner and you could teach me your persuasive ways."

Behind her, the patrolman who had been first on the scene and had called dispatch cleared his throat. "Um, Detective?"

Chagrined, Taylor turned toward the uniformed man. "Why didn't you run this man off?" she asked.

Nervous to be placed on the spot, the patrolman told her, "He said the Chief of D's would vouch for him."

"And you just took him at his word?" she asked incredulously.

"No, ma'am, I called in to check. And Chief Cavanaugh did. He vouched for him. And he told me to tell you that sometimes a little outside help is necessary."

Taylor rolled her eyes. Just what she needed. Her stepfather on this irritating man's side.

She didn't bother suppressing her deep-rooted sigh. Some days it just didn't pay to get out of bed. This was turning into one of those days.

Chapter 6

Taylor, grudgingly accepting Laredo's help, spent the better part of the afternoon interviewing everyone who was at the school when Terrance Crawford's body had been discovered. The primary question was: How did they feel about the dead teacher? The words the interviewees used might have varied, but the essence of what they had to say was the same: Terrance Crawford was a wonderful teacher who was loved by everyone.

Incredibly selfless, the science teacher slash coach gave of himself to the point of exhaustion. If there was an after-school program that needed someone to helm it, Crawford was the first—sometimes the only—one to volunteer his services. And if there was no funding available for the program, he found a way to run it for free.

It quickly became apparent to Taylor that, in his own

way, Crawford was as passionately devoted to his work as Eileen had been to hers. The difference being that there was no king's ransom to be had in the teacher's case. What Terrance Crawford reaped were not exorbitant fees but gratitude and accolades. As in Eileen's case, the main people in Crawford's world were his colleagues. The difference again was that, according to several teachers' testimonies, Crawford could kick back with them. Taylor sincerely doubted that Eileen had kicked back with anyone in years.

Because there were so many teachers, students and, in some cases, parents to interview, Taylor found herself having to reluctantly accept Laredo's help. Otherwise, there was no telling when she would finish and it would be a matter of the proverbial cutting off her nose to spite her face syndrome.

"Glad to see you're being sensible instead of territorial," Laredo had said when she'd relented and told him that he could talk to the teachers without her being present—as long as he showed her his notes afterward. "This way we can probably get the preliminary interviews done in one afternoon instead of two."

There was that *we* again, she thought as she herded off her group of teachers and students. Where did this man get off thinking they were a set? And just what was it about him that got her back up so fast? She was usually a lot more tolerant of people, even when they behaved like insufferable jerks. Since there was no answer, Taylor was forced to drop the matter. But it still gnawed away at her.

She was just getting to her last interview, the vice

principal, Alyce Chin, a diminutive woman who was particularly teary-eyed over Crawford's murder, when Taylor saw Laredo looking into the classroom through the glass window on the upper portion of the door.

Damn, she should have known that he would be finished first. But it wasn't a competition, right?

Doing her best to ignore the man's presence, which still felt intrusive despite the door that separated them, Taylor forced herself to focus on the gut feeling she had about the vice principal.

Alyce Chin wasn't telling her everything.

After getting the standard answers about how well liked the dead teacher had been, Taylor lowered her voice, making the exchange more intimate. "Were you and Terrance Crawford close?"

The young woman began to shrug, denial obviously rising to her lips. And then she sighed. The moment she did, she broke down.

Alyce's lower lip trembled as she hoarsely whispered, "Yes."

Taylor was not about to leave anything in an ambiguous state. She wanted everything to be perfectly clear and spelled out. "Does that mean you were seeing each other outside the school?"

The woman hesitated again, then answered, "Yes," in a small, lost voice.

Thank God, finally something personal. "Then what can you tell me about him?" Taylor pressed, trying not to sound too impatient or eager. "Did Terrance have any enemies, anyone he felt had it in for him?"

The vice principal's dark eyes widened in stunned surprise. "No, no, everyone loved him."

"Not everyone," Taylor reminded her. More tears slid down the other woman's cheeks. Taylor thought of Eileen and how the criminal lawyer had turned her life around after giving birth to her baby. "Was there something in his past that he was ashamed of? That might have come back to haunt him?"

Again Alyce Chin hesitated for a moment, as if debating over something. But then she shook her head. "No, nothing."

"You hesitated," Taylor seized on that, her eyes holding the other woman prisoner. "*Was* there something? Think, this is important, Alyce. It could lead us to whoever killed Terrance."

Loyally, the vice principal shook her head. "No." And then she pressed her lips together, testing the weight of her next words. With a reluctant sigh, she said, "This might be nothing…"

"Let me be the judge of that," Taylor coaxed.

"All right. Once, when he was over at my place and he'd had a few drinks, Terry told me that in his senior year in high school, he'd gotten a girl—another student—pregnant. When he found out her condition, he wanted to marry her. She called him an idiot and said that she wasn't about to compound her mistake by making an even bigger one. She gave the baby up for adoption even though he wanted to keep it. He offered to raise it, but she absolutely refused. It killed him that she could do that, that he had no rights as a father."

She shifted in her chair, uncomfortable about sharing

her late lover's secret. "I think that's why Terry got into teaching. He wanted to make up for not being there for his son. I know it sounds corny, but he wanted to make a difference, to touch as many young lives as he could."

From the first word of the narrative, Taylor felt her breath catch in her throat. Every nerve ending she had was now on high alert. If this was a coincidence, it was one hell of one.

"Did Terrance ever happen to mention the girl's name to you?" Taylor asked, mentally crossing her fingers.

Alyce thought for a moment, her expression indicating that she was having difficulty recalling. "Arlene, Irene, something like that…" Her voice trailed off as she searched for the name that sounded right.

"Could it possibly be Eileen?" Taylor asked.

The vice principal didn't answer immediately. Again her expression indicated that she was thinking. "Maybe. I really don't remember." Her shoulders slumped a little as she wiped away more tears. "I'm sorry. I just can't think right now."

Taylor's heart went out to the woman. How would she feel, losing someone she loved? Wasn't that why she shied away from relationships? Because giving your heart came with a high price tag?

"I understand," Taylor told her gently. "I gave your principal the name of a good grief counselor to call in for the students." Her mouth curved in a soft, sympathetic smile. "He works with adults, too."

Alyce pressed her lips together, nodding. She was struggling not to sob. "Thank you," she murmured.

Finished, Taylor had no choice but to go back into

the hallway—where Laredo was still lying in wait, she thought, bracing herself. Hopefully, he'd learned something useful, although she doubted he'd discovered anything as good as what she'd just gotten.

"That's one hell of a connection," Laredo said the moment she opened the door and walked out.

Taylor stared at him, dumbfounded. He couldn't possibly have heard. She'd had to lean in so that she could hear the vice principal herself.

"What is?" she asked cautiously.

"That the dead teacher is the father of Eileen Stevens's baby." This took the two murders in a whole different direction. He wasn't sure what that new direction was yet.

Her mouth almost dropped open. How did he know?

"You couldn't have possibly heard that," Taylor insisted.

"You're right," Laredo acknowledged. "I didn't 'hear' it. Technically, I read it."

Her eyebrows narrowed over the bridge of her nose. This was in print somewhere? How? "Where?"

"On Alyce Chin's lips."

Just who *was* this guy? "Now you're telling me you read lips?"

Laredo looked at her lips and that same annoying, utterly unsettling sexy smile slipped over his. The one that raised her body temperature by several degrees no matter how hard she tried not to let it affect her. "Yes."

"Is that part of your private-eye training?" she asked sarcastically.

"It's private investigator," he corrected. "And no, it's

not. My mother was hearing impaired. I thought walking a mile in her shoes would help me understand her better, understand what she had to go through every day. For the record," he added, "I also sign."

He also made her feel like an idiot, Taylor thought. She was shooting sarcastic remarks at him and he was telling her about being sensitive to his mother's disability.

"Anything else?" she asked in a flat voice.

Laredo shrugged, amused. "I figure the rest will come out as we go along."

"*We* are not 'going along.'" If he thought he could become her unofficial partner just because she let him question a few people, he was sadly mistaken. "You're only here because my stepfather seems to think that you could be an asset. Obviously, he's not always a very demanding person—"

"I bet you take care of that part for him," Laredo speculated. He saw her open her mouth and he rerouted the conversation before she had a chance to retort. "Why don't we get back to Eileen's mother and verify that the baby's father actually was Terrance Crawford?"

That had already crossed her mind, just not her tongue. "So now you're taking over the lead?" she asked.

Laredo raised his hands as if to surrender. He also attempted to harness his amusement—rather unsuccessfully, she noted. It still shone in the man's eyes.

"Just making helpful suggestions, Detective McIntyre."

She hated the way he emphasized her title. Hated having him hover around. Most of all, she hated that he seemed to always be right.

"If I want your 'helpful suggestions,' Laredo, I'll ask

for them." With that, she turned on her heel and walked down the hallway to the school's front doors.

She heard Laredo murmur, "No, you won't," under his breath behind her, but decided that there was no point in disputing that. After all, he was right. Again.

"Terrance Crawford?" Carole Stevens repeated the name they had put to her less than a half an hour later. "He was the father?"

"That's what we're asking you, Mrs. Stevens," Taylor said kindly.

They were in her kitchen, sitting at the table. Cups of tea Mrs. Stevens had poured cooled in front of them.

"I don't know," she admitted honestly, looking from one to the other. "I always thought it might have been, but you have to understand, back then there were always boys surrounding Eileen." A sad fondness came into her voice as she remembered. "She was like a little Scarlett O'Hara, stringing them all along. She loved the attention," Carole added needlessly.

"And she never confided in you?" Taylor asked. She thought of her own bond with her mother and felt grateful that there was absolutely nothing she couldn't come to Lila with.

An almost tortured laugh escaped the other woman's lips. "I was the last person Eileen would have confided in. Especially after I wouldn't let her have that abortion."

Nodding as if he understood, Laredo asked, "Did your daughter have any friends back then, someone she might have told about the baby's father?"

Carole thought for a moment, then rose to her feet. "Come with me."

She led them back to Eileen's room. Once there, she turned toward Laredo and pointed at the mattress. "Lift that, please. Eileen kept her phone book there, along with her diary," she explained. "For some reason, she thought I wouldn't catch on." Carole shook her head in disbelief. "Don't know who she thought changed her sheets once a week."

There were two small, five-by-six books, worn with time and the weight of the mattress, lying in the middle. One was a faded lavender, the other gray. Propping up the mattress with his shoulder, Laredo picked up the two books before she had a chance.

Damn but he was fast, she thought grudgingly. Laredo let the mattress drop into place.

Holding up the books, he asked Carole, "Mind if we take these with us?"

Carole locked her fingers together. It was obvious that until this moment, she hadn't even given either book a thought. Nor had she sought any comfort from flipping through the diary.

"If it'll help, take them." And then she hesitated. "I will get them back, won't I?"

"I guarantee it," Laredo promised, patting the woman's shoulder as he held the books against himself with his other hand.

"Give them to me," Taylor ordered the moment they were out of the house.

Not waiting for Laredo to hand the books over to her,

she laid claim to the gray bound address book and pulled it out of his hand.

"Yes, ma'am," he answered in a clipped, military voice, saluting her.

She ignored him and flipped through the book she'd secured. Only a few names were scattered through the pages.

All they needed was one, she thought as she drove back to the station house.

As she came to a skidding halt in the parking lot, she looked up into her rearview mirror. There was his car pulling into the lot right behind her. Getting rid of him was harder than exterminating an infestation of ants.

"We can divide the names up," he volunteered.

She stopped halfway up the stairs to the front doors. "Look, what will it take to get this through your head? You're a civilian."

"I know that," he responded amiably.

"And civilians don't work with cops on cases," she continued through gritted teeth.

"Sure they do. Happens all the time. Don't clench your teeth like that, Detective. It'll wear them away. You wouldn't like dentures," he assured her.

Taylor threw up her hands and ascended the rest of the stairs. She was using energy trying to ignore him when she should have been focusing on the case.

Laredo fell into step beside her.

As it turned out, of the few names in Eileen's old address book, only one person had not moved away. Valerie Ames still lived at the same address and had the same phone number as in high school. Valerie had never left her comfort zone. Twenty years after graduation, she still resided with her widowed mother.

Cautious at first, Valerie finally agreed to meet with them, but only in a public place. She chose a coffee shop not too far from her house.

"My mother still thinks she's entitled to know every little thing about me," Valerie complained in a voice that was almost painfully nasal, adding to its whiny quality. She tore open packet after packet of sweetener and poured the contents into her coffee container. "I swear that woman can hear things from the farthest room in the house."

Taylor didn't ask the logical question, if Valerie found living conditions so unpleasant, why didn't she just move out? She didn't ask because she didn't want to antagonize the woman or get drawn into a tedious discussion. All she wanted was an answer to one important question. Was Terrance Crawford the father of Eileen's baby?

"Terry Crawford?" Valerie repeated when the name was put to her. "Sure, he was the father of her baby. Eileen was crazy about him," she confided, then added, "for about three months. A record for Eileen." She made no effort to hide her snide tone. "But then she got pregnant and she was just angry all the time." Valerie paused to take a long sip of her coffee, then addressed her remark to Laredo, with whom, Taylor noticed, she was obviously flirting. "Especially at her mother."

"Because she wouldn't allow Eileen to have an abortion," Laredo said.

Valerie nodded, her chestnut hair bobbing up and down. "That was why."

Taylor cleared her throat. Valerie didn't look in her direction immediately. It was only when Laredo, his eyes on Valerie's, nodded toward her that the woman momentarily shifted her attention.

"We heard that Crawford wanted to raise the baby and was upset when he found out that he couldn't," Taylor said, leaving the statement open for comment.

Valerie shrugged her shoulders. "News to me, but then, Eileen didn't want to have the baby around. If Terry kept the baby, it'd be a constant reminder that she'd made a mistake. She popped that baby out and made sure that there was a social worker right there to whisk it away. Eileen was pretty organized for someone who was so messed up."

"She was messed up?" Taylor pressed.

Valerie nodded vigorously. "Hey, anyone missing a chance to play house with Terry Crawford had to have a few loose screws."

"Doesn't sound as if you and Eileen had much of a friendship," Taylor observed.

Valerie shrugged again as she drained her coffee container. "Hey, you make do." Setting the empty container down on the table, she rose. "Well, I've got to be getting back. Don't want to miss my program," she said cheerfully.

"Wouldn't want that to happen," Laredo agreed.

She paused for a moment at the entrance to the coffee shop. "Unless you'd like to ask me some more questions." Her words were directed at Laredo and it was obvious that questions weren't what was really on her mind.

"Not right now," Taylor assured her. "But we have your number if anything new comes up."

Nodding, Valerie left.

"Think these murders have anything to do with the baby?" Taylor finally asked after a lengthy silence. They were on their way back to the precinct, where Laredo had left his car parked in the lot.

Laredo looked at her now, mildly surprised. "You're actually asking my opinion?"

"Right. What was I thinking?" Taylor shook her head. Maybe she was getting punchy. "Never mind."

"No, I'm flattered," he told her. "Surprised, but flattered."

"I don't want you flattered," she told him wearily. "I just want your take on this."

He'd been going over the situation in his head ever since they found out about Crawford's possible connection.

"On the surface, it looks as if it might have something to do with their past. The baby being the connection would be the logical conclusion, but not necessarily the only one." He laughed shortly. "I don't think this is Planned Parenthood taking drastic measures and striking back if that's what you mean."

"Never mind," Taylor repeated, this time with more feeling. Served her right for lowering her guard and thinking she could brainstorm with this man the way she had with Aaron.

"That, in case you didn't recognize it, was a joke," Laredo informed her patiently. "Loosen up, Detective

McIntyre." He leaned slightly forward in his seat, taking a closer look at her. "And stop frowning. Didn't your mother ever warn you that your face might freeze that way?"

She slanted a dismissive glance in his direction before taking a right turn. "My mother was too busy warning me about scruffy private investigators with big egos trying to horn their way in where they didn't belong."

Laredo nodded solemnly. "Smart lady." It was against his credo to say anything against anyone's mother, even in a joke. "I'll stay on the lookout for one and let you know if I see any."

"Another joke?" she asked warily.

"It's not a joke until you smile," he qualified, watching her.

Maybe he could take a light view of things, but she couldn't. "I've got some nutcase running around, tying wet strips of leather around people's necks and then watching them strangle to death. *And* I've got two dead people to account for. News flash—there's nothing to smile about."

He didn't see it that way. "There's always something to smile about, Detective McIntyre," he told her. "Sometimes you just have to look hard to find it, that's all."

She didn't agree, but she was in no mood to argue. "Right." Feeling suddenly drained, Taylor dragged her hand through her hair.

"Why don't I buy you dinner?" Laredo suggested out of the blue. She glanced quizzically in his direction. "Maybe things'll come together if you don't have to listen to your stomach complaining."

Now what the hell was he talking about? "My stomach?"

"Yeah. Can't you hear it?" He nodded toward it, as if she didn't know where to find it. "It's competing with your thought process—and mine."

Her thought process was being competed with all right, she thought. But it wasn't her stomach that was causing the problem.

Still, he did have one valid point. She *was* hungry. "All right, but you're buying."

"That's what I just suggested. Was I speaking too low for you?"

As a matter of fact, his voice *was* low. And it was getting to her in ways she definitely found distracting. "Shut up, Laredo. Nobody likes a wiseass."

She heard the smile in his voice. "I'll try to remember that."

She took the next turn a bit too sharply, struggling to bank down the unwanted reaction she was experiencing. "You do that."

Chapter 7

"So what do you do when you're not detecting, Detective McIntyre?" Laredo asked her as the waitress retreated with their orders.

When he'd offered to buy her dinner, Taylor had expected Laredo to bring her to one of the dozens of fast-food places that littered Aurora, serving anything from hamburgers to pizza to Asian food, all of which could be consumed on the run.

Instead, he'd brought her to Fiorello's, a well-reviewed, four-star restaurant that specialized in Italian cuisine. She'd always been very partial to Italian food.

Had this been just a lucky coincidence on his part, or had Laredo known about her preference? And if so, how? And why? Why was the private investigator trying to cull favor with her?

What was he up to?

"Your problem is that you overthink things," Frank had told her more than once. But then, little brothers had a tendency to be critical. It was due to the very nature of their position within the hierarchy of the family.

She supposed that maybe Frank had a point. It happened. After all, even a broken clock was dead-on twice a day.

"I sleep," she answered tersely. Before Laredo could say anything in response, she asked, "Do you come here often?"

"No." He took a sip of the ice water he'd requested. "As a matter of fact, it's my first time."

Well, at least he was being honest. So far. "What made you pick it?"

He looked at her for a long moment, as if weighing his answer. And then he laughed, shaking his head. "You don't stop."

That certainly wasn't an answer. Her eyes narrowed. "Excuse me?"

"Being Detective McIntyre. You really don't stop, do you? You just keep on 'detecting,'" he added when she continued to look puzzled.

He was trying to distract her. *I don't distract that easily, Laredo.* "Most people tend to go to a restaurant they're familiar with."

Their eyes locked. "There always has to be a first time."

He wasn't referring to going to a restaurant. As she had to consciously concentrate on breathing, she could feel his words slipping in under her skin, undulating their way through her whole frame. Settling into her very core. It took effort not to let her thoughts drift off.

"You *knew* I liked Italian food."

He'd asked Frank if his sister had any preferences when it came to eating out, but he wasn't quite ready to tell her that. Instead, he looked at her as if this was all news to him.

"You do?"

A two-year-old wouldn't have been fooled by this man, she thought. "You don't do innocent very convincingly, Laredo."

Broad shoulders lifted and fell in a casual shrug. "I guess I've got to practice in front of the mirror more often."

The conversation momentarily stopped as the waitress returned with their dinners. The young woman placed the Italian herb chicken before Laredo and the Alfredo shrimp with angel hair pasta in front of Taylor.

The moment the waitress backed away, Taylor leaned forward and said, "I'll take that as an admission."

She reminded him of a dog he'd once had. His grandfather had bought it for him, hoping that it would help him cope with the loss of his mother. Whenever the dog latched onto something, there was no way to get the animal to drop it.

"You must be hell on wheels in an interrogation room, Detective. I'd like to watch the next time you're up," he told her.

She couldn't decide if he was laughing at her or if he was serious. In any case, it didn't distract her from getting an answer to her question. "Why would you ask what my favorite food is?"

Waiting until after he sampled his dinner, Laredo countered with a question of his own. "Why wouldn't I?"

He was a master of the runaround. She would have expected nothing less. "I asked first."

Hungry, he took another bite of his food. He noted with satisfaction that despite her headstrong attack, Taylor was eating, too. "Maybe I'm just trying to find a way to soothe the savage beast."

"The expression is 'soothe the savage breast,'" she informed him, "and it refers to music, not food."

He paused long enough to grin at her. "Trust me, you wouldn't want to hear me sing."

Wasn't the man capable of a straight answer? If she did have him in an interrogation room, she had a feeling that he would drive her crazy.

"I've got a question for you," she posed gamely. "What do you do when you're not cracking wise?"

"I try to crack cases," he told her seriously. The next moment, the smile was back. Laredo leaned over the small table. Coming much too close to her. "Life's too short, Detective McIntyre. Have some fun with it before it's over." He indicated her meal. "Enjoy your food. Enjoy your diet soda," he added, lifting his glass in a mock salute.

Taylor left her glass where it was as she studied him. She was completely at a loss on how to read this man.

"Did you ask any other questions?" she asked. The query came out despite her resolve to drop the matter. But she suddenly had to know just how deeply he probed, how much he knew about her.

Something akin to goose bumps formed beneath the

sleeves of her jacket. There was no doubt about it, she thought darkly, the man stirred things up inside her.

She didn't *want* to be stirred. Not by someone so damn cocky and sure of himself.

"I ask lots of questions," he answered, again shrouding himself in pseudo innocence.

He knew damn well what she meant, Taylor thought. Although she was hungry, she hardly tasted the dinner she was eating.

"About me," she supplied tersely. "Questions about me."

"Oh, that. Well, yes I did." Without elaborating any further, which he had a hunch irritated her, he asked, "Did I break some kind of rule?"

She was very tempted to use the knife in her hand for something other than her dinner. "Why are you snooping around my life? You're supposedly here to investigate Eileen Stevens's murder."

"No *supposedly*," Laredo corrected in all seriousness. He wound spaghetti around his fork like a pro as he spoke. "I *am* investigating her murder." That was a matter of honor, involving his word. "And yes, I am asking questions about you."

"Why?" she repeated.

Laredo put down his fork, his eyes on hers. He dropped his teasing tone. "Because I want to get to know you, Detective McIntyre. Because I'm attracted to you," he told her honestly, then added what she didn't want to hear. "And, unless my radar's completely off, I think that you're attracted to me, too."

No, no, she wasn't, Taylor thought fiercely. "Your

'radar' needs an overhaul," she informed him in a cool, dismissive voice.

When he looked at her like that, she felt as if he could see right through her. Right *into* her. Could see every thought she had. She knew that was absurd, and yet, she couldn't shake the feeling.

"Does it?" he asked quietly. "It's usually pretty accurate."

The only way she could save herself was if she got angry.

She got angry.

Of all the overbearing, pompous—

Words failed her, even in the deep recesses of her mind.

"Well, I'm sorry. Your 'radar' might be fine and dandy when it comes to the legions of other women in your life, but it shorted out when it came to me."

"There're no legions," he told her mildly, finishing his meal. "I was referring to the gut feelings I have when working a case." He smiled at her. "It's a general-purpose radar," he explained amiably. "Look, I'm used to putting my cards on the table. I don't want to make you uncomfortable."

Too late.

She took a deep breath, as if that somehow signaled a fresh start. "Fine, then let's just finish eating. I've got to be getting back."

Laredo looked at his watch. "It's after six. Aren't you supposed to be off duty by now?"

She worked a case until it was solved. Hours didn't matter. "Not while the case is open."

He watched her thoughtfully, trying to isolate what

it was about her that attracted him so. He couldn't pin-point it. She just did.

"You know," he told her, "even batteries need to get recharged. You've got to take a break sometime. What do you do for fun, Detective McIntyre?"

Her answer was automatic. "I put smart-mouthed private investigators in their place."

Laredo inclined his head indulgently. "What else do you do for fun?"

She didn't want him digging into her life, didn't want him trying to get close because she was afraid that he *would* get close. And that would be disastrous.

"Look, for some reason that escapes me, we're working a case together," she began, her voice strained. "I am not in the market for a new best friend—or anything else—so let's just keep this professional, okay?"

"Too bad. I could make a really good 'anything else,'" he told her teasingly.

Again, his smile slipped under her skin, all but fil-leting her.

And when he leaned over and slowly ran the back of his hand along her cheek, her heart went into double time, all but bursting out of her chest.

She pulled her head back. "That's not professional," she informed him in a voice that wasn't nearly as strong as she wanted it to be.

"Oh, I don't know. *Professional* means business," he told her, his eyes never leaving hers. "And I mean business."

Suddenly she didn't have enough saliva to swallow. "I've got to be getting back," she repeated. Somehow, she got her legs to work, her knees to lock so that they could support her. But as she began to rise, Laredo put his hand over hers.

He vacillated between being amused and being aroused. But whatever state he was in, he knew he was definitely intrigued. And curious. Very, very curious.

"What are you afraid of, Taylor?" he asked her in a low, silky tone.

He was using her first name again, making this feel oh so personal. She didn't want it to. Instinct told her that if she ventured forward, even a few steps, a trapdoor waited for her just up ahead. A trapdoor that would give way when she least expected it, causing her to plummet down to who knew where.

All she knew was that at the end, when she stopped falling, there would be pain. A great deal of pain. The best solution to avoiding pain was not to take that first step, especially not with someone like Laredo.

Someone who could, for reasons she couldn't begin to put into words yet, matter a great deal.

"I'm not afraid of anything," Taylor informed him with a toss of her head, rallying. And then she delivered what she hoped was the final, ego-shattering blow. "Except for maybe being bored."

It didn't have the hoped for effect. Taylor could swear she saw something enter his eyes. She'd seen it before. The look of a man rising to a challenge. And she had just issued it.

"Thank you for dinner," she said, her voice cold enough to freeze over a lake. She left the table—and him—quickly, without a backward glance.

Laredo didn't call out her name the way she'd expected him to. Didn't try to stop her.

Maybe she was rid of him, she thought, at least for the evening. Cheeks flushed as she made her way through the restaurant, she felt oddly feverish. Was that triumph? Or was it simply the result of being so close to him for the length of the dinner?

She didn't know, didn't care, Taylor told herself. All she wanted was to be in her car, driving away from here—and Laredo.

Though she loathed to admit it, the damn, irritating man was right. It *was* past her shift and maybe, just for tonight, she'd go home to ponder over the notes she'd taken and to backtrack over things. Maybe while doing that, she'd find something that would help her untangle these two murders.

Having Laredo hovering around her definitely did mess with her thinking process and she didn't need that. Didn't need a tall, dark, handsome man watching her as if he knew what made her tick—as if he knew what she wanted.

How could he when she didn't know herself? she thought, pushing open the front door and hurrying out of the restaurant.

The breeze that greeted her was a cool one, stinging her heated cheeks. The air was moist and heavy with humidity. Winter was California's rainy season. That was all she need now, rain. Everything seemed to be working against her.

For a moment, she tried to get her bearings, scanning the area for her car. As she stood there, Taylor thought she heard someone coming up behind her. She heard the footsteps half a second before her name was called.

"McIntyre."

She would have swung around on her own, but she never got the chance. The person who'd called out to her caught her arm and did it for her, bringing her around to face him one shaky heartbeat before he pulled her into his arms and brought his mouth down to hers.

If asked, Laredo wouldn't have been able to say just what had come over him. Despite the image he projected, he wasn't the kind who let impulse rule him. At least, not usually.

This time was different.

This time, there had been an almost insatiable need to satisfy his curiosity. To satisfy a strange hunger he had never encountered before. Somewhere deep in his soul, he knew she'd forgive him.

But if he didn't find out what her lips tasted like, he would never forgive himself.

Besides, he had something to prove.

Self-defense reflexes were as automatic to her as breathing. Or, at least, they had been. But they failed her now, freezing and breaking up like so many brittle shards of glass. They might have been as automatic as breathing, but then, she wasn't really breathing, either. Her breath had backed up in her lungs.

Taylor found herself spinning off into a place where neither time nor space played a part. She was only aware of a tremendous wave of heat, beginning in the distance and then suddenly, like a back draft, whooshing over her.

Consuming her.

Making her knees and torso feel so weak that they barely supported her. It took every fiber in her being not to embarrass herself by sinking down to the ground.

But she was certainly sinking into something far greater than she was. If she didn't act, it would overpower her.

Vaguely, the thought occurred to Taylor that she should be angry at Laredo. She should be pushing this egomaniac away with both hands.

And yet, she couldn't.

Didn't want to.

Instead, she wound her arms around his neck and brought her body in closer to his. She could feel the very blood rushing in her veins. Could feel every single rock-hard ridge of Laredo's frame against hers.

Adrenaline raced through her, heightening what she was feeling.

The fact that she was aware of his arms closing around her, of his mouth working nothing short of magic over hers, only deepened her pleasure rather than ignited her indignation.

What the hell was wrong with her? Why was she enjoying this? Didn't she realize that he was pleasuring himself at her expense?

Why wasn't she angry?

Because she was too swept away. And enjoying this far too much.

Somewhere in the back of her mind, Taylor was conscious of the restaurant door opening and then closing again. Of people—a couple—sidestepping them as they left Fiorello's.

Were they staring at them? She didn't know. Didn't

care. All she wanted was for this delicious sensation to continue.

And then it stopped. Just like that, there was space between her lips and his. The contact, the almost spiritual binding of souls, was suddenly broken.

She only realized that her eyes were shut when she had to open them. At the same moment, she heard Laredo say, "Wow."

Had she possessed the strength, she would have pulled back her hand and slapped him. But as it was, her arms hung almost limply at her sides.

Useless.

At least he wasn't smirking.

"You certainly pack some kind of a wallop, Detective McIntyre," Laredo murmured as his eyes swept over her face. There was something different in his voice, something she couldn't identify. "Maybe I should be the one who's afraid."

She cleared her throat, hoping that she wouldn't squeak when she spoke.

"Maybe you should be," she agreed.

"Would it be too presumptuous if I assumed that you weren't bored?"

She stared at him, trying to process what he was asking. Her mind was as numb as her body was not. "What?"

"Bored," he repeated. "Back in the restaurant, you said you were afraid of being bored. You didn't act as if you were bored, but I've learned never to take anything for granted."

Bored? Ecstatic, delirious, excited beyond belief, yes. Definitely not bored.

But she would die before she admitted it. She wasn't in the business of feeding egos and his, she was certain, was large enough.

"Maybe you should learn not to ask so many questions," she told him, turning her back on Laredo and beginning to walk away.

"Can't," he called after her. For the time being, he let her go. He needed time to himself to process what had just happened. "It's the nature of my job."

"See you tomorrow, Laredo," she said without turning around.

"Count on it."

That, she thought, was just the problem.

What she needed, Taylor told herself as she got in behind the steering wheel of her vehicle, was a cold shower and a hot drink. Preferably something to knock her out. And to erase the lingering effects of his mouth on hers.

She wondered if there was an eraser large enough.

Chapter 8

"Something wrong, Johnny?" was the first thing Chester Laredo asked when he opened his front door that evening.

As tall as his grandson and almost as muscular and trim, Chet Laredo had the same bright blue eyes and he sported an identical full head of hair, although his was a mixture of black and gray with just a little white weaving through.

He stepped back now, allowing Laredo to enter, studying his grandson carefully. There was something different about him tonight, but he couldn't quite put his finger on it.

In his seventies, Chet had worked for all of his adult life, but he had never been one of those people, no matter where his work took him, who'd been too busy for his family. Johnny's welfare always had top priority over everything else and he'd lived his life accordingly.

The aroma of something tasty and familiar wafted from the kitchen. No matter where he traveled, this would always be home to him, Laredo thought fondly. More accurately, the man he'd stopped by to see would always be home to him.

Comfortably planting himself on the sofa, Laredo looked up at the older man. His grandfather was studying him. *You can take the man out of the CIA, but you can't take the CIA out of the man,* he thought, amused.

"Does something have to be wrong for a grandson to stop by to see the crusty old man who raised him?" Laredo asked innocently.

About to lower himself into the richly padded armchair adjacent to the sofa, Chet pretended to scowl.

"Hey, watch that 'old' stuff, boy," Chet warned. "I can still take you, you know." And then he added with a fond smile, "Just not with one hand tied behind my back anymore."

"Take me?" Laredo questioned.

"Yup." Reaching for his remote, Chet shut off the early news program he'd been watching off and on for the last hour. "I still have a few moves up my sleeve."

Laredo laughed. "I thought you taught me everything you knew."

A look that could only be described as wicked amusement slipped over the older man's features. "Not everything, Johnny. Some things I kept back for a later date. A man always wants to be useful to his family."

Laredo smiled at that. He couldn't help thinking how

very different his life would have turned out had his father's father not been there for him. Chet had taken both him and his mother in when his father, Bret, a Navy SEAL, was killed on a mission whose exact details he would probably never learn. And then, several years later, his mother had died in a car accident. Laredo knew he would have been deemed an orphan and absorbed by the system had it not been for his grandfather's very large heart.

There were no words to describe how grateful he was—and always would be—to his grandfather.

"I think you went way beyond 'useful' a long time ago, Chet."

Chet smiled, both at the compliment and at the fact that his grandson remembered to address him by his first name. "Grandpa" had always made him feel as if he were being put out to pasture prematurely, something he'd vowed a long time ago would never happen.

That was the reason why he'd taken himself off the active roster at the CIA and opened up his own security firm a little more than five years ago. He firmly believed that work, the right kind of work, kept a man vital.

So did the right kind of woman. He'd shared both thoughts with his grandson more than once, especially the latter. It pained Chet that while his own son had been married and a father at Johnny's age, Johnny was still very much unattached—and appeared to be content to remain that way.

Though he didn't say it, he wanted to bounce his great-grandchild on his knee before he was dispatched on his final mission.

"Flattery will get you nowhere, boy." Piercing blue

eyes narrowed as Chet looked at his grandson. "And it won't distract me. Now, I repeat, is there something wrong?"

There were times Laredo could *swear* his grandfather was clairvoyant. But he kept a poker face as he said, "Why would you ask?"

Chet leaned over the arm of his chair, moving a shade closer to his grandson. "Because you look like something's just rattled the foundations of your world."

Laredo shook his head. "Nope, foundations are just fine and unrattled." Quickly, he changed the subject. Chet had a way of being able to delve right into his head and he really didn't want to talk about Taylor and what had happened outside the restaurant. "Look, I stopped by to let you know that your girlfriend's daughter's murder might not be an isolated incident after all."

That surprised Chet. He slid to the edge of the armchair. Johnny had his attention. "What do you mean by that?"

"There was another murder today." Laredo was surprised that the TV stations weren't carrying the story yet. "A middle-school teacher. They found him in the supply closet. Whoever killed him used the same M.O. that Eileen's killer had."

"You mean there's a serial killer running loose?" Chet asked. Serial killers were not as uncommon as the public might think. It just took the right detective to make the connection between crimes. Being able to share information made the discovery that much easier.

Laredo spread his hands. As far as he knew, the verdict was still out on that. It could just be one person, enamored with a certain method, seeking revenge against a couple of people.

"Maybe, maybe not."

Chet snorted. Some of the tension left his shoulders. "Just like your father. Double-talk. Talk straight, Johnny," he ordered. "If the M.O. is the same for both murders, why wouldn't you think it was the work of a serial killer?"

"Because the two victims had a connection."

A familiar, keen look entered his grandfather's blue eyes. Laredo knew that his grandfather absorbed every word, every nuance and that his mind was factoring it all in.

"A connection? What was it?" Chet prodded.

"Seems that the dead teacher got Eileen Stevens pregnant when they were both in high school."

Chet whistled softly to himself. "Damn, life certainly has a way of surprising you."

The observation had Laredo's thoughts immediately shifting to Taylor. There was no denying that he'd surprised himself when he had kissed her. He'd been even more surprised by his reaction to that simplest of intimate acts. The woman had damn near curled his toes and that didn't happen easily. Or often. Laredo wasn't altogether certain he liked that.

"Yeah, it does."

Chet watched him for a long moment, as if plucking thoughts out of his grandson's head. "You're not talking about the case, are you?"

"Sure I am, Chet." Laredo's tone was deliberately light. "You know, Carole Stevens isn't a bad-looking lady."

"No, she's not," Chet wholeheartedly agreed, allowing Laredo to change the topic.

Laredo had never known his grandmother, other than through photographs. Michelle Laredo had died before he was born. His grandfather could stand a little female companionship in his later years.

"Maybe you could offer her a shoulder to lean on," Laredo suggested.

"Been thinking about it," his grandfather admitted, nodding his head.

"Maybe you should do more than just think," Laredo coaxed.

Chet laughed. It was a rounded, full-bodied sound. "Since when have you decided to play Cupid?" Chet asked. "Seems to me that I haven't seen a lady on your arm for way too long."

Laredo grinned. "I've been busy. Besides, I wouldn't bring them around where an old fox like you could steal them away from me."

Chet doubted that anyone could steal the woman his grandson set his mind to.

"Steal them?" Chet echoed. "Hell, I'd be too happy to see you finally settling down to do anything except hit my knees and give up a prayer of thanksgiving." He eyed Laredo "That going to be happening anytime soon?" his grandfather asked.

"Hitting your knees and praying?" Laredo asked innocently. "I'd say that was entirely up to you, Chet." He took pity on the man and added, "As for the other part, I'll get back to you on that."

"You do that, Johnny." The subject, he knew, was

closed. For now. Chet rose to his feet. "I was just going to sit down and have some dinner. Join me?"

"I already ate. But I can keep you company," Laredo offered.

Chet smiled and slipped an arm around his grandson's shoulders as they both walked into the kitchen. "I'd like that."

Taylor usually slept like a rock. The minute her head hit the pillow, she was out. Zach had once speculated that she could probably fall asleep hanging from a hook in the closet. When she was tired, nothing got in the way of her getting a good night's sleep.

Nothing but the unnerving memory of J. C. Laredo's mouth and the magic it effortlessly wove as it passed over her own.

When she went to bed, Taylor was exhausted, but it didn't matter. Sleep had gone off on a holiday without any warning or forwarding address, leaving her tossing and turning. Every fiber of her being insisted on reliving those few moments in front of the restaurant, when time and the world had stood still and someone had turned up an inferno.

Questions popped up in her head. Questions that would never receive any answers because there was no scenario that would lead to her making love with the tall, sexy private investigator. God knew that she was not about to feed Laredo's ego or blunder into a situation she had no experience with.

There'd never been a man in her life she'd even remotely wanted to plan a future with, or even make love with. And Laredo would probably recoil in horror if he knew she was a virgin.

Besides, she was certain that the longing she felt would bring nothing but disappointment because, in her experience, her imagination was far more satisfying than anything reality had to offer. Turning on her side again, Taylor punched her pillow, vainly trying to find a soothing, comfortable place for herself. There just wasn't any to be found tonight.

Damn the man and his lethal mouth anyway.

She needed all her faculties in top running order, not feeling as if she'd been used to wipe the floor. If she didn't get some sleep soon, she would be a zombie come morning.

Another hour passed and she was still doing a human imitation of a spinning top. Desperate, Taylor got up and went to her medicine cabinet. A couple minutes of rummaging around and she found what she was looking for. It was one of those nighttime headache remedies that tacked the letters *P.M.* to the end of its brand name. She'd picked it up in the store a couple of months ago by mistake, then decided there was no harm in keeping the pills until their expiration date came up. "Just in case."

"Just in case" had arrived.

Resigned, Taylor popped one pill into her mouth, swallowing it without water, an ability that always made her sister shiver when she saw her do it. Hoping that would do the trick, Taylor went back to bed.

Lying down, she willed the over-the-counter medication to work.

* * *

Taylor had no idea what time she dropped off to sleep. All she knew was that when she finally woke up, early sunlight was shining into her bedroom and she felt as if someone had run her over with a double-coupled semi. Twice.

She was also running late. She should have already *been* at work, not getting ready for it.

"Damn, damn, damn."

Bolting out of bed, Taylor hurried into her shower. She was about to turn on the water when she looked down and saw that she was still wearing the jersey she used as a nightgown. Talk about being out of it. No more sleep remedies for her.

"Get with it, McIntyre," she ordered sternly.

Peeling off the jersey, Taylor hurled it onto the floor outside the shower. She turned the cold water on and let it blast her in an effort to get into gear. But she hadn't counted on it to rival the temperature of ice cubes.

A screech sounding not unlike a tortured cat escaped her lips as she quickly grasped the faucet and moved it toward a less-than-subzero setting.

She was just beginning to breathe normally again when she thought she heard a door banging open.

Her door?

Before the thought could actually register, Taylor saw the outline of someone through the frosted glass.

Someone who was running into her bathroom.

The only weapon that was available was the long-handled scrub brush. Better than nothing. She grabbed it just as the shower door was being yanked open.

Outrage flooded through her when she saw who it was. Laredo!

"Are you all right?"

The question, begun in concern, drifted away as the sight of her imprinted itself on his brain. Belatedly, he jerked his eyes back up to her face.

Embarrassed, furious, words failed her. Taylor grabbed the shower door and pulled it out of Laredo's hand, slamming it so hard it popped open again. She bit off a curse as she closed it a second time.

He'd gone too far this time, she thought, outraged.

"What the hell do you think you're doing?" she sputtered.

She heard him answer his own question before he addressed hers.

"I guess you are all right." And then he apologized. "Sorry, I heard you scream and I thought you were in trouble."

"I didn't scream, I gasped," she corrected angrily. "Don't you know the difference? The water was cold. And what are you doing here, anyway?" How much longer did she have to put up with Laredo popping up where he didn't belong?

"Looking for you," Laredo answered simply. His back to the shower stall, he addressed his words to the opposite wall. "I called the precinct, but they said you hadn't come in yet. So I thought I'd swing by your place to see if you'd left yet. When I saw your car parked in your space, I thought maybe you were running late for some reason."

That still didn't answer her question. "Why are you

here?" Taylor enunciated each word with barely suppressed anger.

He had her trapped, she thought. There was no way she could keep her dignity and still step out to get her towel. She stared at the back of Laredo's head. If he turned around, she was going to have him drawn and quartered.

"Hand me that towel that's hanging on the rack," she instructed. "And keep your eyes forward."

There was no missing the warning note in her voice. Laredo took the towel and, still averting his eyes, held it out to her. He felt her grabbing the towel out of his hand, heard her yanking it through the small opening she'd allowed between the frosted door and the shower frame. When he heard the door being shut again, he moved back to the spot where he'd been standing and resumed staring at the opposite wall.

"I didn't mean to startle you," he told her by way of an apology.

She didn't answer.

Wrapping the towel tightly around herself, Taylor secured it. The realization that it was a little like closing the barn door after the horse had run away didn't escape her. She was certain Laredo had gotten more than just a fleeting glimpse of her naked body when he'd yanked the door open.

"I'm waiting," Taylor announced as she opened the door and stepped out of the shower stall.

Very cautiously, he turned around until he was facing her. Damn, but she looked sexy, he couldn't help thinking. Even with dripping hair and no makeup. But, sexy or not, he had no idea what she was talking about.

"For…?" he asked, leaving the rest of it up in the air.

In a perfect world, her answer would somehow dovetail with the sensations and blatant desires now charging madly throughout his system, threatening to overwhelm him if he lowered his guard. With very little encouragement, he would have gladly yanked the damp towel away from her body and set about pleasuring them both. Her first because he knew she had to be won over. But, in doing that, in pleasing her, he would also accomplish bringing pleasure to himself.

Laredo cleared his throat as he struggled to get his mind back on the right track. It took a surprising amount of effort.

The reason why he'd come looking for her in the first place was all but forgotten in the wake of the reason he wanted to be here now. He wanted her. Wanted her in every damn sense of the word, Laredo thought as itches that he wasn't at liberty to scratch ran rampant through him.

Suddenly warmer than she knew the room temperature warranted, Taylor felt incredibly vulnerable. She absolutely hated that.

"I'm waiting for you to tell me why you came looking for me," she choked out. He had no right to be here, shaking her up like this, no right at all.

It took Laredo a second to actually remember what had originally brought him here. "I had an idea."

She'd thought he'd burst in because of something big, like—God forbid—another body being found. Taylor blew out a breath. "I will alert the media, but first, get the hell out of my bedroom," she ordered, walking past him as she crossed from the bathroom to her bedroom. She had to get dressed and she wasn't about to do it with Laredo standing in the room. With her luck, he probably had eyes in the back of his head.

Laredo gave her no argument. He stepped out into the tiny hallway that led from her bedroom into the living room. The second he crossed the threshold, the door behind him slammed shut. It barely missed hitting him in the butt.

"I could have you arrested, you know," she informed him, raising her voice so that it carried through the closed door. Quickly, she hurried into her clothes. "For breaking and entering," she elaborated in case the charges escaped him.

"I had probable cause," he countered. "I heard you scream."

She laughed shortly. "And you were coming to my rescue."

"Yeah, I was."

Finished dressing, Taylor sighed at the answer, then opened the door. Maybe he was telling the truth. Besides, she didn't have time to waste having him booked, even though the idea was more than a little tempting.

"Okay," she told him, walking out holding a pair of shoes in her hand. She dropped them on the floor and then stepped into them. "We'll let it go for now." Adjusting the back of one shoe, she looked at him. "What's this big idea you couldn't wait to share?"

"I don't know how big it is," he prefaced, "but I thought we could take a picture of Crawford and show it to that security guard in Eileen's building. Who knows, maybe Crawford paid her a visit or two and that set off a chain of events."

Offhand, she didn't see how they could follow that up, seeing as how both participants were dead, but stranger things had happened.

After rolling the suggestion over in her head, she shrugged. "Can't hurt, I suppose."

All things considered, the idea wasn't half-bad, but she wasn't about to admit that to him. Not just yet, anyway. She was still trying to come to terms with the fact that he had seen her naked. She knew he had despite the fact that he had been quick to avert his eyes and she had yanked the door out of his hands at lightning speed. There had been a split second. She had almost *felt* his eyes slide over her. Maybe not at length, but still thoroughly.

"Nope," he agreed, "can't hurt—and it might just lead us somewhere." Anything was better than just sitting around, twiddling his thumbs and reviewing notes he'd already committed to memory.

"Maybe," she allowed without feeling. Taylor twisted her still-damp hair into a knot and then secured it with a couple of pins.

He looked at her more closely. "You look a little tired, Detective McIntyre. Up all night working the case?" he guessed.

No, up trying to work you out of my mind. "Something like that," she answered.

"We can stop for breakfast if you want," he offered, following her out of the apartment. "Orange juice might perk you up. I can drive so that you don't run the risk of falling asleep behind the wheel."

If he was trying to ingratiate himself with her, the man was wasting his time. "I don't eat breakfast and I am more than capable of driving my own car," she informed him tersely.

"Shouldn't skip breakfast," he told her cheerfully. "Most important meal of the day."

"So Andrew Cavanaugh likes to say," she murmured under her breath.

"Wise man."

"Yes, he is. You, however, are an annoying man—and on borrowed time," she underscored.

"I grow on people," he assured her.

"So does fungus," she pointed out. "That doesn't exactly make it something to look forward to."

"We're definitely stopping for coffee," he informed her with finality.

Chapter 9

After stopping at the precinct in order to pick up the best photograph from the ones that had been taken of Terrance Crawford at the crime scene, Laredo and Taylor went to see the security guard at Eileen Stevens's building. Taylor insisted on using separate cars.

"I'm beginning to think you don't like my company, Detective McIntyre," Laredo observed when she told him she intended to go in her own car—and he was welcome to follow in his if he wanted.

She smiled, but just barely. "I guess you really *are* astute, Laredo."

"And you, Detective McIntyre, are one tough lady." He noticed that his observation pleased her.

Pressing a button, Laredo released the security

system in his vehicle. It beeped twice in response as all four locks popped open.

"As long as you know," Taylor replied, getting into her car.

Even though he knew the way, Laredo opted to follow behind her. As it turned out, if he hadn't, he would have missed her vehicle suddenly veering off the given course. He watched in surprise as she drove off in an entirely different direction.

What was going on here?

Taking care not to lose sight of her car, Laredo flipped open his cell phone. Eyes on the road, he pressed the number 9, which was the key he had assigned to her cell phone when he'd programmed it in the other day.

The phone rang three times before she answered.

"Trying to ditch me, Detective?" he asked.

Up ahead, he saw her make a sharp right. His was wider as he pushed down on the accelerator, determined not to lose her.

Taylor glanced up into her rearview mirror and saw him narrowly avoid fishtailing. "No, but I can give you a ticket for talking on your cell phone while driving."

"Police business," he pointed out. It was one of the exceptions to the ruling that had recently been passed against cell phone usage in cars. "Besides, I'm using a speakerphone. You can save your ticket, Detective. I've got both hands on the wheel." He heard her sigh and smiled to himself. "By the way, I thought you said we were going to The Villas."

"We were, but that'll have to wait. I just got a call."

He didn't have to guess what the call entailed. Her lieutenant wouldn't have abruptly rerouted her to an entirely different case. That meant that another body, sporting a leather choker, had turned up to be added to the list.

This was getting out of hand. "You're kidding."

"I only wish," she said with feeling, watching the road for the next turn. "Dispatch just got a call that two patrolmen found another body. This time it was in an alley."

He shared her feeling of disbelief. "The same M.O. as the others?"

"Same M.O. And it gets better," she added wearily. This newest development tended to blow the other theories out of the water. "This time, the victim is a homeless man."

She heard Laredo whistle softly under his breath. "Sounds like we really do have a serial killer on our hands," he speculated.

On the outside, yes, but she still harbored doubts. But for now, she'd agree with him. "Looks like it."

Laredo watched as the vehicle in front of him turned right at the next corner. He followed suit. "You don't sound convinced."

The way he could crawl into her head made her uneasy. What else could he intuit? "Could have been done to throw us off," she speculated. "The killer obviously has no problem taking a life. Who better to kill for the purposes of camouflage than some homeless man nobody is going to miss?"

There was silence on the other end, as if he was thinking. She didn't have time for this. But just as she was about to close the phone, he spoke up. "You've got a point, Detective McIntyre."

Detective McIntyre. His usage of her title and last name in almost every other sentence got on her nerves. It was formal and there was nothing formal about him. Besides, he'd kissed her and burst into her bathroom while she was taking a shower. The damn man had seen her naked. Somehow, calling her "Detective" with every other breath felt as if the private investigator was mocking her.

"You can call me Taylor."

"Thank you, Detective McIntyre." Laredo didn't bother keeping the grin out of his voice. In response, he heard the *click* of her phone as she terminated the call.

No two ways about it, he thought, tucking his phone back into his pocket, she was definitely one fascinating woman.

Taylor rocked back on her heels as she studied the dead man on the ground, trying not to let the stench of his body overwhelm her.

It was a homeless man, all right. And he had been murdered in the same fashion as the lawyer and the teacher before him had. The man, roughly in his mid-fifties she judged, had had his hands and feet bound, with duct tape over his mouth and a piece of leather stretched to the limit around his neck.

Taylor didn't need a coroner to tell her that the man had died from strangulation. The ventricular hemorrhaging in his eyes told her that.

A thorough search performed by the younger of the two patrolmen showed that the man had no identification on him.

Rising, Taylor dusted off her knees. "Tell the M.E. I want this man fingerprinted. Maybe we'll get lucky and he served in the military or held down a government job—"

"Or served time," Laredo interjected.

"Yes, there's that, too." At the very least, she could hope that the man'd held a California license in the last ten years. Thumbprints were required and all it took was one match to tell them who this latest victim was. She didn't like the fact that he was anonymous. What if he was the key to it all?

She heard the coroner's van pulling up into the alley. Taylor stepped back to give the attendants who emerged from the vehicle room to work. As she watched, trying to make sense of this latest development, the attendants bagged the body, placed it on the gurney and then withdrew.

That was when she saw it. There was a card on the ground. It had been missed because it had fallen beneath the body.

Was that deliberate? she wondered, taking out a handkerchief. She used it to pick up the card.

"I need to bag this," she told the closest crime scene investigator. The man took a plastic bag out of his case and handed it to her. Taylor slipped the card inside very carefully, sealed the opening and then studied it.

"It's a mass card," Laredo observed, looking over her shoulder.

"I know what it is," she told him. She flipped the card onto its face. There was a picture of St. Thomas More on the other side. "There's a saint you don't see every day," she murmured more to herself than to him.

"The card there by accident?" Laredo voiced the question that was on her mind as well. "Or is the killer trying to tell us something?"

If that was the intent behind leaving the mass card beneath the murder victim's body, a multitude of questions began to spring up in her head.

"Why now?" she asked. "Why with the third victim and not the other two?"

Laredo shrugged. "I guess we're going to have to catch him before we find that part out."

Very carefully, she slipped the mass card into her purse. The fact that Laredo was injecting himself into the investigation on all levels was not lost on her.

"I thought you were just investigating Eileen's murder," she reminded him.

"They all seem to be connected. I might as well try to help."

She didn't see him as the altruistic type. "I bet you were a Boy Scout when you were a kid."

It was meant as a sarcastic remark. She wasn't prepared for him to seriously answer her. "As a matter of fact, I was. My mother thought it would make me a more rounded person. She thought they had a damn fine motto: Always Be Prepared."

A man who spoke fondly of his mother couldn't be all bad—even if he did burst into bathrooms. "Sounds like a nice lady."

A quiet note of sadness fleetingly entered his eyes. "She was."

Was. As in past tense. She hadn't meant to put her foot in her mouth—or to bring up any bad memories for him. She knew what it felt like to lose a parent. The funny thing was, before he was gone, she never thought losing her father would affect her. But it had. No matter what faults he'd had, he'd still been her father.

"I'm very sorry for your loss."

Laredo had come to terms with losing his mother, but there was a measure of pain, firmly entrenched in the background. "She died a long time ago, but thanks."

Taylor found that, despite herself, she was curious about him. "Your father raise you by himself?"

He shook his head. "My father died a few years before she did. He was a Navy SEAL on a mission that didn't quite turn out the way everyone expected," he filled in before she could ask.

"Oh." He'd lost two people in his life—and she had lost her father twice. The first time around, the undercover narcotics detective had faked his death but it had hurt just like the real thing.

"My grandfather raised me," Laredo told her, adding, "when he didn't have to."

Chester Laredo had been under no obligation to take him and his widowed mother in and definitely under no obligation to opt to raise him on his own after his mother was killed. Chet could have hidden behind the demands of his job, which were enormous, but he didn't.

"So anytime he asks me for a favor, I'm more than happy to oblige in any way I can."

Every time she tried to write this man off, he'd unexpectedly display an admirable trait. It was getting harder and harder to actively dislike him—and she felt she needed to for her own self-preservation.

Taylor nodded in response to his last comment. "Yeah, I could see why." She turned to the two patrol-men who had been first on the scene. "I'd like you to canvass the area, please," she requested. "See if anyone knew this man or saw anything suspicious." She gave each man her card. "Call me if you find out anything at all, and I mean *anything*." Done, she turned to Laredo. Funny, she thought, in an odd way she was getting used to having him at her elbow. "C'mon."

"Yes, ma'am." She couldn't make up her mind if he was having fun at her expense or not as Laredo fell into place beside her. "Mind if I ask where we're go-ing?"

"Where we were going before I got this call," she reminded him. "To show the security guard at The Villas Terrance Crawford's picture. It's about time we caught a break."

Maybe, just maybe, the guard, Nathan, would recog-nize the picture and it would make him remember some-thing that would enlighten them.

"What do you mean he's gone?"

Taylor stared at the senior security officer, Ralph Wilson, who was posted at the front desk. When she'd asked to speak to Nathan, Wilson replied that Nathan was "gone."

An uneasy feeling began to tighten in her stomach. "As in gone for the day?" she asked.

"No," the older man said in a voice that sounded raw

from forty years of smoking over a pack a day. "As in forever. The kid quit with next to no notice. Said he felt horrible about that woman being killed on his watch and that he couldn't work here anymore." It was obvious that Wilson saw what Nathan had done as being dereliction of duty, not to mention a lack of discipline and commitment. Wilson shook his head in disgust. "I tried to tell him he was overreacting, but you know these sensitive types." Wilson fairly spat out the words, leaving them hanging in the air.

There was no doubt in her mind that the man didn't think very highly of sensitivity when it came to the male gender. But she wasn't here to argue about the merits of sensitivity or its drawbacks.

"Do you have an address for Nathan?"

A spark of contempt flickered through his brown eyes. "Of course I do. We have all our employees fill out forms when we hire them."

Turning the small computer monitor on the side of the desk so that it faced him and no one else, Wilson slowly pressed several key combinations. Eventually, he pulled up the screen.

"Right here," he announced.

Taylor quickly copied down the address, aware that Laredo was looking at the screen over her shoulder.

Frowning, he addressed the security guard. "You sure this is the address he gave you?"

The guard blustered. "Of course I'm sure. All the forms are scanned into the program." Eyebrows that could definitely use a weeding narrowed, joining together over a very sharp, prominent nose. "Why?"

Laredo saw Taylor eyeing him quizzically as well. "Because, unless the city's found a new way to make buildings go up instantly, as of two weeks ago that—" he pointed to the line on the application with the street address on it "—was a warehouse. Deserted the last time I looked."

Damn it! Taylor scowled. She knew better than to doubt him now, but she still had to ask. "How do you know that?"

"Another case I was working on," he replied vaguely, adding, "nasty business." Client-investigator privilege prevented him from elaborating that he'd tracked down a fourteen-year-old kidnapping victim to the warehouse and rescued her before she could be sold into a foreign prostitution ring.

Taylor sighed. "Nathan," or whatever his name really was, had duped them. Had duped her. She hated being taken. "Are you sure?" she pressed. The sinking feeling in her stomach already gave her the answer.

Laredo glanced at the screen a second time to verify the address, then nodded. "I'm sure."

The news was not received well by the head security officer either. He strung several curses together under his breath before saying, "Why the hell would Nathan give us a false address?"

"To go along with his false name," Taylor answered, trying to bank down her frustration. Everything the so-called guard had told her was now suspect.

Why had "Nathan" lied? Unless—damn it, had she been talking to Eileen's murderer all along?

Because of the information "Nathan" had given her,

she'd wasted precious time calling florists and showing the sketch to see if anyone had noticed the phantom delivery man.

Taylor's exasperation grew exponentially. There was only one conclusion she could come to. "There was no delivery man," she said to Laredo.

He'd already thought of that, but refrained from saying it out loud since it would be like rubbing salt into her wounds.

Instead, he just nodded. "That's a distinct possibility."

Taylor swallowed a groan. Taking out her cell phone, she called the precinct, asking the operator to connect her to one of the computer technicians. Two rings later, she spoke with someone who identified himself as Larry Lopez.

"Larry, this is Detective Taylor McIntyre. I need you to get me everything and anything you can on a Nathan Miller." She paused for a second, then added, "I'm not sure if he exists."

Rather than complain or issue a disclaimer, the man on the other end sounded as if he had just become enthusiastic. "Love a challenge. Hang on, Detective, I can just put you on hold. Shouldn't take too long to find out if he exists one way or another."

Before she could tell him that she preferred being called back, Taylor found herself listening to rousing music that sounded vaguely familiar. She didn't bother trying to place it.

"Anything?" Laredo asked her when it became apparent that she was on hold.

Instead of answering, she held up her phone to his

ear. And watched him smile. She struggled to ignore how the sight stirred her on so many levels. Now was neither the time nor the place to get sidetracked. And certainly not with him. She had no doubt that the man probably thought of himself as charm personified and had a woman for every week of the calendar year.

"*The Magnificent Seven*," he said, nodding his head in approval. When she looked at him quizzically, he couldn't bring himself to believe that she wasn't familiar with it. "Great movie, remake of a Japanese classic, *Seven Samurai*." He watched Taylor to see if any of this rang a bell for her.

It didn't.

Taylor shrugged dismissively. "I wouldn't know about that."

Laredo looked at her in disbelief. "You've never seen it?"

"That would be the implication behind *I wouldn't know*," she agreed. The other members of her family, particularly Riley, were movie buffs. She usually watched and forgot what she viewed once the credits faded to black.

This was not something he could leave alone. "I've got it in my collection. I could screen it for you," he offered.

Oh, no, no personal time with this man. That path, she was now convinced, only led to trouble. "Maybe some other time."

"I didn't mean this minute," he told her, amusement in his eyes.

She took offense. And being on hold always made her impatient. "I don't appreciate you laughing at me, Laredo."

"I'm not laughing," he contradicted. "I'm just enjoying you."

She was spared from responding to that because at that moment, Larry came back on the line.

"I've got some good news and some bad news," the computer tech told her. "Which would you like to hear first?"

Right about now, she could definitely stand to hear some good news. The choice was not difficult. "The good news."

She tilted the cell phone so that Laredo could hear as well.

The second his head bent close to hers, Taylor felt something warm and receptive moving through her. Sharing the phone was a tactical mistake, but pulling it away would be an even bigger one.

She hoped Larry talked fast.

"Okay. The good news, Detective McIntyre, is that Nathan Miller did exist."

Taylor picked up on the only word that mattered. "Did?"

"Yes, ma'am. Nathan Miller died in 2000. He drowned while on vacation. It was a freak accident."

I just bet it was. "Terrific," she said out loud just before she flipped her phone closed.

"Think our Nathan killed the real Nathan?" Laredo asked.

It was as if the private investigator could read her mind. She definitely wasn't comfortable with that parlor trick.

"I don't know," she admitted. With a weary sigh that

came straight from her toes, she said in disgust, "Back to square one."

She expected Laredo to agree and was surprised when he said, "Not necessarily."

Chapter 10

"What do you mean, *not necessarily?*" Taylor asked.

Now that she'd agreed to let him hang around, she couldn't help wondering if he was going to make her resort to dragging information out of him. She wasn't in the mood for games.

Laredo didn't answer her.

Instead, he strode back to the security guard at the front desk. A second before he reached the man, she realized what Laredo had to be thinking.

Of course.

"The logbook," she said out loud.

Laredo glanced at her over his shoulder and grinned. "Exactly."

"Nathan" had handled the logbook, at least once in her presence when he'd picked it up to supposedly look at the previous day's sign-in sheet. That meant the man's fingerprints had to be on the book.

Along with who knew how many others, but at least it was a start.

"I'm afraid we're going to have to impound your logbook for a while," she told the retired policeman just as Laredo reached him.

Clearly on the same wavelength, Wilson nodded. "And you're going to want the fingerprints of all the other security guards so you can rule out their prints on the book."

Taylor smiled, relieved that she wouldn't have any arguments. It was nice dealing with someone who didn't immediately balk at routine police procedures. Far too many people reacted as if their personal space was being violated when asked to cooperate with an investigation.

"Yes, I am," she agreed.

Wilson took out his cell phone and pressed a button on the keypad, getting started. "I'll round them up for you."

She nodded her gratitude. "In the meantime, I'll get someone from CSI out here to collect their fingerprints." But as she took out her phone again, Laredo caught her arm, stopping her. Now what? "What do you think you're doing?"

"No need to call anyone," he told her, releasing her arm. "I've got everything we need in the trunk of my car."

We. She was getting used to that, God help her. She was also getting used to going along with him. Was that a mistake?

"The Boy Scout thing again?" she asked, flipping her

phone closed. She followed him out of the building as he went to his car.

"Absolutely."

She could hear the grin in his voice. He was probably pretty pleased with himself, but since he was being useful, she let it go.

"Your Boy Scout handbook have a theory about why there was a mass card left at the last murder and not at the other two?"

Reaching his car, he pointed his key at it and pressed the button to disarm the security system.

"Our boy is branching out?" It wasn't a statement but a question.

"Maybe," Taylor allowed. "But what does leaving the card mean?" she pressed. Not waiting for an answer, she used him as a sounding board—the way she would have used Aaron had he been there. "Mass cards are given out as keepsakes at Catholic funeral masses. The name of the deceased is printed on the front. There was no name on the card."

He had no theory, not even a good guess. "Odd sense of humor?" he suggested.

She didn't hear him. There were too many questions crowding her head. "And why St. Thomas More? Because the card was handy and he had access to it for some reason—or was there some point to it being St. Thomas rather than another saint?"

Laredo thought for a moment, sorting the vast amount of trivia he'd picked up in his lifetime. "St. Thomas was staunch about his faith. Maybe the guy that was killed strayed from the path and the killer left him

a card so that St. Thomas can show him the way back."
It was only a shot in the dark, a wild guess at best.

Taylor looked at him sharply. "So the killer was
doing a good deed?" That didn't sound likely.

Laredo opened his trunk. There were several plastic
boxes, their contents neatly organized. "Hey, even the
most rotten scum have a little bit of good in them."

Leaning against the trunk, Taylor looked in. What the
hell was this man carrying around? Frustrated in more
ways than one, she blew out a breath. "Speaking from
experience, Laredo?"

"Just the optimist in me." Finding what he needed,
he took the small box out and closed the trunk. He held
the print kit up for her benefit. "Let's get started collect-
ing prints."

Taylor fell into step beside him as they walked back
to the entrance of the building.

"I guess you are kind of a handy person to have
around." It was a compliment she paid grudgingly, but
she knew he deserved it.

Holding the door open for her, he let Taylor walk in
first. "You just beginning to notice that?"

"Don't let it go to your head," she warned, crossing
the threshold.

He followed her in. "No, ma'am."

The way he said it made her smile even though she
tried hard not to.

It wasn't lost on Laredo. He leaned his head in toward
her so that only she could hear. "See, I told you I'd
grow on you."

That was exactly what she was afraid of, she thought,

a shiver racing down her spine. And for the life of her, she wasn't able to explain, even to herself, why.

"ASAP, huh?" the crime scene investigator echoed Taylor's request back to her a little more than two hours later.

Taylor ignored the glib tone. "Sooner, if possible," she added.

The woman in the white lab coat, Wendy Allen, sighed dramatically. She waved at several neat although overwhelmingly high piles all lined up one beside the other on the steel-top table. Hardly any of the table was clearly visible.

"See all this?" she asked. "Same instructions. And they're all ahead of you." It was a blatant dismissal.

"Yes, but they're all complicated," Laredo told her, his low voice pulsing in the otherwise silent area. Taylor saw Wendy raise her eyes up to his face.

Like a flower to the sun, she couldn't help thinking. She watched as Laredo pushed the logbook toward the technician.

"This is just a matter of dusting the book for prints and comparing them to the ones Detective McIntyre's already brought you." His warm smile widened just a touch. "Should be a walk in the park for someone with your education and talents."

Taylor was about to laugh and tell him to save his breath because Wendy Allen wasn't the type of woman to have her head turned by a few flattering words. But even as she began to speak, Taylor saw the other woman, a staunch, no-nonsense technician, visibly melt. The smile on Wendy's lips was reminiscent of the girl she'd once been several long decades ago.

Wendy thought a moment, then asked, "Is this really urgent?" The question was addressed to Laredo, Taylor noted, not to her.

"Really." The single word undulated, warm and caressing, between them.

Impatience drummed through Taylor, but she held her tongue, watching.

The short-cropped hair bobbed just a little as Wendy finally nodded her head in response. "I'll see what I can do."

"That's all we can ask—" Laredo paused half a second as he read her name from the name tag on her coat "—Wendy." He underscored the name with a quick, intimate pat on her hand, and then he withdrew, the words, "Thank you," echoing in his wake.

Her breath all but gone, Taylor turned on her heel and hurried after the private investigator. He was out the door before she caught up.

"Aren't you ashamed of yourself?" she demanded once they were clear of the lab entrance and headed toward the elevator.

He slowed his pace slightly. "Why?"

He asked the question so innocently, for a second she thought he was oblivious to the effect he'd had on the crime scene investigator. But that was like the sun not knowing it cast light.

"Because—because you came on to her to get her to process my evidence first," Taylor accused him.

He still looked like the picture of innocence. "No, I

just stated your case for you." And then, because she seemed not to get it, he elaborated. "I *talked* to her as if she was a talented woman instead of a faceless technician." Reaching the elevator bank, he pressed the button on the wall. "People respond to that."

The man wasn't fooling her. He was anything but innocent here. "Don't you mean that *women* respond to that?"

He looked surprised at the attempt to differentiate. "Women are people, too." And then he smiled. "You're doing it again."

"Doing what?" Taylor demanded. She was struggling to hold her temper in check. What *was* it about this man that set her off so easily each and every time? She could be perfectly fine and halfway into a conversation with him, she started seeing red.

"Shooting sparks from your eyes." He paused to take the sight in. "You know, you're magnificent when you're angry."

Taylor rolled her eyes. She expected more from him than something so mundane. "That has got to be the most trite saying—"

The smile on his lips made the words on hers evaporate. "Doesn't make it any less true."

They stood by the elevator, but it might as well have been in the middle of a deserted island for all the foot traffic there was at the moment. For no particular reason—other than the look in his eyes—Taylor suddenly felt completely isolated.

Completely alone with a man who raised her body temperature with a single raise of his eyebrow. Completely alone and thinking of only one thing. That she wanted him to kiss her.

And then, the next second, Taylor wasn't thinking it. Wasn't thinking at all. She was too busy reacting to having her thoughts suddenly materializing and taking shape.

Laredo had cupped her face in his rough hands and had brought his mouth down to hers, even as his eyes held hers. Her lids fluttered shut at the moment of contact.

Fluttered shut just as her heart stopped beating for a long moment, then resumed with a vengeance, pounding so hard she was afraid that her heart would make a break for freedom and pop right out of her chest.

The rest of her wasn't interested in freedom. It was only interested in prolonging these wonderful sensations that she'd believed were possible only in dreams. Because this didn't exist in real life. She'd kissed enough men to know that. To know that magic and lightning and whatever else went into fictional accounts of men and women lost in the heat of a kiss didn't take place in the real world.

Every man who had ever kissed her hadn't even managed to set off a minor rumble, much less be instrumental in an earthquake that made every part of her weak as it sent her head spinning.

The earth actually moved. And then caught on fire.

Why did this man set her world on fire? Why did it have to be this particular irreverent man who caused such chaos in her world?

"Magnificent," Laredo murmured again as he finally drew back.

The elevator had arrived and its doors had opened. Having stood the obligatory several seconds, the ele-

vator car began to close its doors again. Laredo stuck
his arm in between the two steel plates that were
drawing closer, interrupting the beam that governed the
process. Touching his arm, the doors sprang all the way
open again.

Coming to, still dazed, Taylor managed to turn on her
heel. She crossed the metal threshold, walking into the
elevator car. She was grateful for the several seconds of
silence that ensued as she valiantly worked to pull
herself together.

Had she had the strength, she would have cursed
Laredo from the bottom of her soul.

This was the second time he'd kissed her and both
times he had, she found herself transforming from an
intelligent, highly capable, extremely logical and sharp
police detective to some tongue-tied idiot who was
nothing but a mass of conflicting feelings, functioning
without a single coherent thought in her head.

The silence abruptly ended as they got out on the
third floor.

"It can't end here, you know," Laredo told her as they
started to walk to the end of the hall, where her squad
room was located.

Relieved to be talking about work, she seized on the
topic. "It doesn't. There's a trail out there somewhere
that'll lead us to Nathan-whoever-he-really-is. The way
I see it, he's the most logical candidate for the three
murders." But when she spared Laredo a glance, she saw
that he was shaking his head.

"I'm not talking about that," he told her quietly. "I'm
talking about us."

A blast of heat passed over her, singeing her very soul.

"Us?" she echoed. Trying her best, Taylor banked down the nerves jumping around inside of her. The last thing she wanted was for them to be visible to this man who was to blame for it all. "There is no 'us,' Laredo."

"Oh, yes there is," the infuriating man contradicted. "You can tell yourself anything you like, Detective McIntyre, but there most definitely is an 'us.' Moreover, I think you know where this is going, too."

She stopped walking and glared at him. Why was he messing with her mind this way? "To hell on a toboggan?"

"Maybe eventually," Laredo allowed.

He never looked at relationships beyond a few days at a time, knowing he could count on nothing but himself. The uncertain world he'd lived in as a child had taught him that. After his mother had been killed in that automobile accident, he'd gotten up early every morning for a year and sneaked into his grandfather's bedroom. Not to crawl into the man's bed, but just to assure himself that his grandfather was still alive, still breathing. And then, reassured and relieved, just as quietly he'd tiptoe back out again.

"But before then…" Laredo's voice trailed off, allowing her to fill in the blanks.

"There is no before then, either," she told him tersely. "Look, I'm not one of those women—like Wendy, apparently—who are going to drop like some fly at your feet. For one thing, I have a mind. For another, I've got a killer to catch. Nothing else," she emphasized, "is going to get in the way of that." She took a breath. "Now, if you can help me with that, fine. If you can't,

I'll thank you to get out of my way, stop trying to distract me and let me do my work."

"Distract you?" he repeated, amused.

She threw up her hands and started walking again. Quickly. She'd said too much.

Taylor was aware that Laredo didn't drop back, didn't turn and head back toward the elevator. Instead, he quickened his gait until he caught up and was walking right next to her. Going in the same direction she was. Obviously, he'd opted to keep working with her.

She had no idea if that was a good or a bad thing. To an extent, he had destroyed her ability to think logically and coolly at all times. The man was like a burr under her saddle. And she was going to have to live with that.

For now.

Drawing a deep breath, she marched into the squad room and let the din absorb her.

One of the detectives she occasionally worked with looked up the moment she entered. Kevin Wong rose and crossed to her before she had a chance to toss her purse into her drawer.

"I was just about to call you," he told her. "You got a hit."

It took effort not to look behind her, at Laredo. God, she hoped that she didn't look as flustered as she felt.

"Come again?" she asked Wong.

In response, he dropped a folder with several pages in it on her desk. He smiled, obviously glad to be the bearer of positive news.

"Those prints on the dead homeless guy came back with a hit."

"That was fast." She picked up the folder, opening it. "Criminal record?" she asked just before she began to scan the pages herself.

After making eye contact with Laredo, Wong looked back at her and nodded. "Yeah. His name's Hank Dougherty. Or was. Been in trouble with the law ever since he stole his first car for a so-called joyride at the tender age of fourteen. He was two weeks shy of his fifteenth birthday," Wong supplied. "I was bored," he explained when she glanced at him quizzically. "It looked like interesting stuff."

"If you say so," she murmured. "And he's certainly not going to be in trouble with the law anymore."

Without bothering to sit down, Taylor scanned the next page and the few lines that were on the third before dropping the file back down on her desk.

Just another penny-ante crook, not worth anyone's second glance. Why was he singled out by the killer? Why that method, why that card?

"Okay," she said more to herself than to the detective who'd brought her the file, "I need to find out everything I can about Mr. Hank Dougherty and if there's anything at all that ties him to Eileen Stevens and/or our teacher of the year, Terrance Crawford."

At first glance, her gut feeling was that Hank Dougherty wasn't tied to the other two victims at all. The man was older, homeless, and looked as if the only contact he might have ever had with people from either Stevens's or Crawford's world would be to ask them for any spare change, but you just never knew.

"Why don't I take care of that for you?" Laredo offered, which seemed to surprise Taylor. He opened the file, spreading out the pages so that he could quickly go over each one. "I've got someone who's pretty good about filling in the blanks in people's histories. Especially if," he added, glancing at the first page of the printout, "there's a social security number to work with."

A social security number went a long way in making things easier for his contact. Or rather, his grandfather's old contact.

Old spies didn't die, Laredo thought with a smile, they just went into security work.

Taylor wanted to turn him down, wanted to send Laredo packing and on his way. But she couldn't. She needed help and she knew it. Solving the case took precedence over her pride every time. It was just a hard fact of life. But she didn't have to like it. Especially when something told her that she was allowing herself to slide into a dangerous situation without taking proper precautions.

"Thanks," she said. "But the file doesn't leave my sight," she stipulated.

He seemed all right with that. "Then neither will I," he told her, gathering the pages back together and closing the folder around them.

A catchphrase from a hokey old science fiction series that lived in perpetuity on one of the classic cable channels came echoing back to her: *Danger, Will Robinson. Danger!*

Amen to that. She was stuck with him in close proximity—and it was all her own doing.

Yet, when Laredo sat down at her missing partner's

desk and made himself comfortable as he got down to work, it somehow seemed natural to her.

She wasn't too tired to recognize that was a very dangerous sign. She was really going to have to stay on her guard from here on in.

Chapter 11

Taylor had trouble concentrating. Try as she might to shut out all outside distractions, she couldn't. Ordinarily, she was pretty good at tuning out everything else and focusing only on what demanded her attention front and center.

But this time, her power of concentration had abandoned her.

Most of the people in the squad room had gone home for the night, but Laredo, the source of her distraction, was still there, still sitting across from her. There was a decent separation between them, yet he felt closer than her own skin. At least, to her.

And if that wasn't enough, there were occasional, low-pitched sounds coming from what was really Aaron's computer. What *was* that?

Unable to stand it, Taylor pretended to go to the coffee machine just to catch a glimpse of whatever it was that was transpiring on the computer screen.

Laredo was playing solitaire.

A card game?

"You can do that at home, you know," Taylor informed him tersely, her supposed planned trip to the coffee machine all but forgotten.

"I know," he answered cheerfully, "but then I'd have to come back once I got that information you need, so I might as well just hang around and stay put. Save on gas and all that," he'd added, slanting a quick glance in her direction.

As if I'd believe that he cared about things like the price of gas, Taylor thought, annoyed. What was he, twelve? "Why don't you find something better to occupy your mind? Something intelligent?"

"I'm saving myself for the case," he told her, unfazed by the accusation in her voice. "Besides, cheating in solitaire takes a certain sharpness."

Her eyes widened. The man was unbelievable. "You're cheating?"

"Half the fun," he responded. "Otherwise, this is a deadly dull game." Pausing, he turned around in his chair to face her. "Where're you going?"

Did he think she was making a run for it? She supposed it wasn't such a bad idea, but she had visions of him coming after her, popping up in the most inappropriate places.

She fell back to her initial excuse. "To the coffee machine. I wasn't aware that I had to run that by you first."

"You don't." Leaning forward, he took his wallet out of his back pocket and opened it. Laredo removed a couple of bills and held them out to her. "And I wouldn't mind a cup myself."

Taylor's eyes narrowed. Now he thought she was his gofer? "Then, unless you have some magical ability to make containers of coffee appear when you snap your fingers, I suggest you get up and get your coffee yourself."

"No problem. Lead the way," Laredo said, rising. "It'll be on me."

Now that was a very tempting picture. After a moment, she relinquished the thought.

Taylor walked out into the hall and led the way to the vending machine.

By the end of the day, it felt as if they were all but hermetically joined at the hip. Except for an occasional break, when he paused to talk to one of the detectives— did *everyone* know this man but her?—Laredo remained at Aaron's desk, playing solitaire and occasionally sitting up straighter and hitting a couple of keys or more on the keyboard, pulling up things she couldn't see. He would make notes then and look more serious.

But he volunteered nothing and she'd be damned if she was going to come across like some needy person and ask him what he was doing. After all, it wasn't as if she didn't have anything to do on her own.

But, when six o'clock rolled around and almost everyone from the day shift had left, Taylor decided it was time to stop playing this useless charade.

Taking her purse out of the double bottom drawer,

she placed it dramatically on top of her desk and rose from her chair. "It looks like your friend isn't going to get back to you today."

Laredo raised his eyes from the screen. The next moment, they had locked with hers. "*Today* is not over yet."

Did he have to give her an argument about everything? "Maybe not, but my shift is and I'm going home." She looked at him pointedly. He made no move to get up. The man's middle name most definitely had to be Difficult, not Chester. "Look, I can't just leave you here," she told him flatly. "No matter what you think of yourself, you *are* a civilian and you can't be here without someone on the force babysitting you."

Laredo inclined his head, as if that was logical. And then he suggested, "Then stay."

The hell she would. She was drained and needed a break. All the details she'd been reviewing had begun to run together. She needed some time to let things gel.

"I stopped babysitting when I was a teenager," she informed him.

His smile moved along his lips slowly, unfurling a hint of an inch at a time. And peeling something apart inside of her as she watched.

Most of all, Taylor thought, she needed a break from him.

"You must have been something else back then," he speculated.

She could all but see him envisioning her and nearly told him to stop it. But she had no doubt that Laredo would give her some innocent response and she'd look like an idiot.

Sparing herself the grief, Taylor said, "I was a lot more patient back then. Now let's go. If you have your heart set on it, you can continue playing this game tomorrow—" she tapped the screen "—but for tonight, you—"

That was when his cell phone rang and she was forced to let the end of her statement go unsaid. A part of her suspected he'd managed to get his phone to ring on cue, but she hadn't taken her eyes off him for the last five minutes.

Another reason to get rid of him, she thought. Because the more she watched him, the more he affected her on a deep level. She was more comfortable on her own.

The look on Laredo's face as he talked to the person on the other end of the line told her it was the call he'd been waiting for.

"Great," Laredo enthused. "I knew you'd come through, Levi. E-mail all that to me. Right, I'll tell Chet you said hi. Come over sometime," he invited. "He's itching to talk about the 'good old days,' now that they're in the past," Laredo added with a short laugh. "I owe you one. Okay, two," he amended. And with that, Laredo ended the call, closing the phone and putting it back into his pocket.

It hadn't been easy, holding on to her questions. Now that he'd hung up, Taylor pounced. "Levi?"

Laredo appeared preoccupied as he nodded in her direction. "Someone my grandfather used to work with," he told her as he typed something on the keyboard.

When he said nothing further, she prompted, "You told him to send it to you. That means you have to go home to your computer—"

That was when he actually looked at her. "You're kidding, right?"

She knew damn well so-called guest accounts could be forwarded to other computers and resented his implying that she was a computer virgin. "'Hoping' is more like it," she countered.

One glance at the computer in front of Laredo showed her a screen filled with data. For now, she forgot how annoying she found him and started reading. The amount of background facts was overwhelming.

"Where did he *get* all this stuff?" she asked, stunned as the wealth of information continued to materialize. It looked as if their homeless man had been thoroughly researched from the moment of his birth to a single mom in Kansas City until he'd drawn his last breath sometime last night—if the coroner's estimation was accurate about the latter.

"If he told you, Levi'd have to kill you," Laredo deadpanned, then felt compelled to add with admiration, "The man's good."

"The man's incredible," she breathed, leaning in closer as she read. Without realizing it, she placed her hand on Laredo's shoulder.

"A lot of that going around," she heard him say in a voice that didn't match the one he'd just been using. And then it hit her like a lightning bolt: she was practically bending over him, her hair sweeping along his shoulder. Touching his face.

The second she became aware of how close she was to him, Taylor pulled her shoulders back and snapped into a rigid position—or at least that was the plan.

But for some reason, her body wasn't getting the message and it definitely wasn't cooperating. If anything, it rebelled against her.

As if paralyzed, she remained exactly where she was, her face inches from his. And now that she'd turned her head, she was even closer than a sigh.

Taylor felt his breath on her skin. Her stomach did a backward flip, then was all but lost in the ensuing tidal wave.

"Nice job," she murmured and almost became undone by the smile that began in Laredo's sky-blue eyes and then descended to his lips.

"On behalf of Levi, thank you," he said. "And, in the words of the immortal Al Jolson, 'you ain't seen nothin' yet.'"

The name meant nothing to her. She looked at him blankly. "Who?"

"You're serious?" It was only half a question. Laredo shook his head, doing his best to suppress an amused grin. "Oh, Detective McIntyre, I fear that your education has been woefully inadequate."

He had to be the one who was kidding. "Because I've never seen *The Magnificent Seven* and I don't know who Allen Jolson is?"

"Al," he corrected her. "His name was Al Jolson and he appeared in the first talking picture. His real first name was Asa—"

She held her hands up, as if to physically fend off the

avalanche of words she felt sure was forthcoming. "How do you *know* all these things?"

His eyes crinkled. So did her stomach. Since when were they connected? "I read a lot."

Obviously all the wrong things, she couldn't help thinking. "And just how full of useless trivia is your head?" she asked.

Too late she realized that she had set herself up. Sure enough, Laredo was quick to seize the opportunity. "Why don't we go someplace for a late dinner and you can find out?"

That was the last thing she wanted. Because he was growing on her. Because she didn't have the strength to hold him at bay indefinitely. Because she *knew* she didn't have the strength to hold herself in check.

"Tempting as that is," she told him glibly, "I'm just too exhausted." She pointed to the screen. "Print that up for me and we'll call it a night."

His hands moved. Laredo began the printing process without bothering to look at the keyboard, all his attention focused on her.

"You've got to eat," he pointed out. "Keep your strength up."

Taylor shrugged carelessly. "I'll pick something up on the way home."

His next words stopped her cold. "Sounds good. You talked me into it."

About to go to the printer that serviced her side of the room, Taylor turned around to glare at him. "I wasn't trying to talk you into anything," she protested.

But he winked at her, slicing through sheets of

would-be resistance. "You're more subtle than you give yourself credit for."

Rising, Laredo crossed to the printer before she could. Something else that surprised her. She fisted her hand at her waist.

"How is it that you know where the printer's located and you didn't know where the coffee machine was?" she asked. The printer wasn't out in plain sight but housed in a cubicle against the far wall. The coffee machine, on the other hand, was out in plain sight on the way to the elevators.

"Priorities?" he suggested innocently.

Taylor sighed and shook her head. Though she hated to admit it, she just wasn't up to arguing with this man. Not when she knew that she'd wind up losing. It occurred to her that, like it or not, she had finally met her match.

J. C. Laredo had the ability to effectively wear away his opponent. If she hadn't been on the receiving end of that talent, she might have even admired it. But she *was* on the receiving end and that meant only one thing. She was going to have to stay on her guard.

Constantly.

So what was she doing, letting him tag along as she went home? Somewhere along the line from the precinct to her apartment door, she'd lost her focus. And quite possibly, her mind. Otherwise, she would have sent Laredo packing long before she pulled up into her apartment complex, his vintage vehicle behind her.

Not for a minute was she buying his excuse—that he wanted to read through Levi's pages after she was finished with her initial perusal. If that was the case, they could have printed up two sets. But, if it wasn't for him, she wouldn't have had this information. At least, she wouldn't have been able to get her hands on it this quickly.

Besides, she silently argued, pulling into her parking space, she wouldn't allow herself to be distracted. And as long as they just talked about the case, what could happen?

That she'd wanted to take the night off mentally was not forgotten. The best laid plans of mice and men and homicide detectives…

The tempting aroma of still-hot Chinese food all but surrounded her as she unlocked the door to her apartment. Laredo came in right behind her. He carried an open rectangular box filled to the brim with four different cartons of Chinese food, as well as the obligatory egg rolls, egg drop soup and half a dozen fortune cookies. The last items were thanks to the cashier. The young woman had rained the individually wrapped cookies into the box after the unusually generous tip that Laredo slipped into her hand registered.

He set down the box in the center of the kitchen table.

"Damn that was hard," he said more to himself than to her.

She looked at him over her shoulder. "The box was heavy?" she asked, confused. His comment made no sense to her. While not muscle-bound, she'd noted more than once that the man had one hell of a physique.

"No, but the food was tempting as hell," he told her. He emptied the box, placing the contents around the perimeter of the table. "Took everything I had not to start sampling it in the car."

She laughed shortly. "Your restraint is admirable," Taylor quipped.

She didn't expect to get trapped in his eyes when he raised them to hers and said, "You don't know the half of it."

She made a tactical error by looking into his eyes. She had to avoid that from now on if she wanted her knees to make it through this evening. Taking a breath to hopefully clear her head, she breezed past him to the kitchen cupboards. Another fortifying breath went in, then out and she began to take down two plates and the same number of forks, spoons, napkins and glasses.

Taylor set everything she'd brought back on the table beside the cluster of cartons and announced in a voice that was just this side of hollow, "Well, you can dig in now."

"Can I, now?"

She forgot her promise to herself about not looking into his eyes.

The inside of her mouth turned to cotton but she refused to explore why. Like the man said, she needed to eat to keep her strength up. Right now, she felt as if she had the strength of a newborn kitten.

What *was* wrong with her?

Where were all these adolescent feelings and reactions coming from? She was closer to thirty than twenty, for heaven's sake, and these feelings weren't even worthy of a twenty-year-old. Not even a very *young* twenty-year-old.

"Yes, you can," she said as if he hadn't just begun to melt her inner core. "After all, you paid for it." She was doing her best to focus on the food and not on the way her pulse beat erratically. "And besides, I can't eat all this by myself." As if to tempt him—or was that distract him—Taylor pushed one of the sealed containers toward his plate. "I think that's sesame chicken."

He smiled as he opened the container. "Sesame chicken it is." He took a little onto his plate, mingling it with flavored rice. "You had a twenty-five percent chance of being right."

"Better odds than I usually have," Taylor couldn't help commenting under her breath.

"Oh?" He reached for another container at the same time she did. He withdrew, indicating that she could go first. "Is that professionally or—?"

"That's off-limits, Laredo," she informed him, shoving the second container into his hand to underscore her point. "You're here because somehow you managed to inject yourself into my investigation and I'm too polite to show you your walking papers. But if you think for one moment this gives you a free pass to do or ask anything you damn well feel like—and expect me to answer—you couldn't be more wrong."

"Finished?" he asked mildly. She looked at him quizzically. "Are you finished?" he repeated, then rephrased his question. "Did you get that out of your system? Yelling at me, I mean."

"For now. Although I reserve the right to do it again the next time you deserve it," she informed him as she took a serving of chicken lo mein. There was no question about it, the man aroused her curiosity—among other things. "Why?"

He took the lid off the container of egg drop soup and passed it to her. "Because I have a question for you."

She watched the overhead light dance along the top of the soup. The beams of light mingled with the steam. It was still too hot to eat. "Go ahead."

"Can I kiss you?"

Okay, *not* what she expected to hear. It took all she had not to let her jaw drop. Finding her voice took another good half a minute. She did her best to sound blasé. "Why are you asking? You didn't the other two times."

"Because we're on your home ground now. And because there are other factors that'll come into play this time around," he told her meaningfully. "Now, can I kiss you?" he repeated, his voice low, soft. Caressing her.

Creating incredible havoc throughout her soul.

"Go ahead," she whispered, her breath catching in her throat even before he raised her to her feet and brought her close to him.

Chapter 12

Taylor realized she was a woman standing at the very edge of a narrow ledge. Moreover, she was about to go plummeting without the benefit of even a rubber band to anchor her in place.

When Laredo's lips touched hers, she instantly felt herself free-falling into the abyss, an almost giddy sensation filling every nook and tiny crevice within her. The emptiness Taylor carried within her instantly vanished.

The kiss between them blossomed, drawing in all her senses. She could taste him, feel him, breathe in the particular scent of him. She was vaguely aware of the shampoo he used for his hair, his aftershave and soap.

The subtle mix made her head spin—or was that the effect of the kiss that was ever deepening? Or was it because of the man who was holding her to him as if there were no barriers between them?

All she knew was that they were already mingling, already becoming one even though they hadn't even gone beyond the kitchen, hadn't gone beyond the press of lips to lips.

It felt as if they were already miles beyond that.

He was making love to her with his mouth.

Taylor's pulse raced madly as she tightened her arms around his neck. She kissed Laredo back for all she was worth. There was no way she intended to be the passive one here, the only one who got her shoes knocked off. Although she secretly admitted that she didn't possess nearly the kind of experience as that of the other women he must be used to, her instincts kicked in with full force.

Laredo had known that he'd wanted her even before he'd kissed Taylor in front of the restaurant. He'd known right from the first minute he'd come upon her talking to herself in Eileen's apartment. Something about the sharp police detective with the smart mouth had pulled him in almost immediately. This was what real chemistry was all about.

He could fight it for just so long.

Out in public, he could hold that need, that desire that coursed through his veins whenever he was around Taylor, in check. Even when he was a teenager, he hadn't believed in putting on a show for others to watch, which meant that he developed iron control and never allowed himself to get carried away.

But now they were away from prying eyes.

Behind closed doors, in the privacy of her apartment,

a different set of parameters came into play and he could feel his steely control slipping away from him. It bothered him that his control wasn't relaxing any more because he could finally kiss her. Instead, it just disappeared of its own volition. As if he had no say in the matter.

While there was still a slender thread of control left, Laredo drew his lips away from hers, ignored the frantic hammering of his heart and looked down at this woman who stirred his blood.

"You're sure?" he whispered.

Because her brain was on a holiday, it took Taylor a second to make sense of the words. To focus her mind as well as her eyes.

When she did, she was still confused. Why did he feel the need to question her? Couldn't he sense her willingness?

"I didn't take you for someone so PC," she finally said.

"Not PC," Laredo contradicted. "I just don't believe in taking advantage." The ultimate pleasure came in sharing the experience, not in selfishly focusing on his own needs.

Taylor still would have never believed it if she hadn't actually witnessed it. Even so, she found herself not wanting to be a witness. For once in her life, she didn't want to have time to think, to examine the situation from every single angle. She wanted the sexy investigator to continue sweeping her off her feet.

Most of all, she didn't want to be conscious of making a decision. She just wanted the tidal wave of emotions, of feelings and desires, to carry her away. Right now, the level of passion within her was almost overwhelming.

"More Boy Scout qualities," she murmured, her mouth once more less than an inch from his.

"Hard thing to turn off." Even so, he was having one hell of a time resisting her lips. Especially since she kept grazing his with them. He could feel his pulse quickening each time she did so.

"Try," she breathed just before she kissed him with the full force of everything churning inside of her.

The next moment, she felt herself being raised up off the floor. Taylor took the opportunity to seal her body to his, wrapping her legs around his torso, her arms more firmly around his neck.

When he moved his mouth from hers and began kissing her eyelids, the hollow of her throat, the hint of cleavage that peered out above her blouse, Taylor felt her breathing become even more erratic. A moan filled with pleasure and anticipation escaped her lips.

She would have very easily testified that she was on fire.

On fire and incinerating fast.

Sliding her body back down until her feet touched the floor again, Taylor brought her mouth back up to his. As she did, her fingers worked away the clothing that kept his body from hers.

The feel of his hands on her body rendered her intoxicated with almost painful longing. She hardly recognized herself. But it didn't matter. Nothing mattered except this delicious sensation.

A long, hot shiver shimmied up and down her spine, creating goose bumps on her arms as she surrendered first her blouse, then her slacks. Hurrying to keep up, she tugged the shirt she'd opened down Laredo's arms and then worked his belt loose. All her fingers had turned into thumbs.

Something scrambled within her, rushing toward a goal she couldn't define or even put into words.

This was just about making love, right? The idea that it was more than that terrified her. But she couldn't call a stop to it, couldn't back away.

Her intake of breath was sharp as Laredo's capable, rough hands gently cupped her breasts.

When had he taken off her bra?

Taylor fought to keep up.

The feel of his chest rubbing against hers almost completely undid her, creating bolts of lightning streaking through her.

Damn, he couldn't remember the last time he'd gotten so carried away. Couldn't remember the last time he had to struggle not to go under, losing his very thought process. It wasn't that he laid out lovemaking like a military campaign, but there were definitely steps involved to please a woman, to heighten her pleasure until they finally came together as one.

Right now, the steps, the plan, eluded him. This blue-eyed wonder kept doing things to him that made his brain all fuzzy. She was a living, breathing contradiction in terms, touching him with an urgency that was still almost hesitant. Almost shy.

It was, he thought, as if he was making love with two different women. Taylor McIntyre was far more complicated than he'd initially expected.

But he wasn't complaining. Not by a long shot. He couldn't remember the last time that the very act leading up to the final experience had been so exhilarating, so exciting. He was like an adolescent again, struggling to hold back in order to appreciate the full impact.

With superhuman effort, Laredo drew his lips away from hers. "Where's your bedroom?"

Her knees sinking, Taylor realized that he was asking her a question. For the life of her, she couldn't make any sense of it. His words buzzed in her head.

"What?" she breathed.

"Bedroom," he repeated huskily. "Where is it?"

He didn't know just how much longer he could restrain himself. Although it had never bothered him before, somehow, it didn't seem right to make love with her right here in the kitchen, or even on the living room floor.

He wanted their first time to be in her bed.

That he was thinking in terms of numbers didn't register just then. If it had, he would have realized that he had good reason to be concerned. And afraid, because that was what the thought of commitment did to him.

Rather than answer—she honestly didn't think she could—Taylor pointed in the general direction of her bedroom. And then she took his face in her hands and kissed him long and hard.

Shattering his concentration. Laredo almost lost it then. Despite his latest resolve, he almost took her right then and there on the kitchen table.

Feeling weak-kneed—when had that ever happened before?—Laredo scooped this woman who unaccountably rocked his world into his arms and carried her in the direction she'd pointed.

The second they were in her bedroom, he laid her

down on the bed and then joined her, covering the soft contours of her body with the hardened ones of his. When she twisted beneath him in response, Laredo knew he had very little time left.

With all but his last ounce of strength, he drew back, creating a whisper of a space between them. His body throbbing, he swiftly and thoroughly anointed her damp body with soft, warm, openmouthed kisses along her skin.

Stifling a cry, Taylor began to twist and wiggle more urgently than before.

Something happened to her that she'd never experienced before. For lack of a better description, explosions went off inside of her, originating in her very core. Delicious, mind-melting explosions that bathed her body in heat and ever-growing desires.

Stunned as one explosion flowered into another, growing in intensity, Taylor cried out his name and then pressed her body urgently against his. More than anything, she wanted the sensation of sweet agony to go on forever, even though she knew that wasn't possible.

Her breathing close to erratic, she was only vaguely aware that Laredo had slipped his arms around her, drawing his body up to hers.

And then he entered.

And abruptly stopped.

Stunned, Laredo looked down at the woman who had thrown him for such a loop. He wasn't an expert in this department, but he knew physical resistance when he encountered it.

Pivoting on his elbows, he drew his head back even further, still looking down at her.

It wasn't possible.

Was it?

After a second he found his voice and hoarsely asked, "Are you…?"

Laredo never got a chance to finish the awkward question. Taylor knew she only had a second, maybe two before he pulled back completely. The man had already proven that he wasn't the type to force himself on a woman no matter how aroused he was. And more than anything, she didn't want him to stop.

The moment she had said "Go ahead," Taylor knew she had made the conscious decision that Laredo was the one. The one she wanted to make love with for the first time. No other man had ever gotten her to come even close to this point.

But Laredo had and there was no way she was about to allow him to retreat and abandon her. Not when they both wanted it so much.

"Stop talking," she breathed. Hardly a whisper, it was still a direct order.

Taking his face in her hands again, she brought her mouth up to his even as she began to twist her body urgently against his.

Needs and desires sprang up again, taking up the places they had just temporarily, with the greatest reluctance, abandoned.

Laredo knew the difference between right and wrong. He judged that he probably had a better sense of it than most of the people he encountered in his line of work. But he couldn't do the right thing here, the noble thing, and just walk away. Not when she'd just melted his bones, rubbing that near-perfect body of hers against his.

Biting off a curse, he pushed himself into her, holding her so close his heartbeat became hers. He began to move his hips in time with the near-frantic movement of hers.

Desires and passions grew to unmanageable proportions, absorbing him.

Absorbing her.

When the final moment arrived a handful of heartbeats later, the sensation sent Laredo spiraling off into another world where only pleasure existed. But that world began to fade even from the very moment it had materialized. The real world rose up to greet and claim him. Sadly, all but blotting out the other.

Euphoria receded even though, now more than ever, he wanted it to linger.

As it faded, it ushered in a sense of guilt in its place. A guilt that was so tangible, he could almost touch it.

Falling back, he remained next to her. Searching for words that could somehow make this up to her. None occurred to him.

"I'm sorry," he finally said, his tone all but stilted.

Taylor immediately propped herself up on her elbow and looked at him. So many emotions swirled through her, it almost made her dizzy. She struggled to brace herself for what she knew was coming, but even as she tried, she knew she was woefully unprepared for the way it would hurt.

"You're 'sorry,'" she echoed. "Sorry for making love with me?" she asked.

The last thing he'd wanted to do was to bring her pain—

emotionally *or* physically. "Why didn't you tell me?" When she didn't answer, Laredo repeated the question. "Why didn't you tell me that you were a virgin?"

Right. As if that was the kind of thing you talked about. Why was he putting her through this? Why couldn't he just pretend he'd enjoyed himself?

"The opportunity never worked itself into the conversation," she bit off.

Oh, but it had, he thought. "Just now, in the kitchen, when I asked if I could kiss you, you couldn't tell me then?"

Okay, now she was angry. Anger had come to her rescue, springing out of embarrassment to shield her. "You mean why didn't I say, 'Yes you can kiss me if you want to but you might not want to because I'm a virgin and I'll only disappoint you?'" she asked sarcastically. "Sorry, guess I just wasn't thinking clearly at the moment."

Sitting up, Laredo stared at her as if she were suddenly speaking in some foreign language. "What the hell are you talking about?" he finally demanded. "You think I'm disappointed?"

"Well, aren't you?" she challenged.

"Hell, no."

"Then why are you yelling at me?" she demanded, yelling back. Incensed, she couldn't help herself.

"Because you should have told me." He shouldn't have to explain it to her. As a woman, she should have understood that to begin with. "There's a lot of responsibility, being a woman's first lover."

Was that it? He wasn't disappointed, he was afraid

she was disappointed in him? She would have laughed if she hadn't thought that it might have hurt his feelings. Instead, she fell back on being flippant.

"Don't worry, I won't bill you. On the upside, I have nothing to compare this to." For the first time, she grinned at him. "Which makes you the greatest lover I've ever had."

Now that the euphoria and frenzy had died back, she felt awkward. Nothing a little clothing couldn't fix, she told herself. Turning away from him, Taylor began to get up.

Laredo caught her wrist, holding her in place. His frustration over the fact that he should have gone slower, been more tender toward her, began to abate. "There is that, I suppose."

She looked down at his fingers locked around her wrist. "I can't get dressed if you're holding my wrist." She raised her eyes to his expectantly.

But he didn't release her. "I know."

She took in a breath, then let it out slowly. Some of her embarrassment began to recede, nudged away by another round of anticipation. Was this how it was? Up and down until she felt dizzy?

She looked down at his hand again. "So what is it that you have in mind?"

Taylor heard the grin in his voice. "To give you something to compare your first time to."

"Are you going to yell at me at the end of that, too?" she deadpanned.

"I wasn't yelling at you," he told her. "I was yelling at me."

Funny, it certainly felt like he was yelling at her. But now that she knew why, she wasn't upset any longer. "And what, I just got in the way?"

He lifted his shoulder in a dismissive, half shrug. "Something like that."

Removing his hand from her wrist, he reached up and gently feathered his fingers through her hair. Something stirred within him.

He wanted her again.

"A woman's first time is supposed to be special," he told Taylor. "At the very least, the earth is supposed to move for her."

Taylor pressed her lips together, debating whether or not she should be honest with him or just keep him guessing. But she had always been truthful and games were for people who were careless about other people's feelings.

"So far, so good," she finally said softly.

In response, he grinned. Laredo's smile was so sexy, she could hardly stand it. Feelings began to rush forward again, faster than the first time.

"I don't want to be good," he told her, his voice low. "Do you?"

"Good is in the eyes of the beholder," she managed.

"That's beauty," Laredo corrected, drawing her closer to him as he laid down again. "Beauty is in the eye of the beholder."

The phone could ring at any minute, calling her back to duty. Or he would suddenly realize that he had somewhere else to be. Taylor didn't want to waste precious time discussing a poem she'd long since forgotten.

"Shut up, Laredo," she murmured raising her mouth up to his.

"Yes ma'am," Laredo replied obediently.

And then the next moment, he began to devote himself to showing Taylor the right way to make love to a woman the first time around.

Slowly.

Chapter 13

Laredo considered himself a light sleeper, rendered that way both by nature and out of necessity because of the demands of his vocation. He would have thought, then, that the slightest shift of weight on the surface of the mattress, especially if someone was slipping away, would have woken him up.

But when he did open his eyes to greet the dawn, he found himself alone in the bed. Taylor was gone. From the bed and, apparently, from the room.

Surprised and a little uncertain—just because he'd made love with the woman a record number of three times, as he recalled—didn't mean that she was now an open book to him. With Taylor, he was still feeling his way around.

Right now, he wouldn't have put it past the crafty Detective McIntyre to try to get a jump ahead of him on this case by sneaking out and leaving him here, asleep at the wheel.

Laredo shook his head. He liked his women simpler, he thought as he hurried into the clothes that, unaccountably, were now sitting on a chair in the bedroom instead of scattered throughout the kitchen the way he remembered leaving them. He liked his women more predictable at least, he silently added.

Oh, yeah? I didn't see anyone holding a gun to your head to stay last night. Or urging you to go for a record-breaking performance test, either. That was all on you and you were free to leave anytime.

Zipping up his pants, Laredo sighed. Okay, so there was something about the feisty homicide detective that attracted him more than he was comfortable with. But that would pass soon, he promised himself. And then maybe things could get back to normal again.

There was no denying that he liked his life just the way it was, uncomplicated except when it came to his cases. He was committed to his work and his grandfather. That was where it ended.

As he quickly walked toward the front of the apartment, it occurred to Laredo that he was protesting a bit too strongly.

Never a good sign.

He passed the other, smaller bedroom, came to a screeching halt and then retraced his last two steps. He looked in. His eyes hadn't been playing tricks on him. Taylor was there, wearing something baggy and misshapen—an oversize police T-shirt?—sitting at a desk in front of a computer. All her attention appeared to be focused on the monitor as she scrolled down.

He wondered what had captured her attention so exclusively—but he didn't wonder that nearly half as much as he wondered if she'd bothered to put anything on underneath her T-shirt.

Visions of their lovemaking played vividly across his mind. Whetting his appetite.

Laredo entered the room and, coming up behind her, embraced Taylor lightly with one arm.

Startled, Taylor gasped and swung around.

Seeing that it was Laredo, she relaxed and said, "You shouldn't sneak up behind me like that."

He smiled. "Next time, I'll yell before I walk in." He looked at the screen that had held her attention so intently. "Anything interesting?" he asked, noting a site devoted to the Middle Ages.

"Maybe." Turning her chair around to face him, Taylor leaned back and said, "Did you know that, among other things, St. Thomas More is the patron saint of adopted children?"

She'd lost him. Laredo looked at her quizzically, then remembered the mass card that had been found beside the last body.

"As a matter of fact, no, I didn't. Must have escaped my required reading list." He looked at the screen again, then shook his head. No bells were ringing for him. "Is that supposed to mean something to us?" he finally asked.

She wished she could say yes, but the hard truth of the matter was that she was still trying to connect the dots. "I don't know yet. I just think it's a little odd, given that the first two victims were connected because Stevens was pregnant with Crawford's baby."

He tried to connect that to the third victim. "So you think, what? That our homeless guy got Stevens pregnant, too?"

"No, but our homeless guy did get someone pregnant." It was a thin, almost nonexistent thread, but so far, the only thread they had.

Laredo looked at her. All that from a mass card? He had to be missing something. "Come again?"

Taylor began to shuffle through the array of papers all spread out on the desk beside the computer. "It's right here, in the pages that your friend e-mailed you," she told him, excitement growing in her voice. Finding what she was looking for, she began to read, "It says here that Linda Lawson accused Dougherty of being the father of her baby and tried to take him to court to collect child support. They couldn't find him. Shortly thereafter, Lawson gave the baby, a two-month-old girl, up for adoption." Taking a breath, she looked up at him. "Think it means anything?"

So far, it was just a coincidence, albeit an uncanny one. "Other than, what, there's some superhero out there avenging unwanted kids who were given away by their biological parents?"

Taylor bristled. He was laughing at her. "Not a superhero," she retorted, "but, well—have you got a better idea?"

The corners of Laredo's mouth curved. "That depends."

The way he watched her told Taylor that he might not be talking about the same thing. "On what?" she asked gamely.

His smile grew, slipping into his eyes as they drifted down the length of her. Funny how he hadn't realized sooner just how long her legs really were. "On whether or not you're wearing anything under that baggy T-shirt of yours."

Taylor valiantly ignored the hot shivers suddenly racing up and down her spine. "I'm serious," she told him.

"So am I." And then he sighed, relenting. For the moment. "But maybe your idea isn't that off the wall—insofar as orphaned kids being a connecting factor. It wouldn't hurt to have a few words with the kid that Stevens and Crawford gave up for adoption—if we can track him down," he qualified.

They both knew it was a huge *if.* More and more adoptees were avidly tracking down their birth parents these days in an effort to connect with their roots. But that sort of thing usually took months if not years of diligent work and digging.

Taylor had this uneasy feeling that they didn't have months, that if she was right, another victim was going to surface soon. Most likely, that victim would be Linda Lawson.

Taylor hit a few keys and closed down her computer. "Why don't I get you breakfast," she suggested, "and then we'll see if we can locate this Linda Lawson?" She turned her chair around to face him again. "She might be able to direct us to the agency that took in her baby." Taylor shrugged, anticipating that he would call it a waste of time. "It's a start. Maybe."

About to get up, Taylor found that her limbs were frozen in place. Laredo had begun to slowly run his hand up along her leg, starting at her knee. He was at her thigh now.

Her body tingled in response. "What are you doing?" she breathed.

His smile began to unravel her. Again. "You offered me breakfast," he replied.

"Yes." She had to push the word out as it had gotten stuck in her throat.

"This is what I want for breakfast." "This" being her, she assumed.

Before she could protest, or tell him that he was going to need something more substantial to see him through the day, Laredo swept her up to her feet and against him in one smooth motion.

"Any objections?" he asked.

Because he'd asked rather than taken, he'd melted her resolve and any protest she might have had.

"No."

It was the last word Taylor uttered for quite some time.

A quick search through DMV records told them that Linda Lawson was now Linda Morrow, living not that far away from where she had originally grown up. They lost no time in getting to her.

Linda Morrow answered the door after Taylor had rung the bell twice. The onetime captain of the cheer-leading squad looked as if she had found life after high school hard and unforgiving.

She reminded Taylor of a flower that had bloomed for too long and was now beginning to wilt.

"We have a few questions we'd like to ask you,"

Taylor told her after introducing herself and Laredo. The woman seemed unwilling to step aside and allow them in. "It won't take long," Taylor pressed.

Instead of inviting them in, Linda slipped out onto the porch, closing the door behind her in the furtive manner of a woman attempting to keep her home separate from what had been dropped on her doorstep.

Linda ran her tongue nervously over her lips. "My husband's home today. Sick," she explained. "I can't talk to you," she added in a lowered, pleading voice.

Taylor took a guess. "Your husband doesn't know, does he?"

"Know? Know what?"

"That you gave a baby girl up for adoption," Laredo answered.

The thin, mousy-looking woman's eyes widened, surprised by the question. And then she shook her head. "No, he doesn't know," she said in a flat voice. "And I want to keep it that way. He's a very jealous man. I don't want to set him off."

Because of her father, Taylor immediately jumped to a conclusion. "Is he abusive?"

Again, Linda licked her lips, shaking her head. "No, no, but he's hell to live with when he gets in one of his moods." She glanced over her shoulder toward the door, as if she expected her husband to drag her inside at any second. "Please, just go away."

Taylor didn't want to put the woman in any danger, but then again, if she saw any sort of abusive behavior—whatever Linda wanted to call it—she could arrest the woman's husband.

"We'll leave just as soon as you tell us which agency you gave your baby to."

Linda shook her head. It was obvious that she couldn't remember the exact name. "I gave the baby to a social worker. I don't remember her name." Nervously, she shrugged. "She was with some government agency."

"You mean Social Services?" Laredo asked, peering at the woman's face for recognition.

Linda Morrow had the desperate manner of a woman who would grasp at anything. "Yes, that was it. Social Services. Now please, you have to go," Linda begged. Nervously, she looked over her shoulder toward the closed door again. Fear radiated from every pore.

This just wasn't right, Taylor thought. She was dying to put this woman's husband in his place. No one should have this kind of power over another human being, to make them so afraid.

"Just one more question," she pressed. "Have you seen Hank Dougherty recently?"

At the mention of the name, Linda paled visibly. "No, not since I gave up the baby. Now I really have to get back." Not waiting for a response, the woman quickly darted back into the house, firmly closing the door behind her.

Laredo made no move to leave. "You believe her?" he asked, looking at the closed door.

Taylor shrugged, turning from the door. "For now, we have no other choice." She gazed up at him, curious. "Why? Don't you?"

"I don't know yet," Laredo said honestly. "She seemed awfully jumpy to me."

Taylor laughed shortly. There was no humor in the sound. "Marriage to an abusive husband'll do that to you every time."

Laredo turned away from the house. They began to walk back to the curb where Taylor had parked her vehicle. "She said he wasn't."

"Abused women lie, Laredo. All the time. They don't want the world to know just how bad things really are. A lot of them think that it's all their fault. That if they were perfect, their husbands would have no reason to be 'displeased' with them."

Laredo stopped walking and looked at her for a long moment. He felt a wave of anger rising. Anger not directed at her but at whoever had shown her this ugly side of life.

"Is that just theory, Detective?"

She shook her head. He'd misunderstood. "I haven't been in an abusive relationship, if that's what you're asking. I would never let anyone get close enough for that to happen," she added firmly. "Doesn't mean I haven't seen one, up close and personal."

He wondered if he was included in that emotional embargo and was now on notice. She was suddenly challenging him. More questions occurred to him. He wanted to dig deeper in this stretch of soil she'd just exposed to him.

But for now, he kept his questions to himself. He'd already learned that Taylor was the type who immediately circled the wagons if she perceived an attack coming. Better to just wait and let her volunteer the information on her own. In the meantime, they had a crime to solve.

"You know," he told her, looking back at the house, "you could call that probable cause—thinking she was in some kind of danger because her husband was home." He, of course, needed no such excuse.

She followed his thinking to its logical conclusion. "And just come in like gangbusters, breaking down the front door?"

Laredo shrugged. "Sounds good to me," he said affably.

Maybe he could do it, but she couldn't. "You're a P.I., Laredo. Everything I do has to be by the book."

His smile was wicked. "Everything?"

But just then they heard a woman's scream coming from the house. The moment vanished. He looked at Taylor expectantly. "You were saying?"

"The hell with the book," Taylor retorted, pulling out her handgun and releasing the safety.

He grinned, taking out his own weapon. "Now you're talking."

Measuring the necessary space with his eyes, Laredo took a step back and then kicked in the door, hard. The lock splintered and the door hung drunkenly from the frame with only one hinge holding it up.

Taylor rushed in half a step ahead of him, her adrenaline surging. Laredo, she noted, had his gun drawn, too. She hoped he knew how to hit what he aimed for.

Nothing but eerie silence met them as they swept first one room, then another.

"Linda?" Taylor called out. "Linda, can you hear me? This is Detective McIntyre. We heard you scream and we're here to help you." Still nothing. She exchanged looks with Laredo. He nodded toward the back of the house. She raised her voice even higher. "Where are you?"

No one answered.

Something was very, very wrong. Taylor could feel all her senses going on high alert. Cautiously, they moved from one room to the next. Encountering no one.

"Linda, if you can hear me, say something," Taylor coaxed. "If your husband has hurt you in any way, you can have him arrested. We can keep you safe. He'll never get to you again. You have my word."

There was still no indication that anyone was in the house. They were almost out of rooms. Only one more left in the single-story house. The door to that room, a second bedroom, was closed.

Linda and whoever had made her scream had to be in there.

Taylor exchanged glances with Laredo, indicating that she intended on going into the room first. In response, Laredo nodded. But as she reached for the doorknob to slowly test it, Laredo suddenly rammed his shoulder against the door, causing it to fly open.

Rushing in, Laredo trained his weapon on the center of the room. Just above Linda's head.

The woman was on her knees in the middle of the room. She trembled and sheer terror shone in her eyes. A fresh strip of duct tape stretched across her mouth, sealing in her screams and turning them into whimpers.

Another woman, younger than all of them, stood behind her. Tall, thin, with mousy brown hair that hung limply on either side of her gaunt face, there appeared to be nothing remarkable about her.

Except for the gun she held in one hand and the strip of wet leather she was holding in the other. A drop of water slid down the length of the strip and dripped onto the carpet.

In its own way, the look in the younger woman's eyes was just as terrified as Linda's.

She waved her weapon at the two of them. "Get the hell out of here!" she demanded, her voice cracking at the end of her order.

Laredo's eyes never left the young woman's. "I don't think so." He took a step forward.

"Stay back," she threatened, raising her gun so that it pointed at his chest. Her hand was shaking. "I mean it! This doesn't involve you."

"Oh, but it does," Taylor told her, her voice low, almost soothing. Following Laredo's lead, she took a step toward the young woman as well. "I took an oath that said I couldn't just stand by and watch someone get killed."

"Then turn around and don't watch," the young woman snarled.

"Sorry, can't do that, either. Look—" It occurred to Taylor that she didn't even know the young woman's name. But she thought she had a pretty good idea who the woman was. "What is your name, anyway?"

Suspicion and hatred entered the dark brown eyes. "Why? You want to be my best friend?" she asked nastily.

"Not particularly," Taylor admitted. "But I need a name. Otherwise, I'm going to have to start referring to you as 'hey you.'"

The bony shoulders beneath the shabby yellow sweater rose and fell in a careless, dismissive shrug.

"Why not? I've been called worse," the young woman retorted. And then her eyes narrowed as she looked down at the woman she held at gunpoint. "And it's all this bitch's fault. Every damn bit of it."

Clearly frightened, Linda began to babble as a sob tore from her throat.

"Now is that any way to talk about your mother?" Laredo asked, shaking his head in exaggerated disapproval.

The brown eyes immediately darted in his direction. "How do you know that?" the young woman demanded. "Why did you just call her my mother?"

"Well, isn't she?" Laredo asked. "I saw it right away. The same eyes. The same hair. The same penchant for making mistakes, except that yours carry much bigger consequences for what you're about to do. This is a big mistake," he told her.

"What's a bigger mistake than throwing away your baby like it was yesterday's trash? No, worse than trash," she amended.

"She didn't throw you away," Taylor was quick to point out. "She gave you up so that you could have a better life than what she could give you. It was a huge sacrifice for her to give you up."

The hatred in the young woman's eyes as she looked down at the back of Linda's head deepened. "You believe that crap?" she demanded.

"It's not crap," Taylor countered, as calm as Linda was agitated.

The young woman's head jerked up. "Yes, it is. You want to know how much 'better' my life was because of this bitch's 'sacrifice'? I got to be passed around from one foster home to another. Treated like a servant instead of a kid. Or more like a slave," she corrected, "because at least servants are paid."

Her breathing became audible as she relived the experience. "But that wasn't the worst of it. When I was thirteen, I was sent to the Dobers. Mrs. Dober was an airhead, but she was okay. She even tried to be nice. When she wasn't drunk." Angry tears gathered in her eyes. "Her husband told me it was his job to educate me about the 'pleasures' of life. Every night, after his wife took her sleeping pills, he'd come into my room to give me another 'lesson.' I ran away four times," she said bitterly, "but every time, they'd bring me back." There was agony in her eyes. "And it just got worse."

"Why didn't you tell someone?" Laredo asked gently.

"I did," she shouted. "Nobody would believe me. Dober was a judge. His big thing was family values." The torment melted from her face as her expression darkened. "After I kill this bitch, he's next on my list."

Chapter 14

Clearly terrified, Linda Morrow began to whimper. Her trembling became almost violent, as if she were undergoing a seizure. Huge, frightened brown eyes shifted from Laredo to Taylor and then back again, like dark marbles that couldn't come to rest. They fairly pleaded for help.

"Shut up," the young woman snapped when Linda continued to whimper. She raised the wet strip, holding it in front of Linda like an unfulfilled promise. "It's time for you to pay for what you did."

Trying to divert her attention from Linda, Taylor asked the young woman, "Did you kill that homeless man they found in the alley yesterday?"

Dark, malevolent eyes shifted toward Taylor. "You mean 'Daddy'?" The woman's mouth twisted in a sardonic smile. "Yeah, I did." She paused, as if reliving the experience. "I probably did him a favor, really. The miserable drunk was so out of it, I don't even think he knew what was happening."

Realizing that Taylor was stalling, Laredo followed her lead. "Why did you kill those other two people?" he asked the woman.

The woman scowled. "What other two people?"

"Eileen Stevens and Terrance Crawford," Taylor answered. As she talked, she took in the room, trying to decide their next move. If she and Laredo separated and made their way toward the younger woman slowly enough for her not to notice, one of them might be able to catch her off guard.

The names Taylor said appeared to mean nothing to the young woman. Impatience echoed in her voice. "Who the hell is that?"

Laredo noted that Taylor had managed to move forward. He did the same, then called the young woman's attention to him, allowing Taylor to take another step forward.

"The woman in the penthouse and the teacher," he told her.

The description brought enlightenment. "Oh, them." She laughed shortly, shrugging dismissively. "I didn't kill them."

Laredo's turn to move, Taylor thought. "Same method was used," she said.

The agitated woman seemed close to the breaking point. Any opposition instantly had her temper flaring. "I said I didn't kill them," she snarled, waving the muzzle of her weapon at Taylor.

Linda was on the verge of hyperventilating. And there was no gauging what her daughter was really capable of. She looked as if she was coming apart at the seams, as unstable as a vial of nitroglycerin, Taylor thought. They needed to wrap this up somehow.

"Then who did?" Taylor probed. Out of the corner of her eye, she saw Laredo inching forward. This pace was much too slow. They needed to rush Linda's daughter. But how to keep her from firing wildly? That was the problem before them.

Linda's daughter tossed her head. "Someone who had the right to kill them," she said self-righteously.

She was talking about Eileen's son. Waiting for Laredo to say something so that she could move, Taylor glanced in his direction. He was thinking the same thing she was.

"You mean their son?" Laredo asked.

"Son," the woman snorted contemptuously. "You damn cops make it sound like some kind of PG family movie. Miles wasn't their son," she spat out the last word. "They thought he was just some mistake they made. Some*thing* they were willing to throw away."

"Miles, is that his name?" Taylor asked. She could see that the young woman was working herself up. Desperate, Taylor tried to stop the eruption she could see forming. "That's not true, you know." Taylor kept her voice low, soothing, as if she were trying to gentle a wild animal that had been hurt. And as she spoke, ever so slowly, she moved forward. "Terrance Crawford's girlfriend told us that he tried to get custody of his son, but he was too young and Eileen insisted on giving the baby up. Terrance became a teacher and devoted himself to kids in an effort to try to make up for that. Because he felt so terrible about losing his son," she emphasized.

She saw the young woman's eyes widen as she looked at something that was just behind them. Still on her knees, Linda made a gurgling noise beneath the duct tape.

"Well, well, well, let's bring out the violins," a sarcastic voice behind them said, ending the sentence with a nasty laugh. Taylor froze, as did, she noted out of the corner of her eye, Laredo.

The voice, she thought, sounded familiar.

And then she saw why. The man who'd entered the house was the missing security guard from Eileen Stevens's building.

"Nathan," Taylor cried in recognition.

"Miles," Linda's daughter exclaimed at the same time, lighting up like the proverbial Christmas tree at the very sight of him.

Joining the disheveled young woman, Nathan/Miles slipped his arm around her. In his free hand, he held a gun and aimed it at them.

There was no tremor to his hand. And his gaze was dark, flat. They were in the presence of a stone-cold killer, Taylor thought.

He brushed a kiss against his girlfriend's hair, but his eyes never left the two people still holding their weapons trained on her. "I came to see how you were doing, baby. Didn't think you were going to hold an open house."

"I'm not. I didn't," the young woman protested, irritation and nerves infusing themselves into her voice. "They just came storming in. I don't know where they came from or who they are."

"Then let me introduce you," Miles said magnanimously. "The one with the cute butt is Detective McIntyre. The guy with the scowl's some private eye. Laredo, I think his name is. Don't worry," he reassured his girlfriend, "they're clueless. They came nosing around after I offed dear old Mom."

His easy tone vanished as he raised his weapon, aiming it first at Laredo, then at Taylor. There was no doubt in Taylor's mind that he could shoot them both without the slightest qualm.

"Put your guns down," Miles barked.

"Sorry, that's not an option," Laredo told Miles before she had a chance to. Taylor held her breath. "Right now, we have a Mexican standoff. If we lower our weapons, you just pick us off one by one," Laredo pointed out, his voice deceptively calm.

Miles appeared to think Laredo's words over. "Interesting theory. You mean like this?"

And before anyone could make a move, he fired a bullet into the trembling housewife's leg. Her mouth still taped over, Linda screamed, the sound coming through her nose as she crumbled to the floor. Taylor tried to go to her, but Miles shifted the muzzle of his gun, aiming it at her. Laredo caught her by the arm and pulled her back.

"Miles!" his girlfriend cried in angry protest.

Miles laughed. "Don't worry, baby, I didn't kill her. I wouldn't rob you of the pleasure. You still get to watch her choke to death. I'm just showing these two big, bad detectives that all the cards on the table are mine. Ours," he amended as an afterthought, sparing her a nod.

Slipping his hand all the way around her, Miles deftly

extracted the gun she was holding. With a satisfied smirk, he drew back and aimed one weapon at each of them.

His eyes shifted toward Taylor. "Now put your guns down or the next shot is the kill shot."

His meaning was clear. He meant to kill Linda *and* her daughter.

Very slowly, Taylor put her weapon down before her. After a beat, Laredo unwillingly followed suit.

Triumphant, Miles nodded his head. "Now we can talk. What are our options?" he mocked. "I either snuff out your eager beaver, overachieving, worthless lives, or you end mine." He shrugged carelessly, nodding toward Linda's daughter. "And maybe Donna's."

"It doesn't have to be that way," Taylor cut in, desperately trying to reason with one of them. "We can get you help."

"Get us help?" Miles mocked. His laugh turned ugly. "Lady, are you for real? Where the hell were you when Donna was raped? Growing up in a nice little cushy home where Mama and Daddy saw to your every need?" His tone became menacing. "Where were you when I was being shoved into a wooden box in this maniac's backyard and left there, in the hot sun, for two days because I dragged a chair across the kitchen floor and left scuff marks?"

He all but got into her face, shouting, "Where were you when that son of a bitch the system gave me to beat me just 'to show me who's boss'?"

"I'm sorry that happened to you, to both of you," Taylor began. "If the system is at fault, that should be brought to the public's attention—"

"The 'public' knows. The 'public' doesn't care," Miles shouted. "They just look the other way. Your kind is responsible for everything that happened to me. To Donna. To countless other poor, dumb slobs whose only crime was to be born when they weren't wanted."

"Let the women go, Miles," Laredo requested in a mild, reasonable voice, knowing that to insist would only set the other man off. "I'll stay, I'll be your hostage. You'll need a hostage to get out of here. The police are already on their way."

"If they're as good as you two, Donna and I will be safe," he mocked. "But first—" he glanced toward the sobbing woman on the floor "—we have a little unfinished business to attend to. I went through a lot of work, finding Donna's 'birth parents.' We're not about to just walk away and let her live." Linda's sobs became louder. "Shut up, bitch!" he ordered.

"Can't you see she's sorry?" Taylor asked, taking a step forward.

Miles instantly raised the gun in his right hand. "Sorry? I'll bet she's sorry." Miles sneered at the fallen woman. "But not half as sorry as 'Mama's' going to be, I can promise you that."

"Killing her won't change anything," Taylor insisted. There had to be a way to stop this madman. She had to reason with him.

"Nope, not a thing," Miles agreed. "But it'll make Donna feel better." He spared his girlfriend a smile. "Just like killing those two rutting pigs who were my parents made me feel better."

"Did it?" Taylor challenged.

Miles scowled darkly at her. "Shut your girlfriend up," he ordered Laredo. "Or she's going to be the first to go."

Taylor opened her mouth to say that she wasn't Laredo's girlfriend, but didn't get the chance. Laredo spoke first.

"She's a police detective," Laredo reminded him. "You kill a cop, there's no place in the country that you can hide."

Miles's laugh sent a chill down Taylor's spine. "You've been watching too many cop shows on TV. That's just a lot of hype. The truth is, killers still get away with it all the time. Even cop killers." His dark eyes slanted a glance at Taylor. "They just have to be smart, that's all. And I'm smart," he bragged.

And then his satisfied smile vanished as he glanced toward Donna. "Well, what are you waiting for, Christmas? Tie that leather strip around her throat before it dries out."

Weak, frightened and losing blood, Linda still had the strength to plead for her life. She ripped the duct tape off her mouth, crying out as she did so.

"No. No, please," she cried frantically, putting both hands around her throat to keep Donna from tying the leather strip around it. "I didn't want to give you up, I didn't. You've got to believe me. I couldn't afford to keep you. I had no money, no one to turn to. You were sick. The social worker said they'd take care of you, see that you got treatment."

"Don't listen to her, baby. She'll say anything to save her life. Get this over with. We've got to go," Miles ordered.

"Don't do it, Donna," Taylor implored. Miles cocked

the gun he was aiming at her. Her hands still raised, Taylor ignored him. "Don't let him talk you into doing something you don't want to do."

Her words only incited Miles. "Who the hell are you to tell her what she wants or doesn't want to do?" he demanded.

"I'm the person who's going to go to court to testify that she was under severe duress when she killed Hank Dougherty and didn't know what she was doing." Taylor prayed that she was getting through to the other woman. Donna was clearly a weak person who could be manipulated by someone stronger willed. "They'll send you to a hospital, Donna, where you can get well. If you kill your mother, I can't help you."

"No, no more hospitals," Miles cut in. "No more institutions for us. We're finishing what we set out to do and then we're going away." He cocked his other weapon. "And you two are going to sit here and rot right along with the Mother of the Year."

Laredo knew that it was now or never. That the man on the other side of the revolvers was someone who felt he had nothing to lose. He could see it in Miles's eyes. They were flat, expressionless, as if his soul had long since vacated the premises. He was familiar with the type. Men who did desperate things because they felt they risked nothing. In their eyes, they stood to gain everything.

If he waited one more second, the results, Laredo knew, would be fatal.

With one quick motion, he pulled Taylor by the arm, pushing her behind him even as he tackled Miles. Caught off guard, the latter cursed. At the same time

Donna, afraid, screamed. One of the guns that Miles held flew out of his hand, but he discharged the other, firing wildly as he went down, backward on the floor.

Hitting his head, Miles became enraged. He scrambled up and, with a bloodcurdling shriek, lunged at Laredo. The two were approximately the same size, but Miles had learned every single dirty move in order to survive. Thin and wiry, every ounce of him was dedicated to killing.

A spectrum of colors shifted before her eyes as Taylor struggled to hold on to consciousness. The bullet from Miles's gun hadn't been fired at a target, but it had found one.

Blood was oozing out of her side, taking all her available strength with it.

She didn't have time for this, she thought, desperately trying to steel herself. *If you don't think about it, it didn't happen.*

Grabbing her gun from the floor, Taylor pointed the weapon at Donna. The latter had dropped the leather strip she'd been holding and had picked up the gun that Miles had dropped. Holding it in both hands, she aimed it at the whimpering, pleading woman on the floor.

"Drop the gun," Taylor ordered, her voice echoing in her head.

Donna looked as if she had lost the ability to process what was being said. Instead, she continued pointing her weapon at Linda Morrow. Taylor knew Donna was going to shoot her mother. Miles had told her to do it and it wasn't in the woman to disobey.

God forgive me, Taylor thought. The next moment,

she fired dead center at Donna before she could even think her action through.

Donna went down, her scream dying in her throat as she sank to her knees then fell over, her weapon slipping from her fingers. Inches separated her from her birth mother, who seemed to shrink into herself, sobbing hysterically.

Taylor turned around, trying to orient herself to what was going on behind her. The two men were still locked in combat. The pseudo-security guard had his weapon grasped in one hand. Did Laredo have his gun? She didn't see it.

Quickly scanning the floor, she noticed Laredo's weapon was still on the floor. She didn't remember racing to it, was only aware that when she bent over to pick it up, the entire room tilted dangerously, making her nauseous. She almost fell.

Hang on, Taylor, hang on. You can't pass out now, she upbraided herself sternly. *He needs you.*

Turning back again, she had to blink twice to focus on the struggling men on the floor. She had no opportunity to give Laredo his weapon.

"Back off, Miles," she ordered in what she hoped was a strong voice. "I said, back off! It's time to throw in the towel. Donna's dead. You don't want to join her. Give up. It's all over."

An unearthly, guttural wail escaped Miles's lips as, on his knees, he turned to confirm what she'd just told him. It was all the diversion Laredo needed to get the upper hand. He hit Miles hard, knocking the weapon away. Taylor hurried over and gave him his gun.

Reunited with his own weapon, Laredo motioned for Miles to get up.

Neither he nor Taylor were prepared for what happened next. Lunging forward, Miles grabbed his hand and pushed the finger that was on the trigger back.

Laredo's weapon discharged, hitting Miles point-blank in the chest.

A maniacal smile of deep satisfaction curved the man's lips as he sank back to the floor.

"Looks like I won't be going to any more institutions," were the last words Miles uttered. He fell over, lifeless.

Shaken, Laredo turned to the cowering woman on the floor.

"You're safe now," he told Linda. The woman didn't look as if she understood. He kept his voice low, calm, as he took out his cell phone. "I'm going to call 911. The paramedics will take you to the hospital," he promised.

Just then, someone came on the line. Quickly, Laredo rattled off the necessary information to the dispatch operator, giving the woman on the other end Linda Morrow's address and a thumbnail summary of what had transpired.

Flipping the phone closed, he turned toward Taylor. "Didn't expect him to off himself," he was saying, and then his eyes narrowed. She stood with only her profile visible to him, but he didn't like what he saw. "Are you all right?" he asked, crossing to her. "You look a little pale."

"Pale?" she repeated, then pressed her lips together as she could literally *feel* the word echoing inside her brain.

"Yes, pale," he repeated. "As in no color in your face,"

he further elaborated. Linda was calling to him, crying that her leg was burning, but he barely heard the other woman. All his attention was focused on Taylor. His gut tightened as he voiced his worse suspicion. "Taylor, are you hurt?"

"Oh, you might say that," she allowed in a reedy voice, trying her best to sound nonchalant. She knew she was failing. She was just much too weak to carry the charade any further. It felt as if strength was literally draining out of her.

"Where?" Laredo demanded. "Where are you hurt?" Even as he asked, he was lifting up her jacket. Horrified at what he saw, he pulled it from her arms so he could get to her wound more easily.

"Laredo, please, control yourself," she quipped. She tried to smile, but couldn't.

Taylor desperately tried to be flippant, to show Laredo that she was okay. The problem was, she wasn't okay. Not anywhere *near* okay. Her head swirled around like a merry-go-round stuck in fast-forward and nothing was making sense anymore. Her head felt completely out of focus.

"At least wait…wait until we're alone," she joked.

It became a major effort to remain coherent and say each word. Even now, at the end of the sentence, she wasn't sure what she'd just said to him.

Taking a deep breath, she said, "I'm going to go outside to wait for the paramedics." She said it, but she couldn't seem to make her legs obey.

Confused, she looked down at her legs. Why weren't they moving?

The next moment, everything around her went black.

Before Taylor could open her mouth in protest, the blackness found her and swallowed her up.

It was only because of his quick reflexes that Laredo caught her before she hit the floor.

In the background, he heard the distant sound of approaching sirens and silently offered up his first prayer since he was a child.

Chapter 15

"Really, people, you are going to have to clear the hallway!"

The edict was delivered—not for the first time—by Celia Roberts, the no-nonsense, heavyset head nurse who was a twenty-year veteran at Aurora Memorial. She addressed the overwhelming throng that filled the cheerfully decorated surgical waiting room to its maximum capacity and now spilled out into the passageway before the first-floor operating room.

Every adult member of the Cavanaugh family had been there, marking time the entire afternoon. Ever since word had gone out that Taylor had been shot while trying to bring in the "leather strip strangler," as the killer had been dubbed within the department.

Years of practice had the crusty nurse selecting the

most authoritative-looking member of the group and making her appeal to them. In this case, she made a bee-line for Andrew Cavanaugh, who had arrived with his wife shortly after Taylor had been taken into surgery.

"Sir, can't you pick a spokesperson or a go-between who'll keep the rest of you informed?" She scanned the sea of concerned faces. "This is really getting to be a mob scene."

For a moment, Andrew looked sympathetically at the head nurse, but then he surprised her by shaking his head in response to her question.

"I could, but it wouldn't do any good. We're Taylor McIntyre's family and I'm afraid that, orders or no orders, nobody's willing to leave here until we hear something positive."

"Family?" the woman echoed, stunned as her eyes swept over the crowd. "All of you?"

"Every last one," Andrew assured her. "Except for him." He nodded toward Laredo, who stood closest to the O.R.'s swinging doors. "And I sincerely doubt you could get him to leave without resorting to dynamite."

The woman exhaled loudly, her dark brown eye-brows forming a single, disapproving line above the bridge of her nose.

"Having you all out here like this—" she waved her hand around "—is a fire hazard and a violation of the fire code," she insisted.

People far more adept at it had tried to bully him without success. Andrew merely smiled at her and replied, "I know the fire chief. Trust me, you'll get a pass this one time."

Andrew could only pray that it was this one time. That none of his own would ever wind up here like this again: wounded and in need of emergency surgery. But they all knew that getting shot was a very real part of the job description. Even so, it wasn't anything any of them had learned how to live with.

He glanced over toward his brother Brian and Lila, his brother's wife and Taylor's mother. He couldn't remember Lila ever looking quite this pale and drawn, even the time that she herself had been shot and on the verge of death. And her wound had been far more life-threatening. But those kinds of facts made no difference to a mother, he thought. Having a child get shot was the basis of nightmares.

"She's going to be fine, Lila," Brian told her. Brian had lost track of how many times he'd said that to his wife since they'd gotten the call from Frank.

Lila hadn't taken her eyes off the operating-room doors since they had gotten here. "I know, I know," she murmured now, grasping her husband's hand and squeezing it for strength. Her own was icy. "It's just that things can always go wrong, even in the best of hospitals." There was a hitch in her voice. "God, I wish they were all insurance claims adjusters—or chefs," she added, glancing over toward Andrew and noting the way her brother-in-law was looking at her, concern etched on his face.

"Then they wouldn't be our kids," Brian pointed out. "Like it or not, Lila, this is the family business—keeping the citizens of Aurora safe."

She exhaled, nodded. "And turning my hair gray while they're at it."

Brian leaned over and pressed a kiss to her temple. "I'd love you even if all your hair fell out and you were bald," he told her. And then, giving her another quick kiss, he nodded over toward the figure at the O.R. doors. "I'm going to go talk to Laredo before he gets it into his head to barge into the O.R."

Lila fell into place beside him. "I'll come with you."

Her voice was hollow. He was worried about her. "Don't get any ideas about the O.R.," Brian warned, only half kidding. Lila wasn't the type to hang back. It was one of the reasons he loved her the way he did.

Lila merely nodded.

Making his way through the crowd over to Laredo it occurred to Brian that the private investigator looked like he was ready to shatter into a hundred brittle pieces. He knew what that felt like. It wasn't all that many years ago that he had been in the exact same position in this hospital, only it was Lila's blood that had been on his clothes. The way Taylor's was now on Laredo's.

"We could try to scrounge up a shirt for you, boy," Brian offered once he was beside Laredo. He nodded at the thirty-four people in the immediate vicinity. "One of us is bound to have a change of clothing in the trunk."

Laredo blinked, turning toward Brian. He realized that the older man was talking to him, but none of the words penetrated. He was lost in a fog. And, for the first time since he was eleven, he was scared that he would lose someone.

Back then, it had been his mother he was terrified of losing. He remembered that he'd hoped against hope, as he rode to the hospital with his grandfather, that the policeman who had called to notify them had gotten it wrong. That the car accident had only been fatal for the other driver, not his mother.

And now, despite the optimistic prognosis that the admitting E.R. doctor had given him, bitter memories of that long-ago day came rushing back at him. He couldn't lose Taylor.

Loving someone was a bitch. But then, he'd already come to that conclusion years ago, at his mother's funeral.

How had this even happened? Laredo silently demanded. He'd been so nonchalant, so laid-back, so convinced that he could handle getting close to this sharp-tongued detective because the doors were left open at both ends. Neither of them wanted a commitment. He knew that for a fact. She'd said so.

So what the hell had happened?

How had he gone from having a good time to having his gut squeezed so hard, it felt as if he was being cut in two by a buzz saw?

Shaking his head now, Laredo looked at Brian. "I'm sorry, what?"

"Your shirt," Brian repeated, pointing to it. "I can scout around to get you something else to wear. Something that's not quite so—vivid," he elaborated. The entire front of Laredo's shirt was covered with Taylor's blood. Made you wonder just how much blood a person could lose and still remain alive, Brian thought uneasily.

Glancing down at his chest as if just now becoming aware that Taylor's blood was smeared over a large pa of it, Laredo just shook his head. In some strange way, the bloody shirt made him feel closer to Taylor. "No, thanks, it's okay. It doesn't matter."

Lila gently placed her hand on his arm. "Maybe you should let one of the doctors check you out," she suggested.

Again Laredo shook his head. "No, I'm okay. Really." If anything, his body felt numb all over. And then he saw the torment in Brian's eyes. The burden of guilt he felt was almost more than he could bear.

"I should have never put my gun down," he told the Chief of D's. "I should have just gone ahead and shot the bastard. Damn it, why didn't I?" he upbraided himself angrily.

Brian placed a compassionate hand on Laredo's shoulder. He'd managed to get a very cursory explanation from Laredo when he'd first arrived and one of the first responders on the scene had quickly taken down Laredo's statement, so Brian was aware of the chain of events that had led to finding two dead on the scene and Taylor badly wounded.

"Because you're a decent human being who doesn't just shoot first and ask questions later," Brian told him. "And that is what gives you one up on the bad guys," he pointed out.

"I don't want to be one up on them," Laredo said bitterly, looking at the O.R. doors again. Why wasn't anyone coming out to talk to them? The surgery was taking too long. That couldn't be good. "I just want her to be all right."

"She will be." Brian made the promise so firmly, it

sounded as if his convictions were written in stone. "She will be."

Laredo scrubbed his hands over his face. His brain had turned to mush. "I wish I could believe that."

At that moment, the operating-room doors finally opened and the surgeon walked out. It took less than five seconds for everyone to converge around him.

Dr. Peter Mathias appeared a little surprised at the number of people he saw.

"How is she?" Brian's, Lila's and Laredo's voices mingled together as all three asked the same question at precisely the same time.

"She's a very lucky young woman. The bullet miraculously bypassed all her vital organs. She's going to be fine."

"Can I see her?" Lila asked, her voice throbbing with eagerness.

"Can she have visitors?" Brian asked.

The surgeon addressed the throng of people. "Just one at a time and for only a few minutes. She's still very groggy. Don't be surprised if she falls asleep while you're talking to her." He smiled as he shook his head. "But then, she woke up the second the surgery was over. Tough breed of kids you're raising," he told the petite woman.

"I know." Lila's eyes shone with tears as she took a step forward. And then she stopped to face Laredo. She instinctively knew that this man meant a great deal to her daughter. Apparently more than most. And, judging by the look on Laredo's face, the feeling was mutual. "Would you like to go in first?" she offered.

"No, it's okay," Laredo assured her. "I just wanted to

make sure Taylor was going to pull through. Tell her—
tell her—" He realized that he had no idea what message
he wanted to pass on. Joyful and miserable at the same
time, he'd never felt so damn confused in his life. Seeing
Taylor unconscious and bleeding had turned everything
inside out. "Tell her I'm glad she's okay."

Laredo was about to weave his way through the
crowd in order to leave, but Brian caught him by the
arm. Laredo eyed the chief of detectives.

"Why don't you tell her yourself?" Brian suggested.
And then, lowering his voice, he added, "There are
some things you just can't run from, boy. And you'd be
better off if you don't even try. Trust me."

There was no point in arguing. Laredo knew Brian
was right. Taking a breath, he nodded. "Thanks."

Going through the maze of corridors, which were as
confusing as his thoughts, Laredo followed a talkative
orderly to the room that Taylor had been taken to after
the operation.

When he entered the single care unit, Laredo saw that
Taylor's eyes were shut.

"You asleep?" he asked. There was no response. "Guess
so." He began to back out, then stopped. There were things
he needed to say, to purge out of his system, and what
better time to do it than when she couldn't really hear him?

"Damn it, Taylor, you gave me one hell of a scare
back there." And then he laughed shortly. "For more
reasons than one, I guess." He dragged an impatient
hand through his hair. "I thought you were going to die.
And if you did, everything would just stop. The sun, the

world, everything would just go away. At least for me."
He looked at all the IV tubes attached to her, all the
monitors documenting every step of her progress. "This
wasn't supposed to happen. You weren't supposed to get
shot and more than that, I wasn't supposed to feel this
way about you," he insisted. "Like I couldn't breathe in
a world that you weren't in. I'm not supposed to feel
things. I *promised* myself I wasn't going to feel things."
He glanced out the window. The sky had darkened in
anticipation of night. "There's no room in my world for
feelings. All they do is mess everything up and get in
the way. I can't deal with that."

He looked back down at her. Her eyes were still
closed so he continued. "I can't deal with worrying,
wondering if this is the last time I am going to see you.
That's not me, you hear me? That's not me."

Biting off a curse, he turned to go.

He hadn't realized just how closely he'd been standing
next to her bed. When he turned to walk out, he found
that the bottom of his shirt was caught on something.

Expecting to see something sticking out from her
hospital bed, a jagged edge on the side rails or something like that, Laredo was surprised to discover that the
reason he couldn't leave was because Taylor's fingers
were wrapped around a section of his shirt.

"Taylor?" he questioned in surprise.

It was then, as he bent even closer to peer at her, that
he saw her eyes flutter open. Her lips moved, but he
couldn't hear what she said.

"What?" he asked urgently, bending even closer. His
ear was almost next to her lips.

That was when he heard them. The two words she uttered hoarsely.

"Me, too."

Stunned, he straightened. "Taylor?"

Her fingers became lax, slipping from his shirt, telling him that she had slipped back into unconsciousness.

He stood watching her for a few moments. And then he left.

He didn't come back.

Not during her hospital stay nor during her convalescence, spent, at their insistence, entirely at her parents' house.

In the two weeks since she had been shot, Taylor hadn't heard even a single word from Laredo. At times, his non-appearance made her sincerely doubt that she had heard what she thought she'd heard that day after her surgery. Those times she chalked up her "memory" to the aftermath of the anesthesia, or maybe to hallucinations.

At other times, she was certain she *had* heard him.

And, in an odd way, the fact that he hadn't come to see her proved it.

When she was finally strong enough to move back into her own apartment, her parents, two brothers and sister all came with her. She patiently waited for them all to leave, turning down their offers, tendered one at a time, to spend the first night back with her. The moment they were gone, she sneaked back out to her carport and got in behind the wheel of her car.

She'd missed her independence. And she was about to do something to surrender it again, she thought. Willingly.

Starting up her car, Taylor drove over to Laredo's apartment.

He wasn't home.

Frustrated, she thought about coming back later, then decided to have this out with him once and for all. Making sure no one was around to observe her, she quickly let herself into his apartment, utilizing the skills she'd picked up from her dealings with the less-than-straight-and-narrow people she'd encountered on the street.

It was past seven o'clock and Laredo was bone-tired when he finally got home. But, bone-weary or not, he was instantly alert the second he put his hand on the doorknob. It gave. He *always* locked the door when he left.

Drawing his weapon, Laredo entered the apartment cautiously, prepared to go from room to room, searching for the intruder.

He didn't have far to look. Whoever had come in was still there, sitting on a recliner in the living room. He could just make out the outline of someone in the shadows. Adrenaline roaring through his veins, Laredo flipped the switch, bathing the room in light. He blinked.

Taylor?

No, it couldn't be. His imagination had just kicked into overdrive, that's all.

Terrific.

"Damn it," he muttered angrily, holstering his weapon, "now I'm seeing her."

His comment and the sudden influx of light roused Taylor, who'd dozed off waiting for him. The moment she opened her eyes, they blazed.

"So, you're not dead," she declared as if the discovery was news to her. "I guess that means you're a coward."

Ambivalent feelings battled it out inside her as she rose to her feet. Part of her wanted to throw her arms around him and the other part wanted to throw her hands around his throat for an entirely different reason.

"I figured those were the only two viable options why you didn't come back to see me. You were either dead or a coward. I figured the first was a definite possibility. But I never thought that you might actually be a coward." Disappointment entered her eyes. "I guess I was wrong."

Despite the fact that he'd applied the term to himself several times, he took offense when she did it. "I'm not a coward."

Doubling her fists and digging them into her hips, Taylor glared at him. "Then why didn't you come back to see me?"

He did his best to seem distant. It wasn't easy when all he wanted to do, despite her insults, was to hold her. To bury his face in her hair and inhale the fragrance he knew was there. "The case was over."

Taylor stared at him. She felt her heart splintering. Let that be a lesson to her. Falling in love was tantamount to a death wish. "And that's it?" she heard herself say.

Damn it, woman, why didn't you stay away? "What else is there?"

"Oh, I don't know." Rising on her toes, she was in his face. Some instinct that went deeper than her fear of being hurt said, "Love, maybe."

"Love?" He said the word as if he'd never heard it before. As if, even now, it wasn't eating up his very insides.

"Yeah, love," she repeated. She curbed her desire to beat on him with her fists. Why was he doing this to her? To them? "You said you loved me."

He shook his head, moving away. He became overly interested in removing his weapon and holster. "You were hallucinating."

Taylor moved until she was in front of him again. She wasn't about to allow him to avoid her. "No, I wasn't. And the fact of the matter is, I love you, too, you big dumb jerk, and I want to know what you're going to do about it."

"Do about it?" he echoed. Suddenly, he felt a smile struggling to take over his mouth. Taylor loved him? "What do you want me to do about it?" he asked her.

Taylor shook her head. The ball was in his court and the next move was his. Some things even an independent woman needed a man to do.

"Oh, no, you first."

He took her hand in his, drawing her closer to him. Enfolding her in his arms. Every fiber in his body came alive. Oh, God, but he had missed this. Missed her. The clouds began to lift, disappearing as if they'd never existed. "You love me, too, huh?"

She rolled her eyes. "That's what I said. At least you have decent hearing."

He smiled down into her face. This wasn't nearly as hard as he thought it was going to be. A lot less difficult than imagining his life without her. "How do you feel about marriage?"

Taylor felt her heart skip a beat, but she refused to get ahead of herself. Refused to put words into his mouth. "In general or specifically?"

He laughed, shaking his head. "Damn, for a cop, you sound like a lawyer. Specifically," Laredo underscored, then added, "ours," when she didn't say anything.

She looked at him, puzzled. Had she missed something, or was this some side effect from the medications she'd been taking after her surgery? "We don't have a marriage."

He skimmed his lips along her forehead. "Yet."

She felt herself growing warm. "Are you asking me to marry you?"

And now he grinned at her. "That would seem to be the direction this is going in, yes."

Just because she wasn't shy and retiring didn't mean she didn't want all the trappings that went with something like this. "Damn it, Laredo, say something romantic."

"Something romantic," he echoed, then ducked as she swung to hit him. Catching her in his arms again, he held her close. "Marry me, Taylor. Marry me and make my life a little less miserable than it is right now."

She sighed. So much for a honeyed tongue. "You *can't* say something romantic, can you?"

He lifted his shoulder in a half shrug. "I figure, if you say yes, I've got the next forty years to practice."

"Only forty?"

"After that, we'll negotiate." Warm rays of sunshine threaded all through him. He hadn't thought that it was possible to feel this happy. It almost seemed as if it should be against the law. "Don't want you to get too complacent."

She had a feeling that was never going to happen. Not if she was married to him.

"So?" he coaxed. "Are you going to say yes?"

She laced her arms around his neck, thinking how much she'd missed being this close to him. "Don't rush me, I'm thinking about it."

He kissed her softly even as he began to undress her. "Think fast."

She managed to say yes before they both became too busy to talk.

Epilogue

Reuniting with Taylor, Laredo handed her one of the two glasses of eggnog he'd gone to fetch. Because the noise level in the living room was swelling to epic proportions, he leaned down so that his lips were closer to her ear. "Finished making the rounds?" he asked her.

She laughed, taking a sip. "Not even close."

This was Andrew's annual Christmas party. Not only had the entire extended family shown up, but it felt like at least half the force was here as well. There were people in almost every room, not to mention that they were spilling out into the backyard.

Suddenly jostled from behind, Taylor clutched her drink with both hands to keep it from spilling.

"Sorry," Zach apologized, flashing his sister a grin before merging into the crowd.

"You know, there'd be more room here if the chief had invited less people or gotten a smaller tree," Laredo observed.

Finishing his eggnog, he put the glass down on the closest flat surface and looked up at the heavily decorated tree. It stood more than ten feet tall, thanks to the cathedral ceilings, and there was a story behind each and every one of the countless decorations that hung on every available branch.

Laredo shook his head. "That has got to be the biggest Christmas tree I've ever seen outside of a mall."

Finishing her own drink, Taylor placed her empty glass next to his. "This coming from a man who doesn't even put a tree up."

He shrugged carelessly, drawing her over to a doorway and away from, for the time being, the immediate flow of foot traffic. "It's still early."

She pinned him with a look. "It's Christmas Eve."

"That's my point," he said innocently. "There's still tomorrow."

Yeah, right. "You're planning on putting a tree up tonight?"

He pretended to think it over. "Well, doesn't seem like it's worth the trouble for just one day, does it?"

"It's *always* worth the trouble." Taylor shook her head. She absolutely loved Christmas and the celebration of the holiday was deeply entrenched in her soul. "You should have a tree."

He took hold of her hands in his. "Why?"

Taylor sighed. "If I have to explain it, it loses something." Even so, she tried to get him to come around.

"Don't you just light up inside whenever you look, *really* look, at a Christmas tree?"

This time, he was the one who was jostled. He took the opportunity to move in closer to her. "I don't need a tree to light up," Laredo told her, looking down into her eyes. "I have you."

Taylor could feel herself melting. "That has got to be the nicest thing you've ever said to me."

He grinned in response. "Wait," he told her, pointing up directly over her head. There was mistletoe hanging in the doorway. "There's more."

And then, to underscore his promise and because tradition demanded it, Laredo kiss her. Long and hard.

* * * * *

INTRIGUE...

INTRIGUE...

2-IN-1 ANTHOLOGY

COLORADO ABDUCTION
by Cassie Miles

When Carolyn's ranch is attacked just weeks before
Christmas, the FBI send stubborn JD to safeguard her.
And when the attacks escalate, so does their passion...

IN BED WITH THE BADGE
by Marie Ferrarella

Could detective Riley's new role helping hot-shot cop
Sam cope with his new daughter and his new
department help heal her own damaged heart?

•••

SINGLE TITLE

COWBOY TO THE CORE
by Joanna Wayne

Military man Marcus is returning to his cowboy roots.
Yet his dreams of a quiet life are shattered when he meets
a woman in danger who arouses his protective instincts.

On sale from 1st October 2010
Don't miss out!

Available at WHSmith, Tesco, ASDA, Eason
and all good bookshops

www.millsandboon.co.uk

0910/46b

FREE BOOKS
AND A SURPRISE GIFT

We would like to take this opportunity to thank you for reading this Mills & Boon® book by offering you the chance to take TWO more specially selected books from the Intrigue series absolutely FREE! We're also making this offer to introduce you to the benefits of the Mills & Boon® Book Club™—

- **FREE home delivery**
- **FREE gifts and competitions**
- **FREE monthly Newsletter**
- **Exclusive Mills & Boon Book Club offers**
- **Books available before they're in the shops**

Accepting these FREE books and gift places you under no obligation to buy, you may cancel at any time, even after receiving your free books. Simply complete your details below and return the entire page to the address below. You don't even need a stamp!

YES Please send me 2 free Intrigue books and a surprise gift. I understand that unless you hear from me, I will receive 5 superb new stories every month, including two 2-in-1 books priced at £4.99 each and a single book priced at £3.19, postage and packing free. I am under no obligation to purchase any books and may cancel my subscription at any time. The free books and gift will be mine to keep in any case.

Ms/Mrs/Miss/Mr _____ Initials _____

_____

Surname _____

Address _____

_____

_____ Postcode _____

E-mail_____

Send this whole page to: Mills & Boon Book Club, Free Book Offer FREEPOST NAT 10298, Richmond, TW9 1BR